Unbound

Zoe Moon

Published by Zoe Moon, 2024.

This is a work of fiction. Similarities to real people, places, or events are entirely coincidental.

UNBOUND

First edition. November 11, 2024.

Copyright © 2024 Zoe Moon.

ISBN: 979-8227201188

Written by Zoe Moon.

Chapter 1: Into the Flames

I clench my jaw, breathing in the thick, burning air, feeling it coat my lungs with every shallow inhale. It's too hot to think straight, too loud to hear myself think. The fire's roar is deafening, a guttural sound that vibrates through the bones, rattling everything around me. I glance at the man—no, the firefighter, although I'd be hard-pressed to remember his name under the haze of smoke and fear. His grip on the doorframe is tight, like it's the only thing tethering him to this reality, but his eyes? His eyes are unwavering. They aren't looking at me with pity, or sympathy. They're looking at me like I'm a problem, like a risk, something that needs fixing, or possibly discarding.

I know what he's thinking. I can almost hear the internal argument running in his mind—keep her safe, or get out and do what needs to be done. There's no room for hesitation in this job. Lives are on the line, including his own. And yet, something in me refuses to give in to his silent command to retreat. I can't let go of the fire ladder in my hand. I can't turn away from the smoke curling in the corners of my eyes, even though every instinct screams at me to get out.

I shift my weight, the pressure of the heat pressing against my skin. The fire, it seems to know, is always hungry, always gnawing at the edges of whatever you've built—homes, lives, hopes. It doesn't care if you've only just begun, or if you've lived a lifetime. If you're in its path, it will consume you just the same.

"Move," I say, my voice hoarse from the smoke. It comes out sharper than I intend, but there's something in the air tonight—something about this man.

He doesn't budge.

"Not without you," he answers, his voice calm, unwavering, like he's repeating a mantra, the kind of mantra that's said over and over until it becomes truth.

I stare at him for a long moment, my thoughts a jumbled mess of frustration and disbelief. This isn't what I expected. Not from him. Not from anyone, really. I had assumed, from the first moment I'd seen him—standing tall with that easy confidence, like the flames didn't dare touch him—that he would be the kind of person to push me out of the way without a second thought. To shout orders. To rush me to safety with no hesitation. But this man? He's holding me back. Not physically, but something deeper—something I can't quite grasp yet.

My fingers curl tighter around the ladder. The rough metal bites into my palms, grounding me in the moment. My eyes flick back to the doorframe, the one he's guarding with such intensity. I can feel the shift in him, the subtle pull of tension. It's like he's fighting an internal war, one I'm caught in the middle of. And still, I don't back down.

"Why are you doing this?" I ask, almost a whisper, though the words come from a place much deeper than the fire.

His eyes flash—sharp, quick—and for just a moment, I think I see something break in him. But it's gone in an instant, replaced by that same resolute exterior. "I'm not leaving until you're safe."

The words don't make sense to me. There's no logic in them.

He's here to save people, isn't he? To put out fires and rescue the helpless, not to protect someone like me—someone who barely even belongs in this chaos. I'm not one of those fragile souls who needs saving. I've worked my entire life to make sure I never need anyone. My life was meant to be a quiet one, free from drama or heroism. But now, in this moment, that fragile line I've drawn between my independence and the world around me is blurring. And it's scaring me more than the fire ever could.

I step closer, ignoring the stinging heat against my face. "What are you waiting for?" My voice cracks, but I don't apologize. "There are people who need you. People who need saving. You're wasting time here."

The firefighter's jaw tightens at my words, but he doesn't look away. He stands firm, and I can feel his resolve like a wall between us, unshakable. "And what about you? You think I'll just let you run off into that smoke like it's nothing?"

"I can handle myself!" I snap, the words stinging like acid as they leave my lips. "I'm not helpless!"

There's a flicker of something—amusement, maybe—flashing behind his eyes, before it vanishes just as quickly. "You don't have to be helpless to be in danger."

I'm not sure what he means by that, but the more I think about it, the more I realize something. Something I can't shake. He's not just trying to save me. He's trying to control me. To manage me, like I'm a problem that needs fixing.

It's an impulse—one I can't quite control—but I take a step back. "I don't need you to protect me. I don't need anyone."

For the first time, his eyes soften. There's no pity there, just a quiet understanding that unsettles me. "That's exactly why I'm here."

I want to argue. To tell him I can handle myself. That I don't need anyone. But the truth hangs in the air between us, heavy and undeniable. The fire's roar grows louder. We're running out of time. I can't back down now, not when I've come so far.

And yet, here we are—standing at a threshold. Not just between us and the flames, but between who we are and what we'll become if we let go of this moment. If we let go of the struggle.

I know one thing for sure. Neither of us is leaving this place unchanged.

I take another step back, my boots scraping against the charred floor, the sound lost in the rising fury of the fire. The heat seems to crawl deeper under my skin, leaving a burning trace wherever it touches. It's not just the fire; it's him, too. His presence is a constant, an unrelenting pressure, like he's trying to do more than keep me safe—like he's trying to tame me, to bend me to some unknown purpose.

"I'm not leaving," I say again, but my voice is quieter now, uncertain even to my own ears. It's not a surrender. At least, I don't want it to be. But the pull between us is undeniable. A tug-of-war I never asked for.

He shakes his head slightly, not out of disbelief, but almost as if he knows exactly what I'm going to say next. "I didn't say you had to. I just need you to wait."

Wait. The word hits me like a punch in the stomach. It's one of those simple, aggravatingly dismissive words people use when they want to buy time. When they want to make you feel small, like you don't have enough sense to know that you're already in over your head.

I open my mouth to protest—again—but then the air shifts. The heat intensifies. The walls groan under the strain of the flames, like the building itself is alive and fighting back. It rattles the nerves in my spine, and for the first time tonight, fear pushes its way through the stubborn resolve that's held me together up until now.

A thick wave of smoke engulfs me, suffocating, and I stumble backward, hacking and gasping for air. My throat burns, and for a moment, all I can do is struggle to breathe. There's a wetness in my eyes, and it's not just from the smoke—it's the panic, creeping in at the edges.

He's there, in a heartbeat, pulling me against him, his arms firm, warm, almost possessive as he drags me toward the wall. His grip is like iron, his chest a solid wall against my back, and for a brief, illogical moment, I want to lean into him. It's instinct. The need for something solid, something safe, even though every inch of my body is telling me that I don't trust him. Not like this.

His breath is hot against my ear as he leans in, his voice low, almost a growl. "I told you to wait. I meant it." The words could be a warning, or they could be a promise. I can't decide.

I pull away from him, blinking through the stinging haze of smoke and frustration. "I didn't sign up for this," I snap, words sharper than I mean them to be. "I'm not some damsel in distress. I'm not your responsibility."

For a moment, I think I've pushed him too far. His hand tightens on my arm, and the flames reflect off his eyes like a warning in themselves. But then something shifts. Something cracks, just the tiniest bit. His jaw unclenches, and for the first time tonight, I see a flicker of something more human in him. "I never said you were," he says quietly, the roughness in his tone barely masking the sincerity behind it.

I blink, thrown off balance by his calm, his understanding. He doesn't treat me like a victim. He doesn't look at me with pity. It's confusing—disorienting, really—and for a fleeting moment, I wonder if I've misjudged him entirely. But before I can settle into that thought, the fire crackles louder, pulling me back to the reality of this hellhole we're stuck in.

"There's nothing you can do here, alright?" he says, his voice harder now. "We need to get out. Now."

My heart pounds, thudding painfully against my ribs, as I watch the door behind him. It feels like a lifetime has passed since we started this mad dash through the smoke, and yet, we're still here. Stuck. We should've been through that door by now, out into the relative safety of the hall. But instead, he's standing in front of me, blocking my way, like he's waiting for something.

I know this man. At least, I think I do. Not in the sense that I know his name, or where he's from, or what he likes to do when he's not putting out fires. But I know the look in his eyes. I know the way he's unwilling to let go of his principles, no matter how much the world around him burns. The kind of person who would rather risk his own life than let someone else take a step without him. It's admirable. It's infuriating.

"You're not going anywhere until I say so," he warns, his grip not loosening for even a second.

I glare at him, anger bubbling under my skin like a wildfire of my own. "You think you can control me? You think you have the right to decide what I do?"

"I'm not deciding anything for you," he shoots back, voice hard. "I'm making sure you get out alive."

I want to slap him. I want to tell him to back off, to get out of my face. But instead, I just stare at him, my chest rising and falling with each labored breath. My fingers twitch around the fire ladder, gripping it tighter, wanting to tear myself away from this mess. But there's something in his eyes that stops me—something that's pulling at me in a way I can't explain. It's not fear. It's not even a desire to trust him, though it feels dangerously close to that. It's simply the truth that right now, right here, I don't have a choice.

The fire rages, the heat pressing closer, but the moment stretches on, and I realize we are both caught in the same web of uncertainty, unsure of how to escape, how to move forward. Neither of us willing to let go.

I push against the weight of his hand on my arm, determined to shake off the unwanted sense of safety he's trying to impose on me. My mind is a fog of smoke and confusion, but beneath it is a sense of urgency, of things I still need to do, places I still need to be. "I don't need you to babysit me," I say, the words coming out sharper than intended, but there's no turning back now. "I'm not one of your damn rookies you need to coddle through every step."

He doesn't flinch. Doesn't even blink. His eyes stay fixed on mine, that quiet strength of his an anchor I'm inexplicably tethered to, even though I'd rather be anywhere but here. "You're right," he says, his voice low, barely audible over the crackling flames. "You're not a rookie. You're a pain in the ass."

The words hit me harder than I expected. Not because I'm offended—I'm used to people calling me difficult—but because of the way he says it, with an odd mix of amusement and something I can't quite place. Like he's waiting for me to argue, waiting for the fight.

I almost do.

I take a deep breath, inhaling the heavy smoke, letting it sting my lungs before exhaling it in frustration. "Fine. You've had your little moment. Now let me do my job."

A heavy silence stretches between us, thick as the smoke surrounding us. For a moment, I almost believe he's going to argue, or worse, order me around again. Instead, he simply shakes his head, his lips twisting into a wry smile that barely reaches his eyes. "You think I want to keep you here? You think I'm trying to control you?"

I want to scream, to tell him exactly what I think of his misplaced sense of heroism. But something—some thread of shared understanding or maybe shared resentment—stops me. Instead, I glance over his shoulder toward the door he's guarding like it's the very last lifeline. I could slip past him, push through the flames, and keep going. But it would be stupid. I'd be on my own. And something about this whole mess tells me that being on my own right now would be worse than sitting here, pretending we're in control.

The flames are so close now I can feel their heat pressing against my skin like a cruel joke. Every second we linger feels like it's costing someone their life. The fire is spreading faster than we can keep up, and I know there's no way the building will hold much longer. We've already been in here too long. And yet, the door remains shut.

"We're wasting time," I mutter under my breath, louder than I intended. It's not even the fear creeping in that makes my voice tremble—it's the weight of what we're doing. Or rather, what we're not doing.

"You think I don't know that?" he replies, his voice cutting through the smoke with an edge that surprises me. "But it's not about time, is it? It's about getting you out in one piece."

I bristle at the implication. "I don't need your protection."

He gives me a sidelong glance, the sort of glance that says he's read me a thousand times over, like I'm some worn-out book he's already finished reading but keeps coming back to anyway. "I didn't sign up to babysit anyone," he says quietly, almost like he's talking to himself. "But I'm not leaving until you're safe. Whether you like it or not."

The blunt honesty in his words hits me harder than the fire licking at the edges of the room. I can feel the air growing more oppressive, the heat an unrelenting beast that continues to stalk us, threatening to swallow us whole. It's not just the danger anymore—it's the realization that I'm not as independent as I thought, that I've been carrying too much weight on my own shoulders for too long.

I open my mouth to argue, to spit out another defiant sentence that proves how capable I am, how much I don't need anyone. But the words die in my throat as I glance over his shoulder again. The fire is closer now, just inches from the door. It's spreading faster than I can process. The heat feels more intense, suffocating, and for the first time, I can't ignore the pounding in my chest—the realization that maybe he's right. Maybe, just this once, I need someone to make a decision for me.

I hesitate, standing there in the thick, choking smoke, my heart in my throat as I look into his face. There's something there—a quiet, stubborn kindness mixed with unspoken authority. It makes my stomach twist, makes me wonder why I keep fighting this pull, this strange need to trust him. But I swallow hard, pushing the thought away.

The door behind him groans as if it's about to collapse, the air thickening with the scent of burning wood and melting metal. He looks over his shoulder, back at the door, the silent alarm ringing in his ears. Then he steps aside, just enough to let me see the devastation beyond. It's too much. Too much for even someone like him to handle on their own.

"Now you want me to trust you?" I ask, my voice still hoarse, still full of skepticism. "Now, after all this time?"

He doesn't answer right away. Instead, he just watches me, his eyes unwavering, before stepping fully out of the way. His silence says more than any words ever could.

I take a deep breath. The moment I've been dreading, the one I've avoided all this time, has come. The heat blasts me as I move toward the door, and then, just as I'm about to cross the threshold, I hear it. A sound, soft at first, then growing louder—a creak, a groan, and then the unmistakable crack of something breaking.

Before I can react, the floor beneath me shudders violently, and the world tilts.

Chapter 2: Smoke and Mirrors

The sun feels too bright against my skin, sharp and unforgiving, a reminder that the world keeps moving even as everything else seems to have stopped. The air is still thick with the bite of smoke, a harsh taste on my tongue that won't go away. The kind of smoke that lingers in your lungs, coats your throat, and clings to your skin. It smells like burnt edges and the promise of something lost, and it wraps itself around me like an unwelcome, greasy hand.

I draw in a deep breath and make my way through the debris, my boots crunching on the shattered glass scattered across the sidewalk. It's a wonder anyone was left standing, let alone unscathed. The building, once a proud structure in the heart of the city, now resembles a pile of broken promises. What was meant to be a beacon of ambition and hope is now a testament to the kind of destruction that seems far too easily within reach. I try not to think about the people who might have been inside, about the families who might not have made it out. But then, I can't stop myself, and the guilt clings to me like the smoke, suffocating and relentless.

I stop in my tracks when I see him, standing in the middle of the aftermath, laughing like it's just another day at the office. His broad shoulders, heavy with the weight of too many unsaid things, are hunched slightly as he talks to his team, pointing in all directions, giving orders with a kind of ease I can't quite replicate. His uniform—always crisp, always perfect—seems out of place against the wreckage, as though he's a part of it and yet completely removed from it at the same time. I shouldn't be surprised. Firefighters, like soldiers, have a way of looking at the world that most of us can never fully understand. But that's not the reason I'm frozen in place, watching him.

No, it's because of the way his eyes gleam with something dangerous. And despite every instinct in me screaming to walk away, to let him burn in whatever self-imposed hell he's built for himself, I can't seem to look away.

His laugh is genuine, carefree even. Too carefree, almost. It doesn't fit with the destruction, with the sorrow, with the grief that still weighs heavily on the air. I want to hate him for it. I want to take that laughter, tear it apart piece by piece, and make him feel the gravity of the moment. But there's a flicker in his gaze, a shadow that darts through his eyes when he looks at the ruins, and I wonder if, maybe, he feels the weight of it too. Maybe, just maybe, he's haunted by this, like the rest of us. But he hides it well.

He catches me staring and his grin falters, just for a second. A flash of something—regret? Anger?—clouds his features before he masks it with a smooth, practiced indifference. I can't decide if I'm relieved or disappointed by that.

"Thought you'd run for the hills after that little stunt," he calls to me, his voice carrying across the distance like a challenge. The words themselves sting, but it's the underlying tone that cuts deeper. He's never been subtle with me, always quick to remind me that I'm a civilian—someone who has no business being involved in his world, much less getting in his way. A part of me understands that. The other part? The part that's too stubborn to listen to reason? That part wants to argue, wants to prove him wrong.

But instead of answering, I force myself to take another step forward, my eyes narrowing as I approach him. The crackling of fire hoses being rolled up and the low murmur of his team fade into the background, a mere hum against the rawness of the moment.

"You really think I'm going to just let you get away with this?" I ask, my voice low but steady, not betraying the fire that's bubbling up inside me.

He doesn't flinch. If anything, he stands taller, his posture straightening as if he's already prepared for my words, ready for the confrontation that always seems inevitable when we're near each other.

"Let me?" he asks, a smirk playing at the corners of his mouth. "I didn't exactly ask for your help, you know." His eyes flicker over my face, his gaze weighing me in a way that feels too intimate, too sharp. "And frankly, I'm not sure you're the one who should be talking."

The accusation hangs between us, thick and suffocating, and for a moment, I wonder if I've said too much. If I've made a mistake by confronting him like this. But then I remember everything—the long nights spent trying to clean up his mess, the endless debates with him over strategy, the way he always treated me like an afterthought, like I was just a nuisance.

"Maybe not," I reply, the words sliding out of my mouth before I can stop them. "But I sure as hell think you're going to regret this one day."

His smile fades, and for the briefest of moments, I catch something raw in his eyes—a flash of vulnerability, something he never lets anyone see. It's gone almost as soon as it appears, masked again by the cold, calculated professional I've come to know. But for that split second, I feel a flicker of understanding, an unspoken acknowledgment that maybe, just maybe, we're more alike than either of us are willing to admit.

"You have no idea what you're dealing with," he mutters, his voice suddenly lower, the weight of the words hanging between us like an unsolved mystery.

I want to respond, to say something that will make him feel the same sting I do, but I don't. Instead, I turn, my back to him, the tension between us thick and palpable. I won't give him the satisfaction of seeing me flinch. Not today.

I keep walking, my steps deliberate, but I can feel his gaze trailing behind me, sharp as a blade, slicing through the air between us. He doesn't follow, though. There's something about his presence that stays lodged in the space around me, like a persistent echo that refuses to fade. Maybe it's the way his laughter—still lingering in the dust—doesn't sit right with everything else. Maybe it's because I've spent the last few years watching people who are so much better at hiding their scars. But with him? It's different. His mask slips, even if only for a second, and I can see the brokenness, a flaw that runs deeper than just a bad day at the office.

I pause in the doorway of the nearest café, pushing through the glass with a force that almost makes the bell chime mournfully. The woman behind the counter barely acknowledges my presence as I slide into a corner booth, grateful for the semblance of normalcy. There's nothing about this place that screams danger, nothing about it that suggests a world where flames can consume everything in an instant. But I feel the sting of that world in my skin, in my fingertips as they tap nervously against the worn tabletop. I wish I could say the same about my heart, but the truth is, I know exactly where it's been for the past hour: back there, with him.

The barista finally takes notice of me, offering a half-smile as she slides a cup of coffee across the table. It's supposed to be comforting, I think, the way it warms my hands as I lift it to my lips. But it's not. Everything's a little too sharp, a little too clear. The taste of burnt toast lingers on my tongue, even though I haven't eaten anything since the disaster. A sign, maybe, that I need to learn how to let things go—people, places, bad decisions.

As I sip, the door jingles again, and a gust of wind carries in the last traces of smoke from the fire. It sweeps over the room in a way that no one seems to notice, except me. The scent of charred wood and hot metal mixes with the coffee, and for a moment, it's hard to tell where one begins and the other ends. My breath hitches, my mind flicking back to the way he looked, standing there amid the chaos. There was something unsettling about it all. Something in the way he held himself—calm, collected, like he had been here before. Maybe too many times.

I'm not a stranger to danger. I've learned to navigate it, whether it's in the form of a hurricane of paperwork or a personal storm that's far too close for comfort. But there's something about him—about this man who, to anyone else, might just seem like another person doing his job—that unsettles me more than I care to admit. He isn't just a firefighter; he's the embodiment of something darker, something that doesn't fit into a neat box. And despite every instinct in me screaming to stay away, to draw a clear line between him and me, I can't help but feel that it's too late for that. The line was crossed the moment I stepped into that burning building.

I let my thoughts wander back to the fire—the smell of it, the way it consumed everything in its path like a beast desperate to devour. I was there, running around like a headless chicken, trying to save things I couldn't even begin to understand. But he—he was different. I saw him move through the smoke like it was part of him, his focus never wavering, his steps sure and steady. There was a precision to him that made the chaos feel almost deliberate. Almost like he was controlling it, not running from it.

"Hey, you're not gonna pay for that, are you?" The voice that cuts through my thoughts is sharp, too sharp, and I look up to find the barista glaring at me, her arms crossed as she waits for some sort of reaction.

My mouth goes dry as I glance down at the table, realizing I haven't actually touched my wallet yet. My fingers are still wrapped tightly around the coffee mug, my knuckles pale, my grip white-hot.

"I'm so sorry," I stammer, pushing my wallet across the table. The motion feels disjointed, like I'm moving underwater. "I'll— I'll take care of it."

The barista nods, accepting the payment with a businesslike air that tells me she's seen this before. She leaves me with a pointed look, and I'm left in the aftermath of my own behavior, wondering what it says about me that I let myself drift so far away.

I don't know how long I sit there, letting the world spin on without me. The sun is still out, still glaring too brightly, still beating down on me like I'm supposed to be something I'm not. I should've left already, gotten out of the café and kept moving, but I can't make myself do it. There's something that keeps pulling me back to the fire. Something that keeps tying me to him.

I barely notice the time passing, only that the café has emptied around me, the usual crowd drifting off to their next destination. I'm alone, the sounds of distant chatter replaced by the hollow hum of my own thoughts. And that's when the door swings open again, the bell tinkling as the air shifts. For the briefest of moments, I think I've imagined it—him, walking through the door. But then I see him. His broad shoulders filling the doorway, his face still marked by the smoke.

I freeze. He hasn't noticed me yet, but the tension between us feels like a visible thing, stretching across the room. My heart thunders in my chest, and for a second, I wonder if I should just bolt. But then he looks up, and our eyes lock. He doesn't smile, but his gaze softens, just a little. And that's enough to leave me utterly, helplessly stuck in the moment.

His gaze doesn't soften when our eyes meet again. It sharpens. A flicker of recognition, but nothing else. For a brief, unbearable moment, it feels as if we're caught in a game neither of us knows how to win, each of us holding our breath, waiting for the other to make the first move. I should have looked away. I should have kept my head down, pretended I hadn't noticed him standing there, but I don't. Instead, my pulse quickens, and my fingers tighten around the handle of my coffee mug, as if it might somehow anchor me to this place, this moment.

He doesn't walk over. He doesn't say anything, either. He just stands there, in the doorway, like some kind of shadow refusing to leave. His eyes scan the room briefly, before they land on me again. There's a shift in his posture, just a fraction of a movement, a subtle tension that tightens the air between us.

I open my mouth to speak, but the words don't come out right. Instead, I take a slow, deliberate sip of my coffee, because sometimes, just the act of drinking something hot can give you a few seconds to regain your control.

When I glance back up, he's still staring at me, but this time, there's something more to it. Something that doesn't quite match the hardened look of a man who fights fires for a living. There's something softer—almost like regret, or maybe guilt. It's there, for the briefest of moments, and then it's gone, replaced by that familiar coolness, the mask he wears when he's not sure who's watching.

"You always like hiding in places like this?" His voice is low, the words sliding through the air between us like silk, but there's a sharp edge to them that makes me stiffen.

I can feel the heat rise in my chest, the irritation bubbling up, but I keep my tone even, my words clipped. "Hiding? You think I'm hiding? Maybe you should try it sometime."

He arches an eyebrow, the ghost of a smile pulling at the corners of his mouth. But it doesn't quite reach his eyes, those eyes that have seen too much, that have carried too many burdens for anyone to truly understand. I've spent enough time around people like him—people who wear their trauma like armor, never letting anyone close enough to see the cracks.

But I can see them. I can see the way his jaw tightens when he thinks I'm not looking. The way his hand twitches toward his side, like he's used to something being there that isn't anymore. It's a small thing, but it's enough to tell me he's been through something. Something he's not sharing, something he's buried deep beneath layers of fire and smoke and control.

"Maybe I don't need to hide," he says, the words like a dare. He leans a little closer, just enough to make my breath catch. "Maybe I'm not afraid of being seen."

The challenge is clear, and it shouldn't sting the way it does. I'm not afraid of him. I'm not afraid of anything he could throw at me. But there's something about the way he says it, like he knows more about me than he has any right to. Like he's already figured me out, and all I've done is stand here, pretending not to care.

I push back from the table, the motion abrupt, but not enough to seem desperate. "I'm not afraid of you," I say, my voice steady. But the words don't feel as solid as they should.

He steps into the café, his boots making soft thuds on the worn wooden floor. The door swings shut behind him with a soft jingle, and for a moment, I feel like we're in a world of our own, a pocket of time that has frozen for just the two of us. The rest of the room is oblivious to the tension we're creating, to the way the air seems to hum between us. I'm suddenly very aware of every sound, every little movement—the clink of a spoon hitting a cup, the shuffle of someone's feet as they leave the café, the quiet buzz of the overhead light.

"You sure about that?" he asks, his voice quieter now, a little closer. He's standing at my table, so close I can smell the faint trace of smoke on his jacket, the kind that clings to you even after you think you've left it behind. "You don't seem so sure."

I want to argue, to tell him that he's wrong, but I can't bring myself to. Not when the way he looks at me makes the words feel hollow. I should be angry. I should be furious with him for coming in here and playing his little games like it's all a joke. But the truth is, the fire, the wreckage, the way he makes me feel—it all blurs together, like the smoke I can't seem to shake off.

I let out a breath, my chest tightening as I search for something to say. Anything to fill the silence between us. But before I can speak, the bell above the door rings again, the sound sharp and jarring in the stillness.

I glance toward the entrance, expecting to see someone else walking in, but what I see instead is far worse.

A figure, tall and broad, steps into the café. They're wearing a coat that's too dark, too sleek, and the way they carry themselves is all wrong—too controlled, too perfect. My heart stops. It's him. The one who's been haunting me since this mess started. The one who has answers, but never the right ones. The one who knows too much, and yet too little.

And he's looking directly at me.

Chapter 3: Sparks of Suspicion

The fire station smells like gasoline and ash. It's a scent that clings to your skin and never quite lets go, no matter how many showers you take. I never thought much of it before, but now, every time I step through the doors, it makes my heart beat a little faster, my nerves just a shade too alert. Maybe it's the sheer magnitude of what goes on here—life and death, danger and salvation, all wrapped up in a frantic frenzy of sirens and flashing lights. But today, it's something else. Something heavier, like the air before a storm.

I glance over at the equipment as I try to adjust the straps on the vest. It's too big for me, which is ridiculous because I'm five-eight, not some dainty, small-framed woman. I've worn my share of gear before, but this, this feels like a trap. Every inch of it weighs me down, like I'm being told, in no uncertain terms, that I'm not built for this. Not built for any of it.

I catch his eyes again.

He's standing off to the side, leaning against a pillar with that same damn smirk on his face. I'm not sure what pisses me off more—his lack of concern as I struggle, or the fact that his expression is carved from stone, too unreadable, too impassive. His arms are crossed, and it's hard not to notice how his uniform fits him perfectly. It's too fitted, almost like he knows he's got the body to back it up. But it's not just his appearance that has me rattled. It's the way he watches me, like I'm some puzzle he's trying to figure out, and I'm failing miserably.

"Need some help?" His voice is low, edged with amusement, and it sends a rush of heat straight to my cheeks. He's enjoying this. Enjoying watching me stumble around with the equipment that's supposed to be second nature by now. I clench my jaw and force a smile, though it feels like I'm chewing on glass.

"I'm good," I say, my voice coming out sharper than I meant it to. I'm not going to give him the satisfaction of seeing me flounder. Not today.

The chief calls out from across the room, oblivious to the tension hanging thick in the air. "You're doing great, Julia. We're all here to help." He claps a hand on my shoulder, and I flash him a tight smile, grateful for his enthusiasm but wishing it wasn't so obvious. I can't help but notice how differently he treats me compared to the others. There's something about the way he welcomes me that makes it feel like a performance, like he's checking off some mental list to make sure I'm integrated properly.

But then there's the guy with the smirk, the one who's been watching me with those steel-blue eyes since I walked in. There's a dissonance between his gaze and the chief's welcome. A subtle but undeniable difference, like he's playing a game that I'm not sure I'm invited to.

I try to refocus, turning my attention back to the equipment. But every time I try to adjust my gloves, I feel his eyes on me, weighing me, measuring me like I'm some sort of challenge he's just dying to crack open. It's uncomfortable, and it's starting to get under my skin.

I finally force the vest into place and straighten up, trying to look like I know exactly what I'm doing. I'm sure I look like I've just been through a wrestling match, but I'm not going to give him the satisfaction of seeing me second-guess myself.

"Everything okay?" The chief is too close now, looming just a little too overbearing, too concerned. His voice is light, but there's a heaviness behind it, like he's testing me.

"Just fine," I say, forcing a laugh. "Just working on it."

The guy with the smirk is still watching me, his stance relaxed but his eyes sharp, like he's waiting for me to make a mistake. His arms are still crossed, but there's an air of finality to his posture now, like he's already made his mind up about me. And I don't like it. I don't like feeling like I'm under a microscope, like my every move is being dissected for weaknesses I don't even know I have.

Finally, I can't take it anymore. I turn to the chief, desperate for a distraction. "What's next?" I ask, hoping for some semblance of normalcy to wash over me.

"Next, we're going to go over the protocols for the next fire drill," the chief says with a smile, as if everything is perfectly fine. But I can't shake the feeling that something is off. Something between me and this fire station doesn't sit right.

As we start moving towards the training area, I catch a glimpse of him again, that guy with the smirk. He's not following us. He's not even pretending to be interested. He's got his back to the room, staring out the window with an air of detachment that tells me more than any words could. I can't figure him out, and the more I try, the more it feels like I'm walking into a trap that's been set just for me.

But what does he want? Why is he so bent on making me feel small, like I'm unworthy of being here? The questions swirl around in my head, making my chest tighten with frustration. If I knew what he wanted, maybe I could deal with it. But until I figure that out, I'll have to endure this silent war, the one he's waging with nothing more than a look and a smirk.

And I'm starting to wonder if I'm the only one who doesn't know the rules of the game.

The first few days blur into a haze of sirens and smoke. I'm settling into a rhythm—briefings, drills, and endless training sessions with equipment that I can barely remember the names of, let alone understand. Still, I keep my head down, focus on the tasks at hand. I know what's expected of me, even if the air in this place feels thick with unsaid things. Every time I catch his eye, I feel like I'm failing a test I didn't sign up for.

But it's the little things that make it harder to ignore him—his silence, the way he never seems to make an effort to be friendly, how his eyes always seem to track my every move. His gaze feels like a weight, and I can't shake the feeling that he's watching me the way a hawk watches its prey. It's not the sort of attention that makes you feel seen or appreciated. It's the kind that makes you wonder if you're being sized up for some future blow. What is it about me that has him so invested in my every mistake?

It's on the third day, during a mock rescue drill, that the tension finally snaps.

I'm supposed to be the one leading the rescue—don't ask me why, because even I know it's a bad idea. I don't have the experience to make the split-second decisions that this job demands. But it's too late to back out now. The chief's counting on me, and everyone else is already looking at me like I should know what I'm doing. So I do my best to breathe, to center myself, and focus.

But then he steps in. The guy with the smirk.

"Take it slow," he advises, his voice flat, completely devoid of any real warmth. I glance at him, my heart racing. "You're rushing it. You don't want to make mistakes today. We're not here to fix them."

The way he says it—like he's already written me off—makes my stomach flip. I don't respond. He doesn't deserve the satisfaction. Instead, I take another breath, set my shoulders, and walk toward the mock victim.

The seconds tick by, dragging with every step. I can feel his eyes on me. There's something so unnerving about how he doesn't even try to hide it. He's standing off to the side, arms crossed, his posture casual, yet there's an intensity in his stillness. He's waiting for me to fail, to give him a reason to smirk again.

I can feel my hands shaking as I approach the victim—just a mannequin, but still. I glance back at him, and his gaze is cold, calculating. It hits me in a way that I can't quite explain. It's not like any other look I've encountered. There's no empathy in it. Just a flat judgment. And as I work, struggling with the heavy equipment, trying to maintain composure, I wonder if I'm just a lesson to him, a reminder that not everyone belongs here.

His presence makes the whole thing feel more like a test than a drill. I finish, barely making it through the steps, trying to remember the protocol, trying to appear like I'm not suffocating under the pressure. When I stand up and look around, the others are silent. They're waiting for me to fail, too.

Except for the chief.

"Well done, Julia," the chief says, clapping me on the back with such enthusiasm I almost stumble. He's too loud, too eager. It feels fake—like a show to mask the underlying tension. I force a smile, nodding. "Thanks."

But the guy with the smirk doesn't even look at me. He doesn't need to. He's already decided what he thinks. And that's what gets under my skin the most. The fact that he's written me off without so much as a second thought.

"You got lucky," he mutters, just loud enough for me to hear. "Don't expect the same result next time."

I freeze, just for a second. The others might not hear, but I do. His words cut deeper than any challenge he could throw at me. They're personal, laced with something that feels... malicious. I take a step back, but my legs feel like they might give out from under me. This isn't just about the drills. It's about something else. Something I can't quite put my finger on.

"Is there a problem, Hayes?" the chief asks, his voice sharp, like he's just now noticing the undercurrent. Hayes doesn't answer. He just gives a barely perceptible shake of his head, his eyes never leaving mine. The look in them sends a shiver down my spine.

"No problem, Chief. Just making sure Julia doesn't forget the stakes."

That's the moment I realize: this isn't about the equipment. It's not about the drill. It's not about me making mistakes. It's about him. And whatever it is he's holding onto, whatever reason he's decided I'm not worthy of being here, it's far bigger than any of us are letting on.

The rest of the drill goes by in a blur of motions and instructions. My hands work faster than my brain, and I'm only half-focused on what's being said. Hayes doesn't speak to me again for the rest of the day, which, at this point, feels like a mercy. But the tension is still there, thick in the air, like an unfinished sentence. He's waiting for something. He's waiting for me to fall. And I'm starting to wonder if I want to know why.

But there's no escaping him, not now. He's already planted himself firmly in my world, and I have no idea what he's planning to do next. And, for the first time in a long time, I realize that the real battle has nothing to do with fire drills or life-saving techniques. It has everything to do with him—and whether or not I'll let him burn me.

The days drag on, but I can feel something shifting beneath the surface. The fire station feels different now, charged with an undercurrent that I can't ignore. Every time I walk through the door, I brace myself. The weight of Hayes' presence hovers like a dark cloud, heavy with unspoken tension. His silent judgments are starting to feel like a constant companion, one that lingers in the corners of my vision, waiting for me to slip, to show my hand. I can't figure out if he's trying to teach me something or if he's just out to make my life miserable. Either way, it's wearing me down, and the worst part is—I can't stop thinking about it. About him.

I'm not used to being the subject of someone's disdain, and it's starting to eat at me. It's more than just his icy demeanor. It's the fact that he doesn't even try to hide it. There's no pretension with Hayes. If he doesn't like you, you'll know it within ten seconds of looking into his eyes. And I know that look. The one that says I'm not good enough. Not worthy of his respect. I could stand there, try to prove myself all day, but nothing would change. Nothing ever changes with him.

That realization stings in a way I hadn't expected. There's something deeply unsettling about the fact that, no matter how much effort I put in, I can't break through that wall.

I keep my head down, focus on the work, but it's impossible to ignore the cracks forming in my resolve. Hayes' presence has begun to poison everything. Every moment I spend here, every task I complete, feels like a game to him—one he's already won. Every time I look over, I can see the faintest flicker of amusement on his face, like I'm a joke he's just too polite to laugh at.

I try to push him out of my mind, focus on what I'm supposed to be doing—teaching the community, assisting with fire safety education. But no matter how much I try to pour myself into those responsibilities, I can't shake the feeling that I'm constantly being watched. And not in the good way. Not in the way that makes you feel like someone cares or has your back. No, this is the kind of watching that makes you question whether you've been duped.

It happens one afternoon. The sun is blazing through the windows, the heat almost suffocating, and the rest of the crew is gathered around the table, going over the details for an upcoming community outreach event. I'm taking notes, doing my best to look like I belong, when I feel it—the unmistakable weight of Hayes' stare.

I try to ignore it, keep my focus on the task at hand, but it's impossible. His gaze is like a brand, burning into the back of my neck. Finally, I glance up, meeting his eyes for the briefest of seconds. He doesn't look away. Instead, he holds my gaze, the corner of his mouth lifting in that same irritating smirk.

"Having trouble with the equipment again, Julia?" he asks, his voice cutting through the quiet room like a blade.

There's a collective pause. I can feel the others stiffen, but Hayes doesn't care. He thrives on this. I wish I could come up with something clever, something sharp to throw back at him. But I'm so tired. Tired of the games. Tired of pretending that this doesn't bother me. So instead, I stand, my chair scraping across the floor as I push it back.

"I don't need your help, Hayes," I say, my voice colder than I meant it to be. "If I need advice, I'll ask the chief."

For a split second, his eyes flash with something—surprise, maybe. It's gone as quickly as it came, replaced by that same detached look. But I swear, there's a flicker there, something that I can't quite name.

"Don't waste your time," he says with a shrug, turning his back to me, just as the chief starts talking again. "I'm sure you'll figure it out eventually. Maybe."

The words settle over me like ash, and I force myself to sit back down. But the sting doesn't fade. It lingers, gnawing at my insides, making every breath feel a little harder to take. There's something so personal about it. Something that feels less like a challenge and more like an attack. And it's not the first time.

I push my notebook aside, unable to concentrate anymore. The meeting drones on, but I'm somewhere else. My mind is spinning with thoughts I don't want to have, doubts I can't shake. What did I do to deserve this? What's his problem with me?

I stand abruptly, making the decision before I can second-guess myself. The room quiets as I make my way to the back, towards the small kitchenette where the coffee machine sits. I need something—anything—to distract me from the ache in my chest, from the way he keeps creeping into my thoughts.

The coffee is stale, bitter, and burns my tongue, but I don't care. I'll take anything that numbs the frustration.

"You've got to stop running, you know."

The voice catches me off guard. I don't have to turn around to know who it is. Hayes is standing in the doorway, watching me with those damn calculating eyes.

I don't say anything, just take another sip, feeling the heat radiate through me in a way that's somehow not comforting. He steps inside, leaning against the counter like he owns the place, his presence once again filling the room in a way that feels suffocating.

"I'm not running," I finally reply, though I can feel the defensiveness creeping into my voice.

"Really?" he says, his tone a mixture of disbelief and something darker. "Because from where I'm standing, you're avoiding the one thing that's been staring you in the face the entire time."

The words hang in the air, and for the first time, I realize that whatever he's been holding back—whatever tension he's been building between us—it's about to explode. The walls are closing in, and I have no idea how to stop it.

Before I can reply, the doors to the station swing open with a force that makes both of us jump. The sirens start wailing, cutting through the silence, and just like that, everything else is forgotten. Everything except the next disaster waiting to unfold.

But as I turn to follow Hayes toward the trucks, I can't help but wonder: when the smoke clears, will I still have to face him? Or will it be something far worse than the fire itself?

Chapter 4: Fanning the Flames

The city hums with the pulse of neon lights, their harsh glow painting the streets in shades of blue and red, as though trying to distract from the more insidious things lurking in the shadows. The air feels thick tonight, oppressive and clinging, like a secret begging to be told but too terrified to break free. I shove my hands deeper into the pockets of my jacket, wishing it could somehow shield me from the chill that's crept inside. His words, still ringing in my ears, make the streets seem colder, sharper. Each step feels heavier, weighted with the memory of what he said—what he didn't say.

I try to steady my breathing, but the image of his eyes, sharp and calculating, flashes behind my eyelids. He doesn't know it, but he left a mark on me tonight. His words were like a slap, hard and precise, designed to sting. "Don't get too comfortable," he said, voice low, the kind of warning that didn't sit well with me. I've heard it all before, warnings and threats and things meant to make me retreat, but this? This was different. There was an edge to it, a rawness, that felt almost... personal.

I exhale sharply, the sound a soft echo against the brick walls that line the alley I've found myself walking through. The rhythmic tap of my boots on the pavement is the only sound, save for the occasional distant hum of a passing car or the hiss of a streetlamp flickering out of sync. I should've just nodded, walked out, and left the evening behind me, but I didn't. I stood my ground, as I always do. It's what I've been trained to do—push back, be better, be stronger.

But there's something in the way he looked at me when he warned me, something buried deep beneath the surface, something that unsettles me. It's like he was warning me about more than just the risks. He was warning me about himself, and I don't know what to make of that. He's complicated, wrapped in layers I'm not sure

I want to unravel, but the pull is there. It's undeniable. The fire he tries to smother? It's burning hotter with each passing moment. Maybe he doesn't want to admit it, but I see it. I see the flickers of something else behind that hardened exterior. I'm no fool—I know when someone's hiding more than they let on.

The sharp clink of metal against metal breaks my reverie. My mind drags me back to the present, and I look down at the loose change in my palm. The bus stop ahead of me is empty, as expected at this hour. The usual late-night stragglers are nowhere to be found, leaving me alone with my thoughts, and that's both a blessing and a curse. I shove the coins into my bag and sigh, glancing over my shoulder one last time as if expecting him to be there, lurking in the shadows, watching me. But he's not. He never would be.

The streetlamp overhead flickers again, the dying light casting strange, elongated shadows that seem to stretch towards me, reaching for something I can't quite grasp. I feel it then—the unmistakable tension in the air, thick like smoke, creeping up my spine. My thoughts drift to him again. His harsh words, the way his lips pressed together in a tight line like he was holding something back. I don't think it was just the job he was trying to protect me from. I think there's something about me—something he sees—that I don't even understand yet. I won't lie. It drives me crazy.

I finally pull myself out of the trance, shaking my head to clear the fog. I need to focus, need to remind myself of what I came here for. I wasn't here to play games. I wasn't here to dig into whatever wound he's hiding. But the moment his guard slipped, even just a fraction, I couldn't stop myself from being curious. It's that curiosity, I realize, that's both my greatest strength and my greatest weakness. It compels me to push past barriers, to uncover things I shouldn't.

My heart picks up its pace, and I pause mid-step, the sudden realization almost knocking the air from my lungs. What if I'm wrong? What if there is no hidden depth beneath his stone-cold exterior? What if he's exactly who he seems to be—someone willing to sacrifice everything for control, for power? The fire between us isn't a spark waiting to ignite. It's a trap, carefully set and waiting for me to step into it.

I shake off the thought, just as the familiar hum of the approaching bus draws nearer. The fluorescent lights inside are warm, a sharp contrast to the cold that's taken root in my chest. I step onto the bus, finding an empty seat near the back. As I slide down into the worn cushion, my fingers absently trace the edge of my bag. It feels strange, almost surreal, to be back to the monotony of this life after what happened earlier.

I close my eyes for just a moment, willing the headache building at the base of my skull to recede. This isn't over. Not by a long shot. Something about tonight—about him—won't let me go. And whether I like it or not, I'm about to get much closer to the fire than I ever expected. The question is: when it burns, will I be consumed by it, or will I learn to control it?

I don't have the answer yet, but I know one thing for sure: it's going to change everything.

The night air is thick, sticky with the scent of wet pavement and diesel fumes, clinging to my skin like a reminder that nothing in this city is ever really clean. The bus ride home felt longer than usual, the rhythmic hum of the wheels almost lulling me into a trance. But I couldn't shake the feeling that something had shifted, like the world had tilted just enough to make everything feel off-kilter.

I stare out the window, watching the streets blur by, my reflection caught in the glass. My own eyes seem unfamiliar, dark and heavy with thoughts I don't know how to untangle. My reflection flickers with the passing lights, but I hardly recognize the person staring back at me. Who was I kidding, thinking I could keep my distance? Every moment with him feels like a spark that could either light up the night or burn it all down. And I'm not sure which outcome would be worse.

I glance at my phone, hoping for some distraction, but the screen is blank, the silence deafening. I scroll through messages that hold no meaning, messages from people who don't know how to understand this pull, this unease that's settled deep in my bones. I wonder if anyone else has ever felt like this—like they're walking on the edge of something they can't quite touch but can't escape either.

I shake my head, willing myself to focus, but my thoughts keep circling back to him. The way he stood there, so unmoving, his eyes dark with something I couldn't name. That moment—when his guard slipped just enough to show me that flicker of something real—keeps replaying in my mind. I think I should be angry. I should be frustrated that he's holding back, that he thinks he can intimidate me with his cold demeanor and those warning words, but instead, I'm drawn to him. Not in the way I want to be, but in the way I can't help.

I step off the bus and make my way down the street to my apartment. The neighborhood is quiet, almost too quiet, the kind of silence that makes your ears ring. The old lampposts line the street like silent sentries, their weak light casting strange shadows on the sidewalk. I should feel safe here, in this familiar place, but my mind keeps drifting back to that flicker of pain in his eyes. He didn't want me to see it. He didn't want anyone to see it. But I did. And now I can't unsee it.

By the time I reach my door, I can feel the weight of the evening pressing against me. My hand hesitates over the handle for a moment before I push it open. Inside, the apartment smells like stale coffee and the faint trace of lavender from the candle I'd lit earlier. It's quiet, and for a second, I almost welcome the solitude. I set my keys down, drop my bag on the couch, and kick off my shoes, my body exhausted from the long day. But my mind? It's still running a marathon.

I move through the apartment on autopilot, the familiar rhythm of my evening routine grounding me in something tangible. I reach for the glass of water I left on the counter earlier and take a long sip, feeling the coolness slide down my throat, soothing the parched feeling that's settled there. But it doesn't ease the discomfort in my chest. It doesn't make the tightness in my stomach go away. I pull my phone from my pocket again, considering reaching out to someone—anyone—but I can't bring myself to do it. What would I say? That I'm overthinking things again? That I can't stop thinking about the way he looked at me? No. I don't have the words for it.

I sit down on the couch, my fingers idly tracing the fabric as I let out a long breath. I'm supposed to be in control. I'm supposed to have my life together, to keep my distance from people like him—the ones who have too many secrets and too many walls to break through. But it's impossible not to be curious, not to want to know why he hides behind that mask of indifference. What could have happened to make him this way? Why is it so hard for him to let anyone in?

I set my phone down, frustrated with myself. I don't even know what I'm hoping for—an answer, a sign, something to make sense of this chaos. But I get nothing. The apartment is still, and I'm left alone with my thoughts. The fire is still there, burning quietly in the back of my mind, threatening to flare up if I give it the chance.

Just as I'm about to get up and start pacing, there's a soft knock at the door. My heart leaps in my chest, and I freeze, fingers still gripping the armrest of the couch. I'm not expecting anyone. No one visits me at this hour. My mind races through possibilities—who could it be? My hand hesitates over the door handle, the tension thick in the air. With a shaky breath, I cross the room, trying to silence the noise in my head.

I pull open the door, expecting nothing more than the night's usual quiet or perhaps a neighbor asking for something insignificant. But instead, it's him. Standing there, as tall and imposing as ever, with his dark eyes locking onto mine, unreadable. He's here.

"Can I come in?" His voice is low, almost too casual, like it's nothing. Like it's not as unsettling as it feels. I should say no. I should slam the door in his face and tell him to leave. But I don't.

I step aside, letting him in, the strange, unspoken tension hanging between us like a thick fog. What the hell is he doing here?

The door swings closed behind him with a soft thud, but the quiet it ushers in is anything but peaceful. He stands just inside the threshold, an island of stillness in the small apartment, his presence somehow too large for the space. I can feel the weight of the silence between us, pressing against my chest like the first breath of a storm. My mind is working overtime, trying to make sense of this unexpected turn, but all I can seem to focus on is the way he's watching me, as though every inch of my body is a puzzle he's dying to solve.

I take a half-step back, instinctively putting distance between us. The last time I saw him, he was cold, distant—an enigma wrapped in a uniform of indifference. Now, though, there's something softer about him, like the walls he so carefully constructed are crumbling. And if I'm honest, it scares me more than I care to admit. I've spent years learning how to avoid getting too close to people, too involved. But here he is, undoing all of that with a single glance.

"Is this a bad time?" His voice is casual, but I catch the undercurrent of uncertainty in it, the sharp edge that betrays the calm exterior. It's almost like he's asking permission, though I'm not sure what for.

"Why are you here?" The words are out before I can stop them, sharp and direct. But as soon as they leave my mouth, I regret them. Not because they're untrue, but because they're too loaded with meaning. They're questions I don't want to ask, but I can't help myself. The fire he's ignited in me refuses to be ignored.

He tilts his head, a flicker of something almost amused passing across his features. It's fleeting, gone before I can grasp it, but it's there. "I thought we could talk," he says, and it's the kind of statement that feels too ordinary to be anything but a lie. "About earlier," he adds, like that might somehow explain the strange way his presence is unsettling everything inside me.

I cross my arms, suddenly self-conscious. "We've talked enough," I reply, trying to sound firm, trying to put some of the distance back between us. But the truth is, I don't want him to leave. Not yet. Not when the air feels so thick with unanswered questions and unsaid things.

He doesn't respond at first, just stands there, his eyes searching mine, as though he's trying to gauge whether I'm really as unaffected as I'm pretending to be. His gaze shifts briefly to the couch, and I can tell he's considering sitting down. But instead, he takes a step closer, his movements slow, deliberate. Each step feels like a declaration, like he's claiming the space between us in a way that makes my pulse quicken.

"I'm not here to make things difficult," he says, his voice quieter now, the walls around him crumbling just a little more with every word. "I just... I need you to understand that I'm not the enemy."

His words hang in the air, dense with meaning, and for a moment, I almost believe him. I almost let myself trust the sincerity in his tone. But then the memory of earlier flashes in my mind—his warning, his cold detachment, the way he made it clear he didn't want anyone to get too close. The way he pulled back when I reached for the truth.

I swallow, trying to push down the frustration that's building again. "If you're not the enemy, then what the hell are you?" The question slips out before I can stop it, and I immediately regret it. But it's out there now, and I need answers.

He pauses, his eyes searching mine like he's weighing how much he should reveal. I watch the muscles in his jaw tense, the way his lips press together in that familiar, guarded way. It's like he's holding back some deep truth, something he's terrified to say out loud. And just when I think he's going to open up, to let me in, he shifts, his expression hardening again.

"I'm someone who's trying to keep you safe," he says, his voice low, almost pained. "Even if it means pushing you away."

The words hit me like a slap, and I stagger back, caught off guard by the weight of them. I want to scream, to demand he explain, but something in his eyes keeps me silent. He's holding back, yes, but there's also something in his expression that tells me he's holding onto something much darker than just the weight of his responsibilities.

"Why is it always about safety with you?" I ask, almost pleading, my voice cracking in spite of myself. "Why does it feel like every time I get too close, you push me away?"

His eyes soften for the briefest moment, but it's enough to make my heart skip a beat. "Because, damn it," he mutters, stepping closer, his tone rougher now, "you're not supposed to get involved. You're not supposed to care."

I feel the air shift between us, a storm brewing in the space where I'm standing. I want to scream, to demand more, but I can't seem to find the words. Everything about this feels wrong and right at the same time, and I'm not sure which way is up anymore.

Before I can gather my thoughts, he steps even closer, his face inches from mine. His breath is warm against my skin, and I can feel the tension crackling in the air, thick with something unspoken. I can't look away. I don't want to.

"Just stay away from me," he says, the words almost a plea, a command, a warning all rolled into one.

And before I can respond, before I can even process what he means, the door slams open behind me, the force of it rattling the walls of my apartment.

The room is plunged into darkness.

Chapter 5: Ashes of the Past

The day had started like any other—a gentle breeze that carried the scent of rain, the soft hum of traffic just outside my window. The world was slow to wake, still dappled with the golden light of morning. But there was a shift, something beneath the surface that didn't belong. It wasn't until the whispers started that I realized it wasn't just me. Everyone could feel it.

It was the way the air felt a little too thick, the way the sunlight seemed to catch on something darker, something we were all trying to ignore. I overheard them first—just fragments of conversation, half-hearted murmurs between people who thought they could keep their voices low enough to escape attention. But no one can hide a secret for long. Not in a place like this, where time drips like molasses, slow and sticky, and everything becomes something to talk about.

The fire. A tragedy. The words hung in the air like smoke. People were quick to say that it had happened years ago, that it had been contained, that it was no one's fault. But the way they said it—there was something else there. A tension. Something they weren't willing to touch, yet couldn't entirely avoid.

I should've kept my distance, let the rumors die where they began. But that wasn't in my nature, was it? The moment my curiosity ignited, I couldn't let it go. There were too many pieces to the puzzle, and I had only seen the edges. The man with the haunted eyes—the one who looked at me as if he could see straight through my skin, past all the walls I'd so carefully built—was part of this story. I could feel it.

At first, I thought it was just a passing thought, one of those fleeting notions that we have when something feels off. You know the kind—where you wonder if you've imagined it, or if your mind is just filling in the gaps because it wants something to make sense.

But the more I listened to the whispers, the more it became impossible to ignore. He was connected to it. I could see it in the way his jaw clenched when the subject came up, in the way his eyes darkened, as if he were seeing something far off, something painful that only he understood.

So, I did what any person who's a bit too nosy and far too stubborn would do. I asked him.

We were sitting on the bench by the lake—me, fiddling with a loose thread on my sleeve, trying to look casual, trying not to let him know I had already begun to piece it all together. He sat with his usual stillness, his eyes fixed on the water as if it could offer him some kind of solace.

I turned toward him, hesitated, then said the words that I knew would change everything. "What happened?"

His eyes snapped to mine, and in that instant, it was as if the world stopped moving. The ripples on the lake paused, the birds stopped singing. Everything went silent, save for the sharp intake of his breath. He didn't answer right away. I could feel the tension in the air, thick enough to cut through.

"What do you mean?" he asked, his voice low, guarded.

"The fire," I said, almost whispering. "I've heard things. About what happened all those years ago. What really happened."

His expression hardened, like a wall rising between us. I watched his lips tighten, his hands gripping the edge of the bench like he was trying to anchor himself to something—anything—to keep from being swept away.

"You don't understand," he said, his voice like steel, each word deliberate and controlled. "You don't want to."

It was a warning. One I didn't heed, of course. I never did.

"I think I do," I replied, my own voice steady despite the pulse of adrenaline racing through my veins. "But I need to hear it from you."

His eyes flickered, just for a second, and I caught a glimpse of something—a crack, a break in the armor he had so carefully built around himself. For that brief moment, I saw the man he could've been. Not the quiet, intense figure who stood just out of reach, but someone else entirely. Someone who had been torn apart and put back together again, with jagged edges that never quite fit.

But then, like a switch had been flipped, his expression closed off, the shutters falling down.

"I told you," he said sharply, standing up from the bench, his broad shoulders blocking the sunlight. "You don't know what you're asking for. Leave it alone."

I didn't get up. I couldn't. The pull between us was too strong, the need to understand, to make sense of everything, to fill in the gaps where his silence left them. It was like standing at the edge of a cliff, knowing you shouldn't jump, but also knowing that if you didn't, you'd be left wondering for the rest of your life what it felt like to fall.

"I can't," I said softly, the words tasting like defeat before they even left my mouth. "I can't leave it alone."

His gaze softened, just for a second. But in that moment, something else passed between us—something I couldn't name, something that made my heart beat just a little faster.

"You should," he said quietly. "Because there's nothing left to find. There never was."

But I knew better than that. The truth was buried beneath the surface, and I was determined to unearth it—no matter how deep I had to dig, no matter how many walls I had to break down.

I watched him walk away, the crisp autumn leaves crackling beneath his boots as he left me sitting on that bench, feeling like a fool. I should've let it go, should've pulled myself together and accepted the silence for what it was. But there was something about the way he said it—"You don't understand." It wasn't just a dismissal. It was a challenge.

And for reasons I couldn't quite explain, I was never good at backing down from a challenge.

The days that followed were uneventful, in the most unnerving way possible. It was as though the town had collectively decided to pretend nothing had happened, as if they hadn't shared knowing glances behind closed doors, hadn't let their eyes wander to the empty plot of land that still held the faintest trace of soot. The fire, the tragedy—they were just old stories now, things we didn't need to mention anymore.

Except that I couldn't shake it.

The whispering was getting louder, no longer just rumors but pointed conversations that stopped abruptly the moment I came into view. And it wasn't just about the fire anymore—it was about him. About the way he carried himself, the way people avoided looking him in the eye. I knew that look—every small town had its stories, its skeletons hidden in the closets that no one ever wanted to dust off. And the more I heard, the more I felt the pull. I had to know.

I started with the town library. It was the one place that didn't feel suffocating with its small-town charm. Shelves stacked high with dusty books, the smell of old paper that almost masked the faint odor of mildew, the quiet hum of a ceiling fan that barely managed to stir the air. It was the kind of place that made you feel like you could sit for hours, reading whatever your heart desired—or whatever you had the patience to find.

The librarian, Mrs. Whitfield, was the town's unofficial historian. She knew everything, from the names of families that had come and gone to the exact year the oak tree in the town square had been planted. If anyone would know about the fire, it would be her.

I approached her desk, trying not to feel like a thief. The kind of thief who would steal something far more dangerous than any material object. "Excuse me, Mrs. Whitfield?" I said, my voice more tentative than I'd like to admit.

She glanced up from her crossword puzzle, peering over her glasses with a disapproving look that was practically a town tradition. "Yes, dear?" she asked, setting the pen down and giving me her full attention.

"I was wondering," I began, "if you had any records, maybe some old newspaper clippings, about the fire that happened years ago? The one out on Maple Ridge?"

The moment the words left my mouth, I saw it—a flicker in her eyes, something that wasn't quite surprise, but closer to hesitation. She cleared her throat and stood up, moving to a back shelf that I'd never noticed before. It was tucked away in a corner, as if it were a part of the library people had forgotten existed. She returned with a thick binder, worn and frayed at the edges. It looked like it had been opened hundreds of times, yet the pages inside seemed to hold the weight of the years that had passed.

"Here," she said, opening it carefully and sliding it across the table toward me. "You should know that people don't talk much about that. It's better left undisturbed, if you ask me."

Of course, no one had asked her. But I didn't say that. Instead, I flipped through the pages, scanning the headlines, the photographs of the devastation, the burnt remnants of what had once been homes. The fire itself had been catastrophic. Hundreds of acres reduced to ash. But what caught my eye was something more subtle—a mention of a missing person, someone whose name was listed but whose fate was never fully explained.

My pulse quickened as I read the line over and over, trying to make sense of it. "No trace of the missing resident was found." The words felt like a punch to the stomach.

"Who was that?" I asked before I could stop myself.

Mrs. Whitfield didn't answer right away. Her hand hovered over the binder, her fingers curling slightly, as if she was considering pulling it away from me. Finally, she sighed, a long, drawn-out sound that seemed to come from somewhere deep inside her.

"It was him," she said quietly. "The man you're asking about. He was the one who—" Her voice trailed off as though the memory itself was too painful to speak aloud.

I blinked, the pieces clicking together in a way I hadn't expected. "You're telling me he was—" I stopped myself, unwilling to finish the thought.

But she nodded, once. Just once.

"He was part of it," she said softly. "And no one talks about it anymore. For his sake, and for theirs."

The binder was heavier now, as though the weight of those words alone was enough to make it unbearable. I wanted to ask more, wanted to press her for the details that felt so close to my fingertips, yet always just out of reach. But I could see the way she was looking at me, the pity in her eyes, and I knew it was no use.

"I should go," I muttered, standing up and walking toward the door. The quiet of the library pressed in around me, the weight of it almost suffocating.

As I stepped outside, the cool air hit my skin, the late afternoon sun casting long shadows over the town. The silence felt different now—darker, somehow. As if something had shifted, and the world had become just a little less friendly.

I wasn't sure what to do next. But I knew one thing for certain: the more I tried to stay away, the more tangled I became in the story of the man who haunted my thoughts. And no matter how hard I tried to convince myself to let it go, I knew deep down that I couldn't. Not now. Not when I was this close.

I didn't sleep that night—not really. There were moments when I drifted in and out of restless dreams, but they were filled with fragmented flashes. Images of him, his eyes dark and unreadable, the edge of his jaw clenched tight in that unmistakable way that told me more than any words could. I saw flashes of the fire, too, the orange glow reflecting in broken windows, the smoke curling into the sky like it was trying to escape, like it was begging for forgiveness. But the missing piece—the one that I couldn't get out of my head—was his name. It was there in the back of my mind, always just out of reach, like the thing I needed most to make sense of everything.

The morning came too soon, and with it, the heavy burden of what I hadn't yet learned. I had promised myself I wouldn't push. I had promised myself that I would leave it alone, that I would take his words at face value. But I never had been good at keeping promises to myself.

I found myself standing outside his house later that afternoon, staring at the darkened windows. The house was quiet, too quiet, like it hadn't seen life in a long time. I could feel the weight of it pressing against my chest, the pull to knock, to ask him the questions that had been gnawing at my insides since the library. There was no easy way to do it. No polite way to open a door you were never meant to walk through.

But I couldn't stop myself.

I lifted my hand to the doorbell, paused, and then pressed it. The sound echoed in the stillness, jarring in its suddenness. A moment passed, two, before the door creaked open, and there he stood—his expression unreadable, as always, but this time, there was something else. Something I couldn't quite place. His posture was tense, his eyes darting over my shoulder before they met mine.

"What are you doing here?" he asked, the words not harsh, but still carrying an edge.

"I needed to talk," I said, the words slipping out before I had time to second-guess them.

He didn't move, didn't invite me in. He just stood there, his gaze unwavering, as though he was weighing something—something more than just whether or not to let me in. I stood there, waiting for him to speak, for him to do something. But all he did was watch me, his lips pressed into a thin line.

"I told you before," he said, his voice low and steady. "I don't think you should be here."

I could've left. I should've left. But I didn't. I wasn't ready to walk away yet. Not when I could feel the truth—whatever it was—just under the surface, waiting to break free.

"Tell me what happened," I said, my voice firmer this time, my frustration bubbling just below the surface. "Tell me about the fire. About what really happened. It's all anyone's talking about."

He flinched, but only for a moment. His eyes hardened once again, and he stepped back, holding the door slightly ajar as if to say this conversation was already over. But I wasn't backing down. Not this time.

"I don't want to talk about it," he said, his voice clipped. "And I'm asking you to leave."

I didn't step back. I didn't flinch. I was too far gone now, too deep in the search for answers to let him shut me out again. "I think you owe it to yourself to say it," I said, my words cutting through the space between us like a knife.

His gaze flickered, just for a moment, but it was enough. I saw the hesitation. The part of him that was still human, still haunted by whatever it was he was trying so hard to bury. But then it was gone, replaced by that cold, unreadable mask.

"No," he said, his voice a steel trap. "I don't owe anyone anything."

But something in the way he said it—it made me wonder if he was trying to convince himself as much as he was convincing me.

I took a deep breath, steeling myself for what I had to say next. "If you won't talk to me," I said, "then I'll find someone who will."

For the first time, he looked at me like I had done something he hadn't expected. His eyes narrowed, and a flash of something—anger, fear, maybe both—passed across his face. He opened his mouth, as if to say something, but then stopped.

"Don't," he warned, his voice dropping to a whisper.

I stepped forward, just a little, the heat of the moment catching up with me. "What are you so afraid of? What happened in that fire? What aren't you telling me?"

For a second, I thought he might break. The mask faltered, just slightly, and I could see the man beneath—the one who had carried this weight for so long that it had become a part of him. But then, just as quickly as it came, it was gone, and he slammed the door shut in my face.

The sound was deafening. It reverberated in my chest, a sudden, sharp blow that left me reeling. I stood there for a moment, stunned, my hand still hovering in the air where the door had been. I felt the ache of disappointment settle deep inside me, but beneath it, something else stirred. Something darker.

I turned and walked down the steps, each step heavier than the last. My mind raced with the words I had heard, the silence that had followed, and the truth I still couldn't reach. But I was closer now. I could feel it.

And just as I was about to round the corner, I heard the door creak open behind me. My heart skipped a beat.

"Wait," his voice called out.

I turned, my breath caught in my throat, waiting. Waiting for him to finally speak the truth.

Chapter 6: Heatwave

The sun beat down, relentless in its midday fury. Sweat clung to my skin, slipping down my back in heavy rivulets, the air thick with the scent of asphalt and earth baked under the heat. My shoes scuffed against the gravel as I moved, each step a little slower than the one before, the drill stretching on with no end in sight. It was just another day, another session, another test of endurance, but today felt different. Today, something in the air was off, heavy and charged, like a storm was waiting just over the horizon.

I caught a glimpse of him standing at the edge of the field, his posture taut, like a predator watching its prey. Silent, observant, as always. His eyes never left me as I continued the routine, running drills I could do in my sleep, yet today, each repetition felt like an impossible feat. It wasn't the heat that was making it harder—no, it was the way his gaze pinned me, like he was dissecting every movement, every misstep. I could feel his judgment simmering just beneath the surface, a constant, invisible pressure pushing me forward.

The whistle blew, signaling the end of the set. I slowed to a halt, breathing heavily, trying to ignore the ache in my muscles. The taste of dust and sweat clung to the back of my throat, but I swallowed it down, refusing to let any weakness show. That's what he wanted, wasn't it? He wanted me to break. He wanted to see if I could crack, to test if I was really cut out for this. Every day, he drove me harder, further, like he was trying to break something inside me—and for some twisted reason, it was working.

"Again," he said, his voice low, almost drowned out by the sound of my own ragged breathing.

I looked at him, and for the briefest moment, I thought I saw a flicker of something—an emotion, maybe? But it was gone as quickly as it appeared, leaving only the hard, impassive mask he wore all the time. He was always this distant, this detached. Even when he looked at me, it was as if he was looking through me. And that made me angry. It wasn't just the drills that were getting under my skin anymore. It was him. His presence, his unrelenting focus. I hated the way he made me feel—like I was under a microscope, constantly being evaluated, dissected, and found lacking.

Without a word, I took off again, pushing my body to keep moving, to stay ahead of the discomfort clawing at my chest. Each stride felt heavier than the last, my body crying out for rest, but I refused to give in. If I gave in now, if I slowed down or showed any sign of weakness, I knew exactly what he would do. He'd push me harder. He'd make me feel even smaller. He wouldn't just challenge me, he'd break me down until there was nothing left.

I reached the far end of the field and turned back, my eyes trained on him as I ran. He hadn't moved. Still standing there, unmoving, like a statue, watching, waiting. But there was something different now—something about the way his eyes tracked me, so intently, so carefully. It was like he was waiting for something to happen, something that only he knew would come. And I hated it.

The second the whistle blew again, I stopped, my chest heaving, my legs trembling from the strain. My heart thudded painfully in my chest, and I leaned forward, hands on my knees, gasping for breath.

"Is that all you've got?" His voice was suddenly right next to me, close enough that I could feel the heat from his body, the sharpness in his tone like a knife. I straightened up, but I couldn't bring myself to look at him. I kept my eyes trained on the ground, refusing to meet his gaze. If I did, I'd give him what he wanted—the satisfaction of knowing he'd gotten under my skin.

But then, his voice dropped, so low I had to strain to hear it, like a whisper meant only for me. "You're better than this. Don't make me regret putting in the effort."

The words hit me like a punch to the gut, sharp and unexpected, and for a moment, I couldn't breathe. What did he mean by that? Effort? He'd been pushing me to the edge, every single day, and yet now he was telling me not to make him regret it? My fingers curled into fists, nails biting into my palms as I fought to keep my temper in check. This wasn't about effort—it never had been. It was about control. His control. His need to break me down, piece by piece, until I was nothing but a shell of who I was before.

I finally dared to meet his eyes, and in that moment, the world seemed to shrink. His gaze was intense, almost too intense, and something passed between us—something I couldn't name. It was as if, in that brief second, everything else fell away. The heat, the drills, the tension—it all evaporated, leaving only the weight of his stare, heavy and piercing. The fire inside me flared, not from anger, but something far more dangerous. Something that felt like it was slipping out of my control.

For just one heartbeat, I thought I might actually say something—anything—to break the tension. But before I could, he turned on his heel and walked away, his footsteps steady, his back rigid. I stood there, frozen, the adrenaline still coursing through my veins, my pulse pounding in my ears. What the hell just happened?

The days blurred into a haze of sweat and exhaustion, the rhythm of the drills a steady throb in my chest. I woke up every morning with the taste of grit in my mouth, a dull ache that wrapped itself around my bones before I even set foot outside. But there was something about this place—something about the way the sun rose, scorching the earth as if it had a vendetta, that made me feel alive, despite it all. The mornings were always the worst, the heat like a constant pressure, but I kept going, kept pushing, because what else was there?

And then, there was him. Watching, always watching. He never let up, never let me slip. He was relentless in a way that was almost... clinical, as if he were evaluating something rather than training it. His silence was his weapon, his presence a constant, sharp-edged reminder that I had to prove myself. Each day felt like an interrogation, and I was the suspect, squirming under his scrutiny.

It wasn't that he didn't know how to give a compliment—he just never did. Every time I thought I might have impressed him, there'd be a slight nod, maybe a grunt, but nothing more. He left me to wonder whether he was capable of seeing anything beyond the surface, anything beyond the mechanics of the drills. But then again, maybe that's exactly what he wanted me to think. Because that's the thing with him: nothing was ever just surface-level. There were layers, hidden beneath the surface, and trying to peel them back was like chasing smoke.

One morning, the air was thick with tension even before the session began. I could feel it, vibrating in the space between us. He was standing at the far end of the field, his hands clasped behind his back, his shoulders straight, his gaze locked on me like a hawk eyeing its prey. I knew he was waiting for me to make a mistake. He always did. That was the thing about him—his expectations were always just beyond reach. Always pushing, always demanding more. It made me furious, but there was something in me that couldn't turn away.

The whistle blew, cutting through the quiet, and I snapped into motion. The drills were brutal, like always—sprints, agility, endurance, the same exercises that had become second nature by now. But today, every step felt heavier, every breath more strained. I could feel his eyes on me like a heat wave, relentless and oppressive.

His presence was like a shadow, always just at the edge of my vision, watching, waiting for any misstep.

I pushed harder, faster, but it wasn't enough. It never would be. I could sense him moving closer, the soft crunch of his boots against the gravel signaling his approach. He didn't speak at first, just circled me, his gaze following every movement, dissecting every flicker of hesitation, every stutter of my stride. And then, when I thought I might collapse from the weight of it all, he was there, right behind me, his breath warm against my ear.

"Slowing down, are we?" His voice was a low murmur, just loud enough to make the hairs on the back of my neck stand on end.

I didn't turn to face him. I couldn't. If I did, I'd give in, and I wasn't ready to give him that satisfaction.

"I'm not slowing down," I bit out through gritted teeth. "You just can't keep up."

His chuckle was a quiet, dangerous thing, like the warning of a storm that hadn't quite broken. He stepped closer, until I could feel the heat radiating from his body, his presence surrounding me, pressing in on all sides. "Is that so?" The words were almost a tease, laced with something darker, something unspoken.

It took everything in me not to turn and lash out, but instead, I kept running, my legs pumping beneath me, my heart thundering in my chest. I was so close—so close to breaking through that wall I had been building for months. I could feel it, that moment when everything would click into place, when I could finally prove myself. But the harder I pushed, the more his voice seemed to echo inside my head.

"Are you even trying?"

I snapped my head to the side, catching his gaze for a split second. There was no hint of humor, no trace of encouragement, just that cold, calculating look he always wore. And in that fleeting moment, I realized—he wasn't here to help me. He was here to test me, to push me until I couldn't take it anymore. But why? What was his endgame?

"Give me a break," I muttered, breathless and on the verge of snapping. "I'm not some robot you can program with your perfect little drills."

He didn't flinch. Not even a muscle twitched. "Then stop acting like one." His voice was low, sharp.

And just like that, something inside me shifted. The simmering anger that had been coiling inside my chest all these weeks flared up, hotter than the sun above us.

"Maybe I don't want to be perfect," I snapped, spinning on my heel to face him fully. The words tumbled out before I could stop them. "Maybe I just want to be... enough."

There was a flicker in his eyes—something, a crack in that ice-cold facade. For the briefest of moments, I thought I saw something that resembled... regret? Or maybe it was just a trick of the light.

"Enough?" he repeated, the word hanging in the air like a challenge, like he was daring me to keep pushing. "Maybe you're right. But what if that's not enough for me?"

I swallowed hard, trying to keep my composure, but his gaze was unwavering, pressing in on me with all the intensity of a storm gathering on the horizon. It was then that I realized: he wasn't trying to break me. He was trying to make me stronger. And that thought, that unsettling, confusing thought, made me more furious than I'd ever been. Because if I was honest, I was starting to hate how badly I wanted to prove him wrong.

The following days stretched out before me like an endless corridor, each step echoing with the sound of my own footsteps, each turn bringing me closer to something I couldn't quite name. The drills became a blur of motions, but they weren't just exercises anymore. They had become a battleground—my resolve against his unyielding presence, my will against his silent expectations.

There was no escaping it. No matter how fast I ran, no matter how high I jumped, no matter how deeply I buried the questions that clawed at my insides, he was always there. Watching. Waiting. Silent, but not passive. His eyes tracked me, always calculating, always searching for that moment where he could push me just a little further.

It was the quiet between us that bothered me the most. The space he kept, like some invisible barrier. It wasn't just physical distance—it was something deeper, like an invisible wall that neither of us dared to breach. I caught myself thinking about it more often than I should have, the thought of crossing that line—of saying something, doing something—just to see what might happen.

But that was the problem, wasn't it? He knew how to keep me on the edge.

By the time I reached the end of the field, I was gasping for air, my lungs burning, the sharp tang of metal on the back of my tongue. I slowed, but I didn't stop. Stopping was for failure, and I wasn't about to give him the satisfaction of seeing me fail.

He hadn't moved. I should have been used to that by now—the stillness, the rigidity in his stance. But today, there was something different in the way he was watching me. It wasn't just the quiet observation of a trainer; it was something else. Something that pricked at the edges of my mind like an unanswered question.

I turned back, my legs like lead, forcing my feet to move even though every part of me screamed for rest. His gaze never wavered as I made my way toward him, my chest rising and falling in uneven breaths. He was waiting, but for what? The thought fluttered like a bird caught in my chest, refusing to be ignored.

"You're slowing down." His voice cut through the tension between us like a whip. Low, measured, but somehow, there was an edge to it. A frustration I hadn't heard before.

I stood a little straighter, trying to mask the fatigue that was starting to seep into my bones. "I'm fine," I snapped, though I wasn't sure if I was trying to convince him or myself.

His lips twitched—just slightly—and for a moment, I thought I saw something like... amusement?

"Are you?" He took a step closer, and there was no mistaking the way his gaze narrowed. The distance between us felt like it had shrunk, the space between trainer and trainee suddenly charged with something unspoken. His presence was overwhelming, and I could feel my pulse jump in response, like it was being pulled by some invisible string.

I could have taken a step back. I could have created space. But for some reason, I didn't.

Instead, I stood my ground. "I'm not some machine that can be wound up and told when to stop."

He tilted his head, like he was studying me, his eyes flicking from my face to the sweat-drenched mess of my hair, to the way my hands clenched at my sides. "No," he agreed slowly, "you're not."

There was a pause, a quiet that wrapped itself around us. And then, as if he hadn't already pushed me to my limits, he leaned in just enough to close the last inch of space between us. His breath brushed my ear, a quiet murmur that made my skin prickle.

"Then why do you keep pretending you are?"

The question hit me like a slap, sharp and stinging, leaving me wide-eyed and frozen in place.

I opened my mouth to speak, but the words caught in my throat. I wasn't sure what to say. Was I pretending? Maybe. Maybe I'd been so busy trying to keep control that I hadn't allowed myself to admit how close I was to cracking under the weight of it all.

But I wouldn't show it. I couldn't.

"Why do you care?" The words came out in a whisper, though they were thick with frustration. It wasn't even a question anymore—it was a demand. A need to understand what was happening between us, this strange push and pull that was unraveling something deep inside me.

He didn't answer at first. Instead, his eyes locked onto mine, and for the briefest of moments, I felt it—the thing I hadn't dared name before. The fire, the spark, whatever it was that danced between us, lighting up the space like a fuse on the verge of detonation.

And then—before I could even process it—his hand brushed against mine. Barely a touch. A whisper of skin against skin. But it was enough. Enough to make everything inside me coil tight, to make the heat in the air suddenly unbearable.

His eyes flicked down, his jaw tightening just slightly. And for the first time, I saw something in him that I hadn't expected. Vulnerability? Regret? I wasn't sure. It was gone almost as quickly as it had appeared, replaced by that same cold, impassive mask he wore so effortlessly.

"You need to stop pretending," he said, his voice lower now, more intense.

I opened my mouth to respond, to tell him that I wasn't pretending, but the words faltered as I saw something shift behind his eyes. And that's when it happened. Something cracked. Something unspoken—and before I could stop myself, I reached out, just barely, but enough to make my fingers brush against his arm.

He froze. Just for a second, like time had stopped, and then he stepped back, his eyes narrowing as if he were fighting with himself. I wanted to say something—anything—but I couldn't. My breath caught in my throat, my chest rising and falling with the kind of tension I couldn't control.

The whistle blew then, breaking the moment, but it didn't break the silence between us. It only made it heavier.

"Get back to it," he said, voice strained, and for a second, I thought I saw something flicker in him. Something fragile.

But it was gone before I could grasp it.

And as I turned to walk away, the air between us felt different. Heavy. And I wasn't sure if it was from the heat or something else entirely.

I glanced over my shoulder one last time, catching a glimpse of him staring after me. His expression was unreadable, but in the depths of his gaze, I saw it. Something I wasn't ready to face.

And for the first time, I wondered what it was that made him so afraid of letting go.

Chapter 7: The Inferno Within

The sun slanted low through the thick trees, casting long shadows across the ground. The air was rich with the scent of damp earth, the kind of scent that clung to everything and left a taste at the back of your throat. I wiped the back of my hand across my brow, not caring if I smeared the layer of sweat pooling there. The event was supposed to be a simple one—an outreach to raise awareness about neighborhood safety. The kind of thing you do because it looks good on a resume, or because your neighbors expect you to. But here I was, standing next to him, feeling the simmering heat of something far more complicated than I had anticipated.

I couldn't remember the last time I'd seen him smile. The usual charm he wore so effortlessly—always slightly mocking, like he was too clever for the room—had been absent since the day we first crossed paths. Now, he stood beside me, shoulder brushing mine in the crowded tent, his face unreadable. No smirk. No challenge. Just... silence. A silence that felt like a weight.

"Do you always stand so still?" I asked, my voice louder than necessary in the thickening crowd.

He glanced over, the smallest flicker of surprise in his eyes, before his gaze dropped back to the papers in his hands. "Do you always talk so much?"

"Only when I'm bored." I crossed my arms over my chest, trying to ignore how awkward I felt standing so close to him. His presence, even in this absurdly mundane setting, was a force of nature. A storm waiting to break.

There was a long pause. It was as if he were considering whether to let the tension between us stretch further or slice through it with his usual cutting remarks. Instead, he let out a quiet laugh, the sound almost unrecognizable. It wasn't the smug, self-satisfied laugh I'd come to expect from him, but something softer, quieter.

A laugh that barely made it past his lips. He shifted his weight, his shoulder brushing mine again, and the contact sent a strange jolt through me. It was unintentional, I knew that. But the way he'd done it—how he'd leaned in ever so slightly—felt purposeful. A challenge I wasn't prepared for.

I shook my head, trying to dismiss the thought, but it clung to me anyway. A flicker of something darker moved behind his eyes, something I couldn't place. I wanted to ask him what it was. What had happened to him in the weeks since the incident? Why did it feel like he was always holding something back, something that wasn't for anyone else to know?

"Do you think we'll actually get anything done today?" I asked, hoping to pull him out of whatever internal world he was locked in. It wasn't a great question, but it was the only one that didn't feel too invasive. And with him, I'd learned to be careful with the questions I asked. They tended to ricochet back at me, hitting harder than I expected.

His gaze shifted again, lingering on the way my fingers tapped restlessly against my arm. "I'm sure we will," he said, his voice smooth, but something about the way he said it made my pulse quicken. "You always do."

I didn't understand. He was being too civil. Too... normal. This wasn't the man I'd come to know, the one who spoke in riddles and never told the whole truth. The man who knew exactly how to make you question everything you thought you knew about yourself. I couldn't make sense of him anymore.

But that was the problem, wasn't it? I'd been in the business of trying to make sense of people for far too long. It was what I did, what I prided myself on. And here he was, throwing all the rules out the window, existing somewhere between the lines I was used to.

I couldn't let it go. The doubts. The fear that something was slipping further and further out of my grasp. That maybe the whole charade we were playing—this false pretense of normalcy—was built on something much darker.

The sound of chatter around us blurred into the background, and I turned to face him more directly, lowering my voice. "What aren't you telling me?"

He didn't respond immediately, and for a moment, I wondered if I had pushed too far. But then he looked up at me, his eyes dark and unreadable. "What makes you think I'm hiding something?"

I stared at him, trying to read the line of his jaw, the subtle tensing of his shoulders. The way his lips barely moved as he spoke, like he was trying to keep something buried beneath the surface. But it was there—an undercurrent, a vibration that hummed between us. I could feel it now, that unspoken weight, that silence that was far louder than anything he could say.

"Because I know you," I said softly, almost too softly. "And I know when you're lying."

A flicker passed over his face—surprise? Resignation? Something I couldn't pin down. He took a deep breath, his eyes never leaving mine. "Maybe you don't know me as well as you think."

I swallowed hard, my throat dry. His words, so casually delivered, cut deeper than they should have. It was a challenge, an invitation to dig deeper, to push further. And I hated that it pulled me in. I wasn't supposed to want answers from him. I wasn't supposed to be here, trying to piece together a puzzle that wasn't mine to solve.

But as I looked at him, standing so close yet so far, I realized with a gut-wrenching certainty that I couldn't walk away. Not yet. Not until I had the answers, until I could finally see the whole picture. Because if I walked away now, I'd never know the truth. And that was something I couldn't live with.

The moment lingered, heavy with unspoken tension, before he finally turned away, his voice low and controlled. "We'll see," he said. "You'll figure it out eventually."

But I wasn't so sure.

The late afternoon sun hung heavy in the sky, as if the heat had nowhere else to go but to suffocate the air. The crowd around us shifted and murmured, unaware of the undercurrent of tension swirling between me and him. I tried to focus, tried to make myself care about the brochures I was supposed to be handing out, the statistics on neighborhood crime, the safety tips that everyone had heard a hundred times before. But it was all just noise—background filler for a script I didn't want to be a part of.

I glanced at him again, his figure leaning casually against the side of the tent, his eyes scanning the crowd with an air of detachment that only made my skin crawl more. There was something about him in these moments—something that made him seem like a stranger, even though I had known him longer than I cared to admit. His guarded silence, the way he seemed to exist just on the edge of the conversation, waiting to pull away at any moment, only fueled the confusion that gnawed at me. It wasn't just that he was distant—it was the way his distance felt like an invitation. An invitation to dig deeper, to uncover whatever it was he was hiding.

"You're awfully quiet," I muttered, my fingers clenching around the pile of flyers in my hands. He didn't respond, not immediately, and I could feel the weight of his indifference settle over me. But then, as if he had decided that my comment required an answer, he lifted his gaze from the crowd and met my eyes.

"You talk a lot," he said, a smile tugging at the corner of his mouth. It was a smile that didn't reach his eyes, a smile that was more of a mask than anything else. It was the kind of smile that made you question what he wasn't saying. And in that moment, I realized that his silence wasn't a wall; it was a trap. A carefully constructed one, designed to keep everyone out while giving nothing away.

I swallowed hard, the words bubbling up before I could stop them. "What are you hiding?"

His eyes flickered with something—maybe surprise, maybe something darker—but whatever it was, it was gone before I could read it. "Nothing," he said, too quickly. "Why would you think I'm hiding something?"

"Because you always are," I shot back before I could stop myself. "And you're not fooling me with this... whatever this is."

He straightened, his gaze sharpening. "What exactly is 'this,' then?"

"This," I said, motioning between us, "this game. This charade. You're pretending nothing's wrong, pretending everything's fine. But I know you're lying. You can't hide behind that smile forever."

For a moment, there was nothing but the sound of distant chatter and the rustle of paper. Then, without warning, he pushed off the side of the tent and closed the distance between us, his body invading my space with an intensity that made me catch my breath. My pulse quickened, and I had to force myself to look up at him instead of shying away.

"You don't know anything about me," he said, his voice low, controlled. "And you're right—I don't plan on letting you."

I wanted to respond, wanted to dig deeper, but something in his tone stopped me. There was no anger in his voice, no heat, just... calm. A calm that felt far too deliberate. It made me wonder if I was the one losing control, if the questions I'd been afraid to ask were starting to surface despite my best efforts to keep them buried.

"You think I'm hiding something?" he repeated, his gaze piercing, like he was daring me to press further. I almost did, almost asked him what it was that had changed, what had happened to him. But the words felt like they might choke me if I spoke them aloud.

"Why do you care?" I muttered instead, hating how weak I sounded.

He tilted his head slightly, studying me as if he could see right through the facade I was desperately trying to maintain. "Because, whether you admit it or not, you're just as curious as I am."

I took a step back, suddenly feeling exposed in a way I wasn't used to. He wasn't wrong, not entirely. But I wasn't ready to admit it. Not to him, not to myself.

I crossed my arms tightly across my chest and turned away, my eyes scanning the crowd for anything to latch onto, anything that could give me a moment of relief. But nothing helped. Not the laughter of the children running around, not the familiar faces in the crowd, not the mundane, well-meaning speeches on safety. Nothing could distract me from the reality that, for reasons I couldn't explain, I was trapped in a game that neither of us had agreed to play, and yet here we were—locked in the rules of it, no way out.

I couldn't figure out why he had this power over me. Why his silence, his presence, could twist and pull at the edges of my resolve. It wasn't just that he was good at keeping secrets. It was that I didn't want to know what secrets he was hiding. Not because I was afraid of the truth, but because it meant I was already too far in.

"What do you want from me?" I asked, my voice barely above a whisper. The words felt like they hung between us, heavy and unfinished, waiting for something to fill the space. He didn't answer right away, but I could feel him watching me, his gaze sharp and unreadable.

And then, just as I thought he might turn away, just as I thought I might finally get the distance I so desperately craved, he leaned in. So close, I could feel the heat radiating off his skin. "I want nothing from you," he said, his breath brushing against my ear, sending a chill straight through me. "But I think you're starting to realize that you want something from me."

I shook my head, but the words felt like they were lodged deep in my chest, threatening to burst free. "You're wrong."

He smiled then, the same empty smile he always wore, and took a step back. "Maybe," he said, voice trailing off. "Or maybe I'm right."

I didn't know what to say to that. I didn't know how to walk away from something that was already pulling me under. And so, I stood there, waiting for whatever would come next. The air between us was thick with tension, and I realized with sudden clarity that whatever happened, I wouldn't be able to escape it.

The night had descended before I realized it, the once blistering heat of the day now softened into a damp, suffocating fog. I stood alone at the edge of the event, watching the crowd disperse. Most had gathered their things, exchanged final pleasantries, and gone home to the comfort of familiar routines. But I couldn't seem to leave. Not yet. There was a strange magnetism in the air, a pull that kept me tethered to the space between us.

The gentle murmur of distant conversations grew fainter as my gaze locked onto him again. He hadn't moved from where I had last seen him. His figure, silhouetted by the glow of the streetlights, was still too close for comfort yet too distant to reach. He leaned casually against the post, one hand tucked into his pocket, the other tracing the rim of his coffee cup. A man at ease—or at least, pretending to be.

I couldn't shake the feeling that he was watching me, waiting for me to make the next move, like we were two players in a game with rules neither of us had agreed to. My instincts screamed at me to leave, to retreat to the safety of normalcy, but I wasn't sure I could anymore. Not after everything that had passed between us.

A car pulled up at the edge of the lot, its headlights briefly illuminating his face. The fleeting moment showed nothing but the same unreadable expression, but the faintest tension in his jaw betrayed him. Something was coming, something I couldn't quite grasp, but it was so close I could almost feel it.

Without thinking, I walked toward him. Each step felt like an echo in the quiet night, louder than it should have been. He glanced at me when I drew near, his eyes narrowing just slightly. The small flicker of acknowledgment made my heart race, but he didn't speak.

I wasn't sure what I had expected, but this—this stillness—was almost worse. It was like standing on the edge of a cliff, watching the world spin in slow motion, and knowing that any sudden movement would send everything crashing down.

"You know, you're not very good at this whole social thing," I said, my voice sharper than I intended. I'd been standing in silence for far too long, and it was starting to eat at me.

He tilted his head slightly, eyes lingering on my face for a moment before he spoke. "Maybe I'm just not interested in pretending."

There it was again. That unsettling calm, the controlled indifference. Like he was playing a part in a story he had no interest in telling. It shouldn't have frustrated me as much as it did, but it did. It was a game I didn't want to play, but now that I was in it, I had no choice but to keep moving forward.

"Are we pretending, then?" I asked, voice quieter now, a hint of something more vulnerable creeping through. I couldn't quite hide the uncertainty that clung to the edges of my words.

He didn't answer immediately, and for a moment, I thought maybe he wasn't going to. But then, in that heavy silence, his gaze softened, just the faintest bit, before he spoke.

"Maybe we are."

I almost didn't believe him, but something in the way he said it—something in the space between his words—made me reconsider. Could it be that everything I had assumed was wrong? That this whole situation, everything about him, had been a carefully crafted illusion designed to keep me off balance, to keep me questioning, to keep me wanting more?

I took another step closer, driven by a combination of frustration and curiosity. "And what happens when the pretending stops? When we stop hiding from what's really going on?"

He finally shifted, his shoulders rolling back as if he was waking from a long stupor. The calm he had worn like armor now seemed to crack, just slightly. But only enough for me to notice.

"Then the truth comes out," he said softly, almost too softly. "And you won't like what you find."

His words hung in the air between us, an invisible weight. I could feel the tension in my chest, the deep pull of something dangerous that I couldn't ignore. My heart was hammering, blood rushing in my ears. What did he mean? What truth was he talking about? I opened my mouth to ask, but before the words could form, he took another step back, just far enough that I couldn't reach him without crossing a line.

"I told you, you wouldn't like it." His voice was a low murmur, like a secret he wasn't sure he should be sharing.

I swallowed, fighting the urge to demand more answers, to push him until he cracked and spilled everything he was hiding.

But there was something in the way he said it, something almost final about his tone, that stopped me.

"What if I want to know?" I said, my voice stronger now. "What if I want to hear the truth?"

For a moment, he just stood there, watching me, his gaze unreadable. The world around us had quieted even further, as if it, too, were waiting for something to break. I could see the faintest tremor in his hands as he set his coffee cup down, but his face remained unchanged.

He took a step back, the distance between us growing wider, and in that moment, I realized something—I was afraid. Not of him, but of what he might reveal. Of the darkness that might pour from his mouth, the truth that could shatter the carefully constructed world I had been living in.

"You should go," he said, voice firm, almost commanding.

I blinked, feeling a sudden rush of confusion and something else—something like regret, but deeper. "What?"

"You're not ready for this," he said, almost too softly to hear. "You never will be."

I felt my stomach drop, the words swirling in the air between us. I wanted to argue, to insist that I could handle whatever he was hiding, but as his gaze met mine, something in the pit of my stomach told me that maybe—just maybe—I couldn't.

Then, without another word, he turned away, walking into the darkness that had swallowed the rest of the night. And I stood there, frozen in the same spot, my mind racing with a thousand unanswered questions.

The silence was deafening. And I realized, with a creeping horror, that I wasn't the one asking the questions anymore.

Chapter 8: A Glimpse of Light

I hadn't expected him to invite me into his world. Not like this. Not with such a quiet, confessional weight behind it. The air in the room had shifted ever so slightly, like the world was holding its breath, waiting for him to speak. I'd been around long enough to know when someone was close to breaking, even if they didn't know it themselves. But nothing prepared me for the way his voice cracked when he finally broke the silence.

"I used to think fires didn't just burn things. I thought they could purify them, too," he said, his words low and deliberate, like he was still trying to convince himself of something he hadn't fully accepted. "When I was younger, I... I was stupid, thinking I could control them. I used to play with fire." His hands flexed as if the memories still had a physical hold on him, his fingers twitching as though he could still feel the heat.

I leaned in, but not too much. I didn't want to crowd him, to push him too far too fast. I had learned the hard way that sometimes, the more you pressed, the more people shut down. But something about the way he said it—so small, so quiet—pulled me in like a moth to the flame, and for the first time, I found myself wondering if I could be the one who wasn't afraid of the heat.

He continued, the words spilling out as though he couldn't stop them once they had started. "There was this one night. The fire was bigger than I thought. I thought I could stop it—thought I could outrun it." His voice cracked on the last part, and it was like the earth shifted beneath me. I couldn't decide whether to reach for him or to let him hold on to whatever fragment of control he had left. He gave a bitter laugh, like he knew exactly how ridiculous he sounded. "I didn't outrun it. And I couldn't stop it. By the time I realized it, it had already taken more than just the building."

I was silent. What could I say? The words felt useless, empty in the face of such grief. The only sound between us was the rhythmic thumping of my heart, my pulse loud in my ears. And for the first time, I didn't feel like an outsider to his pain. I didn't feel like I was watching from the sidelines. I was here, now, with him, sharing this moment. I just didn't know what to do with it. I didn't know what to do with him.

"I didn't just lose the house," he said, his voice now barely a whisper. "I lost... I lost myself. I didn't even recognize who I was after that. It was like looking at someone through a cracked mirror and wondering if you could ever piece it back together. But you don't." He shook his head, his eyes narrowing as if the thought alone pained him. "I haven't been able to piece it back together. I don't even know if I want to."

The vulnerability in his words hung in the air like smoke, thick and cloying, and I couldn't breathe for a second. I knew this man—the one who worked late nights, the one who rarely smiled, the one who didn't talk about feelings unless it was to avoid them. The one who held people at arm's length, never getting too close, never giving too much. And yet, here he was, exposing himself in ways that made me ache. His words were like raw scars laid bare for me to see.

"I wasn't there when it happened. I was supposed to be, but I—" His throat tightened, cutting off whatever he'd intended to say. He swallowed, hard. "I didn't make it in time. And I should have."

I wanted to say something—anything—that could fix this. But I couldn't. Because the truth was, nothing would. Not now. Not after everything that had happened. It was like he had let me peek inside a world I wasn't supposed to see, and in doing so, he had taken a piece of me with him. I could feel the weight of it. The burden. And as much as I wanted to pull away, to give him the space I knew he desperately needed, something inside of me pushed against that instinct. Maybe it was foolish, or naive, or just plain dangerous, but I couldn't seem to help it.

"Hey," I said softly, my voice breaking through the silence between us. I could feel his eyes on me, though I couldn't bring myself to meet them just yet. "It wasn't your fault. You can't blame yourself for something you couldn't control."

He snorted, the sound dry and bitter. "Easy for you to say. I can barely look at myself in the mirror without seeing that fire. Without hearing those screams. Every day, I wonder if I could've done something different, something better. And every day, I come up empty."

The words hit me like a slap, raw and jagged. But I wasn't going to let him go on like this, trapped in his own guilt.

"You didn't do anything wrong," I insisted. I reached out, my fingers brushing his arm, tentative, unsure. I wasn't sure if it was the right move, but I had to try. "You're here now. That counts for something. You've done enough."

He didn't respond right away. For a moment, I thought he might pull away, retreat into that hard shell he'd worked so hard to build. But then, slowly, ever so slowly, I saw the tension in his shoulders ease. His eyes softened just the slightest bit, as though he was letting go of something—something I couldn't see, but I felt it shift in the space between us.

"I don't know if I can ever forgive myself," he whispered. "But thank you for saying that."

I wasn't sure what would happen next. I wasn't sure where we went from here. But for the first time in a long time, I was willing to stick around long enough to find out.

I didn't know what to say after that. The words I had rehearsed in my head—the comforting ones, the helpful ones, the ones I thought would make this moment easier—fizzled away, leaving nothing but silence in their wake. Maybe that was the point. Maybe the silence was better than any carefully crafted line of reassurance.

He didn't pull away, not immediately, but I could feel the distance growing between us. It wasn't physical; it wasn't something that could be measured in inches or centimeters. It was subtle, the kind of thing you felt in your chest, that quiet throb of tension in the air. I could almost see the walls going up in his eyes, brick by brick, until he was the man I had met all those months ago—stoic, closed off, unreachable. I watched him stiffen, his jaw clenching, as though he had just decided that this was it. Enough.

I wanted to stop it. I wanted to reach through that invisible barrier and pull him back into the moment we had just shared, where he had been so raw, so human, so utterly vulnerable. But I didn't know how. I couldn't force him to stay in a space where he wasn't ready to be. I knew that. I just didn't want to lose the glimpse of him I had seen—cracked and fragile, like the petals of a flower that had been trampled, but still reaching toward the sun.

"I—I didn't mean to... I wasn't trying to make you feel... uncomfortable," I stammered, suddenly unsure of myself. The words came out awkwardly, like I was stepping on my own feet, and I wanted to slap my forehead for it. I didn't want to take a step back, but I feared I had no choice.

He looked at me then, his eyes heavy with something I couldn't place. Maybe it was regret, maybe guilt, maybe a hundred different things all tangled up in one. Whatever it was, it made my heart clench. He opened his mouth, but before he could speak, the air was pierced by the sudden, shrill sound of a car alarm from somewhere in the distance. It was the kind of noise that made everyone in the room freeze, like a natural instinct to listen for danger. I hated it—hated how it disrupted the fragile bubble we had formed around ourselves, the brief moment of honesty that had connected us.

"I'll go check on that," he muttered, standing up too quickly, as if he couldn't escape the room fast enough. He didn't look back at me, didn't offer anything else, just turned away, his back rigid. The door clicked shut behind him with a finality that felt like a door being slammed in my face.

For a moment, I just sat there, staring at the spot where he had been, the air around me still thick with the remnants of his confession. I ran my fingers over the edge of the couch, as if I could somehow still feel the weight of the words he had shared, the ghost of him that had been just a little bit closer than before.

I didn't know what to do. Part of me wanted to give him space, let him come to terms with whatever demons he was fighting, but the other part of me, the one that had always been a little too hopeful, a little too willing to dive headfirst into the mess of things, wanted to knock on that door and tell him it was okay. That he didn't have to keep pretending he had it all together. But I wasn't sure if I was the person he needed for that—or if I could even handle it. Because whatever this was, whatever thread had connected us for just a brief, fleeting moment, it wasn't something I had prepared for. It wasn't something I knew how to fix.

When he finally came back, there was no apology, no explanation. He just sat down, looking as if he had never left. But the shift in his energy was unmistakable. It was like he had turned into a completely different person, one who had built walls so high they could never be scaled. I hated it. I hated how easily he could slip back into his armor, like he had done it a thousand times before. I hated how easily I let him.

The silence stretched between us, stretching to a point where I felt the need to fill it, to break it before it became a chasm too wide to cross. "You don't have to do this alone, you know," I said, keeping my voice steady, despite the knot tightening in my throat.

He glanced at me briefly, his eyes unreadable. Then he shifted in his seat, avoiding my gaze again. "I'm fine."

I wanted to roll my eyes. Of course, he was fine. "You're fine. Right. That's why you just shut down on me like that."

"Look, I don't... I don't need anyone's pity. Especially not from someone who barely knows me."

I recoiled at the harshness in his tone, but I refused to let it shut me down. I had gotten a glimpse of the real him, and I wasn't about to let that go without a fight. "This isn't pity. It's care. There's a difference."

His laugh was bitter, short, and devoid of humor. "Care? What's that even supposed to mean?"

I leaned forward, meeting his eyes, refusing to let the weight of his defenses push me back. "It means that sometimes, people don't need to be fixed. Sometimes, they just need someone to be there. And that's what I'm offering."

The words hung between us, suspended in the tension of the moment. I could feel the shift in him again, a tiny crack in his fortress. He didn't answer. He didn't need to. I could see it in his eyes, the uncertainty that flickered behind the hardness. Maybe he was starting to believe me. Maybe he wasn't. But I had already decided—I wasn't going anywhere.

I watched him shift, the walls rising again in that slow, practiced manner, like a fortress being rebuilt brick by brick. I almost couldn't blame him. No one wanted to be this open, this raw. Especially not with someone who might end up walking out.

He rubbed his jaw, the movement almost mechanical, as though trying to grind away the emotions he hadn't asked for. I could almost see the gears turning in his head, calculating how much of himself he could afford to give away without losing everything. I didn't know how he had managed to stay this guarded for so long—his anger, his bitterness, his guilt—they were all so thick, layers upon layers of pain, hiding the parts of him that were still soft, still human. And yet, despite it all, there was something undeniably magnetic about him, something I couldn't quite place, but I was hooked on it.

"I'm sorry," he muttered, not meeting my eyes. "I shouldn't have said all that. It's not your problem."

But it was. Or at least, it felt like it was. I wasn't sure what had happened—maybe it was the way he'd let his guard down, or the rawness in his voice—but suddenly, everything felt different. He had let me in, even just a little bit, and I couldn't go back to the way things were before. I wasn't going to pretend I didn't care.

"Stop saying that," I said, frustration creeping into my voice. I leaned forward slightly, making sure he could feel the weight of my words. "You're not alone in this. You've got me, whether you want it or not."

He glanced up at me, his eyes narrow, trying to gauge if I was serious. I could see the skepticism in his gaze, the guarded nature of someone who'd been burned—figuratively and literally—too many times. And yet, something in his expression shifted. The smallest glimmer of hope—or maybe just the tiniest crack in his armor. He swallowed, hard, and I noticed how he clenched his fists in his lap, like he was trying to contain something inside that was trying to get out.

"You don't know what you're getting yourself into," he muttered, the words coming out like a warning.

I tilted my head, watching him closely. "Try me."

His mouth twisted into something that almost resembled a smile, but it wasn't one that reached his eyes. "You think you can handle me? After everything I've done?"

I felt a surge of heat rush to my face, not from embarrassment, but from something sharper, something that made my pulse pick up speed. "I don't care about your past. I care about what you're going to do with your future." I leaned back in my chair, crossing my arms. "And maybe, just maybe, I can help you with that. But you have to let me in. For real."

His gaze lingered on me, his eyes softening for the briefest of moments before that familiar hardness returned. He shifted uncomfortably, rubbing his neck, as though he couldn't decide whether to laugh or be angry. "You really think you can fix me?"

I wasn't sure if that was what I was trying to do, or if I was just trying to make sure he didn't break on his own. I sighed, standing up and pacing the room, trying to gather my thoughts. "I'm not here to fix you," I said, my voice steady, even though my hands were trembling with nerves. "I'm here because I believe in you. And because—" I stopped myself. "I believe that maybe there's more to you than the man you've become."

I felt the silence settle over us, thick and heavy, like it was pushing us both further into our corners. I knew I was asking a lot. More than I should have, probably. But I didn't care. There was something about him, something that kept pulling me back in, even when he tried to push me away. And this time, I wasn't going to run.

He stood up suddenly, making the space between us feel impossibly small. "You don't know what it's like. You have no idea what I've done."

His voice was tight now, the frustration leaking out in a way that made me want to reach for him, to pull him closer, but I didn't. I knew better. The last thing he wanted was for me to feel sorry for him, and yet, that was exactly what I was feeling. But I wouldn't give in to it. Not now. Not after everything we'd just said to each other.

"I don't need to know everything," I said quietly. "But I need to know that you're not going to shut me out. Not now."

There was a long, painful pause, as if he was weighing the consequences of letting me in. The tension in the room was suffocating, and for a second, I almost thought he was going to turn and walk out again. But instead, he reached out, brushing his fingers against mine in a fleeting touch that made my breath catch.

"I don't know if I can do this," he said, his voice barely audible. "I don't know if I can let you in."

For a moment, I thought I had lost him. But then he stepped closer, his hand gently cupping my chin, guiding my gaze up to meet his. The warmth of his touch was almost too much to bear. I couldn't think. My pulse was too loud in my ears, my skin too sensitive to the electricity crackling between us.

Before I could speak, before I could tell him that it didn't matter, that I wasn't going anywhere, the door slammed open with a sudden force, and a figure filled the doorway.

And in that instant, everything between us shattered.

Chapter 9: A Smoldering Attraction

The door clicked behind me with a soft finality, and I stepped into the dimly lit room, my eyes adjusting to the subdued light. The air felt thick with an unspoken tension, a charge that clung to every surface like static, ready to crackle at the slightest disturbance. I could feel it in the way the room seemed to hold its breath, waiting for something, anything, to shift. And I knew, with a certainty that twisted my insides, that it was him. It always was.

He was standing near the far wall, hands stuffed deep into his pockets, shoulders hunched like a man bracing for a storm. His posture was casual, but there was a tightness to his frame, as if he was holding himself together by sheer force of will. And his eyes—those eyes—locked on mine before I even had a chance to fully settle. They were unreadable, always dancing on the edge of something darker, something he kept hidden from the world. But not from me. No, I knew better than anyone that there was a storm brewing in him, a storm that I was dangerously close to being swept up in.

"Back again?" His voice was rough, the kind of rough that hinted at too many late nights and too many things left unsaid. It was a question, but there was no curiosity in it. It was a statement dressed in the form of inquiry, and I hated the way it made my chest tighten.

I shrugged, doing my best to look unaffected, but my pulse betrayed me, racing under my skin as I took a step toward him. "You make it sound like I don't have a choice."

His lips twisted into a half-smile, and for a fleeting moment, I saw the edges of something softer in his eyes. It was gone in the blink of an eye, replaced by the cold indifference he was so damn good at hiding behind. "We all have choices," he said, a challenge hanging between us like a heavy fog. "You just don't like the ones you've made."

I felt the sting of his words, but I refused to show it. Instead, I walked past him, the barest brush of my shoulder grazing his as I made my way toward the window. The city sprawled out beneath me, its lights flickering like stars in the distance, but it felt miles away from where I stood. I could still feel the heat of his presence in the air, like a constant pull, drawing me closer whether I wanted to go or not.

"You think you know me?" I asked, my voice a little sharper than I intended, but the question had been lingering on my tongue for far too long. "You think you've got me figured out?"

"I know what I see," he replied quietly, the words slow and deliberate. "And I don't like what I see."

There it was again—the distance. The barrier between us that neither of us could seem to break. It wasn't just physical, although the space between us was unmistakable. It was the kind of distance that you couldn't measure in feet or inches, but in emotions, in things left unsaid and never quite spoken.

I turned to face him, the words already on my lips, but for a moment, we just stood there. The silence stretched, thick and suffocating, each of us unwilling to make the first move. He studied me like I was a puzzle he couldn't quite solve, and I hated the way it made me feel exposed. Vulnerable. But more than anything, I hated how much I liked it.

"So, what happens now?" I finally asked, my voice steadier than I felt. "Are we just going to keep pretending this—whatever this is—doesn't exist?"

His jaw clenched, the muscles working beneath his skin as if he were fighting to keep his composure. "It's not that simple."

Isn't it? I thought, but the words died on my tongue. Because deep down, I knew exactly what he meant. It was never going to be simple, not with him. Not with this... whatever it was. The connection that hummed between us, as undeniable as gravity, was always there, and no amount of pretending was going to make it go away.

I felt a tug at the corners of my mouth, the ghost of a smile that I couldn't suppress even if I tried. "Yeah," I murmured, taking a step closer to him, "I've noticed."

The air around us seemed to thicken, charged with the electricity that always lingered when we were in the same room. I could feel the weight of his gaze on me, burning through the space, and it made my heart race. But I wasn't the only one who could feel it. I could see the way his body tensed, the subtle flex of his hands at his sides, the way his lips parted slightly, like he was about to say something—but didn't.

"Stop it," he said finally, his voice low, rougher than before, and it sent a shiver down my spine. "You're playing with fire."

I smirked, my lips curling up just a little. "Funny. I was thinking the same thing about you."

He exhaled sharply, as if I'd caught him off guard, and for a split second, I thought I saw something flicker in his eyes. A flicker of doubt? Of something deeper? But then it was gone, hidden behind the mask of indifference he always wore.

"I don't play games," he said, his voice cold now, guarded. "And neither should you."

I tilted my head, studying him closely, watching the way his eyes darkened. "Who says I'm playing?"

The words hung in the air between us like a dare, and in that moment, I knew. I knew that this—whatever it was between us—was only the beginning. It was inevitable, really. The spark was already there, and it was only a matter of time before it ignited into something neither of us could control.

And maybe that was exactly what scared him the most.

I didn't see it coming, not in the way you expect. It wasn't the sort of grand gesture that you see in romance movies, or even in the subtle, lingering touch that people like to say signals a spark. No, it was far more insidious than that. It crept up on me, slow and steady, like a wave inching its way up the shore. And then, before I knew it, I was drowning in it.

It started with a glance—just a quick flicker of his eyes across the room, a momentary hesitation before he looked away. It was enough to make my heart stumble, as if it couldn't quite decide whether to race or stop altogether. I hadn't even realized how much I'd been holding my breath until that moment, and when I let it go, it was shaky, unsure.

"You're avoiding me," he said suddenly, his voice steady but laced with something I couldn't quite place—curiosity? Annoyance? The faintest hint of something else?

I glanced up, startled by the sharpness in his tone. There he was, standing in the doorway like he owned the place, arms crossed over his chest in that way that made everything about him seem too good to be true. And maybe that was part of it. He was too... perfect. Too infuriatingly perfect, with his tall frame, the tousled dark hair that I knew, even in this dim light, had been meticulously arranged to look effortless. He was the kind of person who made everyone around him feel like they were playing in the minor leagues. And I hated him for it, even as I couldn't look away.

"I'm not avoiding you," I said, a little more defensively than I'd intended. "I'm just... busy."

He raised an eyebrow, a small, knowing smile tugging at the corner of his mouth. "You're always busy."

There was something in the way he said it, like he knew me better than I wanted him to. It made the air between us grow thick, as though every word we spoke was another layer added to a growing storm.

"I'm not avoiding you," I repeated, and this time, my voice was a little quieter, a little less sure. "I'm just... being careful."

The silence between us stretched again, the kind of silence that makes you acutely aware of every little thing—the sound of your own heartbeat, the way your fingers itch for something to do, the steady rhythm of his breathing that somehow seems to match your own. It's all too much, and yet, it's not enough. Not when you know it's only a matter of time before something breaks.

"You should know," he said, stepping closer, his voice dropping lower, almost as though he were sharing a secret, "careful isn't the same as being smart."

I turned to face him, feeling the heat rising in my cheeks, but I refused to back down. "And what exactly does that mean?"

"It means you're too busy playing it safe," he said, his gaze locking onto mine, not letting go. "And I'm not sure how much longer I'm going to let you get away with it."

The words hung in the air like a challenge, like a dare, and I wasn't sure whether I should be flattered or furious. But I wasn't about to let him think he had me cornered. Not yet.

"I don't need you to tell me how to live my life," I said, trying to sound more confident than I felt. "I've been doing just fine on my own."

He stepped even closer now, close enough that I could feel the heat radiating from him, like a magnet pulling me toward him whether I liked it or not. His presence was overwhelming, suffocating in the best way, and I hated that I couldn't seem to push him away, no matter how hard I tried.

"I'm not telling you how to live," he murmured, his voice low, almost intimate. "But you're making this harder than it needs to be."

I swallowed, my mouth suddenly dry. I wanted to argue, to tell him off, to make him feel the weight of my words. But when he looked at me like that, when his gaze softened just enough to make my heart beat erratically in my chest, all I could do was stand there, caught in the web he'd spun around me.

"So what happens now?" I asked, my voice barely a whisper, unsure whether I wanted an answer or not.

He didn't say anything at first, just stood there watching me with that look in his eyes—half amusement, half something darker, something deeper that I wasn't sure I could handle. And then, just as I thought he might not answer at all, he spoke.

"I think you know exactly what happens now," he said, his voice tight with something I couldn't quite place. "You're just too scared to admit it."

I shook my head, as if the movement could shake off the growing sense of inevitability settling deep in my stomach. "I'm not scared."

He smiled then, and it was like watching a storm form on the horizon—beautiful, dangerous, and impossible to ignore.

"You will be."

The words hit me like a punch to the gut, and for a moment, all I could do was stand there, breathless, caught in the storm he was creating around us. And I knew, deep down, that I was already lost.

It was already happening.

The tension between us, that spark that had been growing since the first time we'd crossed paths, was too much to ignore now. No matter how much I tried to fight it, it was there, simmering beneath the surface, waiting for the right moment to ignite.

And I had a sinking feeling that, when it did, nothing would be the same again.

He didn't move, and neither did I. The space between us felt like it was shrinking, but neither of us made a move to close the distance. There we were, two people who could hardly breathe in the same room, caught in a standstill neither of us could break. His gaze never wavered, but I could see the war behind his eyes—the battle between whatever it was that drew us together and the part of him that seemed determined to keep me at arm's length.

"I'm not sure how much longer I can keep this up," he said, his voice barely above a whisper.

I tilted my head, looking at him, trying to decipher the meaning in his words. "What do you mean by that?" The words felt brittle coming out of my mouth, like I was walking a tightrope, one misstep away from losing my balance.

"You're not as careful as you think you are," he replied, his voice soft but sharp, like the edge of a knife barely concealed beneath the surface. "And neither am I."

The words hit me like a jolt of electricity. I swallowed, the air suddenly feeling too thick, too heavy to breathe in. Was he suggesting what I thought he was?

I crossed my arms, suddenly aware of how much the room had closed in around us, as though it was daring us to do something we both knew would be impossible to undo. "You think I'm the one making it difficult?"

He didn't respond immediately, but the way his lips curled, just slightly, as if he was about to speak but had second thoughts, made the tension crackle in the air. "You're playing this game, and you don't even realize it. The worst part? You're playing with fire."

My eyes narrowed. "Is that supposed to scare me?"

"No," he said, his voice a whisper now, but it sent a shiver up my spine. "But it should."

It was maddening, the way he stood there, all sharp angles and unspoken truths, challenging me without even trying. I wasn't sure if I wanted to hit him or kiss him, and that was the part I hated most. Because both options felt equally impossible and equally inevitable.

I took a step back, my breath catching in my throat. "So what now?" The words came out quieter than I meant, as if I were afraid of what might happen if I said too much.

He stepped forward, closing the gap between us in one smooth movement. His presence surrounded me, pulled me into his orbit like a planet caught in the gravity of a star. His gaze was so intense, I could feel it sinking into me, into my skin, into the spaces I hadn't even known existed. "Now? Now we stop pretending." His voice was low, rough in a way that made my chest tighten. "Stop pretending that we don't know what's happening here."

The words lingered between us like a spark, threatening to ignite, but I didn't move. I couldn't. Something in me was frozen, and it wasn't fear. No, it was something else—something I wasn't ready to name, something I couldn't afford to admit yet.

"You make it sound so simple," I muttered, taking another step back. But my retreat felt hollow, like it was nothing more than a futile gesture against the force pulling us together. "And it's not."

His expression shifted, just for a second, the hardness in his eyes softening before that familiar mask of indifference settled back into place. "Is that what you want me to think? That it's not simple?"

I could feel my pulse speeding up again, that familiar rush of heat flooding my veins. It was getting harder to think, to focus, to hold on to anything other than the pull of him, the tension hanging between us like a storm just waiting to break.

"I don't know what I want," I said, the words coming out before I could stop them, and I hated the way they sounded. Honest, but vulnerable. "I don't even know what's real anymore."

He looked at me then, really looked at me, his eyes locking onto mine with such intensity that it felt like he was trying to see through me, like he was peeling back every layer I had so carefully built around myself. "You don't have to know," he murmured, his voice barely a breath. "You just have to feel it."

And for a moment, I did. I felt it all—the heat, the pull, the way my heart seemed to beat in time with his own, the way my breath hitched when his hand reached toward me. Every inch of me screamed to let go, to stop fighting it, to let the current take me wherever it led. But something in the back of my mind, that small, rational part of me, kept reminding me why this was dangerous, why this couldn't happen.

"You're right," I said, my voice a little stronger now, even if it was shaky. "I don't know what I'm feeling."

He leaned in just a fraction closer, his lips nearly brushing my ear as he spoke, his breath warm against my skin. "Then stop pretending you do."

The closeness, the heat of his body just inches away from mine, was enough to make everything else in the world fall away. And for a second, I forgot about the consequences, forgot about the mess we'd be making, about the way this could shatter everything I had built. It felt too good to think. Too easy to let myself get lost in it.

And just as my resolve began to falter, the sound of the door creaking open snapped me back to reality. I pulled away instinctively, my heart racing, panic flooding my chest.

But it wasn't him. It wasn't even someone I recognized.

It was a figure in the doorway, half-lit by the glow of the hallway. A stranger. And their eyes were fixed directly on us.

Everything in me screamed to run.

Chapter 10: Playing with Fire

The fire crackles in the background, its ferocity eating up the edges of my thoughts. The weight of the flames is suffocating, but it's the presence of him—tall, determined, and unflinching—that makes it almost impossible to breathe. He's already a silhouette against the orange inferno, but the way he moves—fast, sure, reckless in the way only someone who's faced death a thousand times can be—sends a jolt through me. Every part of me wants to look away, wants to keep my distance, but I can't. I never can.

"Stay behind the line, Sara," he calls out, his voice carrying over the roar of the fire, his tone that unmistakable command I've heard him give a thousand times, and always ignored. It's that combination of authority and care, the knowing that he'll take every risk for the people around him without a second thought. I never have been good at taking orders, especially when it comes to him.

"I'm fine," I shout back, my heart thrumming against my ribcage as I watch him slip deeper into the fire's maw. His form moves fluidly, a blur of strength and purpose, the heat reflecting off his face, his eyes dark and intent.

"Goddamn it, Sara," he mutters under his breath, more to himself than to anyone else. He doesn't look back, but I see it—the flicker of something too sharp and intense in his gaze before he disappears into the thick smoke. There's always a part of me that wants to chase him into the flames, to be closer, to understand the quiet storm that lives inside of him. But it's not something I can touch. Not really.

I want to be angry, to shout at him for disappearing like that, but instead, I just stand there, my feet rooted to the ground. The fire shifts, a sudden gust of wind pushing it toward me, and I find myself rushing forward before I can stop myself, drawn by a force that feels more dangerous than the fire itself.

The heat on my skin is unbearable, making every inch of my body ache with awareness. And then I see him again, emerging from the smoke like some kind of dark angel, his face streaked with soot, eyes wild with focus. He grabs me by the arm before I can even think to run, his grip so tight it feels like he's trying to pull me apart and put me back together.

"Are you out of your mind?" His voice is harsh, rough, full of fire and frustration, and I can't help but meet it with a sharp laugh.

"If you think I'm out of my mind," I say, meeting his gaze, "then you should probably take a look at yourself."

His jaw tightens, and for a second, I think he might push me away. Instead, he pulls me in closer, the space between us vanishing as quickly as the flames that curl around us. I can feel the heat of his body, a live wire that makes everything else—everything outside of us—disappear.

The world goes quiet for a moment, and I think we're both holding our breath, caught in the same strange orbit. But it's broken, shattered by the loud crack of wood collapsing behind him, forcing him to turn away, to step back.

"Don't make me do this again, Sara," he warns, his hand lingering at my shoulder for a moment too long, as though he's battling with himself, trying to decide whether to let go or hold on tighter. His eyes flick to the fire, then back to me, and in them, I see something—a flicker of something dangerous and fragile all at once. A warning. A promise.

I'm not sure which part of him I'm more afraid of: the one who charges into danger with no regard for his own safety, or the one who stands at the edge and dares you to follow.

"I'm not scared of you," I tell him, and there's something in my voice—something raw and unfiltered—that makes him stop.

He looks at me like he's trying to figure me out, like he's weighing the truth in what I've said, and I'm almost certain that he knows it's a lie. But I'm not scared of him. Not really. Not in the way that matters. The fire is the only thing I'm scared of, the only thing that could ever keep me from chasing after him, from getting too close to the flame that seems to burn inside of him.

He doesn't say anything in response. Instead, he takes my hand, his fingers cold against the heat of the night, and drags me back toward the truck. His grip is firm, but there's something tender in the way he holds me, a softness that doesn't fit with the chaos of what's happening around us. The fire roars, hungry and relentless, but he's already moving, already pulling me away from it.

For a moment, I want to argue, want to break free, but then he looks at me again, his eyes dark and knowing, and I wonder if he sees the truth that I can't even bring myself to acknowledge. That I can't keep running. Not from him. Not from the heat that swells between us, the pull that I can't ignore no matter how much I try.

I let him lead me, my heart pounding in my chest, the fire still burning bright in my mind. The world around me might be on fire, but the only thing I'm certain of right now is that there's no escape from the blaze we've set in motion.

We don't speak as we drive back from the scene, the truck's engine humming like a lullaby in the dark. The city is quiet now, the kind of quiet that only settles after a storm has passed. The moon hangs low, silver and sharp against the night sky, and it feels like everything is holding its breath. Even the sirens, the fire trucks, the chaos of the evening, all seem distant now.

His hand rests loosely on the steering wheel, but I can feel the tension in his arm, the way his knuckles tighten every so often, like he's still carrying the weight of the fire. His eyes are fixed on the road, but there's an unreadable quality in the way his jaw clenches, a storm he's keeping buried beneath that cool, composed surface. I'm tempted to ask if he's okay, but I know he won't answer. Not really. Not the way I want him to. Not the way I need him to.

I shift in my seat, trying to get comfortable, but my body feels restless. My arm where he grabbed me still tingles, the heat of his touch searing through my skin like an imprint that won't fade. It's a burn I don't mind. In fact, I almost wish I could feel it longer, but the thought of that is too dangerous, too wild to entertain.

"What is it about fires?" I finally ask, my voice breaking the silence like a sudden splash in a still pond.

His gaze flicks to me for a second, sharp and alert. "What do you mean?"

"You," I say, trying to keep my tone light. "You're always so... calm in the chaos. Like it's where you belong. You make running into a fire look easy. Most people would be terrified, but you..." I trail off, not sure how to finish the sentence without sounding like I'm peeling back a layer of him I'm not supposed to see.

He exhales slowly, his lips curling into a tight smile that doesn't reach his eyes. "It's not easy. But when you've been doing this long enough, you learn to dance with it."

A silence stretches between us, thick and heavy, as the world outside the truck window blurs by. I want to push him for more, for the truth behind that cryptic answer. But I know that if I press, he'll close off, and I'm not sure I'm ready to face that side of him.

"Why do you do it?" I ask instead, my voice a little quieter now. "Why risk your life for people who wouldn't even blink if they saw you walking down the street?"

He glances at me, his expression unreadable. For a moment, I think he might just keep driving, let the question hang in the air like it's a fleeting thought that doesn't deserve an answer. But then he speaks, his voice low, almost like he's speaking to himself.

"I guess someone has to."

It's simple, but the weight of it hangs in the air, and I'm not sure if I'm more struck by the depth of his words or the fact that he's willing to leave it at that. It's like he's revealing something too big to unpack, too heavy to carry on a drive like this. I want to say something, to fill the space with words, but the truth is I don't have anything to offer that would make him feel less alone in this strange, heavy silence.

As we near the outskirts of the city, I feel the truck slow. The lights of the streets start to fade, the buildings growing less dense, the world quieter as we move into the empty stretch of highway leading home. My hands are still slightly clammy, and I wipe them on my jeans, trying to shake the tension that has settled into my shoulders.

"What happens now?" I ask, half out of instinct, half because I need to know.

He doesn't answer right away, his eyes scanning the road ahead, but I can tell he's already processing the question, weighing his response carefully. The way he operates—always cautious, always a step ahead—keeps me on edge, like I'm the one who's being analyzed, not the other way around.

"I'm taking you home," he says finally, his tone practical, but there's an undertone there, something a little more... guarded. Like he's not sure what to say next, like he's wondering if this is the point where everything changes. Or maybe it's just me reading too much into it.

The truck rolls to a stop at a red light, the headlights illuminating the empty intersection in front of us. I can't help but glance at him, at the way his profile is outlined by the soft glow, his jaw still tight, the weight of a thousand unsaid things pressing down on him.

"What if I don't want to go home?" I hear myself ask, the words slipping out before I can stop them. The moment they're out, I wish I could take them back. It sounds too needy, too vulnerable, and I don't know why I've said it. But once it's said, there's no going back.

He doesn't respond right away. For a moment, it feels like time itself is suspended, like the world is holding its breath, waiting for his answer. And then he turns to me, his eyes dark and intent, and for the first time tonight, he doesn't look like the calm, collected firefighter. He looks like a man, a real person, someone who's trying to navigate this strange pull between us.

"You don't get to play games with me, Sara," he says, his voice low but steady. "I'm not that kind of guy."

I nod, trying to swallow the lump in my throat, but there's something in his gaze that makes it hard to breathe. I want to argue, want to say something clever, something that will change the moment. But I don't. Instead, I let the silence stretch between us, a space full of possibilities we're both too afraid to name.

The engine hums beneath us, a steady rhythm that fills the space with a dull, mechanical comfort. We drive in silence, the air in the truck thick with all the things left unsaid. I can feel the weight of his presence next to me, his body tense in a way that tells me he's still miles away, lost in his own thoughts. The moonlight casts shadows across his face, making the lines of his jaw sharper, more defined, as if the night itself is pulling him further into that place he keeps hidden from everyone. Even me.

I've never been good at waiting. I can feel the minutes stretching between us, taut like a wire, and the more I try to ignore it, the more it buzzes under my skin. My hand twitches by my side, aching with the need to reach out, to touch him again, to see if he feels as real as he looks. But I pull my fingers into a fist, unwilling to give in to the impulse. He's always a little out of reach, always just enough to keep me guessing. And I'm not sure anymore whether I want to close that distance or just leave it as it is, a temptation that hangs in the air between us like a fragile thread.

"Where are we going?" I ask, breaking the silence at last. My voice sounds too loud in the quiet truck, but I don't care. I need to fill the space with something, anything.

He doesn't look at me, but I can see the corner of his mouth twitch, like he's holding back a grin. "You really don't know, do you?"

I frown, not sure what he means. I'm not in the mood for games. "What's that supposed to mean?"

His eyes flick to mine for a brief second, and there's something in them—a glint, a spark—that makes my heart skip. "You'll find out soon enough."

I hate how he can do that. How he can make everything sound like a riddle I'll never solve. It's infuriating. And, if I'm being honest with myself, it's part of the reason I keep coming back. He's an enigma, wrapped in that same dangerous charm that always makes my pulse race. The fact that he keeps me on edge like this, keeps me guessing, only makes me want him more.

We drive for what feels like an eternity, the road stretching out before us like some kind of cruel joke, as if time itself is determined to make me suffer through this uncertainty. The truck turns onto a quieter road, the lights of the city disappearing behind us, swallowed up by the darkness. For a moment, I think maybe this is it—this is where we're going to have the conversation that has been hanging over us for weeks, the one where we finally say everything that's been unsaid, where the distance between us gets narrowed to nothing.

But then he pulls over to the side of the road, the truck's tires crunching over the gravel as he shuts off the engine. The sudden quiet feels like a punch to the gut. I stare at him, wondering if I've missed something, if I've been too busy wrapped up in my own head to see the truth of what's happening.

He turns to me, and his face is unreadable, the shadows of the truck cab painting him in sharp contrasts, making him look even more distant.

"We're here," he says simply, and I can't tell if it's an invitation or a command.

My heart beats a little faster, but I can't decide if it's from nerves or anticipation. I look out the window, trying to see what's around us. But all I see is an empty stretch of road, trees lining the sides like silent sentinels, the sky above a dark canvas broken only by the distant stars. It's like we've driven into another world, one where the only thing that matters is the space between us, the tension in the air that refuses to settle.

"Here?" I ask, my voice tinged with disbelief. "This is where we're going to talk?"

He doesn't answer immediately. Instead, he reaches across the seat, his hand brushing against mine for a split second, and the touch sends a jolt through me, as if a live wire has just sparked between us. He pulls his hand back almost immediately, but the feeling lingers. The tension has shifted—gone from quiet and simmering to something sharper, something that feels like it's about to crack open.

"I didn't bring you out here to talk," he finally says, his voice lower than usual, like there's something he's holding back. Something I'm not supposed to know.

My breath catches, and I feel a knot twist in my stomach. I'm not sure what's happening, but it feels like we've crossed some invisible line, like the game has changed without me realizing it.

"You didn't?" I whisper, unable to keep the uncertainty out of my voice.

"No," he says, his eyes dark as they meet mine. "I brought you out here for something else."

And then, before I can ask what that something else is, he opens the door and steps out of the truck. I blink, momentarily stunned, and then scramble to follow him, my heart pounding against my ribs. But by the time I reach the front of the truck, he's already moved into the woods, his figure swallowed up by the trees like he's part of the night itself.

I stand there for a moment, the cool air biting at my skin, the sound of crickets and rustling leaves filling the space between us. I can't see him anymore, not through the darkness, but I know he's out there. Somewhere.

I take a step forward, my pulse quickening with every inch I move deeper into the woods, every step taking me closer to him and further away from everything I thought I understood. The air feels thick, like something is about to happen, like the world is holding its breath.

And then, just as I hear a twig snap in the distance, a sudden realization hits me—the one thing I've been avoiding. I don't know if I'm walking into danger or if I'm walking toward something I've always wanted. And that's the scariest part of all.

The sound of his voice breaks through the silence. "Come closer, Sara."

And with those three words, I feel like I've already stepped off the edge.

Chapter 11: Secrets in the Embers

The air inside the coffee shop was thick with the scent of ground beans and the faintest hint of burnt toast. I could almost taste it, that dryness at the back of my throat. It wasn't an unpleasant smell, just one that clung to you, persistent. The table between us was too small for comfort, but it kept a distance, and in this moment, that felt like the only thing holding me together.

I had always known Alex could be a bit of a mystery. He had that air about him, like a cracked vase still holding together by sheer force of will. The kind of person who said just enough to make you want more, and when you reached for the more, he was already pulling away. But this—this was different. There was something almost desperate in his silence, something I couldn't quite place, not yet. I could see it in the way his fingers hovered over his coffee cup but never quite touched it, like the warmth of it might burn him. His eyes, though—they never left mine. It was almost too intense, the way they latched onto me, as if looking for some kind of solace in a place he couldn't reach.

"So, how's the fire," I asked, my voice steady, though my heart beat erratically in my chest. The words had slipped out before I could stop them, and now they hung in the air, as heavy as smoke. A risky question, to be sure. But it was the only thing that had been occupying my mind since I'd heard the rumors. The fire that had swallowed everything in its path, leaving only ashes. And Alex. His name had come up more than once in the whispers. People didn't speak of him with pity, but they spoke of him in a way that suggested he had lost something—no, someone—important.

He stiffened. The change was subtle but enough for me to catch. I noticed how his lips thinned, the slight twitch of his jaw. And then, just as quickly, he returned to his usual cool detachment.

"It's over," he said, his voice flat, but his eyes betrayed him. They were darker now, shadows pooling where light had once been.

"That's it? Just... over?" My fingers gripped the edge of my cup, the porcelain cool beneath my fingertips, a small comfort in a conversation that was anything but. "What happened, Alex? People are saying... you were there. You saw it happen."

His gaze flicked away, focusing on the window just behind me, where the late afternoon sun cast long shadows over the street. I followed his gaze for a moment, hoping the view would offer some kind of answer, but it was just a blur of pedestrians and the usual hum of the city. The world outside didn't know about the fire. Didn't care about it, really.

"Rumors are like smoke," he muttered, his voice low and controlled, "they swirl around, and by the time you try to catch them, they've already dispersed." He took a breath, a deep one, as if trying to steady himself. "You should stay out of it, Lucy. Trust me on that."

The warning hung between us like a weight I wasn't sure how to lift. "Stay out of what?" I asked, the words tumbling out before I could stop them. "You think I don't deserve to know the truth?"

He winced, but quickly masked it with a half-smile. "You deserve the truth," he said, though it didn't feel like a reassurance. "But the truth isn't always something you want to hear." He stood abruptly, the chair scraping against the wooden floor with a sound that made me flinch. "I've got to go."

Before I could protest, he was already walking toward the door, his coat sweeping behind him like the tail of a storm. I watched him disappear into the street, a whirlwind of questions swirling in my chest. I should've let it go. I should've walked away and let whatever fragile threads of our friendship had been fraying snap cleanly. But I couldn't.

It was the silence that haunted me as much as anything. The way he held back. The way he refused to share, even when I knew he was on the edge of saying something, something important. Something that might explain the darkness in his eyes.

I left the coffee shop minutes later, the cold air of the evening biting at my skin, and I wasn't sure where I was heading. Only that I couldn't let it end there. I had to know. I had to understand what had really happened in that fire, what Alex had lost, and whether it was something I could help him recover.

There was a part of me that feared what I might find, but fear was always a poor excuse for inaction. I had always believed that the truth, no matter how painful, was better than living in the dark. But as I walked through the dimming streets, the chill of the night creeping up my spine, I wondered if this time, the truth would be too much for either of us to handle.

The fire wasn't over, not for him. Not for me. Not yet.

The next few days were a blur, a mix of unanswered questions and persistent, nagging curiosity. I spent most of my time staring at the walls of my apartment, feeling the weight of the truth I didn't have. It hung in the air like an oppressive fog, clouding everything, making even the simplest of tasks feel insurmountable. The sound of my phone vibrating against the counter in the middle of the night sent my heart skittering every time, only to find that it was another missed call from a number I didn't recognize, or a text message that was a little too vague to matter.

But the thing about silence, the thing that gnawed at me the most, was how loud it could be when you were used to hearing a person's voice, their laughter, their touch. Alex hadn't answered my message. He hadn't come by for the usual late-night check-ins, the ones where we talked about everything and nothing at all. He had retreated completely, and I had no idea if it was because of the fire—or because of me.

The knock on my door was sudden, and I nearly jumped out of my skin. It was almost ten o'clock, and in my small world, that was late enough to make someone's arrival feel like an intrusion. I peeked through the peephole, half-expecting to see a delivery guy or some well-meaning neighbor, but instead, there stood Alex, looking as if he had walked straight out of my most persistent dream.

"Lucy," he said, his voice ragged, eyes scanning the interior of my apartment like he wasn't sure whether he belonged there.

"You came." I couldn't help the small breath that escaped me. There was something fragile in the way he stood there, in the way his shoulders slumped just the tiniest bit, like he was holding onto something heavier than he was letting on. "I wasn't expecting you."

He shifted, running a hand through his hair, the stubble on his jaw sharp under the dim hallway light. "I shouldn't have," he murmured. "But I needed to see you."

I stepped aside without thinking, heart pounding at the sheer weight of his presence. I knew he hadn't come here for small talk, for pleasantries. He wasn't here to ask about my day or to share some idle piece of gossip about the neighbors. He had something else in mind, and I could feel it, coiling between us like an unspoken promise.

He didn't sit down immediately. Instead, he paced the small space, fingers brushing the edge of a chair as though testing its solidity. "I've been thinking about what you said," he began, his voice low, quieter than usual, like it was taking every ounce of energy for him to speak.

"What I said about the fire?" I couldn't keep the edge of concern out of my voice. I had tried, after all, to pretend it didn't matter, to act like I wasn't dying to know more. But there was no pretending now.

His jaw clenched. "Yeah. About the fire." He exhaled sharply. "Look, I didn't want to drag you into it. I've been trying to bury that whole thing, bury it so deep no one would ever find it again."

I waited, giving him the space he clearly needed, my stomach tight with anticipation. "But you can't, can you?" The words slipped out, and I didn't apologize for them. He needed to hear them. Needed to hear that I wasn't going to back off, not when he was standing there, so close yet so far.

He finally sat down, his body tense, but there was something in his eyes—something flickering—that I hadn't seen before. Guilt, maybe? Regret? It was hard to tell. "I don't think I can." He paused, letting the words hang between us like fragile glass. "But I don't want to drag you into it either, Lucy. You deserve better than that."

I crossed the room to where he sat, unable to help myself. "Alex, I don't need better than you. I need you to be honest with me. Whatever it is, I can handle it."

He laughed, but there was no humor in it, only bitterness. "You think you can handle it?" His voice was almost a growl now, raw and wounded. "You have no idea what you're asking. What you'll find." He shook his head, his hands curling into fists. "People died, Lucy. People died in that fire, and I... I couldn't save them."

The admission hit me like a blow, and I felt the air go still. My heart sank, but I didn't look away. "You weren't responsible for it," I said quietly, my voice steady despite the rush of emotion threatening to overwhelm me.

He laughed again, this time with a bit of self-loathing. "No? You think so?" He stood abruptly, turning away, running a hand over his face in frustration. "It doesn't matter. I could've done something, and I didn't. And now there's a hole in me, a hole I can't fill. Not with work. Not with anything. You think I wanted to end up like this? You think I wanted to carry that guilt every damn day of my life?"

My breath hitched. "Alex," I whispered. "You're not alone in this. You don't have to carry it by yourself." But I could feel the truth of it, deep in my bones—the truth that this fire, this thing that had taken so much from him, had taken so much from me too.

"I don't know how to let it go, Lucy," he said softly, turning back to me, his eyes wide and lost. "And I don't know if I can tell you everything. Some things... some things are too dangerous to share."

I shook my head slowly, the weight of his words pressing down on me. "I'm not afraid of the truth, Alex. I'm just afraid of what you'll do if you don't let me in."

His eyes lingered on mine for a moment too long, like he was trying to see through me. I almost wished I could disappear, give him the space to pull away, to hide from whatever it was that was eating at him. But I didn't move. The truth had a way of waiting, of sitting in the dark corners of rooms, lurking in the spaces between words. I'd been circling it for days, but now I was too close to stop.

"I'm not afraid of the truth, Alex," I said again, quieter this time. I took a step toward him, aware of every movement, like I was inching closer to something dangerous. "I'm afraid of losing you, of watching you fade into this... shadow that you can't escape."

He flinched, the muscle in his jaw tensing, his fingers tightening around the edge of the chair like he was about to crush it. He exhaled slowly, like he was trying to push the words back down before they could escape.

"You think you want to know, but you don't," he muttered. "Some things are better left unsaid."

I closed the distance between us, my heart racing now, not with fear but with a kind of reckless determination. "I can't help it, Alex. I can't walk away when I know you're carrying this weight. I can't be the person who stands by and watches you destroy yourself over something you're too scared to talk about."

He was shaking his head, but it wasn't denial. It was more like he was trying to convince himself that he was right, that shutting me out was the only way to protect me from whatever it was that haunted him.

"You don't understand," he whispered, voice cracking in the silence. "I wasn't just there, Lucy. I was—" He stopped himself, his words dangling in the air like a broken thread. I leaned in closer, my breath catching in my throat, but he didn't continue. He couldn't.

The room felt smaller now, the walls pressing in, the air thick with the weight of his silence. He wasn't going to give me the rest. I could see it in the way his eyes darted away from mine, in the way his hands gripped the chair as though it were the only thing holding him together.

"I don't want you to get involved," he said finally, standing abruptly, his chair scraping across the floor. "This... this isn't your fight, Lucy. You don't want to know what's really at the bottom of it. You don't."

I stood frozen, my pulse pounding in my ears. The words felt like a challenge, like he was daring me to turn away, to listen to his warning and walk out the door. But I couldn't. I wouldn't.

"Then tell me," I said, my voice firmer now, steady. "Tell me what's at the bottom of it. And maybe, just maybe, I'll listen. But I need to know, Alex. I need you to stop hiding from me."

His shoulders sagged, the fight leaving him in a slow, reluctant wave. He was drowning in something, in a sea of guilt or grief or fear—whatever it was, it was pulling him under, and I didn't know how much longer he could keep it buried. I couldn't let him drown alone.

"I didn't just lose someone, Lucy," he whispered, and for the first time, his voice cracked. "I lost everything. And I was the one who set the fire."

The room went dead silent. My breath caught in my throat, every muscle in my body locking into place. The words hung in the air between us like an accusation, like a confession that had been years in the making.

"You... you set it?" I asked, my voice barely a whisper. "You mean... the fire, you started it? On purpose?"

He looked away, his hands trembling slightly, his eyes unfocused as if he were looking at something far off, something that wasn't here.

"I didn't mean for it to happen. But it did," he murmured. "I thought I could control it. I thought I could make it all go away, but instead..." He ran a hand through his hair, the frustration and self-loathing clear in every motion. "Instead, I lost everything. The people I cared about, the life I had—gone. And I'm the one who's still here, trying to figure out how to live with it."

I felt a chill sweep through me, a coldness that crept into my bones, numbing me. I didn't know what to say. I didn't know how to make him see that I didn't blame him. That this thing, this fire, had taken more from him than he could ever put into words. But the guilt—he was drowning in it, and I didn't know how to pull him out.

"Alex," I said gently, taking a tentative step forward. "You didn't do this alone. Whatever happened, whatever you think you're responsible for, you're not alone in it. We can figure this out. We can—"

He shook his head sharply, cutting me off, his eyes wide with panic. "No, Lucy. You don't get it. I didn't just lose people. I lost something far more important than that." His voice dropped to a low, almost guttural whisper. "I lost the truth. And now, the truth is coming back for me."

The words hit me like a slap, a jolt of realization. "What truth?" I asked, my voice trembling with a mix of fear and urgency. "What are you talking about?"

Before he could answer, the door to my apartment suddenly slammed open with a force that made me jump. A man I didn't recognize stood there, his face hidden by a dark cap and shadows. His presence filled the doorway, too large, too imposing to ignore.

And in that moment, I knew—whatever Alex had been trying to protect me from, whatever truth he had been hiding, it wasn't just his to bear anymore.

Chapter 12: Burning Bridges

I was in the middle of a perfectly mundane Tuesday morning when the tension first sliced through the air like a blade. It wasn't the usual hum of my life that had settled into a comfortable routine. No, it was the quiet before a storm—those subtle shifts in energy that no one ever tells you to watch for.

He had been acting differently, but I had been too busy with my own small battles to notice how deep the cracks had grown. Maybe it was his late nights at the office, the ones that lasted far past the hours of normal people. Or perhaps it was the way his smile no longer seemed to reach his eyes, as if the corners of his mouth were more a mask than a gesture. Still, I convinced myself that it wasn't worth questioning. We had bigger things to focus on.

That morning, I stood by the kitchen counter, absentmindedly scrolling through my phone, trying to block out the ever-present unease. The house felt empty in the way it does when something is very, very wrong but no one has the courage to say it aloud. My fingers hovered over the screen, caught between distractions. And then I found it—the message that felt like a stone thrown through glass.

I don't know why I clicked it. I was tired, yes, but not so tired that I couldn't recognize my own curiosity. It wasn't like me to pry, and yet there I was, the message loading, as though it was meant to happen. I wasn't prepared for the surge of nausea when the words blurred into focus. Not that they were damning—they weren't—but they were enough. Enough to open the door to a truth I hadn't been ready to face.

I didn't want to read them. I didn't want to know what was hidden, but curiosity—a wretched thing, always whispering like a siren—pulled me in deeper. It wasn't just the message itself, but the reminder of everything he'd kept tucked away. The words, innocuous on their own, bled into something bigger, something I didn't understand. And, for reasons I couldn't explain, I knew the lie in the message was only the tip of the iceberg.

I closed the phone, my heartbeat thudding louder in my ears than anything I had ever felt. It was like I had opened a door into a room I wasn't allowed to enter. But I was already there, standing in the doorway, wondering whether it was even possible to walk away.

He didn't come down for breakfast that morning. Not unusual, I reminded myself. His work had been keeping him later and later, each day drawing longer into the night. But it wasn't just his absence that had me on edge. It was the thickening of the silence, the moments when I could almost hear his breath, could almost hear his thoughts pressing against the walls, like a heavy weight pushing from the inside.

I waited, unable to bring myself to start the day. There was nothing to distract me. The lingering, twisted knot of confusion had rooted itself in my stomach, and no amount of coffee would loosen it. When the door finally opened, he stood there in the doorway, his figure silhouetted against the weak morning light. For a moment, I thought he hadn't seen me. He looked tired, his face drawn, his eyes clouded with something I couldn't decipher. But then, there it was—his eyes locking with mine, a flash of something deep and raw that made me swallow back the words I didn't know how to say.

"I'm sorry," I managed to choke out, my voice barely audible against the thick tension. I wasn't sure what I was apologizing for, but it felt like the right thing to do. For all of it. For what I knew, for what I had seen, for how it had changed the air between us.

"You don't have to apologize," he said, his voice low and rough, as if he was trying to stop a storm from escaping. But the words fell heavy between us anyway, and I felt the weight of his gaze as it pinned me to the spot. "You shouldn't have looked."

And just like that, the words crashed into me. Not anger. Not frustration. Something else. Something colder, more complicated. There was a betrayal in his tone, something I hadn't expected.

"What did you want me to do?" I asked, my own voice rising now, echoing off the bare walls. I hadn't meant to sound so defensive, but his words, thick with the kind of reproach I had never heard from him before, stung in a way I hadn't anticipated. "Not know? Not see? You—" I stopped myself, the rest of the sentence hanging in the air.

"I told you not to meddle." The words were like a slap, but it wasn't the kind of slap I could retaliate against. There was a finality in his voice, a depth of pain that hit me harder than I wanted to admit. "You don't understand."

"I don't?" I blinked, his fury churning the calm of my thoughts into something far more volatile. "Then explain it to me. Explain what I don't understand, because I don't think I can keep pretending that nothing is wrong."

He stepped forward then, the space between us shrinking, but it didn't feel like closeness. It felt like a wall was rising between us, one built on things neither of us had said. "Just leave it, okay?" His voice was raw now, shaking at the edges like he was struggling to keep his composure. "It's not your business."

I stood there, my chest tightening, feeling as if I were watching the best parts of my life slip away with every word he spoke. I wanted to walk away. I wanted to slam the door behind me and never look back. But my feet wouldn't move. My mind wouldn't release him.

It was too late for that.

The silence stretched between us, brittle and sharp, like a broken mirror. I wanted to look away, to break the tension, but I couldn't. His anger had carved a divide between us so deep, it was as though an ocean had appeared where there used to be space for everything else—the laughter, the shared moments of quiet understanding, the things that kept us tangled together. Now, there was only the thunderous roar of things unsaid, drowning out any possibility of calm.

I could feel the heat of his stare, and it made my skin prickle. His jaw was clenched tight, the muscles working beneath his skin, but it wasn't just his fury that struck me. It was the look of someone holding back a flood, a surge of emotions so dangerous they could drown us both. It wasn't just betrayal. It was a kind of grief, something that cut even deeper than the anger I'd expected. I felt the weight of it, pressing against me in a way that almost made me wish I had stayed ignorant, let the illusion of peace linger just a little longer.

But then, my mind fought back, demanding answers. Why had he acted so differently? Why hadn't I asked sooner? I had given him room to keep his secrets, room to breathe without question, but it was clear now that my silence had only been a cover-up. A way for me to tell myself I was okay with the distance, that the time I spent reading messages and second-guessing my instincts wasn't a betrayal of everything we had built. But it had been. And so had this conversation.

"You don't understand what this means." His words hit me like cold water, but his eyes—they were a different story. A maze of conflicting emotions, sharp as a knife's edge, and yet so vulnerable that it took all my willpower not to reach for him. I should have turned away. I should have left, just like he had told me to, but I didn't. I couldn't. The truth was out there now, swirling in the air between us, and there was no escaping it.

"Then make me understand." I heard myself say it before I could stop the words, my voice firm despite the shaky ground beneath me. "Because I don't know how we got here. I don't know how we got to this point where you're telling me to leave." My heart pounded in my chest, a wild rhythm that was entirely out of sync with the calm I tried to project. I wasn't calm, not at all. But I wasn't backing down, either.

His eyes softened, just for a moment, before they hardened again. It was like a door had opened, just a crack, but he was shutting it fast, bolting it tight. I could see it, though—the way he was looking at me, as if he didn't know whether he wanted to protect me or push me away. It was an unbearable kind of vulnerability, raw and untamed, and it made me want to do everything in my power to understand him. But I wasn't sure he wanted me to.

"You want to know why I'm so angry?" he asked, his voice quiet, but the edge of frustration was clear. "Because I trusted you. And you ruined that. You went digging around in things that were none of your business, and now look what's happened. You can't just pick at the pieces of something and expect not to break it."

His words stung, and I hated that they did. But there was something there, something I hadn't anticipated. A feeling of being lost, of being unable to control his own world, and the only way he knew how to fight back was by shutting me out.

I shook my head, my hands curling into fists at my sides, fighting the urge to throw them up in defeat. "You're right, I shouldn't have looked. I shouldn't have tried to make sense of something that didn't belong to me. But I didn't do it to hurt you. I did it because—" I stopped, feeling the weight of the confession pressing down on me. "Because I had to know. And now I do. Now I know you're hiding something. But it's not just that." My voice faltered for a second, but I didn't let myself lose the thread. "It's the way you've been pulling away. The way we've both been pretending that things are fine when they aren't."

His lips pressed together in a thin line, and for a moment, I thought he might say something else. But the words never came.

Instead, he took a step back, as if physically distancing himself from the storm that was gathering between us.

"I don't want to talk about this anymore," he muttered, his voice almost too quiet to hear, the weariness creeping into every syllable. "I don't want to do this with you."

It felt like a slap to the chest. I wanted to scream, to argue, to force him to face what we had become. But something in the way he stood there, arms crossed, his eyes filled with both defiance and defeat, told me that I couldn't push him any further.

The air between us thickened, my breaths shallow and quick, but I knew this moment—this was it. The end, or at least the beginning of it. There was nothing left to say, no words that would fix this. No explanation that would bring us back.

"I can't keep doing this either," I said softly, my voice barely above a whisper, but the finality of it hung in the air like a rope, fraying and unraveling. "I can't keep pretending everything's fine when it isn't."

His eyes flicked to mine, and I saw something there—regret, maybe, or guilt. Maybe it was just resignation. But it didn't matter. Whatever it was, it wasn't enough to save us.

With a sharp exhale, he turned and walked away, his footsteps heavy on the floor, each one pulling him further from me. And just like that, the room felt emptier. The silence more oppressive. And I realized, with a hollow kind of certainty, that I had crossed a line. There was no going back now.

I watched him leave, his back rigid, the door clicking shut behind him with a finality that settled over me like dust. The weight of the silence stretched long, curling its fingers into every corner of the room, as if it were a living thing, hungry for my thoughts, for my guilt. I wanted to cry, but the tears stayed hidden beneath the surface. I wanted to scream, to let the anger out the way he had, but my voice felt small now, as though it no longer belonged to me.

He was gone, and for the first time in a long while, the space between us felt wider than just the distance of our bodies. It felt like a chasm, deep and dark, impossible to cross.

I leaned against the counter, feeling the cool granite beneath my palms, trying to steady myself. There had been moments, fleeting glimpses, when everything felt so perfectly right. When the world seemed to fold neatly around us, like a well-worn sweater that kept you warm, even on the coldest days. But now, standing here, with his absence pressing against me, I couldn't remember the last time I'd felt that warmth. It was like a shadow had fallen over the best parts of us, and I couldn't tell if it was something I had caused or something inevitable.

His words echoed in my head, over and over, as though I could somehow make sense of them by replaying them like a broken record. You don't understand. You ruined it. The words stung, but they didn't sit right either. They felt incomplete, like a puzzle missing pieces, and no matter how hard I tried to fit them together, the picture remained broken.

I didn't know how long I stood there, but eventually the sound of a car engine revving outside jerked me out of my reverie. The house, once so full of quiet tension, now felt like a mausoleum, hollow and empty. I had to move, had to do something, or I would suffocate in the weight of everything unsaid. But what could I do?

I grabbed my coat, pulling it on with a speed that felt frantic. There was no plan. There was nothing but the urge to do something, to not be here, alone with my thoughts and the crushing pressure of his absence. The front door slammed behind me as I stepped outside, the cool air hitting me in a rush, a welcome contrast to the stifling heat inside.

The streets were quiet, the sun beginning to dip behind the horizon, painting everything in shades of purple and gold. It was beautiful, almost too beautiful for what I was feeling. I could hear the faint hum of traffic in the distance, but all I could think about was him. Where he had gone. What he was doing. What he was thinking. Was he regretting what he'd said? Was he angry enough to never come back?

I had no answers, only questions, and the longer I walked, the heavier they became.

I didn't realize how far I had gone until I found myself standing in front of a café, the warm light spilling out onto the sidewalk like a beacon. It wasn't a place I would normally go, but the pull of something familiar, something that could offer a small thread of comfort, was too strong. The doorbell jingled above my head as I walked in, the smell of coffee and cinnamon instantly enveloping me. I had no intention of staying, but I needed a moment to breathe, a moment to gather the scattered pieces of myself.

I found an empty table in the corner, and before I knew it, I was ordering something I didn't even want. My hands were shaking, and I had to force myself to focus, to keep the walls from coming down. The waitress, a young woman with tired eyes, gave me a look of sympathy as she brought over a steaming mug of something I couldn't even name.

"Long day?" she asked, her voice light, almost too light for the kind of tension that hung in the air around me.

"Something like that," I replied, forcing a smile that didn't quite reach my eyes. She didn't push it, just nodded and went back to her duties, leaving me alone with my thoughts. I stared at the coffee, the steam rising in curling wisps, as if the answer to everything could somehow be found in the swirling liquid. But I knew better.

I had been here before—sitting in this same spot, feeling like the weight of the world was pressing down on my chest. The difference this time was that I didn't feel like I was on the edge of something. I felt like I had already fallen.

And that's when I heard it—footsteps, slow and deliberate, the sound of someone stopping just behind me. For a moment, I didn't turn around. It could have been anyone, a stranger, someone in the café who was just going about their day. But then, I heard his voice. Low, familiar, laced with an emotion I couldn't quite place.

"You really thought I was gone?"

I froze. My breath caught in my throat, my heart hammering against my ribcage. He was standing there, just behind me, and though I couldn't bring myself to look up, I could feel the weight of his presence like a storm brewing.

I opened my mouth to speak, but no words came. What was there to say? Was I supposed to apologize again? Was I supposed to act like nothing had happened, like everything could just go back to the way it was?

But he didn't wait for me to answer. Instead, I felt him move around to the other side of the table, his presence filling the space like an electric charge, sparking in the air between us. And then, he spoke again.

"I don't know what you're trying to do, but I can't just forget about everything."

The words hung there, suspended in the air, and for a moment, it felt like the whole world had come to a stop.

And then—without warning—he sat down. His chair scraping against the floor was the loudest sound in the room.

Chapter 13: Rekindling the Flame

The night was unusually warm for October, a thin layer of fog clinging to the ground as though the air itself had been given a chance to breathe after the heat of the day. I had just slipped into bed, the soft cotton sheets cool against my skin, when the first crackle of fire reached my ears. At first, it was just a faint, distant rustling, like leaves caught in the wind. But then came the second crackle, sharper, louder, followed by the unmistakable hiss of flames hungry for more.

I sat up in bed, heart pounding. The sound was coming from just a few blocks away. My mind flashed to images of the neighborhood, the buildings, the quiet streets we had grown accustomed to walking together—safe, predictable. A lie. I threw the covers off, my bare feet hitting the floor with a quick slap. A shiver ran up my spine, not from the coolness of the wood, but from the realization that this was real. Something was burning. I grabbed my phone, eyes already scanning the window, and dialed his number without a second thought.

"Jacob," I whispered, breathless as the phone rang through the dark silence of my apartment.

He picked up on the second ring. "Are you okay?"

The concern in his voice broke through the haze of panic in my chest. "I'm fine," I said, trying to steady myself, though my hands trembled. "But there's a fire. It sounds close."

His voice was tight, each word drawn out with a gravity I hadn't expected. "Stay inside. I'll be there soon."

I didn't ask any questions. I didn't need to. He was always the one who could keep his calm in the middle of a storm. That was one of the things I had always admired about him. It wasn't the bravado or the stoic silence that some people thought strength was made of. No, it was his quiet assurance that no matter the fire, the storm, or the weight of the world pressing down on him, he would handle it—without a single crack in his armor.

I didn't wait for him to arrive. My feet were already carrying me down the stairs of my building before I even realized it. The closer I got to the street, the more the air changed—thick with smoke and the acrid scent of burning wood. I could hear the sirens now, closer, the flashing red and blue lights reflecting off the nearby storefronts. There were people standing outside, their faces illuminated in quick flashes of light as they stared at the source of the blaze—an old, neglected building just a few blocks down.

Jacob was there, standing at the edge of the crowd, his face hidden in shadow. I spotted him before he saw me, his posture straight, his eyes scanning the scene in front of him with that sharp, knowing look I recognized too well. The faintest tremor of his jaw gave away the tension that wrapped around him like a vice. This was no ordinary fire. For him, it wasn't just the damage, the destruction—it was the smell of something far more personal, something I hadn't seen before.

"Jacob," I called out, stepping toward him. My voice sounded louder than I intended, as if the word had to break through the haze surrounding us both.

He turned slowly, his eyes narrowing for just a second before recognition flickered across them. His lips parted, but no words came out at first, as though he were searching for the right ones. Instead, his gaze shifted briefly to the building in front of us, and I saw it—the flash of fear, a tightness around his eyes that betrayed a part of him I hadn't realized was still there. A part of him that wasn't the cool, steady man I had come to know, but someone else. Someone burdened by something heavier than the weight of this moment.

"What are you doing here?" His voice was soft, strained.

"I wasn't going to stay inside," I said, moving toward him, the heat from the fire now making my skin feel like it was on the edge of blistering. "I'm not letting you do this alone."

He shook his head, his hand reaching out instinctively to stop me, but I could see the battle behind his eyes. "This is—" he cut himself off, his hand dropping to his side as if he'd lost the strength to argue. He didn't want me here. I could tell that much. But in the same breath, I could see that he needed me.

Before I could say anything more, the fire crews arrived in full force. The sound of their equipment, their voices, the urgency in their steps—everything sharpened around us, making the chaos more real. More present.

"I don't want you getting caught up in this," Jacob murmured, but I could see the look in his eyes now, the shift from resistance to reluctant acceptance. He wasn't pushing me away anymore.

I met his gaze, holding it. "I'm not going anywhere," I said firmly.

And then, despite everything swirling in the air around us, despite the fire that crackled and hissed at our feet, I saw it. The faintest flicker in his eyes, a fleeting softness that he quickly masked, but it was enough. Enough to tell me that this wasn't just about the fire—it was about something much deeper, something neither of us had fully acknowledged before.

The smoke thickened, swirling around us, and I could feel his hand brushing mine in an almost unconscious gesture, just a brief touch, but it grounded me. It was all the answer I needed. We were in this together. Fire, smoke, fear—we would face it all side by side, even if we didn't yet know how.

The fire had swallowed the night in a violent embrace, turning the world into a blur of orange and smoke. My throat burned as the acrid scent of it seared the air. The fire trucks lined the street, their flashing lights bouncing off the slick asphalt, casting shadows that seemed to move of their own accord. I didn't know where to look first—at the flames that leaped and twisted, or at Jacob, whose face had gone ashen in the glow, his eyes darting between the chaos and the ghosts of his past.

I tried to stay close, but the air was thick with heat and the clamor of sirens, each moment more suffocating than the last. I caught him looking toward the fire with an intensity that made my chest tighten. There was something about it, the way the flames raged. It wasn't just the fire. It was the way it seemed to claw at the part of him that still bore the weight of something—something I didn't know, but now felt I was being drawn into.

"Hey," I said, moving in closer, my voice louder now, desperate to break through the fog between us. "We're okay. We're okay, Jacob. Just focus on the now."

He didn't answer at first, his face still locked in that distant, haunted stare. Then, finally, his eyes met mine—those stormy blue eyes, too familiar and yet too distant. There was something sharp in his gaze, like I'd said the wrong thing. I felt the tension coil tighter in my chest, and I fought the urge to step back.

"I don't want you involved in this," he said, his words edged with a quiet anger, but not at me—at something else, something I wasn't part of. "You don't know what it's like."

The words hung between us like smoke. I didn't respond right away. I didn't need to. I just stood there, watching him, hoping he'd see. I wasn't backing down. Not now, not after everything we'd been through. There was too much at stake, and somehow, this—this felt like the tipping point.

"Then teach me," I said, my voice firm. I took a step closer. "Let me understand. Let me help you."

Jacob's jaw clenched, and for a moment, I thought he might say something sharp, something dismissive. But he didn't. His shoulders dropped instead, as if the weight of the fire was too much to bear, too much to carry alone. "You really don't know what you're asking," he muttered, rubbing his hand over his face as if wiping away the fatigue of years.

"Maybe I don't," I said softly. "But I'm here anyway. And I'm not leaving."

He met my eyes then, and for the first time in a long while, I saw it—the real Jacob, not the man behind the walls he'd built. His shoulders sagged, and the intensity in his gaze softened. A tiny, nearly imperceptible nod followed.

"I didn't ask for this," he said, so quietly I almost missed it. "I didn't ask for any of it. But that's what it's always been, isn't it? Every time things get too close, too real, I push people away. Because that's the only way to keep them from getting hurt. The only way to keep them safe."

I blinked, the weight of his confession settling like a stone in my chest. The truth of it was like a blade in the dark. I wasn't sure if I was prepared for it, but I wasn't backing down, not this time.

"You're not alone anymore," I said, my voice soft but insistent. "You don't have to do this by yourself, Jacob."

His gaze flicked to the fire again, his expression flickering between the present and something far darker, something buried deep. The fire was too close now, too threatening for him to hide from. I knew, somehow, that this was a moment of reckoning.

"I've always been alone," he murmured, as if speaking to himself more than to me. "This...this is just another reminder."

I didn't know what to say to that, so I said nothing. Instead, I reached for his hand, the one that had been clenched at his side. His fingers were stiff at first, but then, slowly, they loosened. He didn't pull away.

"Not anymore," I whispered. "I'm not going anywhere."

The moment stretched between us, and for a heartbeat, everything else disappeared—the fire, the smoke, the confusion.

There was only Jacob and me, two people standing on the edge of a precipice, unwilling to let go.

We stood like that for a while, just holding onto each other in the strange, fragile space between fear and something else. The fire raged behind us, but I could feel the shift in the air. The change in him, in us. It wasn't just the flames that burned. It was the quiet breaking of barriers, the slow erosion of the walls Jacob had spent years building.

And then, without warning, he pulled me toward him, his arms wrapping around me in a way that felt both desperate and tender. I could feel the thrum of his heartbeat, rapid and uneven, under my cheek.

"You're crazy," he muttered, his voice rough with emotion. "You really should go. This is too much for you."

I pulled back just enough to meet his gaze, my fingers brushing his cheek. "I'm not going anywhere," I said again, my voice stronger now, more certain. "You don't get to decide that for me."

He didn't say anything after that, but the tightness in his shoulders loosened. The haunted look in his eyes was still there, lurking beneath the surface, but it wasn't the only thing I saw. There was something else—something that felt like the beginning of hope.

We didn't need to speak again. The moment, however fleeting, told me everything. We were no longer two people standing apart. We were two people, facing a fire together, ready to face whatever else came our way.

The fire raged, but I didn't feel afraid anymore. Not with Jacob beside me.

The heat of the fire still hung in the air long after the flames had been tamed. The smoke was thick, clinging to the skin like an unwanted memory, a reminder of everything we had just faced. I was standing in the middle of the street, Jacob beside me, his posture no longer rigid with the same unspoken tension, but still heavy with something more profound. He was different now, a man who had let a part of himself out into the world—and I wasn't sure where it would lead us, but I knew I couldn't walk away now.

The fire trucks had left, their blaring sirens replaced by the low hum of the cleanup crew's chatter. The air had cooled slightly, though the damage to the street and the lingering scent of charred wood was enough to make it clear that the world had shifted somehow. The calm after the storm was always the hardest part, when everything was still, and you had a moment to think about what had just happened, what you'd just survived.

I stole a glance at Jacob. He was staring straight ahead, his jaw tight, eyes trained on the remnants of the fire. The flickering lights from the trucks cast odd shadows on his face, giving him the appearance of someone caught between two worlds—half in the present, half in something darker.

"Jacob," I said quietly, reaching for his hand once more, my fingers brushing his. He didn't pull away this time, but he didn't look at me either. He was somewhere else.

"I'm not going to be the guy you want me to be," he said, his voice low, rough like gravel. The words felt like a confession, as though he was offering a piece of himself that he didn't know how to give. "You're expecting someone else. Someone who can just...forget."

I shook my head, stepping closer, ignoring the distant voices that seemed to fade into the background. "I'm not expecting anything from you," I said firmly. "I'm not here to fix you. I'm here because I want to be."

The words hung between us, like a delicate thread, fragile but strong enough to pull us back together if we let it. And I thought maybe, just maybe, we would.

Jacob finally turned to me, his eyes locking onto mine with a rawness that made my heart skip. There was vulnerability in his gaze now, something I had never seen in him before, not in this way. The walls that had been up for so long were crumbling. Slowly, cautiously, but unmistakably.

"I'm not good at this," he muttered, his voice carrying the weight of all the things he hadn't said in years. "I don't know how to...to let anyone in."

"I know," I whispered back. "But I'm here anyway."

The silence that followed wasn't uncomfortable. It was...understanding. We both knew we were standing on the edge of something. The question was whether we would step into it together or let the moment slip through our fingers.

We didn't speak for a while after that. We just stood there, side by side, watching the last of the embers fade into the cold night air. The crowd had begun to thin, and the emergency lights were finally starting to dim. The fire had been put out, but the lingering tension remained, a reminder of what we had faced—and perhaps, what was yet to come.

I turned my head to look at Jacob again, catching a glimpse of the uncertainty that still clouded his expression. It was fleeting, but I saw it—the way he seemed to be at war with himself, fighting against something deep inside. The question that had been in the air since the moment we'd reunited was still there, lingering, unspoken.

What happens now?

"You should go home," Jacob said suddenly, his voice a little too cold, a little too final. He was pulling away, even if just emotionally, and I could feel the distance forming between us again. It was like the fire had burned through something more than the buildings. It had burned through the illusion that things could stay the same.

"I'm not going anywhere," I replied, stepping closer. His words were like a challenge, a final attempt to push me away, but I wasn't having it. Not anymore. Not after everything. "Jacob, listen to me. You're not getting rid of me that easily."

His eyes flickered with frustration, and for a split second, I thought he might say something sharp, something cutting. Instead, he just sighed, running a hand through his hair. "I'm trying to protect you," he said quietly, almost as if he were talking to himself. "This—" He motioned vaguely to the empty street, the remnants of the fire still casting a dull glow in the distance. "This is me. I don't know how to be what you want. I don't know how to be anything else but...this."

I stepped closer, ignoring the sharpness in his tone. "You don't have to be anyone else, Jacob. I just want you to be you."

His eyes searched mine, a fleeting moment of hope and doubt battling for control. But before he could say anything, the sound of footsteps caught our attention. A figure appeared in the shadows, moving with purpose toward us. My stomach twisted as the figure came into focus—an unfamiliar man, wearing the uniform of the local police department.

"I'm sorry to interrupt," the officer said, his voice steady but laced with a tension that didn't go unnoticed. "We need to speak to the two of you. There's been a development."

I looked at Jacob, who seemed as stunned as I was, his expression darkening again, as if the weight of something unspoken had settled between us once more.

"What is it?" I asked, my heart skipping a beat.

The officer's face tightened. "There's a report of another fire...and it's spreading."

Chapter 14: Shadows of Doubt

I couldn't shake the feeling that the walls were closing in, though they didn't look any different than they had that morning. The same ivory-colored walls. The same heavy drapes, fluttering gently as a breeze pushed in through the cracked window. But something was off. The air had changed—thicker, laden with tension that didn't belong. I wanted to blame it on the coffee I'd had a few hours ago, the one that had left my head buzzing in a way that wasn't entirely pleasant. But I knew better than to ignore the whispers of doubt creeping in from the edges of my mind.

His voice lingered in my thoughts, too smooth, too careful. "Trust me," he'd said last night, the words heavy with a promise I wasn't sure I could keep. But how could I not trust him? He had been my rock, the one constant in a sea of uncertainty. He'd told me everything, hadn't he?

No. The thought rang through my chest like a cold bell. He hadn't told me everything. And something in his eyes told me he knew I was starting to figure that out.

The warning had come from Claire, of all people. I'd always thought of her as a little too eager, a little too sharp. But last night, as we sat together at the bar, the dim lighting doing nothing to hide the unease in her eyes, she'd dropped it casually, like it was nothing.

"You don't know him like you think you do," she'd said, her fingers twisting the edge of her napkin. Her voice had been quiet, almost conspiratorial, but the sharpness behind the words had sliced through the air like a blade. "There are things... dangerous things... he's not telling you. Things you wouldn't understand."

I'd laughed it off then. "You've been watching too many spy movies, Claire. He's a good guy." But even as I said it, I could feel the faintest prickling of discomfort at the back of my mind. It wasn't like Claire to be so cryptic, to suggest something without outright saying it. And she knew me well enough to know that I wasn't the type to be easily swayed.

She hadn't said much more, just a fleeting look of sympathy and a soft, "I hope I'm wrong."

But as I sat in the small café this afternoon, absentmindedly stirring my coffee, I realized I couldn't shake her words from my mind. The weight of them pressed down, pushing against my ribs like a tight corset. I wasn't sure what I was afraid of—what Claire had meant, what she hadn't said. But the more I tried to dismiss it, the louder the question became: What was he hiding?

The door to the café chimed as it opened, and I didn't even have to look up to know it was him. His presence filled the room before his footsteps ever did, an undeniable force that drew my attention like a magnet. I couldn't help the flutter in my stomach, the way my pulse quickened just from hearing the sound of his voice in the next room.

"Morning, sunshine," he said, his voice as smooth and easy as it always was, though there was something in his tone that made me look up.

He was leaning against the doorframe, casually casual in a way that was almost too perfect. The crisp white shirt he wore was just a shade too neat, the sleeves rolled up a little too precisely, the stubble on his chin a touch too rugged for someone who'd just woken up. His dark eyes met mine with that knowing look, the one he always gave me when he thought I was hiding something.

I resisted the urge to look away. This was not the time for me to be weak. Not when the air between us felt like it was filled with all the things we hadn't said yet. I took a long sip of my coffee, feeling the warmth spread through my chest, but it didn't chase away the cold gnawing at my insides.

He smiled, that crooked smile that made my heart do things I wasn't ready to admit, and slid into the chair across from me. His gaze lingered on my face, like he was searching for something.

"Is everything okay?" His voice was careful now, as if the usual banter had been stripped away, and all that was left was the rawness of the moment. "You seem... distant."

My heart gave a little lurch, the type that you get when you've been caught doing something you shouldn't. It was impossible not to feel exposed under that look, that intense, unnerving scrutiny. But the words I'd been holding in for days hovered on my tongue, and I couldn't stop myself from asking, "What's going on, Luke? What aren't you telling me?"

His expression shifted, a flicker of something in his eyes. It was brief, almost imperceptible, but I saw it, and I knew. He knew I was onto him. He wasn't as good at hiding things as he thought. Not anymore.

He leaned back in his chair, crossing his arms over his chest. The usual charm that poured from him was gone, replaced by something I couldn't quite name. Sorrow? Regret? I couldn't tell, but whatever it was made my stomach twist.

"You're asking the wrong questions," he said, his voice low. "Maybe the better question is, what aren't you seeing?"

I didn't know what to say. He was right. I wasn't seeing something, something big, and I was starting to hate myself for it. The worst part? I didn't know how deep the rabbit hole went.

I couldn't help but notice how still the air had become between us, the kind of stillness that precedes a storm. His gaze held mine, and for a moment, the world outside that little café seemed to dissolve into nothing. The weight of everything unsaid, everything hanging between us like a sword ready to drop, became unbearable.

I could feel the familiar ache in my chest, the one that I'd grown used to every time I allowed myself to feel something too deeply, too fully. Love had always been this way—messy, complicated, heavy with implications I never wanted to confront. But Luke wasn't just any man. He was the one I had let slip past every defense I had, the one who had waded into my life like he belonged there, with all of his charm and secrets and that damn smile that made me forget myself.

"I didn't think you'd ever ask," he murmured, his voice low and rough as though he were speaking in a language neither of us understood, but which we both somehow knew.

"I need to know, Luke. I can't keep pretending everything's fine when it clearly isn't."

His jaw tightened, a flicker of something dark passing over his features, but before I could read it, he masked it with a grin. The kind of grin that told me exactly what he thought of my inquiry.

"Did you really think you knew me so well?" he asked, his eyes narrowing as if he were daring me to answer. "Maybe you don't want to know the truth."

I fought the urge to flinch, to give in to the gnawing sense of betrayal creeping up my spine. I'd been here before, in this moment, where I'd stood on the edge, unsure if the person I loved was the one standing before me—or someone I'd only been imagining. But this time felt different, sharper somehow, as if something fundamental had shifted and now there was no going back. My heart was in freefall, tangled between trust and suspicion, love and fear.

"I want to know," I said, my voice shaking more than I cared to admit. "I have to know, Luke."

His expression softened, but there was an edge to it, a sadness that made my heart ache in places I hadn't known existed. "You'll never look at me the same way again," he said quietly, his words hanging in the air like an unspoken warning. He didn't wait for me to respond, didn't give me time to process the heavy weight of his declaration before he continued. "I've made choices... things I can't undo."

I leaned forward, my pulse quickening. This was it. The moment where everything changed, where the veil was lifted, and the person I thought I knew became someone entirely different—or was revealed to have been different all along.

"You're scaring me," I whispered, though I wasn't sure if I meant the words for him or for myself. Because I didn't know anymore.

"I should," he said, his voice now a low rasp, as if the very act of confessing was costing him something more than just words. "I've been keeping secrets. Dangerous ones. Things I've done that can't be undone. You don't want to be caught up in it, not if you know what's good for you."

My breath caught in my throat. There was no going back now. His words, full of menace and regret, hung between us like a cloud, darkening the space we once shared so freely. But then, as quickly as the weight descended, it was gone. His face, etched with something that might have been fear—or maybe it was just the exhaustion from carrying whatever burden he'd been hiding—softened.

"I don't want to lose you," he said quietly, his gaze intense, searching for something in me that I wasn't sure I was ready to reveal.

"I don't want to lose you either," I replied, my voice barely a breath. "But I can't keep pretending I'm okay with what you're not saying."

He reached out then, his fingers brushing mine in a way that felt almost too gentle for the moment. "You'll understand soon enough. Just trust me a little longer."

But that was the thing, wasn't it? Trust.

The word echoed in my head, circling around my thoughts like an endless loop. How could I trust him when everything he said made me question him more? How could I trust him when

Claire's warning still rang in my ears, when the knot in my stomach tightened at the mere thought of him hiding things? But I didn't want to let go. I didn't want to face the terrifying possibility that I had been wrong, that everything I thought I knew about him was a lie.

"I don't know if I can keep doing this," I admitted, the words leaving me before I could stop them. I wasn't sure if I meant the relationship, the waiting, the endless cycle of not knowing, or if I was speaking about something deeper, something I hadn't even fully acknowledged myself. But the silence between us stretched, and I knew the truth had landed hard between us, like a stone sinking into still water.

His eyes flickered, and I saw it then. The chasm between us, wide and insurmountable, though we had both been pretending it wasn't there. The truth hung like an invisible weight between us, and no matter how much I wished it away, it was still there, heavy and undeniable.

"I'll tell you everything," he said, almost to himself, as if making a promise to someone he had already betrayed. "But not today. Not yet."

I didn't know whether to be relieved or more afraid. My heart was torn between the desperate hope that I'd hear the truth—and the sickening fear that I wouldn't like what I heard. But as he stood up and walked out of the café without another word, I was left with nothing but the suffocating silence of the moment. The kind of silence that screamed louder than anything he could have said.

I sat in the empty café long after he had left, my fingers tracing the rim of my coffee cup absently, the bitterness on my tongue nothing compared to the one gnawing at my insides. There was something about the way he'd walked out that had shattered the last fragments of whatever fragile illusion I had left. The finality of his departure hung in the air like smoke, curling around my thoughts, suffocating them until I could barely breathe.

I didn't know what to do with the silence he left behind. He'd told me nothing. Not one word more than what had already been unsaid between us. Just a quiet promise, a vague allusion to truths buried deep under layers of secrecy. But I wasn't stupid. The lack of answers was louder than any revelation he could have given. He had left me in the dark, and that—more than anything—felt like betrayal.

The worst part was that I could still feel the pull. The magnetic force that had drawn me to him from the very first moment. It was a force so strong that it overpowered every reasonable instinct I had, every warning flashing through my mind.

I stood up abruptly, pushing my chair back so fast it scraped across the floor, the sound too sharp in the quiet café. What was I doing? Waiting around for him to make his move? I couldn't do that anymore. But when I walked out of the door, the world outside felt like a foreign landscape, a place where nothing was certain, and nothing was clear.

The city street was bustling with life—people rushing in all directions, the distant honking of taxis, the low murmur of conversation, the smell of street food wafting in the air. But all I could see was his face. His eyes, dark and guarded, looking back at me with a mixture of sorrow and something I couldn't place. It had to mean something, right? But if it did, what was it?

I walked aimlessly, my steps carrying me toward the park by the river. The crisp air did little to clear my mind, but the movement—my own heartbeat keeping time with the rhythm of the city—offered a momentary escape. A space where I didn't have to think about the painful truths that were slowly rising to the surface, one inconvenient revelation at a time.

As I reached the river's edge, I leaned against the railing, staring at the water, which shimmered silver in the fading light of the late afternoon. The motion of the river, constant and unstoppable, reminded me of my thoughts—rushing forward, never looking back, only to be swept along, unsure of where they would end up.

My phone buzzed in my pocket, and I pulled it out with the kind of reluctance you reserve for messages you know you shouldn't open. I stared at the screen for a long beat before pressing the button to read the text. It was from Claire.

"I know you're not going to like this, but I need to tell you something. It's about Luke."

I froze, the words blurring before my eyes. A sick feeling bloomed in the pit of my stomach as my thumb hovered over the keyboard, unsure whether to type back or leave it unanswered. But I didn't have a choice. I had to know. Even if it was the last thing I wanted to hear.

"What do you know?" I typed quickly, my hands shaking, the words feeling like an invitation to disaster.

The seconds ticked by like hours before her reply came through, each one a cruel reminder of how little I truly understood.

"He's not who you think he is. He's in too deep, and I don't think he can get out."

The message hit me like a punch to the chest. I'd known there was something off about him, something I couldn't quite put my finger on, but this? This was different. Claire had never been the type to speak in vague generalities. When she said something like this, there was weight behind it. There was truth, and I had to face it whether I liked it or not.

Before I could respond, my phone buzzed again, but this time, it wasn't Claire. It was Luke.

"I'm sorry. I didn't mean to leave you hanging like that. I know you need answers. But it's complicated, and right now, I can't give you the whole picture."

The words twisted in my stomach. The apology, the admission, the promise of answers—it all sounded too much like a ploy. Like he was trying to keep me tethered to something I didn't even fully understand. And the worst part was that, deep down, I still wanted to believe him. I still wanted to believe that what we had was real, that he wasn't hiding something dark and dangerous.

But if Claire was right, then everything I had been blind to was about to come crashing down around me.

I sent one last message before I could stop myself.

"Tell me the truth, Luke. All of it."

I pressed send and waited, heart in my throat, my breath coming in shallow gasps. There was no going back from this.

The minutes stretched into what felt like an eternity. I waited by the river, staring out at the water, my mind racing, a storm of emotions battling for control. I had no idea how long I stood there—how long I waited for him to respond. But when my phone buzzed again, I nearly dropped it.

This time, his response was different.

"I'm at the old pier. Come alone."

The words were simple, but they sent a chill through me. Why the pier? Why alone? Everything inside me screamed to ignore it, to turn around and go home, but something else—something reckless, something driven by the need for answers—pushed me forward.

I took a deep breath, shoved my phone back in my pocket, and turned on my heel. I couldn't shake the feeling that I was walking into a trap, but it didn't matter. Not anymore.

Chapter 15: Embers of Betrayal

The air was thick, hot with the promise of summer storms, though nothing but a murky stillness settled over the backyard. I could feel the weight of the silence pressing in on me, heavy as the oppressive heat that clung to the trees like a second skin. He had retreated to the far end of the porch, one hand braced against the railing, his broad shoulders tense beneath the faded gray shirt. I couldn't remember when things had become so fragile between us, when each glance, each word, seemed loaded with the weight of a thousand unsaid things.

I wanted to scream at him, to demand some kind of explanation for the walls he'd built between us. But something stopped me. Maybe it was the way his jaw tightened when I moved even slightly, as if he could sense the unrest swirling inside me. Maybe it was the way his silence wrapped around us, turning everything that should have been simple into something complex and unspoken.

I shifted on the porch swing, the wood creaking under me as if it too were unsure of what was happening. I thought about the times we had laughed together, shared quiet moments over coffee as the sun spilled through the windows in the morning. But those days felt like a lifetime ago, faded into something unreal, something distant.

His voice cut through the air, raw and hoarse. "I don't want to do this right now."

I wanted to ask what this even was—the silence, the distance, the strange, aching tension—but I knew better than to push too hard. Not yet. He wasn't ready to talk. And I was starting to realize that maybe I wasn't ready to listen.

I looked at him then, really looked at him. There was a hardness to his features that hadn't been there before, a distance in his eyes that seemed as vast as the space between us. The man I knew, the one who had whispered secrets in the dark and shared his thoughts without hesitation, had evaporated. In his place stood a stranger, someone carrying a weight I couldn't fathom.

And that, I realized, was the problem. The more I tried to reach out, the more he pulled away. The more I offered pieces of myself, the more he buried his.

I slid my fingers over the smooth wood of the swing's armrest, letting the coolness of it soothe the anxious heat building in my chest. There was something lodged in the pit of my stomach—a strange, tight knot that refused to loosen, no matter how much I tried to ignore it. Secrets. That's what I thought about most nights when I lay in bed, staring at the ceiling, willing myself not to succumb to the gnawing doubt.

I wasn't stupid. I knew there were things he wasn't telling me. Things he'd never told me. There had been a shift, subtle at first, but undeniable in hindsight. He used to be an open book, or at least he pretended to be. And I had read every page, every chapter, until I knew his quirks, his fears, his dreams better than my own.

But then came the silence. The late nights. The veiled looks, the words left hanging in the air like smoke, too heavy to be touched. I had convinced myself that it was just a phase, that he'd return to me, the man I had loved so fiercely. But now, as I watched him standing there, his back turned to me as if I were nothing more than a shadow in his life, I felt that hope begin to crack.

The worst part was that I wasn't sure if I even wanted him to turn around. Not yet. Not until I understood why he was doing this. Why he had started pulling away in the first place.

I stood, the swing creaking under my sudden movement. He stiffened, just for a moment, before continuing to stare off into the distance, as though he could will me out of his presence by sheer force of will.

"Don't walk away," I said before I could stop myself. My voice was low, but there was a fierceness in it that I hadn't known I possessed. "Don't do that."

He didn't turn. Not immediately. But when he finally did, his eyes were filled with something I hadn't expected—regret, maybe. Or guilt. But it wasn't enough to erase the shadow of the man who had been slipping away for weeks.

"I'm not walking away." His voice cracked, just once. "I'm just... I'm just not ready."

That word—ready—stung more than I wanted to admit. It was the same word he had used the last time we had tried to talk about whatever this was between us, and it had sounded just as hollow then as it did now. What did it even mean to be "ready"? Ready for what? For me to stop asking questions? For him to stop hiding?

I crossed the porch in three quick strides, standing just inches from him now. My chest heaved, my breath coming in shallow bursts as I tried to steady myself. "I don't need you to be ready," I said, the words biting. "I just need you to stop pretending everything's fine when it's not."

He looked at me then, really looked at me, and I saw something flash in his eyes—something sharp, dangerous. For a split second, I thought he might say something cruel, something that would push me further away. But instead, he simply turned his back again and stepped toward the railing, his fingers curling around the wood as if it could anchor him.

I couldn't just let him go. Not like this. Not without answers. But I knew, deep down, that I would have to fight for them.

I stood there, watching the back of him as he leaned against the railing, his broad shoulders casting long shadows in the late afternoon light. Every breath I took seemed to crackle with the same tension that buzzed through the air between us. It was almost laughable—this distance, this chasm that had opened up like an abyss between two people who had once known each other so intimately. How had we gotten here? And more importantly, why wasn't he fighting for us anymore?

The sound of cicadas hummed in the distance, almost like a mocking lullaby, the world around us too peaceful for the storm brewing in my chest. I hated the silence. I hated how easily he slipped into it, how it swallowed us both, leaving nothing but uncertainty and regret in its wake.

"Stop running," I said before I could talk myself out of it. The words tumbled out, desperate, shaking, and for a moment, I thought he hadn't heard me. But then, without turning around, he sighed—deep and resigned. It was a sound I had grown too familiar with, a sound that signaled he had made up his mind, that no matter how much I fought, I couldn't change his course.

"I'm not running," he said, his voice flat, but the way he said it… it wasn't the answer I wanted, and it certainly wasn't the answer I needed. It was a cop-out. A denial.

"You are," I shot back, taking a step closer. "You're hiding from something. From me. From whatever it is that's been eating away at you."

He didn't answer, not immediately. Instead, he let out another sigh, quieter this time, like a man burdened by something too heavy to carry. It made my insides twist, as though the very air around me had become thick with his secrets. I hated that feeling, the feeling that there were pieces of him, fragments of the man I used to know, locked away where I couldn't reach them.

"Why won't you talk to me?" I pressed, frustration creeping into my voice despite my best efforts to keep it steady. "Why won't you tell me what's wrong?"

A long silence stretched between us, more suffocating than any words could ever be. I could feel his shoulders tense beneath the weight of it, like he was carrying something too fragile to break, something that could shatter if I got too close.

"You wouldn't understand," he muttered, his eyes focused on the horizon as if looking at anything but me would somehow make it easier to breathe.

I couldn't keep quiet. Not anymore. The need to push him, to demand answers, was too strong. It had built up in me for days, for weeks, every time he shut me out, every time he walked away, leaving me with nothing but the ache of unanswered questions.

"Try me," I said, stepping closer until there was barely a foot between us. "I can handle it."

He turned to face me then, and I could see the strain in his eyes, the battle he was waging within himself. There was something in those eyes—something that flickered and died all too quickly. Something raw, and dark, and full of regret. And for a moment, I thought he might crack, might finally say what had been eating him alive all this time.

But instead, he swallowed hard, shaking his head, his jaw tight as he looked away again. "I don't want to do this."

The words hit me like a slap, not because they were harsh, but because of how empty they sounded. There was no fight left in him, no spark of the man who used to fight for us, for this. Just a hollow shell, a shadow of the person I thought I knew.

My chest tightened, and before I knew it, the words escaped me, unbidden and full of heat. "Well, I'm not going to stand here and pretend like everything is fine while you push me away. I deserve better than that. We deserve better than that."

His eyes snapped back to me then, and for a moment, I thought I saw something flicker in them—something desperate, something desperate to say more. But it was gone before I could grasp it.

"Don't make this harder than it already is." His voice was strained, barely above a whisper, as if the very act of speaking the words was a struggle.

But the moment the words left his mouth, I knew they were just another wall, another way to shut me out. And I had had enough of that. Enough of feeling like I was a stranger to the man I had once known so well.

I reached for his arm, my fingers brushing against the warmth of his skin. He stiffened at the contact, his muscles tensing as though I were an intrusion. But I didn't pull away.

"Tell me what's going on," I said softly, my voice almost pleading now. "I won't bite. You don't have to protect me from whatever it is. Just... talk to me."

For a moment, there was only silence. The kind that felt thick, like it was made of something more than just absence. Like it was a space between two people who had shared everything but who now found themselves unable to bridge the distance that had grown between them.

Then, his voice broke through, rough and hoarse. "I can't. I can't tell you." He met my eyes for the briefest moment, his gaze filled with pain, before looking away again. "Not yet."

Something inside me twisted at the finality in his voice. He wasn't going to tell me. He wasn't going to let me in.

I swallowed hard, my pulse racing in my ears. "Then you're leaving me with nothing but your silence. And I can't keep doing this, waiting for you to maybe decide to let me back in." The words stung as I spoke them, but they were true. Every single one.

He seemed to shrink in on himself, the weight of my words landing on him like an anvil. But instead of pushing forward, instead of finally giving me the answers I so desperately needed, he turned away. Again.

I knew in that moment that if I didn't act now, if I didn't find the answers myself, I might never get them. And the idea of living in limbo like this—forever waiting for him to open up, for him to trust me again—was something I couldn't bear.

But as he walked away, leaving me standing in the fading light, I knew this was only the beginning. Whatever was hidden, whatever was buried beneath the surface, it wasn't going to stay buried for long. And I was going to find out what it was. Even if it meant losing him in the process.

I stood there, watching the slow rhythm of his retreat, each step an unraveling thread that pulled him further out of reach. My mind raced with the need to stop him, to somehow bridge this impossible gap between us. But the words felt like weights in my mouth—too heavy to speak, too fragile to hold. I had told myself time and time again that if he couldn't talk, then I would just have to wait. But now, that patience seemed like nothing more than a quiet resignation, and I wasn't ready to resign myself to silence. Not anymore.

I moved, almost without thinking, taking quick, purposeful steps toward him. I reached for his arm again, my fingers skimming the hard line of muscle beneath his sleeve. He stiffened, flinching just slightly at my touch, but I refused to let go. I couldn't let him go—not this time.

"Please," I whispered, my voice thick with emotion I couldn't mask. "Don't do this. I'm not asking for anything I don't deserve. I just need the truth."

He inhaled sharply, like he was preparing for something painful. His eyes flickered to mine, dark and guarded, a flash of something—anguish, maybe—before he turned away. And in that moment, I saw it. The vulnerability. The truth, buried beneath layers of fear and shame.

"I can't, okay?" His voice was low, strained, like each word cost him. "I can't tell you. Not yet."

It wasn't an answer. It wasn't even close to the truth I needed, and the frustration surged within me again, hot and dangerous. I clenched my jaw, fighting the urge to shake him, to demand more, to force him into the open where I could finally see him, truly see him.

But I didn't. Because deep down, I knew that wouldn't work. It hadn't worked before.

"Not yet?" I echoed, the bitterness creeping into my voice. "How long is this 'not yet' supposed to last? A day? A week? A lifetime?"

His shoulders sagged slightly, as if he was carrying an invisible weight too heavy for just one person to bear. "I don't know," he murmured, almost to himself. "I don't know how long."

It was the honesty I had been craving, but it stung like salt in an open wound. I took a step back, retreating slightly as the words circled in my head, desperate to make sense of them. I don't know. It was a confession, a surrender, and it left me reeling in its wake.

"I can't keep doing this," I said, the words rushed and raw, spilling out before I could stop them. "You're asking me to wait for something you won't even explain. You're asking me to trust that you'll come back, that you'll fix whatever is broken. But you're not even giving me a chance to help you."

He turned then, finally, meeting my gaze with a raw intensity that made my pulse quicken. His eyes were stormy, a tempest of emotions swirling just beneath the surface. He opened his mouth, but the words that followed were the last ones I expected to hear.

"I don't deserve your help," he said, his voice barely a whisper. "I don't deserve your trust, not after everything."

The admission hit me like a punch to the gut, stealing the breath from my lungs. Everything? What did he mean by that?

What had happened to make him believe he wasn't worthy of me, of us? The question clung to me, urgent and unanswered.

"You're wrong," I said, my voice shaking, barely audible. "You don't get to decide that. You don't get to push me away just because you're scared or angry or whatever else you're feeling."

He flinched, visibly at the words, but he didn't look away. Instead, he seemed almost... resigned, as though he had already made up his mind about something I wasn't privy to. His gaze softened for the briefest moment, but it didn't last. The mask was back in place, cold and impenetrable.

"I'm not the man you think I am," he said quietly, his words heavy, almost regretful. "And I'm not the man you deserve. Not anymore."

My heart hammered in my chest, the finality of his words echoing in the hollow spaces between us. It felt like the ground had shifted beneath my feet, the world tilting sideways, and for the first time, I wondered if there was no going back.

I shook my head, the words a desperate plea. "Stop saying that. Stop believing that."

But he didn't respond. He just stood there, his face a mask of uncertainty and pain, as though he were battling with something much larger than both of us combined. And in that moment, I realized the truth: he wasn't just pulling away from me. He was pulling away from himself. The man I had known, the man I loved, had vanished into whatever shadow was haunting him.

The silence stretched between us, thick and unbearable, until I couldn't take it anymore. My throat was tight, my chest aching, and I couldn't breathe.

"I don't know how to help you," I said softly, almost in defeat. "But I can't help you if you won't let me in."

He didn't answer at first. But I could see the struggle in his eyes, the battle between something deep inside him—something that was pulling him further away, pushing him into darkness—and whatever part of him still wanted to reach for me, to let me in.

But the longer he stood there, the more that hope slipped from my fingers, like sand in the wind.

And then, just as I thought I couldn't bear it any longer, he spoke again, his voice so low I almost didn't hear it.

"You don't understand."

His words hung in the air, sharp and fragile, like a razor's edge. I opened my mouth to respond, to demand what he meant by that, but before I could speak, the distant sound of a car engine cut through the silence.

I froze, my eyes narrowing instinctively toward the sound. Something about it—the engine's growl, the screech of tires as it skidded to a stop—felt wrong.

Without warning, he turned, his expression hardening once more, and before I could even process what was happening, he stepped away from me, his body tense with a sudden, palpable urgency.

"Stay inside," he commanded, his voice cold, detached. "Now."

I opened my mouth to protest, but his sharp gaze silenced me instantly. I hesitated, my heart racing, but as I saw him move toward the driveway, I realized—whatever was about to unfold, it was going to change everything.

Chapter 16: The Fire Within

The town had been quiet for days, or at least that was the illusion it tried to maintain. People moved through their routines like clockwork, their lives quiet and neat, trimmed at the edges to avoid anything messy. But beneath the hum of daily life, there was something that gnawed at me—something jagged and unfinished, like an old wound that hadn't fully healed. The fire had taken everything from us, or so they said. But there were too many pieces that didn't fit together, too many things that the townsfolk whispered behind closed doors, their words as soft as the smoke that still lingered in the air months after the flames had died.

I could hear it all now—echoes of secrets carried on the wind, too faint to catch in full, but too persistent to ignore. Bits and pieces of conversations floated by, sometimes just a word, sometimes a phrase. "Something wasn't right." "He knew more than he said." "That night—it wasn't an accident." The more I listened, the more I found myself threading together a story that no one else seemed willing to entertain.

The man I needed answers from was the one I least wanted to confront. Jackson. He wasn't just anyone in this town; he was its heart, its pulse. He'd been a hero once. He'd fought the fire with the tenacity of a man who had something to prove. And yet, now? Now, he was a man shrouded in mystery, a man who had withdrawn into himself like a wounded animal. We used to share everything, back when we were young and everything was still possible. But now, our connection was something frayed at the edges, fragile, and yet there was something undeniably magnetic about him. Something dangerous. Something that scared me, if I was being honest with myself.

I knew I had to approach him. I had no choice. But how do you confront someone you've spent so long trying to forget? How do you ask questions you don't really want the answers to, when every part of you dreads the truth?

The morning I decided to confront him, the sun hung low in the sky, casting everything in a golden haze that made the world seem far away, as if it existed in some other reality. His house, a weather-beaten structure at the edge of town, looked almost abandoned, the porch steps sagging under the weight of neglect. But I could see the faintest sign of life inside—a flicker of movement behind the worn curtains. My heart thrummed in my chest, a nervous pulse that kept time with the rhythm of my feet as I walked up to the door.

He didn't look surprised when he opened it, though his expression was unreadable, as always. His eyes—those deep, stormy eyes—locked onto mine with the kind of intensity that made my breath hitch. For a moment, neither of us spoke. The silence between us was thick, almost oppressive. I could hear the sound of my own heart pounding in my ears, my stomach twisting into tight knots. It was as though the years had melted away, leaving only the tension, raw and exposed.

"I need to ask you something," I said, my voice a little rougher than I'd intended.

His jaw clenched. "I don't have answers you're looking for."

But I couldn't back down now, not after everything. "The fire," I said, keeping my voice steady, though my hands were trembling. "There's something you're not telling me. You were the one closest to it, Jackson. The one who should've known. Why won't you talk about it?"

The air between us seemed to crackle, the tension winding tighter with every word. His hands, long and calloused from years of work, tightened into fists at his sides. For a moment, I thought he might slam the door in my face, but instead, he stepped back and waved me inside.

I barely had time to step over the threshold before he whirled on me, his voice low and dangerous. "You don't know what you're asking for. You have no idea what's at stake here."

I stood frozen, the weight of his words pressing against me, but I refused to back down. "I know you're hiding something. You're not just angry. You're scared, Jackson. And I need to understand why."

For a long beat, he said nothing. The only sound was the creaking of the house settling around us, the slow, steady rhythm of the world continuing on while we remained locked in this moment. And then, finally, he spoke, his voice barely above a whisper. "Because I can't lose anyone else."

The words hung in the air, heavy with the kind of pain that seemed to radiate from him like heat from a flame. I had no idea what he meant—no idea what had happened that night, what could possibly have driven him to this point. But something in me shifted, a crack forming in the walls I'd built around myself. The fire wasn't just a tragedy to him. It was something far more personal.

"I'm not going to run from you," I said, my voice thick with emotion. "But you can't keep running from the truth."

The silence between us grew again, but this time it was different. It wasn't just the quiet of a moment stretched too thin—it was the silence before a storm.

And then, just as quickly as it had started, the air between us snapped, and all that simmering frustration, all that unresolved tension, exploded. He grabbed me, his hands fierce on my arms, pulling me against him with a raw intensity that stole the breath from my lungs. For a second, I thought he might crush me with his anger, but instead, the heat of his body was all-consuming, his lips crashing down on mine with a desperation that spoke of far more than just a need for answers.

I should have fought it. I should have pushed him away. But I couldn't. The fire between us—one that had been smoldering for years—had finally ignited. And as his hands roamed, pulling me closer, my own fingers tangled in his hair, I realized there was no turning back now. There was no running from what was burning between us.

The world outside had begun to dull, as though it were retreating into shadows, and we were the only two figures left standing in the center of a long-forgotten story. His breath was rough against my skin, and I could feel the tremors in his fingertips, the urgency in every touch. My heart was thrumming, too fast, too wild, as if it was trying to break free from its cage, and I couldn't seem to stop it. There was something primal about him in that moment, something that set every nerve in my body alight and made me want to scream just to hear myself.

But the words wouldn't come. They couldn't. Instead, I was left staring at him, eyes locked, trying to find the pieces of him I used to know—before everything had changed, before the fire. His chest was heaving under the weight of his emotions, and I could see the flickers of something desperate, something painful, in his gaze.

I shouldn't have let this happen. I shouldn't have let myself be pulled into this, but there I was, tangled in him, both of us caught in something that felt like it was consuming everything around us. His lips brushed mine again, a teasing whisper of a kiss, just enough to make my head spin before he pulled back, his eyes searching my face as if trying to gauge my reaction.

"This—this is insane," I whispered, the words leaving my mouth as if they were something foreign, like I was already losing control.

Jackson didn't answer at first. He just stood there, breathing, his face so close to mine that I could feel the heat of him, a warmth that reached inside and made me ache. His hands were still at my sides, but they didn't feel like they belonged to him anymore. They were a part of me, a part of the night, of the wreckage that we were becoming.

"I didn't want this," he finally said, his voice hoarse. "But you—" He paused, his thumb brushing my lip as if testing the words he couldn't say aloud. "You keep coming back. Keep asking questions."

"Because you're hiding something," I said, the words coming out more forcefully than I'd intended. I took a step back, breaking the contact between us, but the distance between us felt too wide, too impossible to cross.

"You don't get it." His words were low, clipped, like he was trying to hold something back. "I'm trying to protect you."

I wanted to laugh. I wanted to shout that he had no idea what I needed protection from. The fire, the people in this town, even the truth itself—it all seemed to be tangled together in ways I couldn't unravel. But most of all, I wanted to scream at the contradictions that lived inside him, the man who had once been the embodiment of everything good in this town, who had now become someone I didn't recognize.

I could feel the heat of the argument still clinging to us, like smoke that would never clear. There was a tension now, thick and suffocating, that neither of us could shake. His hands clenched at his sides, his jaw tight, but there was something in his eyes that I couldn't look away from.

"I know what you think," he said, his voice suddenly softer, like a sigh escaping him. "You think I'm hiding something, that I'm keeping the truth from you. But the truth? The truth might destroy us both."

I wanted to respond, to ask him what that even meant, but I couldn't. The words wouldn't come because I could feel the space between us growing smaller again. It was as if we were both standing on the edge of something—something we couldn't go back from, something we couldn't walk away from. The pull of him, the magnetism, was too strong. I couldn't ignore it.

I moved towards him again, my hands reaching for him instinctively, and when he didn't pull away, I kissed him, hard and desperate, as though I could drown the questions, the doubt, the fear in the fire between us. It was reckless and unplanned, but it felt like the only thing that made sense in that moment.

He kissed me back, with a force that nearly knocked me off my feet, and it was all fire—raw, urgent, furious. But underneath it, I felt the tremor of something more fragile, something that had been buried beneath all the anger and pain. His hands moved to my back, pulling me closer, and for a moment, I thought maybe this was how we would burn everything down.

And then, just as quickly, he broke away from me, his eyes wide with something that looked almost like regret, and yet, there was no hiding the hunger in them. "I can't keep doing this, with you," he said, his voice trembling. "I won't drag you down into this mess I've made."

I swallowed, the taste of him still lingering on my lips, and the weight of his words pressed against me like a physical force. "You don't get to decide that," I said, my voice more steady than I felt. "I'm already in this. I've been in this since the first time I saw you, since the fire started. You don't get to shut me out now."

He closed his eyes for a moment, as if the words cut deeper than I could have imagined. When he opened them again, the look in his eyes was the same—a storm, a battle between the man he had been and the one he was becoming. "You don't know what you're asking for."

And just like that, the door to whatever was between us slammed shut again. But even though it was closed, I could still feel the heat, still hear the crackle of something burning between us, just out of reach. He didn't say anything more, just turned away and walked toward the window, his shoulders hunched in a way that made my heart ache. There was no solution. No easy way out. And I had no idea what would happen next. But I knew one thing for sure.

There was no going back.

The silence that followed was thick, like a heavy blanket draped over us both, smothering everything except the dull thrum of my heartbeat in my ears. Jackson was still by the window, his back to me, but the tension in his shoulders had eased ever so slightly, as if the weight of the confrontation had left a bruise. My pulse was still racing, but now it wasn't from anger—it was from something else entirely. Something that I couldn't seem to shake off. Something that was starting to feel like it had always been there, waiting for the right moment to come to the surface.

I stood there, watching him, my chest tight with a strange mix of longing and frustration. "You think I'm just going to let this go? Let you shut me out again?" My voice was a little too sharp, and I hated how desperate it sounded. But I couldn't help it. This—this whole situation—was driving me to the edge. I needed him to understand.

He didn't turn around, not at first. The silence between us grew unbearable, stretching longer than I could stand. Finally, he exhaled, long and slow, as though he were trying to summon the words, or perhaps just summon the courage. When he spoke, his voice was tight, as if every syllable were being dragged from somewhere deep inside him. "You think you want to know everything. But the truth? It's not something you can just handle. It's not something you can come back from."

"And you think I don't know that?" I spat the words out before I could stop myself, the hurt rising like bile in my throat. "You think I've spent all these months trying to figure this out for fun?

That I've spent every sleepless night wondering how you—" I stopped myself, suddenly too aware of how far I had gone. I swallowed, trying to keep the heat from my voice, but it was no use. The words were already out there, the damage done.

Jackson turned then, his eyes flashing, and for the first time, I saw something in him that I hadn't expected: regret. It didn't make sense, though, not with the way he was looking at me—like he was already prepared to walk away, to shut this all down before it had a chance to breathe. "You think this is something I wanted?" His voice broke on the last word, a rawness there that was almost worse than his anger. "You think I wanted any of this to happen?" He moved toward me then, taking slow, measured steps, but his eyes never left mine. "But it did. It all happened. And now you're tangled up in it. You think you want to know the truth, but once I tell you, there's no going back. Nothing will ever be the same."

His words hung heavy in the room, a warning I couldn't quite ignore. I wanted to argue with him, to push back, but I couldn't—because in a way, he was right. The truth had already burned its way into my mind. It was already there, gnawing at me from the inside. It had been for days, weeks, maybe even longer, ever since I had started digging, ever since I'd started asking the questions no one wanted to answer. There was something about that fire, about that night, that didn't sit right with me. And no matter how much Jackson tried to push me away, I wasn't going to stop until I had the answers. No matter what it cost.

He was right about one thing—nothing would ever be the same. But that didn't scare me. At least, not as much as the alternative did.

"I'm not afraid of the truth," I said, more quietly now, my words barely above a whisper. "I'm afraid of what happens if you keep hiding from it."

Jackson didn't respond immediately. He stood there, looking at me with something like resignation in his gaze. I wasn't sure if it was pity or anger or some mixture of both, but whatever it was, it felt like he was already writing me off. Like I was another casualty in his twisted game. And that only fueled the fire burning inside me.

"You're not hearing me," he said finally, his voice so low it was almost a growl. "You think you can handle it, but you can't. Not when you find out the truth about that night. Not when you realize the part I played in it. The part I didn't have any choice in."

I took a step toward him, my hands trembling at my sides. "Then tell me. Tell me everything, Jackson. Or are you too scared to face it?"

He flinched at my words, and for a moment, I thought I'd crossed some line. But then his expression hardened, the walls inside him slamming back up, and the door to whatever he had been about to say closed.

"No," he said, his voice firm, final. "I won't do that to you."

For a moment, neither of us moved. The space between us felt like a chasm, a gap I could never cross, no matter how many times I tried. And just when I thought maybe this was the end—maybe this was where he would finally walk away—he spoke again, his voice barely audible, like he was testing the waters to see if the words would drown him.

"You want the truth?" he asked, his eyes flicking to mine. "Fine. But be prepared for what it means."

Before I could respond, the sound of the front door slamming open broke through the tension like a thunderclap, and Jackson spun around, his hand instinctively reaching for something at his waist. I froze, my stomach dropping. The door was wide open, and in the doorway stood a figure—tall, dark, and impossibly familiar. My pulse skittered in my chest.

"Jackson," the figure said, voice smooth and cold, "you're going to want to listen to me."

My blood ran cold. There was something about that voice, something that made every instinct in me scream danger. Something that made me realize, just a second too late, that I hadn't just been digging into the past. I had been digging into something much, much worse. And now, there was no turning back.

Chapter 17: Smoke and Shadows

I walk the streets of our small town like a ghost in my own skin, the air thick with the scent of rain on the horizon. It's quiet, almost too quiet, like the whole world is holding its breath for something that's just out of reach. My boots click against the cracked sidewalk, the rhythmic sound mingling with the rustle of wind through the trees. Each step feels heavier than the last, like the earth itself is trying to pull me back, as if it knows something I don't.

His absence weighs on me like a forgotten promise, heavy and unforgiving. The argument still burns in my mind, a fire that won't go out no matter how much I try to drown it. I can still hear the sharpness in his voice, the way he said things he didn't mean, but I can't forget the way his hands trembled before he left, like he was fighting against something deep inside himself. I should've been stronger. I should've understood. But what am I supposed to do when the man I thought I knew turns into a stranger overnight?

The familiar faces of the town flicker in and out of focus as I pass, each one more haunting than the last. There's no comfort in their expressions—just the weight of time and memory. I stop in front of the old diner, the one where we used to go on lazy Sunday mornings when everything felt simple, when it felt like we were unstoppable. I don't know what I'm expecting. Maybe for him to be there, sitting in our usual booth, grinning like he hasn't just torn my world apart.

But the booth is empty. The waitress behind the counter gives me a nod, but she doesn't ask if I want anything. She's learned not to. She knows better than to offer sympathy. It's not that kind of town. No one asks about what you're really feeling. They just watch. And wait. For the inevitable.

I turn on my heel and head down the street, my mind buzzing with fragments of our conversation. I should've known. I should've seen the signs. But the part of me that still wants to believe in fairy tales—the part that clings to hope no matter how many times it gets burned—refused to acknowledge what was happening. I convinced myself we were just going through a rough patch. That we would work through it, because that's what people do when they love each other, right? They fight, they heal, they move forward.

But he wasn't just running from me. He was running from something deeper, something darker.

The old-timers at the corner shop always know things. You can see it in their eyes, the way they linger over their coffee cups and nod knowingly to each other as if they're privy to some ancient wisdom. I used to think they were just gossiping, spinning tales for lack of anything better to do. But now, as I catch a glimpse of their faces through the window of the hardware store, I realize they've been watching him all along.

"Watch your back, girl," one of them says, her voice gravelly from years of tobacco and secrets. I stop in my tracks, unsure if she's talking about the argument we had last night or something far more dangerous. Her eyes narrow, and her lips twitch like she's holding something back.

"Some fires never die," she adds, her voice dropping lower, almost a whisper. "And you can't outrun the smoke."

I swallow, the words settling in my stomach like a stone. Fires? Smoke? What is she talking about? It's not the first time I've heard talk of flames and shadows in this town, but it always seemed like myth—something the old-timers told their grandchildren to keep them in line. But now... now it feels different. Like there's a warning in the air, one that's been there all along and I've just been too blind to see it.

I don't have time to ask her more; she's already turning back to her work, a brisk dismissal that leaves me more unsettled than before. I should keep walking. I should head home, lock the doors, and pretend like I haven't heard anything. But there's a pull in my chest, a tug that leads me further down the street toward the edge of town.

The wind picks up, and I wrap my coat tighter around me, its worn fabric offering little protection against the chill that's creeping into my bones. The shadows stretch longer as I near the woods, the trees standing like silent sentinels, their twisted branches reaching out like fingers in the dark. There's something unnerving about the way the air feels here, heavy with secrets that refuse to stay buried.

I can't stop the shiver that runs down my spine, and for a moment, I almost turn around. But then I see it—a figure, half-hidden in the shadows, standing just beyond the tree line. My heart skips a beat. It's him.

But no, it's not. The figure shifts, and I realize it's someone else. Someone I don't recognize. They don't move toward me, but I feel their presence, like they're watching, waiting for something. I want to call out, ask who they are, but my voice dies in my throat.

Instead, I take a step forward, my feet heavy, my mind racing with questions I can't answer.

There's a part of me that's afraid of what's waiting in the shadows. But there's another part—the part that still holds onto that thread of hope—that believes I might just find the answers I've been searching for. If only I'm brave enough to face them.

I don't know why I keep walking toward the woods. It's not like there's any sense to it, but it's like I'm tethered to the trees, like something is pulling me deeper into the shadows where I might finally understand. As I approach the edge of town, the old houses grow sparse, and the air shifts, thick with the promise of rain. The sun, barely peeking through the thick clouds, casts an eerie glow, turning everything into a washed-out version of itself. The town feels like a memory, as if it's already in the past, slipping away while I'm still trying to catch hold of it.

The stranger standing in the shadows doesn't move, but there's something about the stillness of them that sends a ripple of unease down my spine. I should call out, demand to know who they are, but my feet are frozen, like the earth has wrapped its roots around my ankles. A part of me wants to turn back, but I can't. I need to know. I have to.

"I see you," I finally say, my voice stronger than I expected, slicing through the silence. "Who are you?"

There's no immediate response. Not even the flutter of leaves in the wind. But then, slowly, the figure steps forward, just enough for me to make out the shape of a woman—tall, sharp features, a cloak of dark fabric swirling around her like it's alive. Her eyes, though, are what catch me. Dark as the space between stars, cold and unsettling, and yet, there's something in them that feels familiar. Something that tugs at the edges of my memory, like I've seen those eyes before, or maybe dreamed of them.

"You don't belong here," she says, her voice soft but carrying the weight of something ancient.

The words catch me off guard. It's not like anyone ever tells me I don't belong. Sure, I've never quite felt like I fit in, but it's different when someone else says it, as if she's speaking some kind of truth I've never been able to face.

"I don't belong where?" I ask, though the answer is probably clear. I don't belong in this town. Not anymore, not with him gone. And now, with her standing there like a manifestation of everything I'm trying to ignore, I wonder if I ever truly did.

She doesn't answer at first. She only studies me, her gaze lingering in a way that makes me want to squirm. Then she steps closer, her movements fluid, too graceful for someone who should be standing alone in the woods, shrouded in shadows.

"Did you really think you knew him?" Her words slice through me, sharp and cutting. "You think you're the first to chase after him, to believe you could fix him? You'll end up like all the rest."

I don't respond right away, because how do you argue with someone who seems to know so much about you and the man you thought you knew? My mind races, trying to piece together her cryptic words, but they're slipping through my fingers like sand.

"I'm not like the rest," I say, though the words feel weak even as they leave my mouth.

She smiles, a thin, almost pitying curve of her lips. "We're all the same. Chasing the same thing. And in the end, none of it matters."

I open my mouth to protest, but before I can, she turns on her heel and begins walking away, disappearing into the shadows as if she's become part of the night itself. I'm left standing there, a mess of confusion and unanswered questions, as the wind picks up, howling through the trees. I don't know whether to feel relieved or more unsettled than ever.

"Wait," I call out, though I know she won't answer. "Who are you?"

But the only response is the rustle of leaves and the sound of my own heartbeat thudding in my chest. I stand there for a moment, too stunned to move, and then it hits me.

She knows something. She knows something about him. About what's been happening.

I don't know why, but I follow. I can't explain it, but there's an instinct in me, something deeper than logic, telling me to keep going. I walk into the woods, my breath coming faster with every step. The air is thick, heavy with dampness, and the path before me disappears into the fog that's rolling in, as though the earth itself is swallowing it up.

The further I walk, the more everything seems to blur. The world becomes a twisted maze of dark branches, shivering leaves, and fleeting moments where the edges of reality seem to fray.

I catch a glimpse of her ahead—her dark figure flitting through the trees like she's part of the night.

"You can't run from this," she calls over her shoulder, her voice drifting back to me on the wind. "No one ever really gets away."

I stop dead in my tracks. The words hit me like a slap, and I feel a chill creep up my spine, but it's not the cold from the wind. It's something colder. Something real.

I should turn back. I should find my way home, call it a night, let the questions burn themselves out like embers in a dying fire. But there's something in her words, something that keeps me rooted in place. She's right, in a way. I can't escape this. Not now, not when I'm so close to the truth, to whatever lies hidden in the darkness.

I push forward, determined to see this through. Because no matter how much it scares me, I know one thing for sure—if I don't keep moving, I'll lose myself completely.

The woods feel more oppressive with each step, the air thickening until it presses down on me like the weight of a hundred years. The trees crowd together, their gnarled branches reaching out like hands eager to pull me into their tangled depths. For a moment, I wonder if this is what he wanted—this strange, suffocating silence. A place where the world can't touch you, a place where no one asks questions.

But I can't stop now. I don't know what it is I'm looking for, but it's almost like I can hear his voice in the wind, calling me forward, urging me to see this through. I shouldn't be here. This place feels wrong, ancient in a way that makes my skin crawl, but the need to understand what happened between us, to finally make sense of all the fragmented pieces, drives me forward.

My boots crunch over the dead leaves as I push deeper, my breath coming in quick, shallow bursts. There's no sign of the woman anymore, no trace of the figure that led me this far. But I feel her presence still, like a shadow at the edge of my vision, flickering just out of reach. She's waiting for something. She's always waiting for something.

And then I hear it.

A soft rustling, barely perceptible at first, like the whisper of fabric against the wind. But it's there, unmistakable now, growing louder as I draw closer to the clearing ahead. My heart speeds up, thudding in my chest like a drum, each beat echoing in my ears.

I stop just before the clearing, holding my breath. There's a figure standing in the middle of it, bathed in the fading light that cuts through the trees like a beam of hope—except this time, it's not him. It's someone else.

My stomach lurches. I take a step back, but my foot catches on a root, sending me stumbling forward into the open.

The figure turns, its eyes flashing with recognition, a flicker of something too familiar. My breath hitches as I take in the face—the one that's haunted me for so long. The face I never thought I'd see again.

"You," I manage, my voice barely a whisper, tangled in disbelief.

The figure doesn't respond. Instead, it steps toward me with a slow, deliberate motion, its eyes never leaving mine. There's something about the way it moves, too smooth, too practiced, like it's done this a thousand times before. I can't look away, even though every instinct is screaming at me to run.

"Did you think you could escape this?" The voice is low, rough, like it's been through too many storms. But there's no mistaking the way it resonates deep in my chest—it's his voice.

I want to scream, but the words catch in my throat. The truth of it hits me like a freight train, and I feel my knees tremble beneath me. He's been here all along. Not gone, not lost—just hiding. Hiding from me, hiding from whatever it is that's been pulling us apart.

"You didn't think I would find you?" I say, my voice breaking despite my best efforts to keep it steady. I can feel the tremor in my hands, and I ball them into fists, trying to hold onto something, anything.

He finally speaks, and the sound of it is like a knife dragging across my skin. "You weren't supposed to find out."

I take another step back, my mind racing to make sense of what's happening. "What are you talking about? Where have you been?"

He doesn't answer right away. Instead, his gaze flickers to the trees, as if he's listening for something—waiting for something. The tension in the air is so thick now, I can hardly breathe.

The world seems to hold its breath with us.

And then, as if on cue, the wind picks up, rustling the leaves, carrying with it a scent I can't quite place. It's faint, like smoke, but it's not from a fire. It smells like... something else. Something ancient.

I feel a chill run down my spine. My heart starts to race again, the pulse of it pounding in my throat.

"What have you gotten yourself into?" I whisper, more to myself than to him, but he hears it.

He steps forward, his presence like a shadow that stretches across the clearing, swallowing the light around him. "You have no idea what you're asking, do you? No idea what's really at stake."

I open my mouth to reply, but before I can, the ground beneath my feet shifts. The earth trembles, just a little, like a warning. I look down, confused. What's happening?

And then, from somewhere deep in the woods, a sound rips through the air—a scream, sharp and desperate, echoing off the trees. It's not human. Not quite.

My blood runs cold. The scream rips through me, chilling me to the bone, and for a moment, I'm paralyzed. I can't move. I can't breathe.

He doesn't flinch. He doesn't even seem surprised.

"Run," he says, his voice low and urgent, but I can't tell if he's talking to me or to himself.

I don't know what's coming, but I can feel it now—the danger, the sense that something is just out of sight, waiting to strike.

I try to turn and run, but before I can take a step, I hear the rustling again, louder this time, followed by the unmistakable sound of heavy footsteps closing in from behind.

I spin around, my heart hammering in my chest, but he's gone. The clearing is empty again.

And then I see it—something moving in the trees, something fast and shadowy, slipping through the branches like a predator. And it's coming straight for me.

I don't know how long I have before it catches up, but I know one thing for sure: I'm no longer alone.

Chapter 18: Fractured Truths

The air felt different that evening. It clung to me with a strange weight, thick and humid, as though the earth itself were holding its breath. I had already set the table for dinner—mostly because I didn't know what else to do with myself while I waited. The leftover scent of burning wood still lingered in the back of my mind, like a smell I couldn't scrub from my skin. I had never been good at waiting, especially not for him.

I should've known he'd return when the light was just about to dip below the horizon, bathing everything in that golden, fleeting glow. He stood in the doorway like a silhouette first, then came into focus, his posture slumped, his face a tired canvas of worry and unspoken words. The faint scent of smoke clung to him, and despite the wash of the day, it felt like the fire still hadn't left him. It clung, wrapped around his shoulders like an old friend, too familiar to shake off.

"Dinner's still warm," I said, keeping my tone light, despite the sense of something heavy pulling at my chest. It seemed, lately, that everything between us had a weight to it. Like we were both standing at the edge of a cliff, pretending not to notice the drop below.

His eyes met mine for a second, and in that flicker, I saw everything I needed to know. There was no escape for him. Not from the fire. Not from the people he couldn't save. Not from whatever dark secret he had wrapped up in that silence of his.

"Thanks," he murmured, taking a step closer. He didn't look at the food, didn't move toward it at all. Instead, he took the seat across from me, dropping into it with a tiredness that wasn't just physical. I wanted to ask, wanted to push the question past the lump in my throat, but I knew better. Not yet.

We sat in silence for a few moments, the clink of silverware against porcelain punctuating the stillness. It wasn't awkward, not exactly, but the air felt thick with unsaid things. He picked at his food, as though the mere act of eating took too much effort.

"I spoke to the guys from the firehouse," he said finally, breaking the silence in a voice that sounded too rough for his usual steady tone. "They... they're struggling too." His hands twisted around his fork like it was the only thing keeping him tethered to reality. "Some of them didn't make it out, and the ones who did... they're not the same."

I nodded, letting him continue at his own pace. My stomach churned at the thought of what he'd seen—what he'd carried home with him. It wasn't just the weight of the loss that held him, it was the knowledge that no matter how hard he tried, he couldn't change it.

"I didn't get everyone out. Some of them..." He paused, his voice thick with emotion, and the words hung there like an unfinished sentence. I knew he wasn't just talking about the fire. He was talking about something else, something deeper, but it wasn't the right moment to pry.

I watched him, studying the lines of his face, the way his eyes flitted between exhaustion and something darker, something more. I could feel him pulling away, could almost see the invisible wall he'd built between us. It was the kind of wall that I couldn't tear down, no matter how hard I tried. But I wasn't about to stop trying.

"You don't have to carry it alone," I said softly, my voice a tentative thread of hope. He didn't respond at first, and I wondered if he'd even heard me. When he finally met my gaze, his eyes were different—more vulnerable than I'd ever seen them. And it took everything I had not to reach across the table and try to hold him, to tell him that the weight of the world didn't have to be his to carry.

But he wasn't ready. Not yet.

"I should've done more," he said, almost to himself. His hand clenched into a fist, the muscles in his arm tight with frustration. "I should've... I don't know... done something differently."

I wanted to tell him it wasn't his fault. That there was nothing he could have done to change the outcome. But the words stuck in my throat. They felt hollow, like they wouldn't reach the depth of the pain he was carrying. So, I stayed silent instead, hoping my presence was enough to speak the comfort I didn't know how to articulate.

It wasn't until after we finished eating, the food cold and forgotten between us, that he finally spoke again. His voice was low, rough, like he had to force the words out.

"I tried to save them," he said, the pain in his voice raw, untamed. "I did everything I could, but sometimes... sometimes it's not enough."

The words broke something inside me. I wasn't sure if it was my heart or my resolve, but the crack was deep, jagged. And I knew—knew with a certainty that scared me—that this was the part of the story where the truth began to slip through the cracks. Not all of it. Not yet. But enough to make me realize how far he'd already gone to bury the rest.

I stood, moving away from the table before he could see how badly his words had hit me. I wasn't sure if I was protecting myself or him, but I didn't want him to see the way the reality of his pain was splintering mine.

"Tell me the rest," I said, my back to him. The words hung between us, but I knew—he knew—that I wouldn't back down. Not now. Not when I could feel the truth pressing against us, like it was just waiting to come to light.

He didn't answer, but I could feel his gaze on me, heavy with something I couldn't place. There was more, I was sure of it. More that he wasn't ready to share. More that I wasn't sure I was ready to hear.

And yet, I couldn't look away. I was already in too deep.

I didn't know how long I stood there, my fingers brushing against the cool rim of the sink, my back still turned to him. I should have said something—anything—but the words I wanted to speak felt like foreign objects lodged in my throat, sharp and unwelcome. It was easier to stay quiet, to let the silence stretch and fill the space between us like a living thing.

I could hear him shifting behind me, the scrape of his chair against the floor like a tremor. He wasn't leaving—not yet—but I could feel the distance growing. It wasn't the physical space between us that mattered; it was the emotional chasm, widening with each passing second, each word unsaid.

Finally, he spoke again, his voice rough like gravel, but this time there was something different. An edge to it that wasn't there before, something that made the hairs on the back of my neck stand up.

"You don't have to wait for me," he said, his words almost too soft to catch, like he didn't want me to hear them. "I've been… I've been keeping things from you. Things I shouldn't."

I turned then, my heart stumbling in my chest at the way he looked at me—eyes dark and full of guilt. There was a storm brewing behind those eyes, one that wasn't going to be easy to weather. But this time, I wasn't afraid. The truth felt close, like it was finally about to break through the surface, and I wasn't about to turn away now. Not after everything.

"Why didn't you tell me sooner?" I asked, the question slipping out before I could stop it. My voice was sharper than I'd intended, but I couldn't help it. I was tired of half-truths, of living in this limbo where everything was left unsaid.

His jaw clenched, the muscle there twitching with something like frustration. "Because you deserve better than this," he said, his voice low but firm. "You don't need this mess. You don't need me dragging you into it."

But I wasn't about to let him push me away. Not this time. I crossed the room in two long strides, the heat of his presence pulling me closer without me even realizing it. Standing in front of him, I felt the urge to reach out, to touch him, but I stopped myself. I needed him to face me. To face what he had buried inside.

"You don't get to decide what I need," I said, forcing the words to come out calm, even though my pulse was hammering in my throat. "I'm not some fragile thing you can protect from the world. I've been in the mess with you since the beginning."

His eyes softened, just for a moment, before the shutters came down again. "I'm not the man you think I am," he said, a sigh slipping from his lips. "And I don't deserve someone like you."

I shook my head, my chest tightening at the way he said it, like he was already writing his own obituary in my mind. "That's not for you to decide either," I replied, my words quieter now, but no less fierce. "I'm the one who gets to choose who's worth my time, and you don't get to push me away because you're scared of what might happen."

He looked away then, as if he couldn't bear to hold my gaze any longer. "I don't want you to get hurt," he muttered, his voice barely audible. "I don't want to drag you into something you can't handle."

And then, finally, there it was—the truth I'd been waiting for. The reason behind all the secrets, the reason behind all the distance. It wasn't just about protecting me from the fire, from the lives he couldn't save. It was about the deeper, darker things that weighed on him. The things that made him think he wasn't worthy of my love.

But that was the part I couldn't let him hide from. Because whether he liked it or not, I wasn't walking away from this. Not after everything we'd shared, not after everything he'd already shown me.

"You don't get to make that choice for me," I said again, my voice stronger now, more resolute. "I'm already in this, and I'm not backing out just because it gets hard. If you're going to pull away, you'll have to do it on your own."

He looked up at me then, his eyes searching mine, like he was trying to decide if I was serious or if this was some temporary surge of stubbornness. But it wasn't a surge. It was something deeper—something that had been growing in me for a while, a certainty that was taking root and spreading like wildfire.

"I can't promise I won't hurt you," he said finally, his voice thick with emotion.

I reached out then, my fingers brushing against his arm, my touch soft but deliberate. "You don't have to promise that," I said, my voice barely above a whisper. "But I need you to promise me something else. That you won't push me away just because you're afraid. That if we're in this together, we're really in it. No more half-truths, no more secrets."

For a long moment, he didn't answer. His eyes were focused on my hand, still resting on his arm, as though the weight of my words had caught him off guard. But then, slowly, he nodded. Once. Just once, but it was enough.

"I don't know what's going to happen," he said, his voice quiet but firm. "But I'm not going to push you away anymore. I'll tell you the truth—whatever that is. No more hiding."

And just like that, the air between us shifted. The wall that had been so carefully constructed crumbled, piece by piece, until all that was left was the raw, vulnerable truth of who we were. I wasn't sure what the future held, or how we would make it through the things he still hadn't told me, but for the first time in weeks, I felt a flicker of hope. It wasn't a big one, not yet, but it was there, growing in the silence between us.

And that was enough. For now.

I woke the next morning to the hum of the coffee maker and the distant sound of rain against the windows. I wasn't sure how long I had slept or what time it was, but the air felt different—cooler, lighter. The tension that had been so thick between us last night still hung in the air like the last vestiges of a storm, but it was quieter now, more subdued.

The kitchen was empty, and for a moment, I let myself believe that maybe things had settled, maybe the words we had shared were enough to patch the cracks between us. But deep down, I knew better. He was still carrying something heavy, something that I hadn't even begun to understand.

I set about making breakfast, the familiar rhythm of it grounding me. But every movement felt mechanical, like I was going through the motions to avoid thinking too hard about what had transpired. The eggs sizzled in the pan, and the smell of coffee filled the room, but neither of those things could quiet the restlessness inside me.

When he finally walked into the kitchen, I didn't look up. I pretended to focus on flipping the eggs, even though my hands were a little too shaky. I could feel him behind me, the weight of his presence pressing against the space between us, and for a moment, neither of us spoke.

"You didn't sleep much," I said, my voice steady despite the knot in my stomach. I wasn't asking a question; it was just an observation. His footsteps had been quieter than usual when he'd moved around the house, like he was trying to avoid waking me—or maybe he was just trying to avoid facing me.

He didn't answer right away. Instead, he leaned against the counter, his eyes fixed on the window. The rain had started to fall harder now, tapping against the glass like it had something to say.

"I couldn't stop thinking," he said finally, his voice a little rough. "About what I told you last night."

I turned then, meeting his gaze for the first time since the conversation had started. "And what exactly was it that you told me?"

His expression faltered for a split second, and I saw the tension in his shoulders before he exhaled a long breath, like he was trying to release something he had been holding in for far too long. "I told you the truth," he said, his voice quieter now. "At least, part of it."

I didn't know what to say to that. I wanted to push him further, wanted to demand more, but something in his eyes stopped me. Maybe it was the vulnerability, the way he stood there, looking at me like he was bracing for impact. Or maybe it was the exhaustion that lingered in the lines of his face, the way he looked worn down in a way that no amount of rest could fix.

Instead, I just nodded, not trusting myself to speak. The silence between us felt different now, heavy with the weight of things left unsaid. I knew he wasn't ready to tell me everything—not yet, not when the pieces of his story were still jagged and unfinished.

The minutes passed in a quiet, uncomfortable stillness, each of us lost in our own thoughts. I couldn't stop thinking about the things he had mentioned last night—the fire, the people he couldn't save. I wanted to understand, but I knew I wasn't going to get there by pushing him. Not yet.

Finally, he moved, crossing the kitchen to grab a mug from the cabinet. His fingers brushed against mine as he reached for the handle, and for a second, the world outside us faded away. The brief touch lingered, a spark in the air that neither of us acknowledged.

"Did you ever think about what you'd do if you couldn't save them?" he asked, his voice distant, almost to himself. It wasn't a question I expected, and I found myself pausing, unsure of how to answer.

I thought about it—really thought about it—and then shook my head slowly. "No," I said quietly. "I try not to."

He glanced at me then, his eyes searching mine as if trying to find the answer he needed. "I couldn't stop thinking about it," he said, his voice thick with something raw. "Every time I saw someone—every time I knew I couldn't get to them in time—I just... I couldn't stop wondering if I could have done something different. If I could have saved them."

I felt a pang in my chest, the words cutting through me like a knife. But there was something else in his eyes, something deeper, something that wasn't just about the fire. There was guilt there, yes, but also fear. Fear of something that went beyond the blaze, something that he hadn't spoken of yet.

"You've been carrying that around for how long?" I asked before I could stop myself. I knew the question was too blunt, but it had been eating at me since last night—the way he kept skirting around the real reason for his pain.

He stiffened, and for a moment, I thought he might shut down completely. But then he looked at me, his eyes dark with something I couldn't quite read.

"Since before the fire," he said softly, his voice barely above a whisper. "Since I left the last one."

My heart skipped a beat, and the air between us thickened. I could feel the weight of his words, the heaviness of a past that had been buried for too long. He wasn't just talking about the fire. He was talking about something else, something I hadn't even considered.

I opened my mouth to ask, to demand an explanation, but before I could speak, the sound of the doorbell cut through the air, sharp and unexpected.

We both froze.

"I wasn't expecting anyone," he muttered, his voice tight.

Neither of us moved for a moment, the tension thickening in the room. The doorbell rang again, this time more insistent. My heart thudded in my chest as I glanced at him, trying to gauge his reaction.

He didn't look at me. Instead, he stepped toward the door, his movements quick and purposeful, like he knew exactly what was coming. And when he opened it, I couldn't see who was on the other side. I couldn't see anything but the shadow of him stepping into a past that wasn't done with him.

And just like that, everything I thought I knew was turned upside down.

Chapter 19: The Spark Ignites

The apartment smells of cedarwood and the faintest trace of something sharp, like old books left in the sun too long. A contrast, I think, to the warmth that floods the room. Or maybe it's just him. I can feel his presence like a soft pressure, an anchor to the ground, and yet it's so light that I sometimes wonder if I'm imagining the whole thing.

His hand slides from my wrist to my palm, tracing the lines as though reading a book he's long studied, like he knows every twist and turn. I shiver, and the tiny gasp that escapes me is the only sound for a moment.

"I wasn't sure you'd come back," he murmurs, his voice low and soft, like the hum of a guitar string just before it snaps. The firelight catches his face in fleeting bursts of amber, making it hard to read. Not that I need to. I can feel the weight of his words. The hesitation, the longing that always lingers behind his gaze. There's a question there, an unspoken plea, but I don't know how to answer it.

I pull my hand away, folding it in my lap as if it could somehow stop the electricity between us.

"I wasn't sure I would either," I admit. The truth tastes like smoke on my tongue, burning but necessary. "But I'm here now."

His eyes flicker for the briefest second, like something fragile has just been touched. "You're here," he says, like it's the only thing that matters. But there's a question behind the words, as if he's searching for confirmation, looking for something deeper than what the surface offers.

I could say it. I could tell him I'm here because I'm tired of running, tired of pretending like I can stand still while the world around me collapses. But I don't. Instead, I lean forward, my hand finding his once more, a quiet plea for something neither of us is ready to voice aloud.

The silence that falls between us is thick with possibility, each breath heavier than the last. He leans in, slowly, as if testing the waters, and when his lips finally meet mine, it's not the firestorm I expect. It's soft, almost tentative, like two people feeling each other out in the dark. But then there's a shift, a click in the space between us that suddenly ignites everything. He pulls me closer, and this time, it's not gentle—it's desperate. It's everything I've been denying myself for far too long.

The kiss deepens, his hands slipping beneath my jacket, warm fingers skimming across the bare skin of my back. It's so much that I can't process it all at once, the heat, the need, the overwhelming certainty that this is more than what I bargained for. And I realize—just in that moment—that maybe I was never meant to just survive this. Maybe I was meant to feel it all. To be it.

His chest presses against mine, and I lose track of time, of everything. There's only the sound of his breath, the rush of blood in my ears, the sharp edges of reality falling away. And for the first time in a long time, I stop wondering if I'm worth this. If he is worth it. I stop asking questions that don't matter.

It's when the fire flickers low, its crackle turning to a soft pop, that the weight of the room changes. The night is starting to bleed into dawn, the first tendrils of morning slipping beneath the curtains. He pulls away first, his forehead resting against mine, both of us still gasping for air as though we've run a marathon we didn't sign up for.

"I wasn't sure," he whispers, his voice rough, "but now... I'm sure."

Sure of what, exactly? I want to ask. Sure that I'm here? Sure that this is real? I could tear myself apart with the questions, dissect this fragile moment, but I don't. Because in the stillness, in the aftermath, there's something else—something heavier than both of us combined.

I swallow the words on the tip of my tongue, the ones that threaten to ruin this. I don't need to ask, because I already know the answer. I'm here, and he's here. And maybe that's enough for now.

But as he runs a hand through his hair, looking away for the first time all night, I catch a glimpse of something—something I didn't want to see. There's a distance in his eyes now, a shadow that wasn't there before, and it pulls at me like a dark tide. It's the way his smile falters, the way his body shifts just slightly away from mine, as though he's bracing himself for something.

I feel it in the pit of my stomach, that flicker of doubt. That creeping suspicion that maybe this is all just a beautiful illusion, one I'm too afraid to shatter.

He catches my gaze again, and for a moment, it's just us, two people standing at the edge of something that could change everything—or nothing at all.

"I'm glad you came back," he says softly, like it's the simplest truth in the world. And maybe it is.

But as the sun starts to rise, painting the room in soft gold, I wonder if we've both already crossed a line. And if so, whether we'll ever be able to go back.

The room is alive in the stillness, the last embers of the fire casting warm, dancing shadows along the walls. There's something intimate about it, almost sacred—the way the fire's glow turns the room into a secret world where nothing outside can touch us. The hush of the night is thick with the things we haven't said but somehow both know all too well.

I can't stop thinking about how his lips lingered on mine, how his hands moved with such purpose, as though every second of it was meant to stitch something back together. But what, exactly? Was I broken? Was he?

I pull the blanket tighter around me, the fabric soft against my skin, and shift, feeling the weight of the bed beneath me, the familiar pull of exhaustion and contentment that wants to lull me into sleep. But my mind won't let go, twisting and turning, caught in a snarl of what's real and what's not.

"Why do you always overthink everything?" His voice, low and familiar, slices through the quiet like a knife dipped in honey. He's leaning against the doorframe, a half smile tugging at his lips. It's one of those smiles that makes my heart do a stupid little flip in my chest. "We were fine until your brain started going in circles."

I turn to look at him, my brow furrowing. "I don't think I was going in circles," I say, attempting to sound nonchalant, though I know I'm failing miserably. "I was just... thinking."

"Thinking." He says the word with such mock disbelief that I can't help but laugh, the tension lifting, if only slightly. "About what? How I'm probably hiding a second set of tattoos that say 'I'm an emotional trainwreck'?"

I smirk, shifting so I can sit up and lean back against the pillows. "It wouldn't surprise me. I mean, what else could be under that nice shirt?"

He laughs, a rich, warm sound that fills the room, and for a moment, it's like none of the complexities that swirl around us exist. Just this—him, the warmth, and the ease of something not trying too hard. I feel a sudden rush of affection, unexpected and fierce. But then it's gone, as quickly as it came, replaced by the ache of wanting more than what we've allowed ourselves. More than just these stolen moments.

"I'm glad you're here," he says quietly, and the way he looks at me, his eyes soft but steady, makes something tighten in my chest.

Like he's trying to say more than the words, but the moment is fragile.

I force myself to look away. I don't want to read too much into it. I've been wrong before, assumed things I shouldn't, and it always stung when the reality didn't match.

"I wasn't sure what to expect, but... here I am," I murmur, not quite meeting his gaze. "I just don't want it to be temporary." The words slip out before I can stop them.

There's a pause, just long enough to feel the weight of them hanging between us, before he steps closer. He's careful, like he doesn't want to cross some invisible line I haven't even drawn yet.

"Temporary," he repeats softly, like he's testing the word on his own lips. "You're asking if this is real."

I nod, the motion quick and sharp, as though I could force myself to believe it if I just asked the question enough.

"Everything feels real. For a moment, I thought... I thought maybe you didn't want this to be real," he says, his voice threading with something unspoken. "But you're still here, and I'm still here. So maybe it is."

I can feel his proximity now, the heat of his body radiating like a tangible thing. I want to pull back, to escape the weight of his words, but I can't. I can't pull away from this, not when it feels like everything I've ever wanted is on the other side of that uncertainty.

I laugh, a soft, breathless sound that feels like a mistake the moment it leaves my lips. "I'm a mess, aren't I? You must be regretting this by now."

His eyes soften, the sharpness in them fading. "No regrets here. Just... patience. I'm not going anywhere, but you need to figure out what you really want."

It's blunt. Too blunt. And I hate him for being right, for saying the thing I've been avoiding with every twist of my mind. The thing I already know. I don't know what I want, not entirely. But I know that he's here, and this—whatever this is—feels like it might be the one thing I can't walk away from.

I look up at him again, the vulnerability I've tried to shield slipping through. "What if I don't know how to figure it out?" I ask, and it feels like an admission I should be ashamed of, but somehow, in this moment, I'm not.

He sighs, a small, almost imperceptible exhale that seems to carry the weight of everything we've been dancing around. "Then I'll help you." The words come easy to him, but there's a sincerity there, one that makes my throat tight. He's offering me something I didn't know I needed, but now that it's here, I realize how desperately I want it.

I open my mouth to say something—anything—when his phone buzzes on the table beside us, sharp and intrusive. He glances at it, and the expression that crosses his face is one I don't quite understand. It's subtle, but it's enough to make me pause, my own breath hitching in my chest.

"Who's that?" I ask, trying to keep the casual edge in my voice, but there's an anxiety creeping in now, curling in my gut.

"Just work," he mutters, reaching for the phone, though the way his fingers linger on it tells me something's wrong. Something's shifting in the air, and I feel it—harder than any kiss or lingering touch.

"I'll be back in a minute," he says, his tone suddenly guarded, closed off in a way that I can't quite place.

But I don't need to know. Not yet. What I need now is to hold onto the feeling of him, before it all slips away. Before I can think too hard about what I'm about to lose.

The moment he leaves, the silence in the apartment seems to stretch out in all directions, an emptiness that presses against me like a physical force. I pull the blanket tighter, though it's hardly needed—my own heat is enough to fill the space, to make me feel like something is still alive between us, even if only in my mind. It's the kind of silence that brings with it the weight of questions, too many for me to unpack all at once. How much of this is real? How much of it is just the kind of thing we build in our heads when we're desperate to escape? I roll over, burying my face in the pillow he'd just been leaning against. It smells faintly like him—woodsy, with just the hint of cologne—and I allow myself to take a breath, a deep one, as if somehow that will make everything clearer.

It doesn't.

His absence is like a vacuum. The kind that feels like it should be permanent, like nothing can ever fill it, even though I know the minute he walks back through the door, everything will snap back into place.

I close my eyes and try not to wonder why I feel the overwhelming need for him to return. It's not that I don't have my own life, my own sense of independence. I've always valued that, held it close like a shield. But there's something about him that makes me want to put down my armor, if only for a moment, and let someone else hold the pieces.

The soft buzzing of his phone earlier still lingers in my mind. I can't shake the feeling that it wasn't just some random work call. There had been a hesitation, something about the way he picked it up, the look on his face when his thumb hovered over the screen before he answered it. I don't know why, but I feel like it was something more than just business. Maybe I'm overthinking it. Maybe I'm just looking for a reason to back away before things get too real.

But even as I think this, I know it's not true. I know I'm already too deep. The spark that lit between us, that sudden, overwhelming connection, wasn't just some fleeting thing. It's something that's stayed with me, the remnants of it still swirling in my chest like smoke.

A soft knock on the door snaps me out of my thoughts, and I freeze, my heart racing as I look toward the door. It's too soon for him to be back, right? It's been less than twenty minutes. My fingers curl around the edge of the blanket as I wait, trying to calm my breath.

"Are you going to answer that, or just sit there looking like you're waiting for a ghost?" his voice calls from the other side of the door.

I let out a sharp laugh, part disbelief, part relief. "You came back that fast?" I stand up and cross the room, pulling open the door to find him standing there, looking both familiar and strange in the quiet morning light. His hair's a little messier than before, his shirt slightly untucked. It's the same look he had when he'd first walked into this room—like he's been caught off guard by the reality of the situation.

"Something came up," he says, stepping inside and giving me an apologetic smile. "I know I said I'd only be a minute, but—"

"But work?" I cut him off, not able to resist the sharpness in my tone. It's not that I don't understand, but there's something about his distance that sets me on edge, like he's hiding something. I'm not used to being kept in the dark, especially not by him.

"Yeah," he says, a little too quickly, his eyes darting away from mine for the briefest moment. "I'm sorry. It wasn't what I expected."

I nod, though the movement feels robotic, as though I'm trying to convince myself this is just a small blip. "It's fine." I smile, but it feels forced, the edges of it a little too sharp.

"Look," he says, his voice lowering as he steps closer. "I really didn't mean to leave like that, but something came up that I couldn't ignore." His hand brushes against mine as he reaches for the couch, and I feel that familiar spark again. It's easy to let myself get lost in the heat of it, to let him pull me in, but this time, I can't ignore the twinge of doubt that's threading its way through the space between us.

"What happened?" I ask, trying to keep the curiosity from spilling into something darker. There's a weight to the question, one I'm not sure I want the answer to, but I ask it anyway.

He hesitates, his mouth opening and closing like he's trying to decide whether or not to speak the truth. And that, in itself, is enough to send a ripple of unease through me. "It's nothing. Really." But his eyes tell a different story, the flicker of something I can't quite identify dancing across his face.

The tension stretches thin between us, and for a moment, it feels like the air has thickened, wrapping itself around both of us in a way that I can't escape. "I know when you're lying," I say softly, my voice barely above a whisper.

He doesn't flinch, but his jaw tightens, the muscles in his neck flexing. "It's not what you think," he says, his voice clipped now. "I just need some time to figure this out."

"Figure what out?" I ask, the words tumbling out before I can stop them. I want to take them back, to swallow them and pretend like I'm not unraveling at the seams, but it's too late. His expression darkens, a flicker of something I can't quite name flickering in his eyes.

"I'll explain later," he says, but I don't think he believes it. Neither do I.

And just like that, the silence grows again—thick, oppressive, and full of things left unsaid. But before I can ask him to explain further, the doorbell rings, loud and insistent, and everything inside me freezes.

Chapter 20: Ashes of the Past

The light from the setting sun filtered through the dusty blinds, casting long, slanted shadows across the room. I leaned against the windowsill, my fingers lightly grazing the edge of the glass as I stared out at the world that had felt so still lately. The gentle hum of the city outside—distant, almost forgotten—sounded like a far-off memory. In here, everything was too quiet. Too contained. My thoughts spun in a circle, unwilling to settle.

I should have been relieved. I should have been savoring the feeling of being close to him, of finally feeling like I was part of his world. But there was a nagging sensation in the back of my mind, an itch that I couldn't reach, no matter how hard I tried. The closer we got, the more he revealed, the more I felt a distance. A distance I couldn't quite place, but that was there all the same.

He had always been an enigma. The way his eyes would narrow when he spoke of the fire, the way his hands would shake just slightly when he talked about anything from his past—it wasn't subtle. I'd caught it, but I hadn't pushed. I had let him guide the conversation, like a quiet river carrying me along, gently but relentlessly. But that tension in his voice when he mentioned the fire—it echoed in my head, in the silence of the room, now that he was gone again.

He'd left only hours ago, his presence still lingering in the air like the scent of his cologne that had clung to my sheets. I didn't want to admit it, but the feeling of abandonment was creeping in, filling the gaps where his warmth had been. And when I saw his name flash up on my phone—another emergency call—something inside me snapped. It wasn't the urgency of the message or even the brief, clipped tone of his voice. It was the quiet suspicion that had been building in the back of my mind for days.

I wasn't sure what I was hoping to find—if anything at all—but I needed to understand. I needed to know if I could trust him fully, if there was anything in the shadows of his past that could undo everything we had started to build. I couldn't afford to be blindsided. I couldn't allow myself to become tangled in something I couldn't escape from, not again.

I pulled open the drawer of my desk, the one filled with old receipts and forgotten trinkets, and reached for the phone book. It felt absurd in the age of the internet—old-fashioned, almost—but there was something comforting about it. The yellowing pages. The names and numbers that had been scrawled in ink, each one a thread to something unknown.

I flipped through the pages slowly, my eyes scanning for a name. And then there it was, hidden between two others like an afterthought. Lucas Green. The name was like a jolt to my chest. It was a name I'd heard before, a name I knew had been associated with the fire. He had been there, the one person who had been close to him during that time, and now, he was the one person who might know what had happened.

The weight of the decision settled on me. I could feel my pulse quickening, my fingers trembling as I dialed the number, even though I was fully aware of how absurd it was to reach out like this. I wasn't sure what I was expecting—some sort of revelation, maybe, or at least an explanation of the things I hadn't been able to understand.

The phone rang three times before the voice on the other end spoke. It wasn't the warm tone I'd imagined in my mind, but something guarded, like someone used to keeping their distance. "Hello?"

I swallowed, my heart racing. "Is this Lucas Green?"

There was a long pause before he answered. "Who's asking?"

I took a breath, trying to steady my nerves. "I... I'm looking for information. About the fire. About someone who might've been involved."

His voice dropped a notch, becoming more cautious. "I don't know what you're talking about."

I took another deep breath, refusing to back down now. "I think you do. You were there. You knew him—him."

I heard the rustle of paper, followed by a muffled sigh. "I'm not sure what you want from me. That was years ago."

I pressed my lips together, frustration bubbling up. "I want to understand him. I need to know the truth."

Silence stretched between us for a long moment. Then, finally, he spoke again, his voice softer, more resigned. "You don't want to go digging into that. It's not something you need to know."

"I do. Please. He's not the man he was before—whatever happened, I can see it in his eyes. I need to understand why he's so haunted."

Another pause. I could hear him breathing, the sound filling the silence between us. "I'm not going to tell you everything," he said, finally. "But if you really want to know, you should meet me. In person. I'll tell you what you need to hear, but only then."

The words hit me like a punch. I didn't know what I was expecting, but this wasn't it. "Where?" I asked, my voice tight.

There was a soft chuckle on the other end, dark and low. "You'll know when you get here. Just make sure you're ready for it."

The city's pulse thrummed in my ears as I made my way through the winding streets, the humid air clinging to my skin like a heavy cloak. My stomach churned with something that wasn't quite dread, but wasn't far from it either. I didn't know what to expect from Lucas, and yet I couldn't shake the feeling that this was something I had to do. I could already hear his voice, dark and knowing, replaying in my head. The way he'd warned me not to dig into the past. His reluctance had only fueled my determination.

The address he had given me was tucked away in a part of town I hadn't even realized existed. It wasn't the kind of place you stumbled across unless you were looking for it—or running away from something. Old brick buildings lined the narrow streets, their windows shrouded in thick curtains that blocked out the dying light of the evening. The air smelled of oil, rust, and something I couldn't quite place—something forgotten, like the town had given up on itself long ago.

When I arrived at the address, I took a moment to steady myself. The building loomed above me, its rusted iron door slightly ajar, as if it had been waiting for someone to push through it. My hand hesitated just above the handle, my mind racing through every possible scenario. It was stupid. It was reckless. But then again, what wasn't reckless about everything that had led me here?

I stepped inside, and the door creaked shut behind me, sealing me into the dim, musty room. There were no windows, just walls lined with shelves of dusty old books, a few chairs scattered around like they'd been left in a hurry. The faint sound of a clock ticking somewhere deep within the building echoed in the silence, adding to the strange sense of urgency in the air.

I was about to call out when I heard footsteps, slow and deliberate, approaching from the back of the room. My heart skipped a beat, and I turned, expecting to see someone who might offer answers—or at least some semblance of them.

Instead, Lucas Green stepped into the light, his face a mask of unreadable emotion. His expression was guarded, eyes flicking over me with an intensity that made the hairs on the back of my neck stand up. He was taller than I remembered, his broad shoulders filling the doorway as if he were holding the weight of the entire room within him. He didn't smile, didn't offer any pleasantries.

His gaze lingered on me for a moment too long before he gestured toward the chair nearest him.

"Sit," he said, his voice a low rumble. It wasn't an invitation; it was an order.

I obeyed, easing myself into the chair with far more poise than I felt. There was something about the way he looked at me that made me feel like an intruder. A trespasser in a world that wasn't mine, trying to dig my fingers into the edges of a secret he didn't want me to unravel.

Lucas moved across the room with that same deliberate pace, as if he had all the time in the world. I watched him carefully, my pulse quickening. When he finally spoke again, his voice was softer, almost detached. "You want to know about the fire. About what happened."

I nodded, trying to steady the fluttering in my chest. "I do."

He took a deep breath, as if considering something—or perhaps just weighing whether it was worth the effort. "People don't talk about it. Not because they don't want to. But because the memories... they don't fade. They never do."

I swallowed. "You were there, weren't you? You knew him."

Lucas looked away, his jaw tightening in a way that suggested the words were lodged somewhere deep in his throat, unwilling to come out. When he finally spoke again, his voice was barely above a whisper, and it felt like the room had shrunk in on itself. "I knew him. He was... different then."

The finality of the sentence hung in the air like a heavy fog, but I wasn't satisfied. I wasn't ready to let him pull back into the shadows, where everything seemed more dangerous. "What happened?" I asked, unable to keep the urgency from creeping into my voice.

Lucas exhaled sharply, rubbing his hand over his face. "It's not a story you want to hear. People like you don't need to know things like this."

I leaned forward, feeling the weight of my own resolve pulling me down. "Maybe I do."

His eyes flickered to mine, and for a split second, there was something in them that looked like fear—raw, naked fear. But it was gone before I could pinpoint it, replaced by the cool, unflinching gaze of someone who had learned to hide their emotions well.

He sighed again, this time with a sharp edge to it. "You should've stayed away. You should've just walked out, gone home, and never looked back. But you didn't, and now you're going to regret it."

I raised my chin, a surge of defiance rising up from within. "I don't believe that."

Lucas smirked, though there was no humor in it. "I don't give a damn what you believe. You came here because you thought you could handle it. You think you're prepared for what you're going to hear?"

I hesitated, feeling a knot tighten in my stomach. But I forced myself to meet his gaze. "Yes."

He let out a short laugh, bitter and hollow. "You're more naïve than I thought. That fire... it wasn't just an accident. And he—" He paused, his eyes narrowing, as though even saying the words might cause something inside him to break. "He wasn't the man you think he is."

The air in the room seemed to thicken, a tension so thick that it became almost impossible to breathe. "What do you mean?" I asked, though I could feel the fear creeping into my own voice now. "What aren't you telling me?"

But Lucas only shook his head, his eyes distant, as if the answers were already too far gone for him to retrieve. He stepped back into the shadows, his silhouette a mere outline in the darkness. "Some things are better left buried, trust me."

And just like that, I was left in the silence, the weight of his words hanging between us like a storm ready to break.

The silence of the room wrapped around me like a thick blanket, suffocating, almost too heavy to bear. I sat there in the dim glow of the single hanging light, watching Lucas disappear further into the shadows as though he had been a figment of my imagination all along. Every inch of him had exhaled something—fear, regret, shame—and I could feel it seeping into the walls, into the air I breathed. For a moment, I thought I might suffocate in it.

I waited for him to speak again, but his back was turned, and he didn't seem inclined to offer any more cryptic warnings. I could feel my pulse hammering in my temples, a drumbeat urging me to do something, anything, but sit still. So, I stood, my hands trembling slightly as I pushed myself to my feet. He hadn't told me what I needed to hear, hadn't given me the clarity I was so desperate for. And yet, something about the way he had spoken, that hesitation in his voice, still clawed at me.

I stepped forward, trying to ignore the tightness in my chest, the unease swirling at the pit of my stomach. "What happened?" I asked again, my voice softer now, more insistent, though I hated how raw it sounded. "Lucas, I'm not leaving until you tell me."

His shoulders stiffened at the sound of my voice. Without turning to face me, he spoke through clenched teeth. "You should've gone home."

I shook my head. "I'm not going anywhere until I understand."

For the first time, Lucas turned to look at me. There was something in his gaze—sharp, dark, painful—that made my heart stumble in my chest. He exhaled slowly, as though considering whether he should even say more. His eyes darted to the door, to the window, and then back to me, as if he were calculating whether he could walk away from this moment.

Finally, he seemed to make up his mind. "You want the truth?" he asked, his voice low and jagged, as though the words themselves scraped against his throat. I nodded, refusing to show any sign of hesitation. He gave a bitter laugh. "Truth doesn't come without a price. You want to understand who he really was, you want to know what happened? You'll have to accept the cost of it."

I couldn't breathe. "I can handle it."

His gaze sharpened, a flicker of doubt passing through his eyes. "Can you? You think you can handle everything that comes with it? The darkness? The loss?" He took a step toward me, his words now quieter, more dangerous. "Because once you see the truth, there's no going back."

A shiver crawled down my spine, but I stood my ground. "I'm not afraid of the truth."

For a long moment, he just stared at me, as if waiting for me to change my mind. But then, with a resigned sigh, Lucas reached for something hidden in the folds of his jacket. He pulled out an old photograph, yellowed with age, and handed it to me without a word. It was a faded image of two men, one of them younger than I had ever seen him, standing side by side in front of a charred building. The man beside him was smiling, his arm slung casually over my man's shoulder. But there was something in their eyes—something unspoken—that made my stomach tighten.

I turned the photo over, expecting to find a name, a date. Instead, there was only a single word scratched in uneven handwriting. Together.

I glanced back up at Lucas, confusion pulling at my insides. "What is this? Why are you showing me this?"

He didn't answer immediately, his eyes clouded with a depth of regret that sent a chill down my spine. Then, his voice broke the stillness, thick with an emotion I couldn't quite place. "That man in the photo," he said slowly, "he's not who you think he is."

I could feel my heart constrict, my body tensing as though bracing for a storm. "Who is he, then?"

Lucas stepped closer, the weight of his presence heavy in the air. His gaze darkened, and he seemed to hesitate before he spoke again, his voice barely above a whisper. "He was a fireman. A hero, they said. But there's more to the story than that. Much more." His words were measured, as though he had to carefully choose each one. "The fire—it wasn't an accident."

My breath caught in my throat. "What do you mean? Are you saying—"

"The fire was intentional. It was set. By someone we knew." His voice grew tight, like a noose wrapping around his throat. "By someone who knew exactly what they were doing."

I could feel the weight of his words pressing down on me, suffocating, until my thoughts were scattered and I couldn't make sense of them. My mind raced with questions. Who would do such a thing? Why? What had they been trying to achieve?

But before I could ask anything else, Lucas moved away from me, his hands shoved deep into his pockets, his back to me once more. "You really want to understand everything?" he asked, his tone now flat, emotionless. "Then go find out. Go ask the people who were there. But be prepared for what you might uncover."

I stood frozen, unable to move, the photograph burning a hole in my hand. His words hung in the air, unanswered, unresolved, like a riddle that refused to be solved. And just when I thought I might shatter from the weight of it all, the door behind me creaked open, and a sharp, unfamiliar voice cut through the tension.

"You shouldn't have come here."

I spun around, heart leaping into my throat. The man who stood in the doorway was someone I didn't recognize—but there was something unmistakable about the glint in his eyes. Something dangerous. Something familiar.

I tried to speak, but the words stuck in my throat. Lucas didn't turn, didn't even acknowledge the newcomer.

But the stranger wasn't finished. "I warned you." He stepped into the room, and with that single movement, everything shifted.

Chapter 21: Flickering Doubts

I wish I could say the silence between us settled like a comfortable blanket, the kind that wraps around you on a chilly evening, but it didn't. The air was thick, each second heavier than the last, suffocating in its own unspoken tension. I stood there, staring at him, feeling the remnants of the world I had once known slipping like sand through my fingers. The man I thought I knew, the man I had trusted with everything, was no longer that person.

I had come into this conversation full of fire, a blaze of righteous indignation burning bright in my chest. But now, as he stood there in front of me, his posture rigid and his eyes darker than I remembered, I felt small—like a child caught with their hand in the cookie jar, though I wasn't sure who the thief was anymore.

"I found the letters," I said, my voice sounding more fragile than I wanted it to. "The ones from years ago. They don't make sense. Why didn't you tell me about them?"

He didn't flinch. Didn't even move. There was a tightening of his jaw, but that was the only indication that anything was stirring within him. And yet, his gaze, once warm and inviting, now seemed like a wall—unreachable, impenetrable.

"You shouldn't have looked," he said, his voice low. Calm. Too calm. It was like he was trying to soothe a storm that had already hit, but there was no storm. Not from me, anyway. He was the one who was storming, quietly, quietly enough to make my heart race.

I could feel his discomfort, not just in the way he spoke, but in the way he avoided my eyes, as if they might burn him with their questions. He took a step back, the faint sound of his shoes against the wooden floor somehow louder than any words I had said. I swallowed hard, but my throat felt dry, like the words I wanted to say had been swept away by a current I couldn't fight.

"Why would you hide this from me?" I asked, my voice barely above a whisper.

"I didn't hide anything." His words were clipped, like he was trying to maintain control, but it wasn't working. I could hear the tremor in his tone, a subtle crack in the veneer he was so desperately trying to uphold.

"Then what was it?" I challenged, my pulse quickening, urging me to push. "You think I won't understand? You think it's too much for me?"

His silence stretched longer than I was prepared for. The minutes felt like hours as I stood there, my breath caught in the tight knot of uncertainty that had formed in my chest. The only sound was the faint hum of the refrigerator in the kitchen and the irregular thump of my heart.

"I told you once," he said finally, his voice tight, "some things are better left buried."

"And I told you," I countered, stepping closer, despite the warning bell ringing in my head, "the truth has a way of coming to light. I can't ignore it now. Not after everything."

He closed his eyes for a long moment, and I thought I saw something—something more than anger flicker in the depth of them. Regret? Fear? It was gone too quickly for me to pinpoint, but it was there. It was enough to send a chill crawling up my spine.

"You don't understand," he muttered, shaking his head. "You think you do, but you don't. You don't know what it's like to live with the weight of something like that."

The confession hung in the air like a death sentence. I felt it settle over me, heavy and suffocating, and I had to fight the urge to step back. Instead, I stood my ground.

"I don't need to understand. I just need you to tell me the truth."

He met my gaze then, and the look he gave me was as cold as ice. It was like a door had slammed shut between us, the finality of it sending a shudder through my limbs. He turned away, his back to me now, as if he couldn't bear to face me anymore.

"You're better off not knowing," he said, his words barely audible, as though speaking them out loud might make them too real. "Digging into the past will only bring pain. You'll wish you hadn't."

The warning felt like a dare, like he was challenging me to back off, to drop it all and pretend I hadn't seen anything, heard anything. But I couldn't do that. Not when everything inside me was screaming to push further, to expose whatever it was he was hiding. The doubt gnawed at me, growing larger with every second. What had he done? What was he hiding from me? I wasn't sure I wanted to know anymore, but I couldn't stop now. I had crossed a line, and the only way forward was to walk through whatever truth waited on the other side, no matter how painful it might be.

But as I stood there, in that too-quiet room, I realized something. The hardest part wasn't going to be uncovering the truth. It was going to be facing what I might find once I did.

I'd always thought I could read him like an open book. Every smile, every flicker of his eyes, every tone in his voice—each detail had seemed like a small piece of a puzzle I could solve. But now, standing here in the silence that had swallowed us whole, I felt as if the book had turned into a riddle I couldn't even begin to decipher. The man who had held me close and whispered sweet promises in my ear was suddenly someone I didn't recognize. His warmth was gone, replaced by a coldness that seeped into the room, chilling everything it touched.

"Are you going to keep pretending this doesn't matter?" I asked, though the words felt too fragile, like they might break if I said them too loudly.

He didn't answer immediately. Instead, he stood there with his back to me, staring out the window as if he could find solace in the view. The moonlight fell across his silhouette, casting long shadows that seemed to stretch across the floor, just like the distance that was now growing between us.

"I never wanted this to come between us," he said finally, his voice so low it could have been the murmur of the wind outside. "But some things... some things are better left buried."

I could almost hear the plea in his words, though it was buried deep beneath a layer of something harder—something I couldn't quite touch. The kind of thing that made the hairs on the back of my neck stand up. I could feel it, too, that undeniable sense that there was more he wasn't saying, something he was keeping locked up tight, and I was too close to the key now to walk away without finding it.

I stepped forward, just a little. Enough to close the gap but not enough to touch him. Not yet. "You don't get to decide what I can or can't handle. Not anymore."

That was it, wasn't it? The moment the line had been crossed. The moment he realized I wasn't going to let it go.

He turned around then, his face shadowed in the dim light, but there was something in his eyes that made my stomach twist. Guilt? Fear? I couldn't tell. Maybe it was both.

"You think you can handle the truth?" he asked, his voice a mix of bitterness and something else—something darker.

The question hit me like a punch to the gut. Could I? Could anyone? But I wasn't going to back down now. Not when I could feel the pressure of all the questions pressing in on me like a vice.

"Try me," I said, trying to keep my voice steady. "I'm not afraid of the truth."

He let out a sharp laugh, but it wasn't the kind that carried any humor. It was jagged, almost mocking.

"You should be."

The words hung between us, and for a moment, all I could do was stare at him. What did he mean by that? Was it a warning, or was he daring me to dig deeper? Whatever it was, the weight of it landed heavily on my chest, and for the first time since all this started, I wondered if I'd made a mistake—if I was better off never uncovering whatever lie he was hiding.

But I couldn't go back. Not now. The truth was like a magnet, pulling me toward it with a force I couldn't resist.

"You've always been the one who told me to face things head-on," I said, trying to get some of the confidence back that was slipping through my fingers. "So, what's different now? What's so dangerous about facing the truth?"

His gaze hardened, the warmth from before now completely extinguished.

"I said some things are better left alone. For your own good."

His words were so final, like a door slamming shut, but I could see the tension in his jaw, the way his hands clenched at his sides. There was something in him—something deep—fighting against this conversation, fighting against me.

I had seen it before, the way he could shut down when he didn't want to deal with something. But I wasn't the same person who had fallen for him all those months ago. I wasn't the naive, trusting soul that believed he had all the answers. I wasn't going to let him keep me in the dark anymore.

"Tell me," I demanded, stepping even closer, until the space between us felt impossibly small. "Tell me what you're so afraid of."

For a moment, he didn't speak. His eyes drifted to the floor, then to the window, then back to me. He was trapped in the web of his own making, and for the first time in our entire relationship, I wasn't sure which of us would be left standing when it all unraveled.

The silence stretched out, long and suffocating. I could see his mind working, could almost hear the arguments playing out behind his closed eyes. But in the end, it was his reluctance that told me more than any words ever could.

"I don't want to lose you," he said, the admission so quiet it was almost lost in the space between us.

That was the moment I realized—he wasn't afraid of the truth. He was afraid of me.

The realization was a knife to the heart. It twisted deep, and for a second, I didn't know how to breathe.

"You won't," I whispered, though even I didn't know if I meant it. How could I promise that? How could I promise that when everything inside me screamed that I couldn't unlearn what I was about to find out?

"You might wish you had," he murmured, his voice so soft it almost didn't reach my ears.

And just like that, I understood. Whatever he was hiding—whatever truth he was so desperate to protect—wasn't something I could walk away from. Not without it breaking me.

I could feel the floor shift beneath me, like I was standing on the edge of something dangerous—something that could topple me over if I wasn't careful. The words hung in the air, thick with unsaid things, and the silence between us stretched taut like the string of a bow, ready to snap at any moment. The room felt colder somehow, though I couldn't remember if I had ever felt warmth here.

I took a step back, trying to regain some semblance of composure. It wasn't working. I could still feel his eyes on me, their heaviness pressing against my chest, and the feeling of being too close to a truth that would tear everything apart made my hands shake. It was his fear that unnerved me the most. He had always been so confident—so sure of everything. But now, in the dark corners of his gaze, I saw something I hadn't expected: vulnerability. And for a second, I almost felt pity. But pity wouldn't save me. Pity wouldn't uncover whatever secret had been locked behind those carefully constructed walls.

I didn't want to pity him. I didn't want to feel sorry for him or give in to the urge to back away. I had come too far, and whatever this was—this thing that loomed between us like an impossible riddle—had to be solved.

"What is it, then?" I asked, my voice trembling slightly, though I tried to make it firm. "What's so bad that you'd rather keep it from me? Why not just tell me?"

His eyes flickered, just for a moment, before he closed them like he was shutting me out completely. "You don't need to know."

"I don't need to know?" I repeated, incredulous. "You think I'm going to just walk away, pretend I didn't see the letters? You think I can forget what I've learned? I'm not a child, you know."

"I never said you were," he muttered, his voice rough. "But this... this isn't something you can handle."

I was shaking now, my hands clenched at my sides as the weight of his words pressed down on me. "Then why did you bring me into this in the first place?" I demanded, the frustration I'd been holding back finally breaking free. "If I'm not supposed to know, then why did you drag me into your mess?"

His gaze shot up, his face hardening. "I didn't ask for you to get involved, but you did. And now it's too late. The past doesn't let go that easily."

The way he said it made the hairs on the back of my neck rise. The past. The words hung in the air like a warning, an echo of something I couldn't quite reach, no matter how hard I tried.

"You're making it sound like something... terrible happened," I said, slowly, almost cautiously. "Something that's not just a mistake, but something I can't forgive."

He flinched at that, just a tiny shift in his expression, but it was enough. And in that instant, I understood—this wasn't just a misunderstanding. This was something dark, something that would destroy everything I thought I knew about him if I pushed too far.

But I couldn't stop. Not now. Not when I was standing on the brink of unraveling a secret that could change everything.

"You've been hiding it from me, haven't you?" I said, my voice a little steadier now, though it trembled with the weight of everything I had just begun to piece together. "You've been hiding something so big, so terrible, that you think I can't handle it."

His lips tightened into a thin line, his face shadowed. "You don't want to know, trust me."

"Try me," I shot back, my tone sharper now, biting with the frustration I could no longer keep inside. "What is it? What are you so afraid of?"

His eyes flashed, something dangerous flickering behind them. "I said, you don't want to know."

A silence settled between us, thick with tension. I waited for him to speak, to say something—anything—to make sense of the chaos spinning in my head. But he just stood there, his eyes fixed on the floor, unwilling to meet my gaze. The seconds ticked by like hours, and with every passing moment, the feeling of the unknown pressed harder against my chest. I couldn't breathe, couldn't think, couldn't do anything except wait for him to finally break.

And then it happened.

"Fine," he said, his voice barely above a whisper. "You want to know? Fine. But don't say I didn't warn you."

I blinked, taken aback. This wasn't what I had expected. I had expected more resistance, more of the stone wall he had been hiding behind. But now—now he was giving in.

But was he giving in, or was he preparing to bury me with the truth?

He took a deep breath, his hands still clenched into fists at his sides. "I didn't just leave. I didn't just disappear. I did something—something I can't take back." His voice broke on the last word, and I saw it—the flash of regret, of guilt—before he buried it again. "I hurt people, people who trusted me. People I loved."

I wanted to say something, wanted to reach for him, but I was paralyzed. His words, his confession, cut deeper than anything I had imagined. What had he done? What had he been hiding so carefully for all this time?

"I should never have let you get this close," he muttered, almost to himself. "But now it's too late. And I don't think you'll forgive me. Not after this."

I opened my mouth to respond, but before I could speak, there was a sharp knock on the door. And just like that, the world shifted again—pulling me further into the unknown.

Chapter 22: Stoking the Flames

The doorbell rings, sharp and insistent. I barely look up from my laptop, the low hum of my thoughts wrapped tightly around the work I've been burying myself in for the last few days. The numbers, the reports, the endless emails—anything to distract me from the ache in my chest, the one that still carries his touch like a brand. I swear, it's like his scent is stitched into the very fabric of my clothes, trailing behind me, a constant reminder of what I'm trying so hard to forget.

The doorbell rings again, and this time, the urgency in the sound cuts through my fog. My fingers hover over the keyboard as I freeze, a knot tightening in my stomach.

"Don't," I mutter under my breath, even as I push myself up from the desk. My bare feet meet the cold floor with a soft slap, the chill of it grounding me, if only for a moment. There's only one person who would ring my doorbell at this hour. Of course, it had to be him.

When I open the door, he's standing there, framed by the soft glow of the hallway light, his jaw set, eyes like ice. The sharp angles of his face are almost too much to bear—like a sculpture carved from granite, but with the edges too jagged to touch. The fire in his gaze sends a shock of warmth through my chest. That's the problem with him, isn't it? Everything about him makes me want to burn.

"What do you want?" I ask, but my voice is quieter than I'd intended, betraying the twist of something else that flutters beneath my ribs. Anger, maybe. Or something like it.

He steps forward, and I instinctively back up, but the hallway is too narrow. "I need to talk to you."

I narrow my eyes, every inch of me wary. "We've done enough talking, I think."

He exhales sharply, running a hand through his messy hair like he doesn't know whether to pull it all out or shove me out of his way. "You're being reckless."

I laugh, a dry, humorless sound. "I'm being reckless? You're the one who keeps showing up."

His eyes flash. "You're in danger, and you don't even see it."

I tilt my chin, the defiance surging up through me like a tidal wave. "I can handle myself, thank you."

"Really?" He takes a step closer, the scent of him—something dark and dangerous—washes over me, and for a moment, I can't breathe. "You think you can just keep doing what you're doing without consequence? Playing with fire like it's nothing?"

His words land heavy in the air between us. I bite back the flood of emotion I feel rushing to the surface. "Maybe I like fire."

His gaze hardens, every inch of him suddenly a storm. "This isn't some game. You don't get to play at being fearless when it's not just your life on the line."

I cross my arms, trying to mask the tremor in my chest. "You don't get to lecture me. You're not my—"

"Not your what?" He cuts me off, his voice low and dangerous, like he's been holding something back for far too long. "What exactly do you think I am? Some kind of savior? Or maybe the one thing you can't have?"

There's a crack in his voice, something raw, and I swear I almost feel sorry for him. But I shove it down, bury it under the layers of resentment I've been nurturing. Because he's right about one thing. I can't have him. And maybe that's what hurts the most.

"I'm not scared of you," I say, even as my hands tremble at my sides, betraying the lie I'm trying to sell.

His lips curl, a flicker of something dark passing across his face. "You should be."

He's close now, too close. I can feel the heat from his body, the pressure of his presence like a force I can't fight against. It's intoxicating. But I can't—won't—let him win this time.

"Leave," I say, my voice barely a whisper, but it carries the weight of everything I'm trying to hold on to. "Before this goes any further."

For a moment, he doesn't move. The space between us crackles with unspoken tension, and I swear the air is thick enough to cut. Then, finally, he steps back. His eyes don't leave mine as he does, and for a fleeting second, I think he might say something—anything—but then he's gone.

The door clicks shut behind him with finality, and I sink to the floor, the cold tiles pressing against the warmth of my skin. My chest is tight, my breath coming in short bursts, and for the first time in days, I let myself feel it—the frustration, the rage, the desperate longing I can't seem to shake.

I throw myself back into the work, because if I don't, I'll drown. But even as I stare at the screen, the flickering cursor mocking me, my thoughts drift back to him. To the fight. To the way his eyes blazed with something I couldn't name.

This is dangerous, I remind myself. He's dangerous.

But the truth is, I'm not sure anymore. I'm not sure of anything when it comes to him.

The hours stretch long and uneven, like the sluggish drip of water from a leaky faucet. I've poured myself into the task at hand, but my concentration keeps snapping away from the screen. It's a maddening dance—type a few lines, glance at the clock, stare at the wall. My thoughts dart around the room like restless insects, unwilling to settle. I pull at the collar of my shirt, as though I could physically shake off the memory of his hands, of the hard, determined look in his eyes. It's all tangled up in me, the way he made me feel like I was on the edge of something terrifying and exhilarating. It's like trying to chase a storm in the middle of a drought.

I was doing fine, wasn't I? I told myself I was moving on, that I could handle things. It was supposed to be simple—just keep my head down, stay busy, pretend I wasn't haunted by the ghost of his voice in my head. I'd thrown myself into work because that was safe, wasn't it? Numbers don't touch you the way people do. They don't breathe down your neck or make you feel like you're in the eye of a storm that might rip you apart.

But there's no ignoring the feeling of his eyes, hot and steady, on the back of my neck. I'm not sure if it's anger or something else, but I'd be lying if I said I wasn't addicted to it. He had that way of pulling you in, and once you were in, there was no getting out. I could see it, like it was already written in the lines of his clenched fists and the set of his jaw. He wanted to break me. And maybe that was the problem. I didn't know how to resist it.

I stand up abruptly, the chair scraping back on the floor. My movements are sharp, calculated. I should keep working. I should stop thinking about him. But my feet carry me to the window, and I look out into the night. The street below is empty, the lamplights casting long shadows on the pavement, stretching and twisting like they have secrets to keep.

A knock at the door. It's soft but insistent, like it knows exactly what it's doing to me. I freeze, the blood in my veins turning to ice. No. Not this. Not again.

But I know exactly who it is before I even open the door. I could feel him out there, waiting, the electricity in the air thick with something neither of us wants to acknowledge.

When I open it, he doesn't say a word. His presence fills the doorway, strong and overwhelming. He's not here for pleasantries. I don't think he ever was.

"I told you to stay away," I say, my voice sharper than I intended. I step back, giving him just enough room to slide through the threshold. The tension is immediate, palpable—coiled and ready to snap.

"I couldn't stay away," he replies, his tone low and urgent. "Not when you're making mistakes."

I cross my arms, keeping my distance, but he's too close, his presence too overwhelming. "I'm not the one making mistakes here."

He laughs, but it's not a laugh—it's the sound of someone who's already lost. "You think you can keep doing this, keep pushing everyone away, and nothing will happen? You're reckless. You don't even know what you're courting."

I raise an eyebrow, willing my pulse to slow. "And what exactly am I courting?"

"The kind of trouble that doesn't just go away." His eyes are dark, intense. "You think you're untouchable, but everyone has their limits. And you're about to find yours."

My pulse spikes at the implication, but I push it down, unwilling to let him see how much his words are getting under my skin. "I can handle it," I say, and even I can't believe the confidence in my voice.

"No, you can't," he insists, his voice a low growl. "I've seen people like you. You think you're invincible until it all falls apart, and then you're left with nothing but the wreckage of your own making."

I step back, my heart thudding in my chest. "I don't need your help, and I don't need your judgment. So, if you came here to lecture me, you can leave."

For a moment, he doesn't move. The air is heavy between us, thick with the electricity of something unsaid, something raw. Then, just when I think he's about to back down, he steps forward, his gaze locked onto mine like it's the only thing in the world. His breath comes shallow and quick, but it's not anger—it's something else entirely.

"You don't get it," he mutters, barely above a whisper. "You're playing with fire, and it's not going to end the way you think it will."

I stand my ground, my hands trembling at my sides. "Maybe I like fire."

He shakes his head slowly, as if he's watching something he can't control, something that's already slipping out of his grasp. "You think you're strong because you don't care. But there's a difference between strength and stubbornness. And one of them is going to break you."

His words land like a slap, sharp and final. I can feel the weight of them pressing down on me, but I refuse to let it show.

"You don't know anything about me," I snap, even as a piece of me wonders if he does.

He opens his mouth to respond, but then he stops, his lips pressing together in a thin line. His frustration is so obvious, it's almost painful to watch. He runs a hand through his hair, exhaling sharply.

"I'm not leaving," he says, his voice steady now, like he's made up his mind.

I open my mouth to argue, but I can't. The words stick in my throat, heavy and unnecessary. For the first time since this whole mess began, I'm not sure if I want him to leave.

The silence in the room stretches, thick and uncomfortable, as he stands there, the weight of his presence pressing against me like a storm waiting to break. I've never seen him this still, his usual restlessness replaced by something darker. It's in the way his shoulders are tense, his jaw clenched tight as if holding back something dangerous. It's unnerving how easy it is to read him now, as if all the walls he's built between us have come crashing down, leaving me exposed to everything he's been hiding.

"I'm not asking you to leave," I finally say, my voice steadier than I feel. "I'm just asking you to stop pretending like you can save me."

He laughs, but it's bitter, lacking the usual warmth that I've come to associate with him. "Save you? I don't think you need saving. I think you need to stop pretending you're invincible."

"I never said I was invincible," I shoot back, crossing my arms over my chest. "I'm just trying to live my life without you swooping in every time I do something you don't approve of."

"I'm not swooping in," he growls, taking a step closer, closing the gap between us until I can feel the heat from his body radiating into mine. "I'm trying to keep you from making a mistake you can't undo."

"You're the one who's making a mistake," I snap, feeling the fire rise in my chest. "You think I don't know the risks? You think I don't know what I'm getting into? This isn't some fairy tale, and you're not my knight in shining armor."

The words hit harder than I expected. There's a brief flicker of something in his eyes—hurt, maybe, or recognition—and then it's gone, masked by his usual calm demeanor. But I see it, and for a moment, I regret the sharpness of my tone.

"I never said I was," he replies quietly, his voice softer now, almost like he's trying to reach me, trying to break through the armor I've wrapped around myself. "But you're playing with fire, and sooner or later, it's going to burn you. And I won't just stand by and watch it happen."

I swallow hard, the weight of his words sinking into me, twisting into the pit of my stomach. I want to argue, to tell him that I can handle it, that I've been handling it just fine without him. But the truth is, I don't know. I don't know if I'm strong enough to resist whatever pull he still has on me, whatever fire we've started that I can't seem to put out.

"I'm not asking you to save me," I repeat, though this time, it sounds more like a plea than a declaration. "I'm just asking you to leave me alone."

He doesn't answer right away. Instead, he looks at me like he's trying to figure out if I mean it or if it's just another defense mechanism I've put up to keep him out. And maybe it is. But I'm so tired of this—of him, of the constant push and pull, the dance we've been doing for so long that it's starting to feel like we're only circling the same dangerous path.

"Fine," he says after a long pause, his voice tight with something unreadable. "But don't think for one second that I'm going to stop watching over you."

Before I can respond, he turns and walks out, leaving me standing there, the cold silence wrapping around me like a blanket I don't want, but can't shake. I watch him go, my heart pounding in my chest, unsure of what just happened or what it means. All I know is that the door clicks shut behind him, and I feel emptier than I did when he walked in.

I don't know how long I stand there, staring at the empty space where he stood. Minutes? Hours? Time seems to bend and twist in his presence, like it's out of my control when he's around. All I can focus on is the hollow ache in my chest, the one that's been growing since the moment he showed up in my life, and how it's impossible to ignore it now.

I try to shake it off, to push it down, but it's no use. The damage has been done. I can't erase him, no matter how hard I try.

The next few days blur into each other. Work becomes a lifeline, a distraction from the thoughts that keep creeping back into my mind like unwelcome visitors. I bury myself in spreadsheets, emails, phone calls, anything to keep me from thinking about him, about how he's been embedded into the fabric of my life without me even realizing it.

But then, as if by some twisted fate, I get a call from a number I don't recognize. I pick up without thinking, my stomach dropping when I hear the voice on the other end.

"I need to talk to you."

It's him.

My breath catches in my throat, my hand trembling around the phone. "What do you want?" I manage to choke out, trying to steady myself, to stop the rush of emotions from flooding in.

"I'm outside," he says, his voice quiet but insistent. "We need to talk."

I don't know what I'm doing when I grab my coat and head out the door. I don't know why I'm walking toward the sound of his voice, toward whatever he's about to say, but I do it anyway. Maybe I'm tired of pretending I don't care. Maybe I'm tired of fighting the inevitable.

But when I step outside, he's not standing there, waiting for me like I expected. There's no sign of him at all.

Just a note, written in familiar handwriting, left on the ground at my feet.

I bend down to pick it up, my heart hammering in my chest.

I never said I was done with you.

Chapter 23: Shattered Trust

The rain had begun in the early hours of the morning, turning the streets into slick mirrors that reflected the dull, pale light of a sky weighed down with clouds. It was the kind of rain that made everything feel heavier, as if the world were holding its breath, waiting for something to change. I stood under the awning of an old diner, watching the water dance across the pavement. My fingers were numb, curled tightly around the envelope I had just pulled from my bag—the one that had changed everything.

There had always been something about Ben that felt too polished, too perfect. His smile, the way he touched my arm when he thought no one was looking, the way he could recite my thoughts before I even voiced them. It had been intoxicating, drawing me in with a magnetic pull I couldn't name, couldn't understand, and certainly couldn't escape. I used to think he was a man with nothing to hide, a steady, constant force that had somehow appeared in my chaotic life at exactly the right moment. But the truth had a way of twisting, turning under the surface, slipping through the cracks like oil in water. And now, I had proof of what I had long suspected.

My heels clicked against the wet pavement as I made my way toward the small, quiet apartment we'd shared. The familiar creak of the door handle, the warm smell of coffee drifting from the kitchen—it all felt wrong now, like a movie that had gone off-script. I took a deep breath, one last attempt to steady my shaking hands, before pushing the door open.

He was there, standing in the kitchen, the same spot where we had spent countless mornings together. His back was to me, his movements slow, deliberate, as though he knew what was coming but couldn't bring himself to face it. The air between us was thick, charged with something I couldn't name—regret, guilt, fear.

Whatever it was, it hung in the room like a fog, suffocating and undeniable.

I didn't waste time. I didn't need to. There was no more room for questions, no more pretending I hadn't seen what I had seen.

"Ben," I said, my voice steady despite the storm in my chest.

He froze, his broad shoulders tightening as though bracing for impact. "I didn't want you to find out," he muttered, his voice low, rough with a weight I hadn't expected.

"You didn't want me to find out," I repeated, my words sharp as they cut through the silence. "You didn't want me to know that everything you told me, everything we built, was based on a lie."

He turned to face me then, and I could see it in his eyes—something hollow, something regretful, but no explanation, no apology. His lips twisted into a grimace, but there was no denial. I had him. The pieces were all there, laid out before me like the remnants of something fragile, broken beyond repair.

"Why didn't you tell me?" I asked, though I wasn't sure I wanted to hear the answer. Part of me—more than I cared to admit—was hoping he would say something that would make it all make sense, something that would bring back the man I thought I knew.

"I couldn't." His voice cracked, the words barely audible. "I thought I could bury it. That it wouldn't matter. But it does." He stepped closer, but I didn't move. I stood rooted to the spot, the paper in my hand trembling as I held it out for him to see.

The connection was there, undeniable in its simplicity. The fire. The one that had changed everything for so many people. The one that had scarred families, taken lives, and left the rest of us in its wake, wondering how something so brutal could have happened so close to home. And there it was—his name, tied to the blaze in ways I couldn't ignore. The paper didn't lie.

His eyes fell to the envelope, the final nail in the coffin, and I saw the realization dawn on his face.

"Why?" I asked, though I wasn't sure I could stand to hear the answer. "Why hide it from me, Ben?"

"I didn't want to lose you," he said, his voice raw, vulnerable in a way I had never heard before. "You don't understand what I've been trying to outrun. What I've been trying to protect you from."

"Protect me?" The words were bitter on my tongue, each one a reminder of the trust that had slipped away like sand through my fingers. "You've been lying to me, Ben. You've been hiding a part of yourself, and now, I don't know who you are anymore."

"I never meant for it to go this far." His hands were clenched into fists at his sides, his jaw tight as if fighting against whatever emotions were threatening to break free. "I never wanted you to find out. I thought I could keep it hidden—keep you safe from the truth. But it's too late now. You know, and you're right to be angry. You should be."

I felt a tremor of something deep in my chest. Something darker than anger, something that burned hotter than I could name. Betrayal. The trust we had built over months, over every quiet moment shared in the comfort of our apartment, was crumbling before me. And with it, everything I had believed about him.

I took a step back, the room suddenly feeling too small, the air too thick. "I don't know if I can forgive you for this."

His face twisted, as if the words themselves were a physical blow. "I never wanted to hurt you."

"No," I said, shaking my head. "But you did. And I have to figure out how to live with that."

I turned, the door creaking open behind me, the sound of the rain pouring down outside calling to me like a lifeline. The world had never seemed so distant, so unreachable. The space between us was filled with all the things we could no longer say, all the things we could no longer fix. And as I stepped into the storm, I knew one thing with certainty: I would never trust him again.

The streetlights flickered in the distance, their dim glow barely cutting through the rain that had begun to pick up in intensity, slashing against the windows like a thousand tiny knives. I hadn't realized how heavy my steps had become until I was already out on the sidewalk, the echo of my heels on the wet pavement the only sound in the world. The world outside felt foreign, hostile—like I had stepped off a cliff into someone else's life. My life, once wrapped in the comforting illusion of knowing who I was with, had turned into a place of raw, uncharted terrain.

I didn't know where to go, or what to do next. I just kept walking, and that movement, the rhythm of my feet against the ground, became my anchor. I didn't have to think, didn't have to confront the ocean of emotions that had swelled inside me like an unforgiving tide. I let the rain sting my skin, hoping it would wash away the nagging feeling that clung to me—self-doubt, fury, and something else I couldn't put a name to.

It was his words that had stayed with me. He never wanted me to find out. He never meant to hurt me. The irony of it burned deep, like salt in a wound. Every part of me, every piece of my soul that had believed in the version of him I'd crafted, shattered with each of those words. Because I knew, deep down, that it wasn't the lies that hurt the most. It was the idea that he had thought I wouldn't see through them. That I wouldn't question, that I would simply accept the picture he painted.

I had never asked for perfection, but I had asked for honesty. And now, I wasn't sure if that was too much to ask for.

The sound of my phone vibrating in my pocket pulled me from my thoughts. It was a text message—Ben's name lighting up the screen like an insult. I stared at it, my fingers itching to throw the damn thing into the nearest puddle. But there it was, his message waiting for me to give it the dignity of a reply. Part of me wanted to ignore it, to block him out completely. But another part of me, the one that had trusted him without question, was curious.

I didn't answer. I couldn't. I just shoved the phone back into my pocket, feeling it vibrate once more as if it was trying to drag me back into the mess I had just walked away from.

The night felt heavy, laden with the unanswered questions I hadn't been able to ask. I had been so certain of him, of us. Now, all I could see were fragments of lies floating in the dark, and the painful truth was that they didn't just shatter the person I thought he was. They had cracked something deep inside me too.

I pushed through the fog in my mind, my feet taking me through streets I hadn't noticed in years—those quiet alleyways and familiar corners where memories used to feel safe. It was as though the city had closed in on me, pressing in with the weight of everything I had ignored for so long.

The diner was still open when I passed by it—its warm, inviting glow a stark contrast to the chill in the air. The smell of freshly brewed coffee drifted toward me, and I hesitated for a moment, the pull of comfort almost too strong. I had spent so many mornings there, wrapped up in conversation and companionship that seemed so effortless. But today, it felt wrong. The place that had once been a sanctuary now seemed to hold too many memories, too many traces of the life I had built with him.

I kept walking.

But the quiet hum of a life I had known began to gnaw at me, and before I knew it, I found myself standing outside his building. I hadn't planned to come here, hadn't thought I would even be able to face him again after what had happened, but here I was. The decision was a sudden, irreversible pull, as if something in me was unwilling to let go.

I raised my hand to knock, but the door swung open before I could touch it. Ben stood there, looking as if he had been waiting, though I couldn't imagine why. He looked different, his eyes rimmed with shadows that made him seem older, tired, as if he hadn't slept in days. I hated that I felt a pang of sympathy. I had walked away, convinced that there was no coming back from what had been broken, but standing there, facing him, that feeling of connection had surged again, just long enough to make me doubt myself.

"You're back," he said, his voice low, wary.

"I came to get my things," I replied, my own voice steady but not entirely sure. The words came out before I had time to second-guess them.

He stepped aside, opening the door wider, and I felt a rush of cool air sweep through, a reminder that the world outside was still there, still waiting, despite the wreckage inside. I didn't want to cross the threshold. I didn't want to feel the remnants of him in every corner, in every lingering smell of cologne and half-forgotten dreams. But the promise of closure, of seeing him face-to-face one last time, anchored me to the moment.

"I don't know what you think you'll find here, but I'm sorry," he said, his voice thick with something raw that I couldn't place. "I never wanted to hurt you."

I swallowed hard, forcing myself to look past the apology in his eyes, the vulnerability that was spilling out of him like a broken dam. "You think sorry is enough?"

"No," he said quietly, his gaze never leaving mine. "But it's all I have to offer."

I stared at him, at the man I had once trusted, once loved, and for a brief, fleeting moment, I wanted to believe him. I wanted to believe that he was truly sorry, that the lies hadn't been deliberate, that I hadn't been some casualty in his quest for redemption. But the cracks were too wide now, and no apology, no matter how sincere, could ever bridge the gap.

"Goodbye, Ben," I whispered, my heart shattering just a little more with each word. I didn't know if he heard me, didn't know if he understood. But I knew, with a certainty that had taken root in the darkest corners of my soul, that this time, there was no coming back. Not for us. Not for me.

I walked out, the sound of the door closing behind me as final as the last breath of a long-held secret.

The night stretched on like an endless shadow, swallowing the world around me as I walked aimlessly through streets that no longer felt familiar. Each step seemed to echo in my chest, thudding louder than the rain that pelted the ground beneath my feet. I couldn't stop thinking about Ben, couldn't escape the image of his hollow eyes, the ones that had once looked at me with a kind of tenderness that now seemed like a lie. How had I not seen it? How had I not known?

The city seemed to mock me, its lights flickering as if to highlight the fracture in my own heart, the jagged lines of disappointment and betrayal that carved through me with every breath. I hadn't expected this. Hadn't planned for it. When I'd first met Ben, he had been my constant, my anchor. Now, he felt like a ghost, haunting me with every word he hadn't said, every moment he had concealed. I thought I had understood him, but it turned out I had only understood what he wanted me to believe.

My phone buzzed again, the screen lighting up with another message from him. The words were brief, desperate even, but I didn't need to read them to know what they said. "We need to talk." Of course, we needed to talk. I had no idea what there was left to say, no idea what kind of explanation could salvage any part of what we had been.

I had to leave. I needed space. But a part of me couldn't walk away completely. I wanted to hear him try to explain. I wanted to hear him say the words I already knew were coming—words that wouldn't fix anything but would somehow make everything more real. That was the thing about pain, wasn't it? It had a way of making the truth impossible to ignore.

I stopped at a small coffee shop, the warmth from the overhead lights spilling onto the sidewalk like a promise of comfort I wasn't sure I deserved. Inside, it was quiet, almost peaceful, the hum of the espresso machine and the soft murmur of the barista's voice a far cry from the storm in my chest. I slid into a corner booth, my hands shaking as I set my phone down. I hadn't realized how tightly I had been holding onto it until I let go. It was strange, how small the world felt in those moments. Just me, a phone, and a lifetime of unanswered questions.

The door opened, and a gust of cold air swept through, but it was the figure in the doorway that made my heart stutter. Ben. His face was drawn, eyes still clouded with the same guilt that had haunted him earlier. His lips parted, as if he had been about to speak, but he stopped when his eyes met mine. He must have seen something in my expression—something that made him hesitate, because he didn't approach immediately. Instead, he stood frozen, as if waiting for me to say something, anything.

I felt the sting of a thousand emotions, sharp and raw, clawing at me from every angle. Anger. Hurt. Confusion. I was so tired of feeling like this. So tired of trying to make sense of things that didn't make sense. But there he was, standing in front of me, the very man who had ripped my world apart, and still, a part of me wanted him to explain it all away. To tell me that this wasn't what it seemed, that there was some reason behind it that I just didn't understand.

"I didn't think you'd be here," he said, his voice low, almost too soft, as if he were afraid of breaking whatever fragile thread still connected us.

I didn't know what to say to him. The words felt heavy on my tongue, as if they had taken root deep within me, unwilling to come out unless I meant them. I opened my mouth, but before I could speak, the door swung open again, and another figure entered, this one even more unexpected than Ben.

Eliza.

Her eyes flicked over to us, narrowing when she saw us together. A flicker of something—anger?—passed through her expression before she schooled it into something unreadable. My heart sank. I hadn't expected her to be here. Not tonight. Not now. She wasn't supposed to know about any of this.

"You," she said, her voice sharp, her gaze cutting through the space between us. She didn't need to say more. The way her eyes landed on Ben told me everything I needed to know. She knew. Of course she did. Eliza always knew.

"What are you doing here?" I asked, the words out before I could stop them. The tension in the room thickened, and I could feel it—their history, the undercurrent of something that had always existed but had been left unspoken until now. It was all out in the open. The secret Ben had tried to keep hidden, the one that had caused so much damage—it was right there, laid bare for both of us to see.

"I could ask you the same thing," Eliza snapped, taking a step forward, her eyes locked on mine with a fierce intensity. "You don't know him the way I do."

I looked at Ben, who stood motionless, caught between the two of us, like a man who had no idea how to escape the trap he had set for himself. His lips were tight, his hands fisted at his sides, as if he were bracing for something, waiting for something to give.

"What is she talking about?" I asked, turning to him, my voice cracking. I didn't care about his excuses anymore. The questions I had were too much to hold back. "What's going on, Ben?"

His gaze met mine, but it wasn't the familiar, comforting look I had come to know. There was nothing in his eyes now except regret, something darker—something that made my stomach twist.

"I never wanted this to happen," he murmured, but the words felt empty. He had already said that once, and it had meant nothing then. It meant nothing now.

I stood up, my heart racing, a thousand thoughts swirling in my head. Eliza's presence, the tension in the air, and Ben's silence were too much. I couldn't breathe. Not anymore.

I turned to leave, but just as my hand reached for the door, I felt it—someone grabbing my wrist from behind.

It wasn't Ben.

It was Eliza.

Chapter 24: Beneath the Ashes

I had never been one to dwell on things, but this... this gnawed at me in a way that felt almost physical. It was as if every corner of my mind had become an echo chamber, amplifying every word he'd said, every glance he'd thrown my way. He was sorry, so very sorry, but his apology didn't come with any answers. It didn't come with a map of how to move forward, or a simple 'this is how we fix it' that I could cling to.

Sleep became a foreign concept. The bed, once my refuge, now felt like an interrogation chair. Every time I closed my eyes, the shadows of his confession stretched like tendrils around me. I couldn't even tell if the tears on my pillow were from anger, grief, or confusion. Maybe it was all of it. It was a strange feeling, a heaviness that crawled up my spine and nestled in the back of my skull. I was too tired to think clearly, too restless to sit still.

And yet, when the sunlight finally broke through the curtains in the early morning, when the world outside seemed to breathe without me, I couldn't shake the thought: something didn't add up. His guilt was palpable, yes. But there was something off about it. Something that didn't match the man I thought I knew. His eyes, wide and mournful, his hands shaking as he reached out to me—it all made sense on the surface. But beneath that was a truth I couldn't touch, something buried so deep that even he had yet to unearth it.

I pushed the covers back with a sense of purpose that surprised me, my feet hitting the cool floor with a sharpness I hadn't expected. I stood in front of the mirror, my reflection hazy, the dark circles under my eyes giving away my lack of sleep. It wasn't a pretty sight, and yet, I couldn't bring myself to care. Not now. I needed answers, and if that meant tearing apart every conversation we'd ever had, every word he'd ever spoken, then so be it. There had to be something I missed. He wasn't the villain. Not in the way I'd believed. But who was he, really? That was the question that rang through my mind like a bell.

The days stretched on, the weight of my thoughts growing heavier with each passing hour. I found myself back in the places we'd been—his favorite diner, the little bookstore he liked to drag me into for hours, even the park bench where we'd sat for so many lazy afternoons. Each one was a puzzle piece I hadn't fully examined, a photograph I hadn't looked at long enough to notice the smudges on the edges.

The diner was the first stop, its neon sign flickering in the early morning mist like some tired promise of comfort. The smell of coffee and sizzling bacon greeted me as I walked in, the clang of dishes and soft murmur of conversation blending together in a symphony I once found soothing. Now, it felt like noise—a distraction. I slid into our usual booth, the worn leather creaking beneath me as I stared out the window, watching the world bustle past in a blur of people with places to go, lives to live. I was too frozen in place to be one of them.

I looked at the menu, though I had no intention of ordering. My eyes drifted over to the spot by the counter where we had sat the day after his confession, the spot where his hands had trembled, his eyes darting around as if searching for something to hold onto. I could still hear his voice, low and tortured. "I never meant for it to happen."

Meant for what?

A woman in her fifties, with bright red lipstick that seemed almost too bold for the morning hour, approached the counter, her heels clicking against the tiled floor. She ordered without hesitation, a routine she performed every day without a second thought. For some reason, I envied her. She was living in a world where things made sense. The coffee was strong, the food predictable, and her life—at least from where I stood—seemed as orderly as her polished boots.

I ran my fingers over the edge of the table, feeling the scratches in the wood, the marks of time passing in subtle, unnoticed ways. There was nothing in this diner that told me what I needed to know. No hidden messages in the walls, no truths waiting in the stale air between the clinking of coffee cups. Just the same old scene, the same old routine, and a growing sense of frustration that knotted tighter with every minute.

I stood up abruptly, the chair scraping against the floor as I pushed it back. The movement startled a nearby waitress, her surprised gaze meeting mine. I gave her a tight smile, though it felt more like a grimace.

"Excuse me," I said, more sharply than I intended. "Do you remember the man who used to come in here with me? About a month ago, tall guy with dark hair?"

Her eyes flickered with recognition, but then she frowned, as though trying to place the face in her memory. "He was in here a lot, wasn't he? That guy... yeah, I remember. He wasn't a talker. Just sat there with you, kind of lost in his head, you know?"

I swallowed, the pit in my stomach deepening. "Lost in his head," I repeated softly, almost to myself.

The waitress nodded, clearly uncomfortable now. "He seemed... well, like he was carrying something. Heavy, I guess. But I never asked. People come and go, and I don't pry."

I could feel the tension building, rising like the sharp sting of an open wound. I nodded, thanked her, and walked out. There was nothing else to say. Nothing else to hear. But now, more than ever, I needed to know what he was running from.

I ended up back at his apartment, standing in front of the door, my hand hovering just inches from the knob. I hadn't planned on this—on showing up uninvited—but there it was. I could practically feel the hum of the air in the hallway, a soft buzzing, a reminder that life was happening beyond the thin walls that separated us. The apartment smelled faintly of lavender and something woodsy—he'd always had an affinity for candles that didn't quite match the rest of the decor. It was part of the charm, that odd little mismatch of his world. But today, that scent only made me feel sick.

I knocked three times before I could change my mind, the sound of the knocks echoing in the hallway like some strange metronome, ticking away at my resolve. Seconds passed, too many of them, before the door finally opened. He stood there, looking as if he hadn't moved since the last time I'd seen him—the same tired eyes, the same worn-out look. But his expression? That was different. Something was off. There was wariness now, mingled with the confusion that had been there the last time we'd spoken. And beneath it all, I swore I could see something else—something darker, something he didn't want me to know.

"Hey," I said, voice too calm, too controlled for the chaos spinning inside me. "I need to ask you something."

"Sure," he replied, his voice rough, like he hadn't used it in a while. "Come in."

I stepped over the threshold without waiting for an invitation. I could feel his eyes on me as I moved past him, his gaze heavy on the back of my neck like a weight I could never quite shake. I sat down on the couch, the familiar cushions sinking under my weight. The room still held the ghosts of us—the coffee-stained books we'd laughed over, the map we'd pinned to the wall, tracing imaginary trips we never took. But there was also something else now, something lingering in the air that hadn't been there before.

He followed me into the living room, standing there in the doorway, his hands shoved into his pockets as though he were trying to hide the way they shook. I didn't wait for him to speak.

"I've been thinking about what you said," I started, my eyes locked on his, searching for any crack, any weakness in his facade. "About the guilt, about the regret. But it doesn't add up, does it?"

He stiffened, a slight twitch of his jaw the only sign he was affected. I didn't give him time to deflect, to hide behind that wall of his.

"I've known you long enough to know when you're lying, even when you don't say a word. And I've seen that look on your face before. I've watched you crumble under pressure, I've seen you hold back from the truth like it might choke you if you let it out. But this? This is something else. This is..." I paused, trying to find the right word. "Not just guilt. It's something deeper. And I need to know what it is."

His lips parted as though he was going to say something, but then he closed them again, as if he were weighing his next move. The silence stretched between us like a tightrope, and I could feel my heartbeat picking up pace, a drumbeat in my chest that threatened to drown out everything else.

"I didn't mean to hurt you," he said finally, the words coming out in a rush, like he'd been holding them back for too long. "I never wanted to. But I did. And it—"

"It's not just about that, is it?" I interrupted, my voice sharp, cutting through his defenses like a blade. "This isn't just some mistake you made, some careless thing that got out of hand. There's more to it. You're not just sorry for what you did, you're sorry for something else. Something you haven't told me."

I could see the flicker of panic in his eyes, that same helplessness I'd seen when he'd confessed before. But this time, there was a twist—something about the way he looked at me made me think I wasn't the only one drowning in this.

"I don't know how to explain it," he said, his voice tight, strained. "I just—" He stopped, shaking his head, like the words were stuck in his throat, trapped in some place he couldn't quite reach.

I stood up, pacing now, my mind racing as fast as my feet. The room felt smaller suddenly, the walls closing in on me, pressing in from every direction. There were pieces missing from the puzzle, things I couldn't quite fit together. He was holding something back, something that wasn't just about his past, but about what had been building between us.

"You keep saying you're sorry," I said, my voice quieter now, though still edged with frustration. "But I can't fix this if I don't know what I'm fixing. I need you to be honest with me, all of it. Not just the pieces you think I'll want to hear. Not just the stuff that's safe. What really happened?"

He looked at me for a long moment, as if weighing the consequences of telling me the truth, as if he were considering how much of himself he was willing to expose. And then, just when I thought he was about to open up—just when I thought I might finally get the answer I was begging for—he shook his head, a bitter smile playing at the corners of his mouth.

"I can't do that," he whispered, barely audible. "Not yet."

The words hung in the air, thick and heavy, like smoke from a fire that wouldn't die. I felt my breath catch, a sudden realization creeping up on me, sinking into my chest like a stone. The distance between us had never been more apparent, and for the first time, I wondered if I'd been wrong all along. What if I wasn't the one who needed to be fixed? What if it was him—and the part of him he couldn't bear to let me see?

I spent the next few days circling the edges of my thoughts like a vulture waiting for the right moment to swoop down. The apartment felt colder now, emptier, as if the space itself was holding its breath along with me. The silence between us had become an uncomfortable thing, stretching its limbs across every corner, filling the air with an absence that didn't feel natural. I couldn't tell whether it was him pulling away or if I was just unwilling to step closer, but there was something strange about the way we existed in the same room without speaking. It wasn't peaceful. It was tense. And that, more than anything else, made me wonder what we were really doing here.

I avoided the phone, avoided any conversations with friends or family. I didn't want to hear their assurances that he was just going through something, that we all make mistakes, that love was supposed to forgive it all. I didn't care for their words of comfort. What I wanted was clarity. I wanted the truth, the whole truth, wrapped in honesty—no more lies wrapped in well-meaning apologies. But there was something in his eyes, something in the way he was slipping further away from me, that told me he couldn't give me what I was asking for. Or maybe he just wouldn't.

The phone buzzed beside me, cutting through the quiet. I ignored it at first, my gaze fixed on the half-empty cup of coffee in my hands. The screen lit up again, the name flashing in bold, familiar letters. It was his. I didn't pick up right away, my thumb hovering over the screen as if I could somehow decipher the meaning in that simple message without opening it. I'm sorry. Again. Always the same. I let the words hang in my mind for a moment, like smoke that wouldn't clear.

Finally, I pressed the green button, holding the phone to my ear.

"Hey," his voice cracked, strained in a way I hadn't expected. "We need to talk."

I exhaled, the frustration rising like bile in my throat. "You're right, we do."

A brief pause, then, "Not here. Can we meet?"

"Where?" I replied, already knowing the answer. He was always vague when it mattered most.

There was another beat of silence, but this time, I could hear the rasp in his breath, the hesitation that made me think twice. "The pier," he said finally. "Tonight."

The words hit me harder than I expected. The pier. That damn pier, where we'd spent hours talking about our future, about our pasts. It had always been our place—untouched by the chaos of the world, a quiet haven that felt like it belonged only to us. I wanted to protest, to tell him that everything between us had become too messy to revisit that spot, but instead, I found myself agreeing. "Fine. I'll be there."

The evening rolled in like a blanket, heavy and thick, obscuring the sky with its bruised clouds. I could feel the chill in the air, the weight of the moment pressing in as I stood on the edge of the pier, the wooden planks creaking beneath my feet. The water stretched out before me, black and endless, the only sound the lapping of the waves against the pylons below. I had expected to feel a sense of anticipation, but all I felt was dread—an aching gnawing sensation that curled around my chest and wouldn't let go.

And then I saw him.

He was standing at the far end, his silhouette dark against the shifting light of the distant streetlamps. He hadn't changed much, still the same figure that I remembered, yet something about him seemed... off. The way he moved was hesitant, like a man walking in a dream, disconnected from the reality that surrounded him. As he drew closer, I noticed how his jaw was clenched, how the muscles in his neck twitched with the tension he was carrying.

"You came," he said softly, his voice rough, like gravel scraping against stone. I didn't reply right away, just watched him with a gaze that felt more like an interrogation than anything else.

"I said I would." My words were cold, sharper than I meant, but I couldn't help it. The closer he got, the more the weight of his confession seemed to press down on me. I wanted to hate him, I wanted to feel the anger I knew I was entitled to, but all I could feel was an unbearable heaviness.

"I'm sorry," he repeated, the words coming out like they were falling from his lips against his will. "I've been running from this. From you. From everything."

I swallowed hard, a knot of frustration lodging in my throat. "Stop. Don't give me that. I've heard it too many times. I need more than just words, more than just apologies."

"I know." His voice broke then, the crack sending a jolt of surprise through me. I wasn't prepared for that. I wasn't prepared for him to be as fragile as he sounded. "I wish I could give you more."

"Then tell me why you've been avoiding me," I demanded, the question bursting out before I could stop it. "Tell me what's been eating you alive for so long."

For a moment, he didn't say anything. His eyes were fixed on something far away, something that only he could see. The wind whipped through his hair, and I watched the uncertainty flit across his face. It was clear—whatever he was hiding, it was too much to bear alone.

"I never wanted this," he said, his voice barely a whisper. "I never wanted you to find out."

My heart skipped a beat. His words sent a shiver up my spine. "Find out what?" I asked, my voice dropping to a near hush, the danger of it hanging heavy in the air between us.

He finally met my eyes, the depth of his regret so raw that I felt like I might drown in it. "That I'm not the person you think I am."

And just like that, the ground beneath my feet shifted.

Chapter 25: Rekindling Hope

I barely recognize the voice when he answers, the rasp of it unfamiliar and thick with the weight of silence. It's as though time has worn it down, strained it like an old rope. I sit back in my chair, fingers curled around the edge of the phone, half expecting him to hang up before we get anywhere. After all, it's not like I've given him much reason to believe I'm still in this, that I could ever be in this again.

"You didn't have to call," he says. It's not defensive, just... resigned, as if the thought of anything else has long since slipped from his grasp.

I don't know what to say to that. There are so many things I want to say, but the words hang in my throat like stones, too heavy to dislodge. Instead, I breathe deeply and force the first thing out that comes to mind. "I want to understand."

The pause that follows feels endless, the kind that stretches across an ocean, and I wonder if he's preparing to lie, or worse, to disappear without another word. But then he speaks again, and this time his voice cracks—just a little, just enough for me to hear the fissures in it.

"I never meant to hurt you," he begins, and I know without a doubt that he means it. The words come so slowly, as though each one requires a monumental effort to find its place. "But sometimes life makes choices for you, and the ones you make in those moments... they follow you."

I close my eyes, squeezing them shut as if blocking him out could erase everything. But of course, it doesn't. It never does. The memories rush in like a tidal wave, taking me back to a time when he used to laugh, when I'd hear that sound like the first notes of a familiar song. When I could trust the warmth of his hand in mine without wondering if the other shoe would ever drop. But life has a way of twisting things, doesn't it?

He lets out a sigh, and I can almost picture him on the other side of the line, probably sitting in some dark corner with his elbows on his knees, shoulders hunched like he's bracing himself for an impact he's not sure he can survive.

"I wasn't always who you thought I was," he continues. "I didn't know how to handle it. I didn't know how to explain it without breaking everything."

There's a flicker in his tone—something like regret, something like pain. I wonder for a split second whether I can still be the person who holds his heart the way I once did, but the thought fades just as quickly as it came. I open my mouth to say something, anything, but the words tumble away, falling short of the tangled mess in my chest.

"I never wanted to be a monster," he adds, the bitterness in his voice now sharp enough to slice through the tension between us. "I made the choice, and I can't take it back. But I never asked for what happened next."

There's a sharp edge to his words now, the rawness of a confession turning into something else. A kind of resignation. And I'm not sure if that makes me angry or sad.

"But why didn't you just tell me?" The question slips out of my mouth before I can stop it, the sting of it harsh and biting. "Why let me live with all the lies? Why make me question everything we were?"

I can hear him swallow, the movement so loud in the quiet of the call that it makes my pulse quicken. "Because it wasn't just my secret. I couldn't drag you into it."

I can feel the heat of frustration crawl up my spine. He never was good at understanding what I could handle, was he? "I'm not some fragile thing to protect," I snap. "I can handle the truth."

"I didn't think you could." His voice is softer now, as if he's just realized the mistake he made in underestimating me. "And I didn't want to see you break."

Something about that makes my chest ache. Not the apology—no, that's too little, too late—but the way he still believes he can fix things by protecting me from the worst of it. He never quite got it, did he? That the worst of it was never the truth itself; it was the silence, the lies.

"Then tell me," I whisper, my voice quiet, almost pleading.

And so he does.

His story unfolds in jagged pieces, the kind that cut through you when they land, and I realize, with a start, that I've been holding my breath the entire time. I listen, and I try not to imagine the pain in his eyes, the way his hands must've trembled when he made the decisions that brought us to this moment. There's so much more to it than I ever could have guessed—so much more than I wanted to know.

But it's there, all of it, bleeding out in a raw confession that reveals him in ways I didn't expect. In ways I'm not sure I can ever truly understand. The man I thought I knew, the one I had loved with reckless abandon, is someone entirely different, and the world he's trapped in now is not the one I ever imagined. It's a prison of his own making, a place where every choice is a double-edged sword.

And in that moment, I see him—really see him—not as the man who broke my heart, but as a man broken by choices that no one should have to make. It's tragic. It's complicated. And it's nothing like the fairy tale I once thought we had.

But maybe, just maybe, it's something worth fighting for.

His words swirl in my head like a storm, each sentence striking harder than the last. As much as I want to walk away, to slam down the phone and shut him out completely, something keeps me tethered to him. Maybe it's the raw honesty, the way he's not trying to defend himself, not trying to spin the truth into something more palatable. He's just letting it all fall where it may, and I can't decide if I'm angry or relieved. Or both.

"Are you... are you done?" I ask finally, my voice sounding alien to me—strained, tight, as though it's carrying the weight of the world.

There's a hesitation, a long, drawn-out breath from his side of the line. "I never meant for it to go this far. If I could take it all back—if I could make a different choice, I would. But that night... it's done, and nothing can undo it."

I want to scream at him, to tell him how selfish he is, how reckless, how blind to everything he left in his wake. But the words aren't there, not anymore. They evaporate into something softer, something I can't quite reach but can feel creeping along the edges of my heart. He's speaking, but I'm not listening in the way I thought I would.

"I don't know how to fix this, how to make it right. I never have," he adds, and the sincerity in his voice has the power to crack me wide open, spilling all the things I've kept locked inside. The truth is—if I'm being honest with myself—part of me never wanted this to end. The thought of a world where we were strangers again, where we couldn't even look at each other without pain, was unbearable.

"It wasn't just about us," he continues, his voice quiet now, almost gentle. "It was about so much more than that. There were things I couldn't control. Forces outside of us. And I couldn't ask you to bear that, not when everything was already falling apart."

I picture him then—his face worn with the weight of years, his hands maybe trembling, just like his voice. I wonder how long he's carried this, how many nights he's stayed awake, tormented by the very things he's kept from me.

"Then why didn't you let me help?" I can't stop myself from asking, the question tasting bitter on my tongue. "I would've done anything. I would've stood by you."

Another pause. A moment that seems like it could stretch into infinity if I let it. But then he speaks, and I know the words are harder than anything he's said so far.

"Because you didn't deserve to be dragged into it," he murmurs. "I wanted you to have a life. I wanted you to have the freedom to make your own choices without being suffocated by mine."

There it is, that self-sacrificing nonsense he's always believed in. That martyrdom he wears like armor, pretending it makes him noble, pretending it makes everything easier. And I used to fall for it—used to admire him for it, even. But now, it just feels like another excuse.

"You didn't give me a choice," I say, my voice tight, an edge of bitterness seeping in. "You made it for me. You kept me in the dark and then... you let me walk away, thinking it was all my fault. It wasn't fair."

He doesn't argue, doesn't try to defend himself. And for that, I almost respect him. But that respect comes with its own brand of pain, a pain I'm still learning to navigate. His silence stretches out again, thick and heavy, until I wonder if he's said all he can say. But then, as though he's trying to reach through the airwaves, his voice breaks the stillness once more.

"I didn't want to hurt you," he says, and there's a tremor in it that makes my heart ache in ways I don't know how to explain. "I wanted to protect you. I thought that by keeping you safe, by keeping you away from it all, I was doing the right thing."

"You thought you could make decisions for me?" I ask, incredulous now. "That's not protection. That's control. It's manipulation."

There's no answer to that. There can't be. It hangs in the air between us, unspoken but understood.

"And I was wrong," he admits softly. "I was wrong to think that."

The confession lands in my chest like a stone, sinking deeper and deeper into the ocean of regret. Part of me wants to shout at him, to tell him how much I've suffered, how much I've agonized over the mess he left behind. But another part of me—the part I can't quite quiet—just wants him to keep talking. To keep explaining himself, to keep trying, because somehow, I still want to hear it.

The tension between us feels different now, heavier in a way I can't describe. It's like we've both crossed a line, and there's no going back to the way things were before. I can't tell if it's a good thing or a bad one. All I know is that it's real now—the weight of everything we've been through, the distance we've traveled, and the fact that we're both still standing on opposite sides of a chasm that feels too wide to bridge.

"I don't know how to fix this," he says again, as though admitting it out loud will somehow change the facts. "But I'm willing to try. If you are."

And just like that, the world shifts. Not in a grand, sweeping way, but in the quiet, fragile way that things do when they might be on the verge of falling apart—or might be on the verge of coming together again.

The air between us feels electric, charged with all the unspoken things that have haunted the spaces where we've stood apart. His words—his raw honesty—are stirring something inside me, something that I can't quite name. Maybe it's hope, or maybe it's just the promise of closure, the idea that I might finally have the answers I've been searching for. But in the back of my mind, I know better. Hope is fragile. It's one wrong word away from shattering into a thousand pieces. And I've already had too many pieces of my heart scattered across the ground.

"I don't know how we're supposed to move forward from here," I say, the words tumbling out before I can stop them. "I don't know if I can believe in us again."

There's a long silence on the other end, one that stretches taut and thin between us. When he speaks, it's with a quiet strength, the kind that comes only when someone's had to carry more than they ever should have. "I'm not asking you to forget. I'm not asking you to forgive me, not yet. But I'm asking for the chance to prove that I can be someone worth trusting again."

I want to tell him that I don't know if I can give him that chance, that everything inside me is screaming to protect myself from getting hurt again. But there's something in his voice—something that feels like a lifeline, pulling me back from the edge I've been teetering on. I take a breath, trying to steady my shaking hands, and find the words that will either build a bridge or burn it down.

"Prove it, then," I say, my voice steadier than I feel. "Show me that you're worth it."

A small, almost imperceptible chuckle escapes him. "I thought I was supposed to be the one making the demands here."

I can't help but smile a little, despite myself. The familiar banter between us, the one we used to share so easily, still lingers beneath the surface. It's a fleeting reminder of a time when we could laugh without consequences, when love didn't come with a heavy price tag.

"Life's different now," I reply, my voice softer. "And so are we."

There's a long pause, one that seems to stretch on forever, and I wonder if he's regretting the words he's just spoken. But when he finally speaks again, his voice is firm, resolute.

"I know," he says. "And I know I've messed up. But I'm willing to fight for this, for us."

I lean back in my chair, staring at the empty room around me, the silence heavy with the weight of everything unsaid. I've spent so many nights asking myself if it was worth it, if the love we shared had been real or just a fleeting illusion. I've watched that love twist and change, morphing into something unrecognizable, and I've wondered if I could ever go back to the way things were before. But the truth is, I don't know if I can. Not anymore.

"You're asking a lot," I say, my voice barely above a whisper.

"I know." He doesn't back down, doesn't flinch. "But I'm asking for one more chance. One more shot at proving that I'm more than the mistakes I made."

The words settle into me, wrapping around my heart like an old familiar song, one I can't quite shake. I can feel the weight of the decision pressing down on me, and for a moment, I'm paralyzed by the fear of choosing wrong. What if he's just saying what I want to hear? What if this is all a lie—a beautiful, heartbreaking lie that will leave me shattered all over again?

But then, something shifts. Maybe it's the sincerity in his voice, or maybe it's the thought of never knowing what could have been. Whatever it is, I find myself moving closer to the edge of hope, reaching for something I thought I'd lost.

"Okay," I say, my voice barely audible, a breath between us. "One chance."

The line is silent for a moment, as though he's waiting for me to change my mind. And then, finally, he speaks, his voice thick with something unspoken. "Thank you."

I don't say anything in return. What's there to say? He's thanked me for the thing he should have been fighting for all along—the thing he almost lost forever.

"I won't let you down," he adds, and I can hear the sincerity in it, even if I'm not sure I believe it yet.

But just as I start to let myself believe, to think that maybe—just maybe—this could be the start of something new, something repaired, the doorbell rings.

I freeze. My breath catches in my throat. The timing feels too perfect, too impossible. I glance down at the phone, the screen lighting up with his name. It's still him, still his voice I hear on the other end, and yet—something doesn't feel right.

"I'll be there soon," he says, the words clipped, like he's trying to hold something back. "I'm not giving up on us."

I stand up, my heart pounding now, the tension in the air thickening. I glance toward the door, my pulse quickening with an unshakable sense of dread.

Before I can speak, there's a loud knock. And then the door swings open, the sudden intrusion slicing through the fragile moment we've created.

I turn to face it, my breath caught in my chest.

Chapter 26: Rising from the Ashes

The air was heavy with the scent of burning wood and damp earth, an intoxicating mixture of something alive and yet on the verge of dying. I stood there, barefoot, on the edge of what used to be a garden. What had once been a riot of color and warmth was now an expanse of charred remains, the remnants of a fire that had consumed everything in its path. But even in the ashes, there was life, a quiet promise of rebirth.

I didn't look at him right away. I couldn't. Not yet. The crackle of the dying fire behind me was enough to remind me of the heat we had endured, both literal and metaphorical. It had all started in flames, after all. A year ago, it was our words that had burned, a fire fueled by lies and half-truths. Today, though, it was different. There were no words left to betray. Just the rawness of who we were and what we had become after the fire had swept through us.

He was standing behind me, close enough for me to feel the heat radiating off him, but not so close that he was intruding on the space I needed. For now, I just needed the distance. The silence between us stretched, thick and awkward, but not uncomfortable. I had grown to love these silences—how they weren't just about the absence of sound, but the absence of expectations. Neither of us had to fill the space with unnecessary words anymore. The silence was honest in its own way.

"You know," I said, without turning around, my voice soft, "I always thought I would find a way to rebuild all of this. The garden. The house. Everything." I motioned vaguely toward the remnants of the fence, the skeletal remains of the rosebushes, the lone oak tree that had somehow managed to survive the flames. It stood tall now, a symbol of defiance against the destruction that had nearly consumed it. "I didn't think about how hard it would be to rebuild myself."

He didn't speak at first, and I couldn't decide if I was grateful for the pause or if I wished he would just speak, say something that would make it all feel easier. Finally, he did. "You've already started, haven't you?" His voice was low, not quite a question, more like a quiet observation. He always knew me better than I liked to admit.

I shook my head, though he couldn't see the motion. "I thought I had. I thought if I just kept busy, kept my hands in the dirt, I could fix everything that had gone wrong. But I didn't understand how much of it was inside me. I wasn't looking at the right things."

The sound of his footsteps on the gravel reached my ears, slow and steady, and then, finally, his hand was on my shoulder. I didn't flinch. The warmth of his touch was a strange comfort, a reminder that, despite everything, we were still here. I turned to face him, then, meeting his gaze for the first time in what felt like an eternity. His eyes were shadowed, still haunted by their own ghosts, but there was something else there now. Something softer. Something more real.

"I never thought I'd be here again," he admitted, his voice rough, like he hadn't used it in too long. "With you. With all of this." His hand dropped from my shoulder, and for a moment, I thought he might walk away. But he didn't. He just stood there, waiting for me to speak. Waiting for me to say something that would make sense of this chaos.

I smiled, the edges of my lips trembling as I tried to push past the weight of everything that had happened. "Funny, I never thought I'd be here either. But here we are."

For a long time, neither of us moved. The wind began to pick up, the remnants of the fire swirling in the air like tiny embers trying to hold on to the heat of the past. I didn't know how long we stood there, but it didn't matter. In that moment, nothing else existed except for the two of us, standing on the precipice of everything that had been lost and everything that could still be found.

"You're not the same person you were when you left," he said, his voice quiet but steady. "Neither am I."

I nodded, unsure whether I should say something in return, unsure if there were words for this. For the way we had both changed, for the way we had both learned to carry our scars instead of hiding them. It wasn't about forgetting the past. It wasn't about pretending it hadn't happened. It was about accepting it, about understanding that we were stronger because of it. Or maybe, despite it.

"Maybe that's the point," I said softly, my eyes drifting toward the horizon where the sun was beginning to dip, casting everything in a golden light. "Maybe we weren't supposed to be the same."

He looked at me, really looked at me, as though seeing me for the first time in a long while. "You know," he said with a small smile, "I think that might be the most honest thing you've ever said."

I couldn't help but laugh, a sound that felt foreign after everything. But it felt good, too. Real. Like a first step forward. "Well, I guess that's progress."

We both stood there for a while, the weight of the past heavy but no longer suffocating. There was still so much to rebuild. So many things we still needed to figure out. But in that moment, with the sun setting behind us and the ashes of everything we had been scattered at our feet, I realized that maybe, just maybe, we could rise from all of it.

Together.

The moon hung low, casting a pale light over the ruins, transforming everything into something almost unrecognizable. The darkened landscape around us looked as if it had been painted in charcoal strokes, the shadows long and stretching like forgotten memories. But there was something else in the air now—a sense of possibility, like the world itself was holding its breath, waiting for us to decide what would come next.

I looked at him again, but this time, there was no hesitation, no doubt in the way I met his gaze. His face had softened, as though time itself had carved out the sharp edges, leaving only the man who stood before me now. The man who had, despite everything, come back. I wasn't sure how we had reached this point, how the space between us had narrowed from an insurmountable distance to a single breath that connected us.

"I was angry," I said, the words slipping out before I could stop them. "I was angry, and I didn't know what to do with it. All that time, all that energy... spent trying to hold on to things that weren't real anymore."

The night air was cool against my skin, and for a moment, it felt like the world was moving slowly, giving me the time I needed to say what had been left unsaid for far too long. His lips parted as if he might say something, but I raised a hand to stop him. "Let me finish. I need to get this out before I can move forward."

He only nodded, the movement slow, deliberate.

"I thought if I could just keep moving, if I could bury the anger somewhere where it couldn't hurt me, I'd be fine. I didn't realize that I was just... avoiding the truth. About you. About me. About what really happened."

The words hung in the air between us like smoke, thick and impossible to ignore. The fire in my chest had long since been extinguished, but the scars it had left still burned. They weren't the kind of wounds you could heal overnight, and I knew that now. I wasn't looking for perfection anymore. There was no such thing. But I had learned, in ways I never expected, that it was the imperfections that made us whole. They made us real.

"You weren't the only one avoiding the truth," he said, his voice steady but carrying an edge that made me look at him again. His hand dropped from my shoulder, but the weight of his words hung heavier than any touch. "I couldn't face it either. The mess I made, the choices I'd turned into mistakes." He paused, and there was something in his eyes, something darker than regret, something more... permanent. "But running from it didn't make it go away."

I wanted to say something, anything that would make it easier, but the words failed me. They always did when it mattered most. Instead, I closed the distance between us, stepping forward, just enough so I could reach him. I didn't need to say anything. We both knew what this was. What it had always been.

The ground beneath my feet shifted slightly, the soft rumble of earth shifting into new forms, a reminder that even the world around us was still changing, still learning to breathe again.

"I don't expect things to go back to how they were," I whispered, the words catching in my throat. "But maybe that's not the point. Maybe we weren't supposed to stay the same."

"No," he agreed, his hand finding mine again, a steady warmth against the chill of the night. "We weren't. And that's the hardest part. Accepting that we can't unmake what's already been done."

I nodded, but my mind was already somewhere else, lost in the complexities of everything that had brought us to this place. The choices we made, the ones we hadn't made, the things we had said and left unsaid. If I was being honest, I wasn't sure what was scarier: the thought of moving forward or the thought of being stuck in this limbo of what could have been.

"There are days when I'm not sure who I am anymore," I said quietly, looking down at the remnants of my garden, the blackened soil barely recognizable. "I thought I could rebuild it all. Piece by piece. But some things... they don't come back. Not the way you want them to."

His grip on my hand tightened slightly, like he understood what I meant. "You've always been more than what you lost, you know."

That was the thing about him—he always saw the parts of me that I couldn't see. The strength I'd buried, the courage I'd hidden behind walls of frustration and anger. For the longest time, I hadn't been able to understand how he could still look at me like that. After everything, after how badly we'd broken each other, he still saw me. The real me.

It wasn't until now that I realized I'd been looking for someone to save me. I thought I needed him to be my hero. But what I needed was for him to stand beside me, not in front of me, not behind me. Equal. And maybe, just maybe, that's what we were becoming.

"I don't want to be the person I was before," I said, meeting his eyes once more. "I don't want to keep pretending like everything's fine. But I'm ready to face whatever comes next. With you. I don't know what that looks like, but I want to try."

The faintest hint of a smile tugged at the corner of his mouth, and for the first time in so long, I saw something familiar there. Hope.

"Then we'll figure it out," he said, his voice rough with something I couldn't quite name. "Together."

And that was the moment. The moment when I finally let go of the past, when I stopped trying to hold on to the idea of who we were and started embracing who we could be. The fire had burned us both, but it hadn't destroyed us. It had reshaped us, forged us into something stronger, something better. It wasn't about rising from the ashes anymore. It was about building something new—together.

The night was uncomfortably still, and yet, beneath the silence, I could hear the pulse of the world—slow and steady like the beat of my own heart. Everything had changed. It was strange how I could feel the shift in the air, like the weight of it pressing against me, demanding acknowledgment. I squeezed his hand, the warmth of his touch grounding me, and for the first time in what felt like forever, I didn't feel the weight of all the years we had spent apart.

But that didn't mean I was ready to face it all. Not yet.

"I've been thinking," I started, my voice a little too quiet in the stillness. "About how we got here. About the moments we missed, the things we couldn't fix, the things we should have done."

He tilted his head, not out of confusion, but out of understanding. "I think about that too," he said. "What we did wrong. What we left undone. But it's hard, isn't it? Trying to untangle the mess of it all."

I nodded, my fingers tracing patterns on his hand, as though that simple act could put everything back together. "It's like... I've spent so much time trying to figure out what went wrong that I didn't stop to ask myself what went right. And maybe that's why I'm still stuck. I've been focusing on all the broken pieces instead of the ones that are still intact."

He let out a breath, a sound that was part laugh, part sigh. "That sounds a lot like you," he said softly. "Always trying to fix things. Even when they can't be fixed. But I think... maybe you're starting to get it. Sometimes, things don't need to be fixed. Sometimes, we just need to learn to live with them."

I looked up at him, the faint moonlight catching the sharpness of his features, softening them just enough for me to see the man who had always been there beneath the armor. "Is that what you think? That I just need to live with it?"

His eyes softened in response, and for a moment, I could see everything that had passed between us—the hurts, the regrets, the laughter, and the shared silences. "I think we both need to learn how to live with it. Whatever 'it' is."

I blinked, suddenly overwhelmed by the gravity of what he was saying. "And what if 'it' is too much? What if 'it' is all the things we've tried to bury?"

For a moment, he didn't answer, and I wondered if my question was too raw, too dangerous for him to consider. But then he stepped closer, his hand gently cupping my face, and I realized I didn't need an answer right then. Not yet. What I needed was the space to breathe, to just exist in this moment of fragile possibility.

"I don't want to rush this," I whispered, more to myself than to him. "I don't want to force us into something we're not ready for."

His thumb brushed against my cheek, slow and deliberate, as if trying to erase the remnants of doubt from my skin. "Then don't rush. We don't have to have all the answers right now. All we have is tonight. And maybe that's enough."

There was a vulnerability in his words that caught me off guard, a shift in his usually steadfast demeanor that made my heart ache. For a second, I wanted to push him away, to run, to do anything to avoid the impending storm of emotions I could feel brewing. But then I realized, for the first time in ages, I wasn't afraid. Not of him. Not of the storm.

I leaned into him, our foreheads touching, the soft heat of his breath mingling with mine. "I don't want to hide anymore. From you. Or from myself."

His hand slipped to my waist, pulling me closer until we were pressed together, the closeness startling and comforting all at once. He was right. It didn't have to be perfect. We didn't have to have it all figured out, not in this moment. But there was something in this silence, something that wasn't quite comfortable, yet felt more real than anything I'd experienced in years.

"You don't have to hide," he said softly, his voice a low promise. "Not from me. Not anymore."

The words lingered between us like a touch, a subtle weight that kept us anchored, even as the night seemed to shift around us. But then, just as the quiet seemed to settle into something more peaceful, a sound—a rustle in the shadows—pierced the stillness. I tensed, pulling away slightly, my senses on high alert.

"Did you hear that?" I asked, my voice barely a whisper.

He didn't answer right away, but I saw the way his eyes darted to the darkness, the way his posture stiffened. "Stay close," he said, his tone sharp, commanding.

I didn't have to be told twice. My heart skipped a beat, the calm that had surrounded us suddenly replaced by the prickling awareness of something lurking just beyond our reach. Something unfamiliar. Something we hadn't anticipated.

I grabbed his arm, my fingers tightening around his sleeve. "What is it?"

Before he could respond, a figure stepped into the dim light, a silhouette in the distance. Tall, imposing, and shadowed, it loomed in the clearing like an unexpected intruder. I couldn't make out any details, but I knew enough to recognize that we weren't alone anymore.

And in that moment, everything shifted again.

Chapter 27: Smoldering Suspicions

The air was thick with the scent of rain, fresh and metallic, clinging to the damp earth as if the world itself were holding its breath. The house creaked under the weight of history, its wooden bones groaning in protest. The shadows in the hallway stretched longer than they should, slinking toward corners I hadn't noticed before, lurking with the kind of quiet patience I'd only ever seen in wolves. And here I was, standing at the heart of it all, pretending it didn't feel like the walls were closing in.

I should've been satisfied. After everything that had happened, after the storm and the wreckage, we'd managed to carve out a space for ourselves, a small sliver of peace in the midst of chaos. His presence was a balm I never expected, a steadying force that made the uncertainty feel almost bearable. But the more I tried to settle into the fragile tranquility, the more the quiet whispered—unwelcome, unnerving. There was something I was missing, something I hadn't seen, and that gnawing feeling in my gut wouldn't leave me.

We were sitting in the living room, him lounging on the couch, fingers tracing the rim of his glass with an absentminded grace that spoke of days long gone. I could hear the low hum of the television, but my mind was elsewhere. I'd told myself a hundred times that I was being paranoid, that the calm of his steady gaze, his slow smile, was enough to silence any lingering doubts. But the past had a way of sneaking up on me, its claws sharp and unforgiving.

"Another drink?" he asked, voice smooth, offering the bottle between us like it was nothing more than a casual gesture. His smile never faltered, and I almost envied the ease with which he wore it. If only it were that simple for me.

"Sure." I took the glass he offered, fingers brushing his for a fraction of a second, a spark igniting that I quickly ignored. I looked away, the sharp edge of my unease refusing to let me fully relax.

He hadn't seen it. The shift in the air, the subtle tightening of my chest. Or maybe he had, but chose to pretend it wasn't there, just like he always did. Always smooth. Always calm. Always untouchable.

"Are you okay?" he asked, his voice soft, as though he could sense something slipping through the cracks of my composure.

I swallowed hard, my eyes tracing the pattern of the rug beneath my feet, avoiding his gaze. "I'm fine," I lied, even though I knew he could see through it. But he didn't push. He never did. Instead, he leaned back into the couch, the lines of his body stretching in a way that made him seem more comfortable, more untouchable than ever.

"I heard some things," I said, the words slipping out before I could stop them. "About that night. About—" I faltered, my voice trailing off as I picked at the fabric of my sleeve, unwilling to look at him. There it was again, that unwelcome sensation that lingered like smoke in my lungs.

His face remained unreadable, the quiet strength in his expression never wavering. "You know how people talk."

"Not like this," I murmured, the words tasting bitter on my tongue. "It's not just talk, is it?"

He set his glass down with a soft clink and turned to face me fully. The shift in his demeanor was subtle but there, like the quiet before a storm. The warmth that had settled between us was gone, replaced by an undeniable tension that crawled beneath my skin.

"You're letting it get to you," he said, his voice gentle but firm, as though he were trying to protect me from something I couldn't see. But I knew better. "It's just rumors. People don't know what they're saying."

"I don't know if that's true." I looked up at him then, my eyes locking with his, and for the first time in weeks, I saw something flicker behind his gaze. Something I couldn't name. "You haven't heard what I've heard."

He didn't respond at first, his jaw tightening just enough to make the muscles beneath his skin twitch. The silence stretched between us, heavy and laden with all the things we hadn't said, all the truths we were still dancing around. He leaned forward, and I could see the intensity in his eyes, a flash of something dangerous that made the hairs on the back of my neck stand on end.

"They're trying to turn you against me," he said, his voice low, like the warning of a predator.

I didn't flinch. I didn't retreat. But I couldn't help the shiver that ran through me. "Why would they do that?"

He stood then, pushing himself up with a fluid grace that made the air around him crackle. "I don't know," he admitted, the words coming out gritted and raw. "But I'm not going to let them. Not again."

I stood too, heart pounding in my chest as I met his gaze. Something in the room felt too still, too quiet, as though we were both standing on the edge of something, teetering just out of reach.

"And what if they're right?" I asked, the question slipping out before I could stop it, sharp and unforgiving. The moment it left my lips, I regretted it, but there was no taking it back.

His expression darkened, a flash of pain crossing his features before it was quickly masked by his usual cool exterior. "You don't believe that."

"I don't know what to believe anymore," I said, my voice trembling slightly despite my efforts to keep it steady.

There was a moment of stillness, the weight of our silence pressing down on us. And in that silence, I realized something I hadn't wanted to face. The questions I'd buried, the fears I'd shoved deep inside, were rising to the surface, clawing their way through every crack, every whisper of doubt that had begun to cloud my thoughts.

I didn't trust him. Not fully. Not anymore.

And I didn't know if I ever would again.

The house felt smaller today, as if the walls were inching closer with every breath I took. Each step echoed too loudly in the hallways, a constant reminder that nothing was truly silent—not anymore. Even the air around us seemed heavy, like it had been soaked in all the words we'd never spoken, thick and suffocating, clinging to the corners of every room. I could almost hear it, the soft rustle of the past pressing against the present, whispering its secrets through the cracks.

I turned from the window where I'd been staring at nothing in particular, lost in the movement of the trees outside. They swayed gently, indifferent to the chaos I felt brewing just beneath the surface of everything.

"You're distracted," his voice cut through the stillness.

I couldn't help but raise an eyebrow, trying to summon a playful tone even though my insides were in turmoil. "I'm not distracted. I'm just... contemplating the meaning of life."

He laughed softly, but there was a sharpness to it that didn't escape me. He knew something had shifted, and it was only a matter of time before it all came spilling out. His eyes met mine, steady, searching.

"I don't think I've ever seen you stare at trees for so long," he teased, his tone light, but his posture was too tense, the muscles in his arms flexing like they were ready to spring into action. Something was off.

"Maybe it's because I've got nothing else to look at." I wasn't sure if I was trying to convince him or myself. The truth was, my gaze kept straying to the shadows, to the spaces where I knew things were lurking—things we weren't talking about. Things he didn't want to talk about.

His lips twitched into a smile, but it didn't reach his eyes. "You always know how to make a joke, don't you?"

I wanted to laugh back, to shove the tension between us aside, but instead, I just nodded, my fingers gripping the edge of the countertop, the cool marble grounding me. But it didn't feel grounding—it felt cold, as if even the world had turned its back on us.

"I'm just trying to keep things normal," I said quietly, meeting his gaze. "It's hard to do that when you know something's... wrong."

His expression hardened, the lines of his face sharpening like the contours of a weapon. "You're letting your mind run wild again. It's not healthy."

I bristled at his words, even though I knew he meant them in the kindest way possible. He always did. But it felt like a dismissal, like everything I was feeling was just... irrational. A fleeting thought that could be dismissed with a soft smile and a change of subject.

"You think this is all in my head?" I asked, the question hanging in the air like smoke.

"No," he said quickly, his eyes flicking away, too fast, too guarded. "I think you're overthinking it. You always do. You always get lost in the details. It's not healthy."

I couldn't stop the laugh that bubbled up, dry and without humor. "Not healthy?" I repeated. "We're talking about something that happened. Something real. And I'm supposed to just pretend it's not there?"

He didn't answer right away, his eyes shifting uncomfortably as he turned away, looking out the same window I'd been staring at earlier. I could almost feel the tension in his muscles, the restraint, as if he were holding himself back from something, something he didn't want me to see.

"Maybe," he began slowly, "we just need to let things go."

Let things go. The words felt like a slap, and for a moment, I was paralyzed by their weight. Let things go. If I let things go, if I closed my eyes and pretended none of this ever happened, then what would we have left?

I felt my pulse quicken, the pressure of my thoughts pushing against my temples. No. I couldn't let it go. Not now, not when I could feel it closing in from all sides. I stepped forward, my voice quieter but no less insistent.

"You don't get it, do you? There are people who don't want this buried. They don't want it forgotten. And no matter how many walls you build around us, no matter how many times you tell me to 'let things go,' they're not going to stop. You're not the only one with a past, you know."

He turned to face me then, his eyes flashing with something—frustration, maybe, or fear. "I know that," he said, his voice low. "But you can't keep living like this. We can't live like this."

"And yet, here we are," I replied, my voice colder than I intended. "We're not living, we're surviving."

The silence stretched between us, thick and suffocating, until I felt like I might choke on it. I could feel the weight of everything I had yet to say pressing against my chest, threatening to spill out, but the words were trapped. Trapped between the fear of what they might unleash and the need to speak them.

I took a step back, my arms crossed defensively over my chest, unwilling to let the space between us collapse completely. "You don't get it. You don't understand what it's like to have your entire world torn apart, piece by piece, until nothing is left but questions and whispers."

"I'm trying," he said quietly, and there was something in his voice that stopped me. Something vulnerable, raw, a crack in the armor I hadn't expected. "But I can't fix everything. Not everything can be fixed."

"I don't need you to fix it," I said, my voice softer now. "I need you to see it. To understand what's happening. To see that we're not the only ones fighting to keep this—whatever this is—alive."

His jaw clenched, and for a moment, I thought he might say something else, something that would close the door between us once and for all. But instead, he just nodded, his expression unreadable. "I'm listening," he said. "But I need you to trust me. I need you to believe that we're not in this alone."

I shook my head, the weight of the past pressing down on me harder than ever. "Maybe that's the problem," I whispered. "Maybe we are."

The tension was like a string pulled taut between us, neither of us willing to be the first to let go. I could feel the heat of it in the air, the kind that burns, but it wasn't the kind of heat that promised resolution. No, it was the kind that left everything frayed, still hanging, waiting for something to snap. His gaze was locked on me, but there was a distance in his eyes that wasn't there before, as if the person I had spent these months with was slowly being erased, replaced by someone else.

I took another step back, instinctively putting more space between us. My fingers gripped the edge of the counter, knuckles white. "You think I'm paranoid. That I'm reading into things too much."

His silence, the way his eyes followed me without saying a word, made my pulse thrum in my throat. It wasn't disbelief, not exactly. It was more like he was waiting for the storm to pass, like it always did. He didn't understand. Maybe he never would.

"You don't know what it's like, do you?" I said, the words spilling out, cutting through the air with more force than I intended. "To be constantly watching your back, wondering if the peace you're finally starting to feel is just a trick. Wondering if the past is just waiting for the right moment to come crashing back into your life."

His jaw tightened, but he didn't respond, his lips pressing into a thin line. I didn't want to look at him anymore, didn't want to see that stoic mask he wore like armor. I needed something—anything—that told me I wasn't crazy, that my instincts weren't just a side effect of too many sleepless nights and too much time spent in my own head.

"You don't even care, do you?" I whispered, barely recognizing my own voice. It was sharp, raw. The anger came from somewhere deep inside, somewhere buried under the weight of too many unanswered questions. Too many things I couldn't shake off.

He was at my side in a second, too fast for me to process, his hand reaching out to steady me when I didn't even realize I was swaying. "I care," he said, his voice thick with something that could have been frustration, but also something else—something softer. "I care more than you know."

I swallowed hard, trying to blink away the lump in my throat. "Then why don't you understand that something is wrong?" I asked, my voice breaking despite myself. "Why don't you see what's happening?"

He stepped back, his fingers falling away from my arm, but the coldness between us was sharper now, like ice spreading under my skin. He didn't answer. Not right away, anyway. I could feel the weight of his gaze on me, but I didn't dare look up. I couldn't face him. Not when I knew that whatever this was, it was far from over.

"Maybe you're right," he said finally, his voice so quiet I almost didn't hear it. "Maybe something is wrong. But it's not just what you think. It's... more than that."

I froze, the air in my lungs refusing to move. "What are you talking about?"

His gaze flicked toward the door, like he was measuring the distance to freedom. I felt it then, a shift, a subtle change that made my skin crawl. There was something he wasn't telling me, something that had been hidden for far too long, buried under the same thick layer of silence that had been smothering us.

He took a deep breath, as if steeling himself for something, but his words still caught me off guard. "You're right about one thing. The past doesn't stay buried. It never does." He glanced back at me, his eyes searching mine, like he was looking for something—an answer, maybe, or a reason to explain away the tension that hung in the room. "But there's something you don't know. Something about that night. Something... important."

I shook my head, the confusion in my chest quickly turning to something else. "What are you saying? What happened that night? What are you hiding from me?"

For a moment, I thought he was going to walk away. He took a step back, his hand gripping the doorframe, his face an unreadable mask. "I never wanted you to find out," he said quietly, his voice carrying an edge I hadn't expected. "But now I think you're going to have to. For both of us."

I felt my heart stumble in my chest. "What does that mean? What do I have to find out?"

He was already halfway to the door when he turned back to look at me. The weight of his words hung between us, more suffocating than any silence could be. He opened the door just enough to step out, and for a brief moment, I thought I saw something flicker in his expression—something that looked like regret, but it was gone too quickly for me to decipher.

"I'll be back," he said simply, as though his absence was something I could prepare for, something I could handle. The words were light, but the weight they left in the room was anything but.

I didn't move. I didn't breathe. He was gone before I could say anything else, before I could ask the questions that were building in my chest, threatening to explode. The door clicked softly behind him, and I stood there, alone, feeling the ground shift beneath my feet.

The quiet in the house was deafening, a stark contrast to the noise inside my head, where the questions swirled faster than I could catch them. And the worst part? I knew deep down that I wouldn't have the answers I needed until it was far too late.

I turned toward the door, fighting the urge to follow, to demand more answers. But a sudden movement caught my eye—an envelope, half-hidden on the table where we'd sat earlier. My stomach twisted, cold fingers wrapping around my heart as I picked it up, the handwriting unmistakable.

I tore it open, the paper crinkling in my hands. My eyes scanned the note, my pulse racing with every word.

"You're not the only one looking for the truth."

Chapter 28: Dancing with Shadows

The smell of burnt wood lingered in the air, thick and acrid, curling around me like a specter. The room had the unmistakable silence of a place that had seen too much, its walls steeped in whispered confessions and half-remembered promises. I stood in the center of it, my hands still trembling from the encounter with the man who had walked out of the flames, a ghost from the past who could unravel everything I had come to believe.

His name was Isaac Malone. Tall, broad-shouldered, with a face that seemed to have been carved out of the very darkness he'd emerged from. His hair, a wild mess of black curls, framed eyes so piercing that they seemed to see through me, past all the layers I'd built. I had expected him to be a simple answer, a missing piece of the puzzle, but he wasn't that. Not even close. He was the whole damn box—complicated, fragile, full of twists I wasn't ready for.

The moment our eyes met, I knew it wasn't the first time he'd seen me. There was something in the way his lips tightened, a flicker of recognition—or was it contempt? I wasn't sure, but I knew then that I hadn't stumbled into this confrontation blindly. No, this was all deliberate, and the shiver that ran down my spine wasn't entirely from the cold draft that whispered through the cracked windows.

"So, you're the one who's been poking around," he said, his voice low, gravelly, like it had been ground down by years of secrets. "I didn't think anyone would care enough to ask the questions you're asking."

I swallowed, the tension between us thickening the air. My mind was racing, piecing together the story I thought I knew, but his presence twisted it, contorting it into something else. "What do you mean?" I asked, though I was certain I already knew the answer.

He stepped closer, his boots barely making a sound on the wooden floor. The soft creak beneath his weight was the only thing that kept the silence from smothering us completely. "You're digging for something, and I don't think you realize just how deep this hole goes," he said, his eyes narrowing. "Not everyone wants the truth to come out, and some of us aren't so eager to let it."

I took a step back, the back of my legs hitting the edge of the old desk. The movement was almost involuntary, the distance between us offering some small comfort, though it didn't feel like it. In his gaze, there was a strange pull—something magnetic, dark, and dangerous. He wasn't just a man of the past; he was a shadow that threatened to swallow the future I thought I was building.

"I'm not afraid of the truth," I replied, though even as the words left my mouth, I questioned whether that was still true. "I'm not afraid of you either."

He chuckled, low and guttural, the sound wrapping itself around me like a too-tight embrace. "You should be. You've no idea what you're getting into, sweetheart." His lips barely moved when he spoke, his words edged with something that could have been a threat—or an invitation.

It was maddening, the way he wove himself into the space between us, the way he made me second-guess everything I'd thought I knew. But I wasn't going to give in—not yet.

"What happened that night?" I asked, my voice steady despite the storm churning inside me. "Why was there a fire? Why did you leave?"

He didn't answer right away. Instead, his eyes flicked to the side, as if the walls themselves were listening. His lips parted, but instead of speaking, he seemed to inhale deeply, the air around us charged with something too heavy to ignore.

"You don't want to know," he muttered. "Not everything is meant to be uncovered, not if you want to keep breathing."

There it was again—the warning. It was as if I could hear it, echoing through the room, through the very fibers of my being. It was a rhythm, an undercurrent of threat that had followed me ever since I stepped into this mess. But the pull was stronger than the fear, stronger than the hesitation gnawing at my insides.

"I'm not scared of the past," I said, lifting my chin, even though my heart was slamming against my ribs. "I need to know what happened."

For a long moment, we just stared at each other, the space between us heavy with something that felt like inevitability. And then, just as quickly, the moment passed. Isaac stepped back, his hands lifting slightly, palms open in a gesture of surrender—or was it mockery?

"You'll regret it," he said, his voice losing the bite it had once held. "People like you don't survive when they go looking for things that were meant to stay buried."

I held his gaze, my pulse quickening, my chest tightening. "Then I guess I'll just have to prove you wrong."

His lips twisted into a smile that didn't reach his eyes. "Maybe. But remember, not everyone wants the truth to come to light. And not everyone gets to decide what happens next."

With that, he turned, disappearing into the shadows that clung to the edges of the room, leaving me with nothing but the faint echo of his warning. And as I stood there, my skin still humming from the exchange, I realized one thing—there was no turning back now. Not for me, not for anyone. The dance with shadows had begun.

The door creaked shut behind him with a finality that rattled my bones, but I couldn't let the echoes of his words settle inside me. They were dangerous, like a long-forgotten key trying to unlock something better left untouched. I was used to the sting of secrets, the tension of hidden truths, but this felt different. Isaac wasn't just a player in the game. He was the one who had set the board, and now I was tangled in the threads of his design.

The room was cold in his absence, the heat from the old furnace cutting off with a soft thud as if it, too, had realized there was no comfort to be found here. I looked around, my gaze falling on the cluttered desk, the scattered papers, and the burnt edges of the worn chair. It all seemed so... insignificant now. The files I'd thought might hold the answers didn't seem to matter, not when the man who could give them to me was standing in the shadows, waiting for me to make a mistake.

I ran my fingers over the surface of the desk, letting the wood grain ground me. The cool, steady texture did little to calm the storm in my chest. What had I walked into? More importantly, what was I prepared to do with what I found?

The only sound in the room was my own breathing, deep and deliberate, as if I could force my thoughts into alignment if I could just concentrate long enough. I had come here with purpose. I couldn't let fear take that away. I'd promised myself I wouldn't back down, no matter how high the stakes got. But with Isaac's warning hanging in the air like smoke, I felt the first whisper of doubt.

I should've been smarter. I should've known that some things weren't meant to be uncovered. But here I was, standing at the edge of a precipice, my fingers itching to push further. The question now was how far I would go.

A knock at the door interrupted my thoughts, sharp and quick, followed by the unmistakable sound of someone entering without waiting for permission.

"Didn't think you'd be here long," a voice said, smooth and insistent, with the unmistakable edge of someone used to getting what they wanted.

I turned to find James standing in the doorway, his suit sharp and crisp, his face unreadable, as always. His gaze swept over me with the practiced ease of someone who had made it his business to observe, to know.

"I didn't take you for the type to enjoy long, drawn-out visits," he added, his smile polite but edged with something darker.

I raised an eyebrow, resisting the urge to sigh. Of course, he would show up now. "I'm not here for pleasantries," I said, my voice firm, not entirely steady, but close enough. "What do you want?"

James leaned against the doorframe, his arms folded in a casual but deliberate manner. "Is that how we're going to play this?" he asked, a small, amused smirk dancing at the corner of his mouth. "You could at least pretend to be glad to see me."

I wasn't sure if it was the way he stood there, like he owned the room, or the way his gaze seemed to track every movement I made, but something about him made the hairs on the back of my neck prickle. I wasn't here to play games, not anymore.

"I'm not interested in pleasantries, James," I repeated, meeting his eyes with an unwavering determination that I didn't entirely feel. "I'm looking for answers. I need to know what happened that night. I need you to tell me."

The smile slipped from his face, replaced by a flicker of something I couldn't quite place. It was the briefest of moments, but it was enough to make my pulse spike. James didn't do vulnerability, didn't allow himself to be caught off guard. But there it was, something slipping through the cracks, revealing just a sliver of the man behind the façade.

"You're still chasing shadows, aren't you?" he said, his voice suddenly softer, tinged with something I couldn't identify. "What's it going to take to make you stop?"

"Nothing," I replied, the word firm on my tongue. "I can't stop now. Not when I'm so close."

James let out a long breath, his shoulders shifting slightly, as though he was deciding something. When he spoke again, his voice was lower, almost reluctant. "You think you know what happened, but you don't. You're walking down a path that's been paved with lies. It's not going to lead you where you think it will."

"I don't care where it leads," I said, my voice sharp, more confident than I felt. "I need the truth. It's the only thing I can hold on to right now."

There was a long pause, and for a moment, it felt as if the room itself was holding its breath. Then, without warning, James took a step forward, his presence filling the space between us. The air seemed to crackle with something unspoken. He was close now, close enough that I could feel the heat radiating off of him, his breath steady and controlled.

"You really think you're prepared for this?" he asked, his voice barely above a whisper, though there was a rawness to it that made my pulse race. "Once you open this door, there's no going back. You can't unlearn what you're about to discover."

His words hung in the air like a challenge, a dare. And for a moment, I found myself wondering what would happen if I stepped back. What if I did walk away now, turned my back on this madness? But the thought was fleeting. There was too much at stake. Too many people who needed answers. Too many lives tethered to this lie.

"I'm already too far in," I said, the words coming out more sharply than I intended. "There's no turning back now."

James didn't respond immediately. Instead, he studied me for a long, tense moment, his eyes searching mine as if looking for something, some hint of doubt or fear. But there was nothing.

Finally, he spoke, his voice steady and quiet. "Then brace yourself. You have no idea what you're about to walk into."

And with that, he turned, leaving me standing alone, once again at the edge of the unknown.

The silence that followed James' departure was the kind that pressed against your chest, thick and suffocating. I stood there for a long moment, staring at the door he'd just left through, the echo of his words still reverberating in my mind. "You have no idea what you're about to walk into." The warning seemed so simple, so direct—but it felt like more than just a caution. It felt like a threat wrapped in concern, a warning disguised as a plea. And something about it gnawed at me, tightening my stomach, urging me to pause, to reconsider.

But I couldn't. Not now.

I moved, my feet heavy on the wooden floor as I headed toward the file cabinet in the corner of the room. There was a drawer I hadn't yet touched, a place I'd avoided, instinctively knowing that if I opened it, I'd find something that might change everything. But I wasn't in the mood for instinct anymore. I was done walking around the edges, skirting the truth like a scared child. It was time to face whatever was waiting for me at the bottom of this particular rabbit hole.

The drawer opened with a soft protest, and I slid the folder out, its edges frayed, the paper inside yellowed and brittle. I hesitated before flipping it open, the weight of what might be inside pressing against my ribs. The first sheet was a list of names—names I recognized from the fire. People who had vanished into the smoke, or so I'd been told. But there, at the bottom of the page, was something new. A note, scrawled hastily in black ink: He didn't die that night. Neither did she.

My hand shook as I read the words again, trying to make sense of them, trying to find a way to reconcile what I was seeing with everything I thought I knew. I reached for the next page, but a sudden noise from behind me froze my movements—a soft thud, the kind of sound you hear when someone's trying to be quiet, but failing miserably.

I didn't turn immediately. I didn't need to. I could already tell who it was, the tension in the air giving him away before the faint scent of leather reached my nose.

"Do you always snoop around in other people's things, or is this just a new hobby of yours?" Isaac's voice came from the doorway, low and smooth, the kind of voice that slid beneath your skin like velvet and made your heart skip a beat.

I didn't move, not even an inch. "What do you want?"

There was a pause, then the sound of his boots scraping against the floor as he crossed the room. "You were never good at letting things go," he said, his tone almost wistful. "Don't you ever get tired of digging? Of poking around in things that don't concern you?"

"Maybe I don't get tired of it because it does concern me." My voice was steady, though there was a part of me, the small part I kept buried under layers of bravado, that was waiting for him to tear me apart. "This isn't just about you anymore. This is about what happened that night. It's about the truth."

I could hear him move closer, could almost feel the heat of his presence as it curled around me like smoke. He was standing right behind me now, close enough that I could hear his breath, shallow and measured, just like mine.

"You don't know what you're asking for," he said, his voice dropping lower. "Some things are better left buried, trust me."

I closed the folder and slid it back into the drawer with a swift, decisive motion. "I don't trust you," I said quietly, standing up and turning to face him. "And I don't trust anyone who tells me to stop looking. What happened to her, Isaac? What happened to him? What's the truth?"

For the first time since I'd met him, Isaac seemed to hesitate. His gaze dropped to the floor, and I watched his jaw tighten, the muscle working beneath his skin. He was a man built on secrets, a man who had learned to bury his emotions deep beneath the surface. But for just a moment, a crack appeared—a brief flicker of vulnerability that disappeared as quickly as it had come.

"You think you're ready to hear it?" he asked, his voice low, almost dangerous.

"I don't think," I replied, stepping closer, my resolve hardening with each step. "I know I am."

Isaac's eyes met mine then, and for a heartbeat, the room seemed to shrink, the space between us charged with something I couldn't quite define. It wasn't just the past we were dancing around anymore—it was something else. Something darker. He had an answer, and he wasn't ready to give it to me.

"You don't get to choose when the truth comes out," he said, his voice tight. "And you sure as hell don't get to decide who gets to hear it."

I opened my mouth to respond, to tell him that I didn't care about his rules anymore, but before I could speak, the door slammed open with a force that made the walls shake. Both of us turned, startled, and I immediately knew something was wrong. The air in the room shifted, the tension breaking as my gaze flicked to the man standing in the doorway.

It was James.

But this time, his expression wasn't the usual unreadable mask. It was something far worse—something like fear.

"You need to leave," James said, his voice sharp, almost frantic. "Now. Both of you."

I took a step toward him, confusion blooming in my chest. "What's going on?"

James didn't answer, his eyes flicking between me and Isaac, and then, without another word, he turned and disappeared into the hall, his footsteps rapid and urgent.

Isaac didn't move, didn't speak. But the look on his face was enough to make my heart skip a beat. Something had changed. And whatever it was, it was bigger than all of us.

I didn't hesitate. I grabbed my coat and followed James into the hallway, my pulse pounding in my ears, wondering just how deep this rabbit hole went—and what would be waiting for me at the bottom.

Chapter 29: The Edge of the Flame

The late afternoon sun filtered through the blinds in a faint golden haze, casting long shadows across the room. My fingers lingered on the rim of my coffee cup, the warmth seeping into my skin, grounding me to the mundane world I was desperately clinging to. But nothing in this world, nothing as simple as a hot cup of coffee, could keep me tethered now. Not with him in the room.

His presence was like a storm gathering on the horizon. Unseen yet felt, it wrapped itself around me, leaving no escape. I had learned to read him like the back of my hand, yet there were corners of his soul that remained stubbornly concealed, places where the shadows crept in and refused to be banished.

"Just let it go," he said, voice low, carefully measured, as if the very words might break apart at the seams if he pushed too hard.

I set the cup down with deliberate slowness, my gaze never wavering from his. "You're asking me to pretend nothing's wrong, aren't you? After everything? I know you're not the type to back down from a fight. So why are you acting like this is some minor inconvenience I should ignore?"

He stiffened, the muscles in his jaw clenching as if his teeth were the only things keeping him from shattering. I had always wondered what would happen if I pushed hard enough—if I dug deep enough to uncover the jagged edges of the man who stood before me, constantly shifting under the weight of a past I could never fully understand. The threat of that past loomed like a shadow, darkening everything between us.

"Because it's not your fight," he finally said, the words coming out with a weight that felt like a confession. "You don't need to be dragged into this."

I leaned forward, crossing my arms, defiant. "Don't you dare try to protect me. Don't even think about it. I've lived through worse than anything you could ever imagine, and I'm not about to start running now. Not because of some stranger with a grudge."

His eyes, once so confident and unyielding, flickered. There was something raw there, a vulnerability that made the hairs on my neck rise. It was a look I hadn't seen from him before—one that suggested not danger, but a terror so deep, it shook him to his core.

"You think I'm doing this to protect myself?" His voice dropped, a jagged edge to it that made my stomach twist. "No. I'm keeping secrets to protect you. To keep you from seeing the things that—" He broke off, his fingers curling into fists at his sides. "To keep you from knowing the truth."

I shook my head, disbelief washing over me in waves. "The truth? What truth? You've been lying to me this whole time, haven't you? About everything."

He looked at me then, really looked at me, as if searching for something in my face that would give him the courage to go on. But there was no turning back now. The dam had broken. The floodgates had been opened, and no amount of pretending could shove it all back inside.

He exhaled sharply, his shoulders slumping just slightly. "It's not about lies. It's about the things that happened before you—before us. Things that are... better left forgotten. If you knew everything, you wouldn't want to be near me. And I can't lose you. I won't lose you."

His words hit me like a cold wave. The silence that followed was thick with the unsaid, a million unspoken stories swirling between us. There was a heaviness to the air, an ache I could almost feel in my bones. I could see the war inside him, the battle raging between the man he was and the man he feared he had become. I wanted to ask more, to demand the truth, but something stopped me. A fleeting thought, like a whisper in my ear, told me that maybe I wasn't ready for what I might uncover.

"But I deserve to know," I finally said, my voice barely more than a whisper. "If we're going to have any chance at this... at us, I need to know who you really are. I can't keep living in the dark."

He didn't answer right away. Instead, he ran a hand through his hair, the action so familiar, so casual, that it almost felt like the calm before the storm. I could see his mind working, fighting with itself, wrestling with the decision of how much to reveal. Finally, he spoke, his words measured and slow, as if he were testing each one before it passed his lips.

"The truth is," he began, his eyes not quite meeting mine, "once you know everything, once you see what's been hidden, there's no going back. You won't be able to look at me the same way again. And I can't bear the thought of losing you. Not because of something I did, but because of who I was."

I felt the air shift between us, thick with the weight of his confession. "You think I can't handle it?" I said, my voice sharpening now, an edge of steel creeping in. "You think I'm too fragile to face whatever it is that's lurking in your past? I'm not afraid of your past. I'm afraid of the future—the one where you keep shutting me out. The one where you keep lying to me. That's what scares me."

He opened his mouth to respond, but the words never came. Instead, he closed his eyes, as if trying to block me out entirely, like the truth itself might burn him if he dared to speak it. But we both knew that the silence between us was only temporary. And when he finally did speak, I knew the truth would change everything.

The silence hung heavy between us, the kind of silence that presses against your chest, makes it harder to breathe, harder to think. He wasn't looking at me anymore. His gaze was fixed on the floor, his jaw clenched tight enough to crack. I could almost hear the grind of his teeth, the way the tension hummed in his muscles, trying to hold something back that wanted to break free.

I didn't know whether to push further or let him retreat into whatever dark corner he'd been hiding in. He was acting like the man before me wasn't the one I'd known, the one who cracked jokes on lazy mornings, who made me laugh so hard I forgot what day it was. He was acting like the man before me wasn't the one who made my heart skip with a touch, who whispered secrets in the dead of night when it was just the two of us. But whatever else he'd been, whatever stories and shadows had followed him here, they were still his to keep—if he insisted on keeping them.

I crossed the room, slow steps measured, like I was walking on fragile ground that might crack at any moment. My fingers brushed the edge of the counter, the cool granite against my skin almost soothing as I fought the urge to pull him back from whatever cliff he was teetering on. I wanted to wrap my arms around him, tell him that it didn't matter. That whatever past he was hiding could stay buried, that I could still love him, no matter what. But something in the way his shoulders were hunched, in the tightness of his lips, told me that wasn't the answer he needed.

"You don't get to decide what's best for me," I said, quieter now, trying to find my footing in this shifting world between us. "You don't get to protect me by keeping secrets. I've been in the dark enough. I don't want to stay there."

He looked up then, eyes meeting mine, but they weren't the eyes of the man I thought I knew. They were darker, haunted. "You don't understand. If you knew—" His voice broke, just a little, and the weight of his vulnerability hit me harder than I was ready for. "I can't let you walk into this. You won't come back out the same. And I won't be able to live with that."

The words hung in the air like a promise, an impossible truth that neither of us could escape. His fear, raw and unfiltered, twisted something deep inside me. This was no longer just about the threats hanging over us. This was about him—about his past, the ghosts that were clawing at his heels, threatening to drag him down if he let them. But it wasn't just his past anymore. It was mine, too. Because if I was going to keep walking this path with him, if I was going to keep loving him, then his shadows would become mine, and I couldn't pretend I wasn't already tangled in their pull.

"I'm already here, aren't I?" I said, my voice catching. "I'm already in this, with you. You're not the only one who has something to lose."

His eyes softened, just for a moment, and I felt it—a crack in his armor. But then it was gone, sealed tight again, as if nothing had ever shifted. "You don't know what you're asking for."

"Maybe not," I admitted, taking a step closer. "But I know what it feels like to hide, to bury things so deep you think they'll never come back. And I'm not running from it anymore. Not now. Not with you."

He stepped back, his hand brushing against the doorframe like he needed the solid support of it, something to hold him up when the ground beneath us felt like it was caving in. "You don't get it," he muttered, his voice low, barely audible. "Once you know... once you see it, there's no going back. You'll never look at me the same way again."

I shook my head, my own heart thumping hard in my chest. "You're right. I might not look at you the same way again. But it won't be because of your past. It'll be because you decided to push me away. To keep me in the dark."

He didn't answer immediately, just stood there, his eyes clouded with regret and something else. Maybe fear, maybe anger. But beneath all of it, there was something more—a longing, a desperation to break free of whatever chains had kept him bound for so long.

And then, for the first time in days, he smiled. It was brief, like a flicker of light in a dark room, but it was there—small and uncertain, yet still enough to make my heart stumble.

"You really think you can handle it?" he asked, his voice a mixture of disbelief and something else I couldn't quite place.

I met his gaze steadily, letting him see everything in my eyes. The truth. The fear. The love. "I'm not afraid of you," I said, letting the words sink into the space between us, each one heavier than the last. "But I am afraid of losing you. So, whatever this is, whatever you're hiding, it's ours now. You can't keep me out. Not anymore."

He was quiet for a long moment, the silence stretching until it felt like it might snap. I watched the battle unfold across his face, the conflict between the man who wanted to protect me and the one who feared what would happen if I truly knew him.

"You really want this?" he asked, his voice barely a whisper, like he was afraid the words might break something fragile if they came too loud.

"I want you," I replied, the answer so simple, so absolute that it left no room for doubt. "And I want to know you. All of you."

For a moment, it felt like the world held its breath, waiting for something to shift. And then it did—slowly, painfully—like the first crack in an old foundation, threatening to tear everything apart. But I wasn't afraid. Not anymore. Because this was the truth. The kind of truth that could shatter everything, but also the kind that could rebuild us from the ground up. And I was ready.

He looked at me then, his eyes intense, burning with a mixture of something I couldn't quite place—guilt, perhaps, or regret—and yet, there was something else there. Something desperate. The muscles in his neck tightened as he swallowed, his throat moving in a slow, deliberate motion. His hands, which had been clenched at his sides for what seemed like an eternity, now flexed, as if he were fighting the urge to reach out to me, to pull me into the quiet chaos that lived between us.

"Once you know, it changes everything," he repeated, almost pleading. His voice was raw, like it had been dragged through too many sleepless nights. "There's no going back from that. You can't unknow something like this, and I can't lose you. Not because of me."

I took a steadying breath, feeling the weight of the room press down on me. My pulse quickened, and for a second, I wondered if I'd bitten off more than I could chew. Maybe I hadn't been ready for this, for what was waiting on the other side of that door he'd been keeping shut for so long. But I couldn't walk away. I wasn't that person anymore.

"Then show me," I said, my voice steady, but my heart hammering in my chest. "You want me to understand? Then show me the truth. Don't keep me locked out."

His eyes darted to the window, to the sliver of sky beyond the glass, as if he could somehow escape through it. For a moment, he didn't move, didn't speak, and the silence was unbearable. But I held my ground. I couldn't look away. I couldn't look at anything else.

Finally, he exhaled, a sharp, ragged breath, and turned toward me. His gaze softened, and I saw it then—the exhaustion in his eyes, the kind of tiredness that ran so deep it lived in the very marrow of his bones. The kind of tiredness that came from fighting battles no one else could see, from carrying burdens that weren't his to bear.

"I wasn't always... this," he said, the words coming slowly, like he was pulling them from some dark, tangled place in his past. "I wasn't always the man you think I am."

I nodded, keeping my expression open, though inside, a storm was building. I had always known there were pieces of him I couldn't reach, parts of his soul that stayed tucked away, hidden behind walls he'd put up long before I ever came into his life. But now, I had to wonder—what kind of man had he been before? What had he done? What was so awful that he couldn't share it with me?

"It's not what you think," he added quickly, almost as if sensing the questions spiraling through my mind. "I didn't hurt anyone. Not in the way you're thinking. But there are... things. Things that are better left buried."

I shook my head, the anger bubbling up inside me. "You don't get to tell me what's better left buried, and you certainly don't get to decide what I can or can't handle. You've been making choices for both of us for too long. You want to protect me from what? The truth? That's not your decision to make."

He stepped back, his jaw working as though he were biting down on something sharp, and I could see the shift in him. The battle inside him had reached a boiling point, and I wasn't sure which side was going to win.

"I never wanted this for you," he said quietly, his voice barely a whisper, but the words felt like a punch. "I never wanted to pull you into this world. But it's not that easy. You can't just—"

But before he could finish, a loud banging noise from the hallway cut him off, sharp and insistent, like a hammer striking metal. Both of us froze. My heart skipped a beat, and the air suddenly felt thick, charged with a kind of electricity that made the hairs on my arms stand on end. He looked at me with wide eyes, his pupils dilating in shock and fear.

Before I could say a word, the door slammed open, and in stepped the last person I ever expected to see. A man. Tall, dark-haired, and wearing a leather jacket that looked like it had seen too many rough nights. His expression was unreadable, but his eyes—his eyes were cold, cold in a way that sent a shiver down my spine.

"Well, well, well," the man said, his voice smooth but edged with a threat. "I always wondered when you'd let her in, but I didn't expect it to be this soon."

I took an instinctual step backward, the adrenaline rushing through me. My pulse roared in my ears as my mind scrambled to make sense of the sudden intrusion. Who was this? And why did his words sound like a promise?

The man's gaze flicked over to me, taking me in like I was something to be examined, something to be judged. Then, without even acknowledging me further, he turned his attention to the man beside me, his expression hardening.

"You really think you can keep this from me?" he sneered, his lips curling with disdain. "You think you can protect her from the truth?" He glanced at me again, a sly, knowing look crossing his face. "You should have let her stay out of this. But now? Now, you've made it personal."

The words hit like a punch to the gut, leaving me breathless, confused, and suddenly, deeply afraid. My stomach churned, and I glanced at the man beside me, seeing the way his face had gone pale, his fists clenched again, his body tense.

I opened my mouth to say something, anything, but my voice faltered. I had no idea who this man was or what he was talking about, but the fear in the air was palpable. This wasn't just a random interruption. This was the beginning of something far more dangerous.

And as the man stepped further into the room, closing the door behind him with a chilling finality, I knew that nothing—nothing—would ever be the same again.

Chapter 30: A Scorching Revelation

I sat in the dim light of the living room, the silence pressing in around me like a heavy blanket. My fingers trembled as I turned the pages, eyes scanning the documents in front of me with a growing sense of dread. The air felt charged, thick with something dangerous, like the quiet before a storm, when you can feel the world tipping on the edge of something terrible. And then, there it was. The proof.

It was an old newspaper clipping, faded at the edges but clear enough to leave no room for doubt. The headline screamed of a tragedy—a fire that had ravaged a small town, leaving nothing but ashes in its wake. The flames had consumed everything, including lives, leaving families shattered and communities forever scarred. I knew the story well; it had haunted the region for years, whispered about in hushed tones whenever someone dared speak of it. But what I hadn't known until now was the connection—the man I had come to trust, the one I had allowed myself to care for, was tangled in it, his name etched into the very fabric of the tragedy.

My stomach twisted painfully, a sickening realization creeping up my spine. There was no denying it now. The fire that had haunted my nightmares for years—the one that had stolen everything from so many—was no accident. And he... He wasn't just a witness. He had been there, involved in a way I couldn't yet comprehend. But it wasn't just the past that sent a chill down my spine. It was the undeniable truth that the man I thought I knew—thought I understood—was still hiding something from me. A part of him, a dark, suffocating part, had been lurking in the shadows all along, manipulating everything in his life with a precision that left me breathless.

I set the papers down, my mind whirling as I tried to process the weight of what I had just uncovered. He had known, had always known, that I would find out. The game he had been playing, the charming, mysterious man who had swept me off my feet, had all been part of his plan. Every glance, every touch, every carefully crafted moment, was calculated. And what's worse, I had fallen for it—had fallen for him.

But why? Why now? What had made him feel like this was the right time to let the truth slip out, to let me see the man beneath the facade? Was this his way of testing me? Seeing if I would stand by him even when the truth of his actions came to light? Or was it something darker—something more insidious that he knew I would never be able to untangle on my own?

I paced the room, the soft creak of the floorboards beneath my feet the only sound in the stillness. The weight of the decision I now faced felt like a thousand-pound anchor dragging me down into the depths of uncertainty. Should I confront him? Should I demand answers, knowing full well that the truth might shatter everything between us? Or should I keep silent, bury it deep, and pretend like I hadn't seen what I had? The thought of keeping quiet gnawed at me, a bitter taste in the back of my throat, but the idea of exposing him—of unraveling everything he had so carefully built—felt like a betrayal of my own heart.

I ran my fingers through my hair, frustration mounting. I didn't know what to do. The truth was a double-edged sword. If I confronted him, I would have to face the consequences of that knowledge. I would have to live with the reality that I had once loved a man capable of such deception, of such manipulation. And if I kept it to myself, I would always wonder whether I was complicit in his lies, whether my silence made me as guilty as he was.

But the worst part wasn't the fear of what might happen if I exposed him—it was the fear that maybe, just maybe, I was beginning to understand him. That the man I had come to know, the man I had believed in, was a victim in all of this too. His hands were tied, bound by a past he couldn't escape, a past that had shaped every decision he made. I had never once considered that maybe he wasn't the mastermind behind his own life, but rather a puppet, controlled by strings he couldn't sever.

It was then that I remembered the small details, the subtle inconsistencies in his stories, the way he'd look away just a moment too long when asked about certain things. The pieces of the puzzle had always been there, scattered in plain sight, but I had never put them together. He had been hiding behind lies, behind half-truths, all to protect something—or someone—he was terrified to expose. But what if, in his own twisted way, he was trying to protect me too? What if everything he had done, every step he had taken, was a calculated effort to keep me out of harm's way, to keep me from the very truth that could destroy us both?

The more I thought about it, the more I realized the full scope of what he had done. He wasn't just connected to the fire; he had been running from it his entire life. And now, it seemed, he was trying to drag me into the ashes with him.

The question burned in my mind: Should I stand by him, or should I run? Was it even possible to escape once you'd discovered the truth? And if I stayed, what would it mean for me, for us, for the life I had dreamed of building? Was I strong enough to face the storm ahead, or would it sweep me away, leaving nothing but ruin in its wake?

As the first hint of dawn crept through the curtains, casting a faint glow over the room, I made my decision. But the consequences of it, I realized, would haunt me forever.

I didn't know how much time had passed. The hands of the clock in the corner had become nothing more than a blur as I paced the room, every step echoing in the silence that felt heavier with each passing second. My fingers were still trembling, and though I could hear my own breath in the thick quiet, the question swirled around me, relentless and insistent: Why hadn't he told me?

The longer I thought about it, the more it gnawed at me, like a wound that refused to heal. How many moments had he spent lying to me, wrapping his lies in a disguise so carefully crafted, I had never once thought to question them? He had built his life on secrets, on the quiet manipulation of everything and everyone around him, including me. Was I just another piece of the puzzle? Another pawn in his game? The thought twisted my stomach, and I stopped pacing, standing still in the center of the room like a statue caught in the middle of an unfinished dance.

A voice inside me screamed that I had to confront him. I couldn't live in this kind of limbo, with half-truths hanging in the air like an unspoken threat. I wanted to scream, wanted to throw everything in his face and demand the answers that were now so painfully out of reach. But there was something else—a voice, much quieter, urging me to tread carefully, to think before I acted.

Maybe it wasn't just the lies I was angry about. Maybe it was the betrayal of everything I had believed in. Because it wasn't just his secrets that hurt; it was the fact that I had allowed myself to get so close to him, to trust him, without ever knowing the truth. In my mind, I had painted a picture of a man who had lived through his demons, who was simply trying to outrun his past. But I had been wrong. So wrong. His past hadn't just been something he was running from. It had been something he was still controlling, pulling the strings of his life like a marionette, and I had been blind to it.

The house felt colder now, the chill creeping under my skin, making every step heavier than the last. But as much as I wanted to hate him for what I had discovered, there was still a part of me that hesitated. A part of me that remembered the way his hand had felt in mine, the way his eyes softened when he looked at me, like I was something worth saving. How could someone who had orchestrated so much destruction also make me feel so safe, so seen? How could the same man who was tangled in a web of lies also look at me with such honesty, as if I were the only thing that mattered?

I shook my head, willing myself to stop thinking in circles. I couldn't afford to get lost in him—not anymore. Not when I was standing on the edge of a truth that could unravel everything.

I moved toward the door, almost as though my body had made the decision for me. I had to see him. I had to hear it from his own lips, no matter how much it hurt. I had to know if everything I thought I knew had been a lie, or if there was some shred of truth left in him that wasn't tainted by the past he could never escape.

The night air hit me like a cold slap as I stepped outside. The city felt too quiet, the streetlights casting long shadows on the pavement, the air heavy with a kind of tension I could feel in my bones. My steps were purposeful now, and yet my heart seemed to race in the opposite direction, tugging me back, telling me to turn around, to forget what I had learned. But I couldn't. Not when the weight of the truth was so suffocating.

His place wasn't far, but with every step, I felt like I was walking toward something I couldn't undo. I had no idea what I would find when I got there, no idea how I would react when I finally stood face to face with him. But I couldn't turn back now. Not after what I knew.

When I reached his door, my breath caught in my throat. The soft hum of the city around me seemed to fade into nothingness, leaving only the sound of my pulse in my ears. My hand hovered over the doorbell for a moment, my mind racing with a thousand different scenarios, each one worse than the last. But I pressed it anyway.

He opened the door so quickly, I almost didn't have time to react. His eyes were dark, tired, and for a moment, I thought I saw something in them—something like regret, or maybe even fear. But before I could say anything, before I could demand the truth from him, he stepped back, his gaze flickering over my shoulder as if waiting for something.

I pushed past him, my voice cold and sharp. "We need to talk."

He closed the door behind me, his gaze never leaving mine. "About what?"

"About the fire," I said, and the words felt like lead in my mouth, as though saying them aloud might somehow make everything real.

His face didn't change, but there was a tension in his posture, something that told me he knew exactly where this was headed. He didn't try to deny it, didn't try to run from the truth. He just stood there, watching me, as if he knew I was about to tear everything apart with a single sentence.

"I know everything," I said, my voice trembling, though I tried to keep it steady. "I know what you've been hiding. I know what you did."

His expression shifted then, just slightly, like a crack in a façade that had held for years. But he didn't speak, didn't try to explain. He just waited, his silence pressing in around me, daring me to continue.

"Tell me why," I whispered, my heart in my throat. "Why didn't you tell me the truth?"

His lips parted, but the words that came out weren't what I expected. "Because the truth wasn't mine to tell."

His words hung in the air, thick with something I couldn't quite grasp. "The truth wasn't mine to tell."

I wanted to scoff, to laugh in disbelief, but the weight of his gaze held me in place, pinning me to the spot like a moth caught in a web. It was a ridiculous statement, one that defied everything I thought I knew. But as I looked at him, the lines of his face softer than I had ever seen them, I realized that something deeper, something more complicated was unfolding right in front of me.

"Then whose truth was it?" My voice was sharp, a flicker of anger dancing in the corners of my words. "If you're not responsible for it, who the hell is?"

His gaze shifted, flickering momentarily to the side, like he was grappling with something just below the surface. The man I had thought I knew so well—the one who had smiled in my direction, shared intimate details of his life, made me feel like I was the only thing in the world that mattered—was now standing there, completely foreign to me. I had spent so long trying to fit him into a box that made sense, a box that told me he was good, or at least trying to be. But now, the edges of the box were crumbling away, revealing something dark and unnameable beneath.

"You don't understand," he finally said, his voice quieter now, the sharpness gone. "You think this is about me, about what I've done. But it's not. I'm just the messenger. The one who had no choice but to play the part I was given." His voice wavered for the briefest of moments before he cleared his throat, a hollow sound. "If I had told you, if I had tried to explain, you would have never believed me. You would have turned away. And maybe you're right to do that."

I shook my head, frustration welling up in my chest. "So this is it? You're just going to keep me in the dark forever? Let me believe that the worst possible version of you is true?"

"I never wanted that," he whispered, taking a slow step toward me, his eyes pleading for understanding I wasn't sure I could give. "You think I've been lying to you, but the truth I carry isn't just about me. It's about everyone. And if I told you, it would cost you everything. It would destroy everything."

The words hit me like a slap, cold and sharp. I stepped back instinctively, as if to distance myself from the weight of what he was saying. Destroy everything? What did that mean? Was he talking about us? Or was there something bigger at play, something much darker, pulling the strings of his every move?

"What do you mean by 'destroy everything'? What the hell are you involved in?" My voice trembled, the edges fraying as my heart began to race, the fear creeping up from the pit of my stomach to my throat.

He took another step closer, but I held up my hand, a silent plea for him to stop. I didn't know if I could hear more—if I could process it. The entire room seemed to tilt, everything around me spinning like a carousel I couldn't stop. But he didn't retreat. He stayed there, in front of me, as if rooted in place by something far stronger than my resolve.

"I never wanted this for you," he said, his voice breaking. "But I've made choices, bad choices. Choices that weren't just mine to make. And now, those choices are coming for us. I never wanted you to be part of it. But you've already been pulled in." He swallowed, his throat working, like he was struggling to breathe.

I stared at him, the anger slowly draining away, replaced by something deeper, darker—something colder. What was he saying? What had he done? And why had he let me get so close to the edge of the abyss without ever warning me?

"Pulled in? Pulled in by what?" I demanded, each word weighted with more disbelief than the last. "What the hell are you hiding?"

He didn't answer immediately, but the way his jaw clenched told me more than words ever could. He was terrified, genuinely terrified, of whatever was coming next. And the fact that I was standing here, trying to understand it, made me feel like a fool. I should have walked away the moment I found those papers, the moment I uncovered the lie. But instead, I stood there, frozen, waiting for him to tell me something that would make sense of the mess he had created.

Finally, he spoke, his words slow and measured. "There are people who would do anything to keep the truth buried. People who—" He stopped himself, the words catching in his throat. His face twisted, like the very thought of it made him sick. "If you want to walk away from me now, you can. But you won't be safe, not from this. You'll never be safe."

"From what?" I almost whispered, my voice barely a breath, but he didn't answer.

Instead, he reached into his pocket, pulling out something small—something shiny. It caught the dim light from the hallway, a glint of silver. He dropped it into my hand, and I stared at the small object, trying to make sense of it. It was a key. A simple, unassuming key. But the weight of it felt too heavy, too significant.

"What is this?" I asked, my voice faltering as I looked up at him. "What am I supposed to do with this?"

He didn't answer immediately. Instead, he turned away from me, his shoulders sagging like a man who had carried the weight of the world for too long. He didn't look back as he spoke, his words barely above a whisper. "If you want the truth, you'll find it there."

And with that, he walked out of the room, leaving me standing in the middle of the floor, staring down at the key in my hand.

The silence that followed felt oppressive, suffocating. My heart hammered in my chest, and the question that burned in my mind was no longer just about him, about what he had done. It was about what was waiting for me at the end of that key. What did it unlock? And why was I so sure that finding the answer would change everything?

Before I could think about it any further, the sound of a car screeching to a halt outside caught my attention. My blood ran cold as the front door slammed open behind me.

Chapter 31: Hearts Ablaze

The moment the door clicked behind me, I knew there was no turning back. The weight of the words I was about to speak settled in my chest like a stone. My breath felt shallow, but there was no room for hesitation. Not anymore.

"There's something you need to know," I said, my voice betraying none of the anxiety that twisted like a knot inside me. He looked up from the papers scattered across the desk, his brows knitting in that way they always did when he sensed something was off. His dark eyes were sharp, intense, always searching, as though he could read me in a way no one else could.

I watched him carefully as I continued. "I've learned something—something that changes everything. And I can't keep it from you any longer." The words sounded foreign on my tongue, as if they belonged to someone else.

He didn't move, didn't speak, just studied me with that familiar gaze. The clock ticking behind him was the loudest thing in the room. It seemed to echo through the silence, each second dragging like the slow creep of dawn, too drawn out, too painful.

"Whatever it is, you can tell me." His voice was steady, but there was an edge to it—something sharp that made my pulse quicken. He leaned forward, his hands clasped together, resting on the desk. He always had this way of looking at me that felt like he could see through my soul. But I wasn't ready for what his eyes might uncover now.

I swallowed, feeling the words burn their way to the surface. "It's about your brother."

At the mention of his name, I saw the briefest flicker of something dark pass across his face. His jaw tightened, the muscles in his neck shifting, and for a split second, I wondered if I had made a mistake. His brother—always a sore subject. A ghost that lingered in the corners of every room they shared, every conversation they had.

"Why would you—" His voice broke, the question hanging between us, suspended in disbelief.

"I know about what happened," I said, my voice firmer now. "I know why he left. Why he cut you off, why—"

"No." He stood abruptly, pushing the chair back with a loud scrape. "You don't know anything." The words came out harsh, laced with something like panic.

I remained rooted in place, watching him, my heart aching at the sight of the raw emotion flaring in his chest. The air was thick with the tension between us now, the weight of all the unsaid things crashing over me like a wave. I could feel his breath, ragged and uneven, his fists clenching at his sides.

"You think you can just walk in here with your 'truth' and fix things?" His voice was low now, a dangerous calm beneath the fury. "You don't get it, do you? You don't know the first thing about what it's like to lose someone you trusted—to have everything torn apart by lies and betrayal. How could you possibly understand?"

I took a step forward, my heart thudding louder in my chest. "I understand more than you think," I whispered. "I understand that love isn't built on lies. You don't have to carry this alone."

He was silent for a moment, his chest rising and falling in rapid breaths, before he spoke again, his words strained and quiet. "You don't know what it's like to watch someone you love walk away and leave you behind."

The words cut deeper than I expected. A flicker of guilt stirred in me—because he was right. I didn't understand, not in the way he needed me to. I didn't know what it felt like to have someone you trusted betray you so completely that it turned your entire world upside down.

But I wasn't going to let that be the end of our story.

I reached out, my hand trembling slightly, but I steadied it before it touched his arm. "I know you're angry. And I know you're hurt. But pushing me away isn't the answer." His body tensed under my touch, but he didn't pull away. "I'm not leaving. Not because of this. We can face this together. Whatever it takes."

He turned to face me, his expression a mix of rage and desperation, but I could see the cracks forming, the rawness of his pain just beneath the surface. "You don't know what you're asking for," he said, his voice hoarse. "You're asking me to trust again. And I don't know if I can."

"I'm not asking you to trust me," I said, my voice steady despite the storm raging between us. "I'm asking you to trust us. To trust what we have. I won't let you fight your demons alone. You don't have to carry this burden by yourself."

For a moment, there was nothing but silence, thick and heavy, pressing down on us from all sides. Then, slowly, almost imperceptibly, I saw his shoulders relax, the tension easing out of his frame.

"You think this is easy for me?" His voice was softer now, a hint of vulnerability breaking through the anger. "You think I can just let go of everything I've been holding onto for so long?"

"No," I said, my heart aching for him. "But I believe we can rebuild it. Together."

The air shifted then—something between us snapped into place. His gaze softened, the fury in his eyes flickering and fading into something else, something I couldn't quite name but that made my chest tighten with hope.

And then, without a word, he pulled me into him. His arms wrapped around me tightly, his chest rising and falling against mine as if he, too, was trying to steady his racing heart. I held onto him, feeling the heat of him seeping into me, our bodies pressed together as though we had no other choice but to be here.

He buried his face in my hair, his breath warm against my skin. "You don't have to do this," he murmured, his voice low and broken. "You don't have to fight for me."

I tilted my head up, meeting his eyes. "I'm not fighting for you," I whispered. "I'm fighting with you."

And in that moment, I knew that whatever came next, we would face it together.

The warmth of his embrace didn't quell the storm inside me. His body, taut with unresolved tension, pressed against mine like a force I couldn't escape, though I wasn't sure I wanted to. The hum of quiet moments that had once filled our shared spaces now felt distant, replaced by a churning undercurrent of unsaid things. His breath, uneven and shallow, whispered in my ear like a confession I wasn't ready to hear.

I stayed still, my hands on his chest, feeling the beat of his heart against my palms. It was frantic, the rhythm of his pulse too fast, too erratic, like the thunder before a storm. He wasn't letting go. Neither was I.

"Why didn't you tell me?" His words were a rasp, thick with the weight of years spent buried beneath layers of pride, pain, and secrets. "Why keep it from me? Why now?"

I leaned back just enough to look into his eyes. They were darker than usual, something wild simmering in their depths. "Because I didn't know how." The truth was uglier than I wanted it to be, but there was no use hiding from it now. "Because I was afraid. Afraid of what you might think, of what it might do to us."

His lips pressed into a thin line, and I could see the muscles in his jaw working, the fight in him still simmering just beneath the surface. "You should've trusted me," he muttered, his voice trembling with the raw edges of his hurt.

"I trusted you with everything," I countered, the words leaving my mouth before I could think them through. "But this? This was too much. It felt like I was opening a door that might swallow us whole."

The silence that followed was almost unbearable. The weight of it hung between us, like a suspended breath, fragile and pregnant with meaning. Finally, he released me, stepping back just enough for his hands to fall to his sides. His gaze remained locked on me, but his expression was closed off, guarded.

"You think this is easy for me?" His voice was cold now, stripped of the fire it had held moments before. "You think I can just forget everything?"

"I'm not asking you to forget," I said softly, my heart aching at the distance that had crept in between us, even in this moment of closeness. "I'm asking you to trust me. To trust that we can move through this, together."

He scoffed, the sound bitter, cutting through the space between us like a blade. "Together? You think you can just waltz in and save me from my demons?"

"I don't think I can save you," I said quietly, but with conviction, stepping closer, closing the gap he had created. "But I think we can help each other face them."

He shook his head, a cynical laugh escaping his lips, though there was no humor in it. "You have no idea what you're getting yourself into."

His words stung more than I wanted to admit. I wasn't blind. I knew his past wasn't just a string of unpleasant memories; it was a wall, a fortress that he'd built around himself for years. But I wasn't willing to let that wall become a barrier between us. Not when we were so close to breaking through it. Not when the truth was right there in front of us, waiting to be untangled.

"I'm not afraid," I said, my voice steadier than I felt. "And I'm not going anywhere."

He turned away then, his back to me, shoulders stiff with the weight of whatever thoughts were brewing in his mind. I could hear his breath, still ragged, but underneath it, I could feel the shift. Something had cracked, even if it was just a hairline fracture. And I would take that.

"You think this is love?" he asked, his voice low, almost distant. "You think love can survive after all of this?"

I watched him, my chest tightening. "I don't think love is something that just survives. I think love is something you fight for."

His silence was almost louder than his words, thick with something I couldn't name. But I wasn't about to back down. Not now.

I took another step forward, until the space between us was almost nothing. His back was still turned, but I wasn't afraid anymore. "I'm not going to let you push me away," I said firmly. "Not when we've come this far. Not when I know what we're capable of. I don't care about your past. I care about what we build from here."

He stiffened, his shoulders set like iron, but I didn't flinch. "You can't just pretend like everything is fine. Like I'm not broken."

"No one's ever fine," I said, my voice quieter now, a touch of vulnerability creeping in. "We're all broken in some way. But it's how we choose to put ourselves back together that matters."

Finally, he turned to face me, his eyes stormy and filled with a mixture of anger and something else. Hurt? Hope? It was hard to tell. "And what if you can't put me back together?"

"I don't have to fix you," I whispered. "I just need to stand by you while you find your way."

For a long moment, neither of us spoke. There was no dramatic flair, no tearful confession. Just the weight of what was between us, and the quiet understanding that perhaps the hardest part was admitting that we didn't have all the answers. But maybe, just maybe, we didn't need them.

He closed the distance between us then, slowly, carefully. His hand reached for mine, hesitating just for a second before he cupped it, his touch soft but firm. "I'm sorry," he said, the words rough in his throat, but they were there. "For everything."

I didn't say anything at first. There was nothing to say that could take away the ache, the years of tension between us. But I didn't need words. Not right now. I just needed him to know that this—us—wasn't over. Not by a long shot.

"We're not done," I said softly, the certainty in my voice surprising even me.

And in that moment, as his thumb brushed across my knuckles, I knew we would face whatever came next—together.

The room felt impossibly small, the air dense with unsaid things, with words that hovered on the edge of our lips but refused to break free. He had drawn back, but we remained tethered by the thread of something that neither of us could name—not quite love, not quite hate, but something close enough to both to make the space between us electric with unspoken promises and unresolved pain.

"You don't get it," he muttered, running a hand through his disheveled hair, frustration seeping into every line of his posture. "I can't just let go of this. I can't pretend like I don't see the damage. It's not just water under the bridge, you know?"

"I'm not asking you to forget," I said, my voice calm but sharp, cutting through the thick silence. "I'm asking you to move forward with me. To stop living in the wreckage of your past. It's over, all of it. And you don't need to carry it anymore."

He glared at me, the muscles in his jaw working overtime as if trying to will himself to believe my words. "And what makes you so sure you have all the answers?" His voice was a growl now, and

I saw a flicker of something darker behind his eyes. "You think you can just waltz in here, pretend to fix everything, and we'll walk off into the sunset? It doesn't work like that."

"Then help me understand," I shot back, more forcefully than I intended. "Help me understand why we're standing here—on the brink of something real—and you're holding on to ghosts that have no place in this. You want to punish me for the past, but I'm not the one who's responsible for it. And I refuse to let you drag me down into the ashes of something that's long since burned out."

He flinched at my words, his gaze dropping to the floor like he was fighting a war inside his own head. I could almost hear the internal battle raging behind his quiet, clenched form. Part of me wanted to shake him, demand that he see what was right in front of him—what we could have, what we could still build. But I knew better than to push him too hard. He wasn't ready, not yet, but I could see the glimmer of something. A crack in the armor.

"Why do you care so much?" His voice was barely above a whisper now, almost too soft for me to catch. "Why do you want to fix me when I've got nothing left to give?"

I stepped closer, the space between us practically nonexistent now, and placed my hand over his, still trembling slightly from the storm of emotion running through me. "Because I see you. Not the angry man who thinks he's too broken to be loved. I see the guy who made me laugh, who made me feel safe when the world felt like it was spinning out of control. The one who held me close and made me forget my fears for just a moment. That's who I care about. And I'm not going anywhere."

His eyes flickered to mine, a storm of conflicting emotions crashing behind them—doubt, pain, and something softer. Something more vulnerable. "You can't fix me," he said, more to himself than to me, the words hanging in the air like a bitter truth neither of us wanted to face.

"I don't want to fix you," I said, my voice steady now, but my heart thundering in my chest. "I want to help you find your way back to yourself. I can't do it for you, but I can walk beside you while you figure it out. And if you need time, I'll give it to you. But I'm not running away from this. Not from you."

He looked at me then, really looked at me, and for a moment, the walls between us seemed to fade, the anger and hurt melting away like snow beneath the heat of the sun. There was still hesitation in his gaze, but it was different now—fragile, uncertain. He wasn't pulling away. He was... considering.

Before he could speak, the phone on the counter rang, shattering the moment like a glass slipping from a high shelf. We both froze, the sound of the ringtone suddenly too loud in the otherwise silent room. I looked at him, a silent question in my eyes, but he was already shaking his head.

"Ignore it," he muttered, his voice rough, still thick with the remnants of everything we'd just said.

But the phone continued to ring, insistent, like an unanswered plea. I could feel his hesitation, the unwillingness to break the fragile peace that had just started to settle between us. But something in my gut told me this wasn't just another call. This one mattered. I reached for the phone, my hand trembling just enough to make me second-guess it.

"Don't," he said, his voice low, a warning in his tone. But it was too late.

I answered, the phone pressed to my ear, and before I could say a word, a voice that I didn't recognize filled the space between us. It was gruff, unfamiliar, but the message it carried was clear.

"I don't know what you're mixed up in, but you need to be careful. This thing you're involved in? It's bigger than you think. If you don't want blood on your hands, you'll stay out of it. All of it."

I pulled the phone away, blinking in disbelief. The line went dead before I could respond, leaving nothing but the eerie silence that followed.

I looked at him, my mind racing, the weight of the words still sinking in. But he was already moving, his face drained of color, his eyes wide with a new kind of fear. "Who was that?" he demanded, his voice barely a whisper.

"I... I don't know," I said, still trying to process what I had just heard.

He grabbed my shoulders, shaking me gently, but urgently. "What did they say?"

I repeated the words back to him, and his face paled further. The air between us shifted, thickening with something I couldn't name—an unspoken dread that gnawed at the edges of everything. The ghosts of his past? Or something much darker, something that we hadn't yet begun to understand.

Before I could react, the sound of a car engine roared to life outside, followed by the screech of tires, fading into the distance. And in that moment, I knew, deep in my gut, that everything was about to change.

And neither of us was ready for what was coming next.

Chapter 32: Burning Bridges

It's funny how quickly a place can go from familiar to foreign. The coffee shop was supposed to be my sanctuary, a quiet little corner where the scent of ground beans and warm pastries was the only thing demanding my attention. But today, it felt more like a stage set for some private performance I wasn't prepared for. My fingers curled around the mug in front of me, its ceramic surface cool against the heat of my palm, as I watched him from across the table.

Liam was pacing. Back and forth, back and forth, like a caged animal, his movements sharp and jittery, the way they always were when something was brewing beneath the surface. His jaw was set in that tight line that told me he was at war with himself, and every muscle in his body was screaming to fight. But there was no enemy here. No villain. Just him, locked in some internal battle with ghosts I didn't know how to help him face.

"Liam," I said, my voice softer than I'd intended, the tension between us palpable. I hated when he did this—this unpredictable, sudden withdrawal into himself. It was like I was living with a tornado, always on the brink of destruction. But I stayed still, hoping that maybe, just maybe, he would let me in this time.

He froze, eyes narrowing as if he'd only just realized I was still there, watching. I was used to that—his ability to shut out everything and everyone when his mind locked into something. But what he was about to do... I knew it wasn't going to be good.

"I need to do this, Chloe," he muttered, barely above a whisper, but the words hit me like a slap.

Do what? The question hung in the air between us, unanswered. I wanted to reach out, to say something, anything, that would pull him back from the edge. But I knew it wouldn't be enough. Whatever this was—whatever this meeting with the man who had been nothing but a shadow in his life for so long—there was no stopping it. He was already too far gone.

"I'll be fine," Liam added, his voice rough, strained, but a lie nonetheless. His eyes flicked to the door behind me, the glass still fogged from the chill outside. The man was coming. I could feel it. The storm was coming, and I was standing right in its path.

I could tell by the way he adjusted his shirt, pulling at the sleeves as if trying to smooth out the chaos he carried with him. I couldn't help but wonder if it was more than just nerves. Maybe he was trying to convince himself. Maybe he was trying to convince me.

I shook my head, almost against my will. "You don't have to do this. Whatever it is, whatever you think you need to prove... you've already proved it. You've shown me who you are. And it's not him. You're not that man anymore, Liam."

He didn't look at me then. His gaze remained locked on the door, waiting. And I knew, with a certainty that chilled me, that the man on the other side was someone Liam had once been. Someone he didn't want to acknowledge. Someone he was about to face again, head-on, and I wasn't sure if he'd survive the encounter.

The door swung open, and the bell chimed a little too loudly for my liking. My breath caught in my throat as a tall figure stepped inside, his silhouette dark against the bright sunlight outside. He wasn't what I expected—at least, not in the way I'd imagined. He wasn't the hulking presence I'd thought of when Liam had first spoken of him, but there was something about the way he stood, about the way his eyes scanned the room, that made my stomach tighten.

I could see the old tension rise in Liam's body. He straightened up, his posture rigid, every muscle locked tight as he stepped toward the newcomer. There was a flicker of something in Liam's eyes, something that looked almost... desperate. Like he was waiting for something to break, for the fight to finally erupt.

I swallowed hard, my heart pounding in my chest, unable to tear my gaze away from the scene unfolding before me. The air between them was thick with unspoken history, and the noise of the café seemed to fade away, leaving only the two of them—pitted against each other, like two gladiators with nothing left to lose.

"You showed up," Liam said, his voice low but clear, the words hanging in the air like a challenge.

The man—Marcus, I assumed—smirked, a sharp, knowing expression that made me uneasy. He stepped closer, his shoes clicking against the hardwood floor in an almost mocking rhythm.

"I told you I would," Marcus replied, his voice dripping with something I couldn't quite place. I didn't like it. There was a darkness in his tone that sent a shiver down my spine.

The space between them seemed to shrink, even though neither man made a move to touch the other. It was like the air itself had thickened, charged with electricity, waiting for the storm to break.

"You think you're better than me now?" Marcus sneered, crossing his arms. "You think you've won?"

I wanted to look away, but I couldn't. The words were already too loaded, too painful, and I could feel the weight of them pressing against my chest, making it harder to breathe.

Liam's hands curled into fists at his sides, his knuckles white, and for a moment, I thought he might lash out. But instead, he swallowed, his eyes locking onto Marcus's with a fire that frightened me.

"I'm not better than you," Liam said, his voice barely above a whisper, but it was the quiet kind of anger that scared me more than anything. "But I'm done with you. And I'm done with all the shit you made me carry."

Marcus's eyes flared, and in that instant, I could see it—the exact moment when the past fully consumed Liam. It wasn't just the words, it was the way his whole body seemed to collapse in on itself, a crack in his armor I couldn't mend. And I realized then—I wasn't just watching a confrontation. I was watching Liam burn his bridges. And this time, there was no going back.

I wanted to scream at him. I wanted to shout, to tell him he was making a mistake. I could see it happening, the slow burn of rage eating away at him, turning his every word into something poisonous. But instead, I stayed silent. Because, in that moment, I realized something I had been too afraid to admit: this wasn't about Marcus. This was about Liam. About everything he had carried with him for so long, the darkness that had followed him like a shadow, too close, too heavy to escape.

"Do you hear yourself?" Marcus's voice cut through the tension like a knife, smooth and mocking, a sharp edge coated in sweetness. "Still playing the victim, aren't you? You've been free for how long now, and you still can't let go of it. Still chasing after ghosts, still hung up on things that don't matter anymore."

The words stung. I could see them landing, each one digging deeper into the old wounds Liam had worked so hard to bury. I knew Marcus wasn't just trying to provoke him—he was trying to break him. The smile on Marcus's face didn't reach his eyes. There was no warmth there, no understanding. Just the cold satisfaction of seeing someone squirm, of watching them unravel in front of him.

Liam's nostrils flared, his jaw working as if he were trying to hold back something, but it was clear he was losing control. I could almost feel the heat rising off him, like the simmering rage inside was about to boil over.

"You don't get it," Liam muttered, his voice dangerously low. "You never did."

"You're right," Marcus said, leaning in closer. I could see the way his eyes narrowed, like he was savoring the moment. "I never did. Because unlike you, I didn't waste my time drowning in self-pity. I moved on."

I didn't want to watch this anymore. I didn't want to see Liam fall back into the trap that had almost destroyed him, back into the same cycle of anger and regret. But I stayed still, my hands trembling around the cold ceramic of my mug, my heart racing. I wanted to pull him away from this, to wrap him up in something that wasn't poison. But I knew, deep down, that this was something only he could face.

Liam exhaled sharply, his eyes flashing with something dangerous. "You don't get to tell me what I've been through, Marcus. You don't get to act like you know me."

Marcus chuckled, the sound dripping with bitterness. "I know you better than you know yourself. You're still that same kid, just a little older, a little more beaten down. You've been playing this game, trying to make everyone think you're better, that you've moved on. But I know the truth. You're still chasing after the things you can't change. And that makes you weak."

The words hit Liam like a slap. His hands twitched at his sides, and for a split second, I thought he might explode, might finally unleash everything he'd been holding back. But instead, he stood there, frozen, his eyes darkening with something I couldn't place.

"Stop," I whispered, though I knew neither of them could hear me. "Please. This isn't you."

But it was too late. The words had already been said, the damage already done. I could see the flicker in Liam's eyes, the shift in his posture as he let the past take hold of him, just like it always did. He was drowning in it again, unable to let go of the pain, the betrayal. And I was just watching him sink.

"Do you really think you can just walk away from this?" Marcus said, his voice rising, like he was enjoying every second of this torment. "Do you think you can just leave all of it behind, like none of it ever mattered?"

Liam's hands balled into fists, his body rigid with restraint. I could feel his breath coming faster, quicker, like he was ready to explode. His shoulders tensed, his entire frame coiled tight, and for a moment, I thought he might just lash out, let the fury take over completely.

But then he did something unexpected. Something that knocked the air right out of me.

He turned his back on Marcus. He didn't say anything. Didn't shout, didn't storm out. He just... walked away.

I didn't know what to think. Part of me was relieved, but another part of me—something deep inside—was scared. Terrified. Because I knew that walking away from Marcus wasn't enough. He had to walk away from everything that tied him to that dark place, everything that had kept him shackled for so long. And I didn't know if he could do it.

I followed him, almost instinctively, as he made his way to the door. His pace was slower now, almost deliberate, like he was trying to keep himself composed, to hold it together just long enough. I could hear the heavy beat of his footsteps, each one echoing in the quiet space between us. He reached for the door, pushing it open with a quiet creak, and I stepped out into the cold air right behind him.

It wasn't until we were standing outside, the world still and silent around us, that I saw it. The weight in his eyes, the heaviness that had settled there, pulling him down like gravity. He wasn't free. Not yet. Not while the fire of revenge still burned inside him.

"Liam..." My voice trembled, but I didn't care anymore. I reached for his arm, but he pulled away, his back still turned to me.

"I have to do this," he whispered, his voice low but firm. "I can't keep running from it. I can't keep pretending like it didn't matter."

I watched him, the man I loved, and I realized with a sickening clarity that this wasn't just about Marcus anymore. This was about Liam facing a past that had never let go of him. And I wasn't sure if I could be the one to pull him out of it.

But I had to try.

I could feel the tension in the air long after Liam had walked away. It pressed down on me like the weight of a thousand thoughts, each one heavier than the last. He wasn't free, not yet. His voice still rang in my ears, his words echoing with the fury of a man who was trying—desperately trying—to break free of something that had shaped him, scarred him, controlled him for too long. And I couldn't tell if he was on the verge of healing or spiraling deeper into the wreckage of his past.

The street outside was quieter than usual, the usual bustle of traffic muted by the cold, crisp air. I wrapped my coat tighter around myself, though it didn't seem to help with the chill spreading from the inside out. I wanted to follow him, but a voice inside told me I shouldn't. He needed space, needed to figure this out on his own, but that didn't make it any easier to stand here, watching him disappear into the distance.

His footsteps had slowed, but he didn't turn back. He never did when he was in this kind of mood, when the storm inside him had made him blind to everything around him, including me. It was the only thing I hated about him—the way he could shut everything out when things got too heavy. And it was the one thing I could never fix.

I stood there for what felt like hours, the cold creeping into my bones, until the sound of a car door slamming shut startled me. I spun around, my heart leaping into my throat. The last thing I needed right now was for someone to see me standing there like a lost soul, but then I saw who it was. Marcus.

I hadn't expected him to follow, much less to show up now, when everything was still hanging by a thread. He was leaning against the car, arms folded across his chest, his eyes glinting with a smugness that was almost too much to bear.

"You look lost," he said, his tone laced with that same irritating superiority he'd worn like a second skin back in the coffee shop.

I ignored him, focusing instead on the path where Liam had disappeared into the distance. I didn't need this right now. Didn't need his games, his taunts, the way he was clearly enjoying the chaos unfolding between us.

"You think you're helping him?" Marcus's voice was sharp, cutting through the silence that had settled between us. "You think you can save him?"

I turned slowly, my eyes locking onto his. "That's none of your business."

Marcus raised an eyebrow, a smirk curling at the corner of his lips. "I think it is. You're wasting your time, you know. He'll never let you in. Not completely. He's too far gone. And you'll only end up getting hurt."

My hands tightened into fists at my sides, and I felt the heat rise in my chest, but I refused to let him get to me. Not now. Not when Liam needed me more than ever.

"You don't know him," I said, my voice low but firm. "You don't know anything about what's inside of him. He's not like you."

The smirk on Marcus's face faltered, just for a second, before he regained his composure. "Oh, I know him. Better than you do. Better than anyone." He pushed off the car, stepping closer. "You think you're the one who's going to fix him? You think you're the one who's going to make everything right? You're fooling yourself."

I swallowed hard, the anger building inside me. "I'm not fooling myself. But you—" I took a step closer, my voice shaking slightly with the force of my words. "You're the one who's been holding him back all these years. And you don't get to just waltz in here and act like you have some kind of right to tear him apart."

Marcus's eyes darkened. "I'm not tearing him apart. He's doing that all on his own. I'm just here to remind him of what he's really capable of."

The finality in his voice made me stop in my tracks. He wasn't just trying to provoke me. He was trying to provoke Liam, to drag him back into a world he had no place in anymore. The thought of it made my stomach twist with unease.

"I'm not going to stand here and argue with you," I said, turning on my heel. "If you want to keep playing games, go right ahead. But I'm not doing this with you."

I heard him laugh behind me, the sound cold and cutting. "You're wasting your time, Chloe. You're already too deep in it. You'll never get him out."

I didn't look back. Didn't let him see how much those words hurt, because I knew he was just trying to bait me. I had bigger things to worry about than Marcus, and right now, those things were walking further and further away from me.

I was halfway down the street when I heard the familiar sound of footsteps behind me. I didn't turn around, didn't need to. I knew exactly who it was. But this time, I didn't stop.

"Chloe." His voice, rough and hoarse, called my name.

I finally stopped, my heart lurching in my chest as I turned to face him. He was standing there, a few feet away, looking at me with an unreadable expression. His eyes were wild, stormy, and there was a darkness there that I wasn't sure I could pull him out of.

I wanted to run to him. To reach out and take his hand, to tell him it was going to be okay, but something held me back. Maybe it was the look on his face, or maybe it was the sense that I wasn't enough anymore, that I didn't have the power to pull him from the edge.

"I don't know if I can do this, Chloe," he said, his voice strained, his words heavy with regret.

I felt my chest tighten, the air between us thickening with all the things left unsaid. "You don't have to do this alone."

Liam's gaze flickered toward the street, his jaw clenching as if he were wrestling with some internal battle. "I don't know how to let it go. To just... move on."

I took a step toward him, my heart aching for him, but before I could say anything else, a car screeched to a halt beside us. And just like that, everything stopped.

The door swung open, and a man stepped out. My heart dropped into my stomach as I saw who it was.

I didn't know if I was ready for this.

Chapter 33: Ashes of Redemption

The scent of rain lingers in the air, sharp and fresh, mingling with the earthy musk of wet asphalt. It's the kind of night that makes everything feel like it's just on the edge of transformation, as though the world itself is holding its breath, waiting for something to change. I can hear the tap of my heels against the pavement as I make my way toward the old warehouse, the one that's seen too many secrets and far too much pain. There's no mistaking it now. He's here.

I take a deep breath, willing the doubt to slip away, but it doesn't. Not this time. The uncertainty has settled into my chest, a cold weight that tightens every time I think of him. Of us. The man I've loved, the one I've fought for, the one who has become a stranger under the weight of his own demons. He used to be a flame, bright and fierce, but now he's nothing but embers, glowing faintly in the dark. And it's all because of that one thing he can't let go of. That one thing that keeps pulling him under, no matter how much I try to reach for him. Revenge.

The warehouse door creaks as I push it open, the familiar scent of rust and old wood greeting me like an old, unwanted friend. Inside, the dim light from a single hanging bulb flickers, casting long, spindly shadows across the floor. I don't see him right away, but I know he's here. I can feel him, the way his presence fills up the space, like a storm cloud hovering just above.

Then I see him, sitting in the far corner, his back to me, as though he's waiting for me to make the first move. His shoulders are hunched, as if he's carrying the weight of the world—or perhaps the weight of all the years he's spent drowning in his own fury. His hands are clenched into fists, the muscles in his arms taut under the thin fabric of his shirt. He doesn't move when I approach, doesn't even turn to look at me.

"Evan," I say, my voice steady despite the tremor I feel in my chest. I've come here, to this godforsaken place, to make him see reason. To make him realize that we have a life worth fighting for. That there's more to us than this endless cycle of pain and rage. But it's harder than I thought. It's harder because he's not the same man I fell in love with. He's someone else now, a stranger who wears his face.

He doesn't respond right away, but I can hear his breath, shallow and quick, like he's trying to steady himself. The silence between us stretches, thick and heavy, until I can't stand it any longer.

"Don't do this," I whisper, stepping closer. "You don't have to keep punishing yourself. You don't have to keep chasing this—this shadow."

He finally turns to me, his face a mask of torment, the lines of his jaw tight with restraint. His eyes are dull, clouded with something darker than sorrow, something I can't name. Anger, maybe. Or maybe it's regret. Or maybe it's both.

"You don't understand," he says, his voice rough, like he's been chewing on broken glass. "You don't get what it's like to want something so badly, to need it so much that it consumes you."

I swallow hard, fighting the sting of the words. "I understand more than you think." I take another step, closer now, so close I can feel the heat of him, the tension radiating off his skin. "I've watched you destroy yourself, Evan. I've watched you spiral, over and over, while I've stood here, waiting, hoping you'd come back to me. But you're not coming back, are you? Not unless you let go of this. Let go of this need for revenge."

His lips curl into a bitter smile, the kind that doesn't reach his eyes. "You think I can just let it go? Like that? Like it never happened?" He stands up then, his movements sharp and jagged, as though he's ready to explode. "You don't get it. I don't have a choice anymore. I made a promise."

I shake my head, my heart pounding. "You made a promise to someone who isn't even here anymore, Evan. You're not just punishing them. You're punishing yourself. And you're punishing me. You're punishing us."

He steps forward, his eyes burning with something dangerous, something I don't recognize. "What if I can't? What if it's already too late?"

I stand my ground, meeting his gaze, trying to hold onto the thread of hope I have left, but it's slipping through my fingers like sand. "Then you'll never be free," I say, my voice soft but firm. "You'll never have what you want. You'll never have us. Not if you keep dragging this weight behind you."

He flinches, the words hitting him harder than I intended, but it's too late to take them back. There's no softening the truth now. He has to choose. And so do I.

For a long moment, neither of us speaks. The air between us is thick with the unsaid, with everything that's been left unresolved, hanging in the balance. But then, slowly, almost imperceptibly, his shoulders drop. The fire in his eyes dims, just a little, and I wonder if it's because he's finally hearing me—or if it's because he's too exhausted to keep fighting.

"I don't know how to stop," he murmurs, his voice a low, broken whisper.

"Then let me help you," I say, reaching out, my hand trembling just slightly as I offer it to him. "Let me help you find your way back."

And for the first time in what feels like forever, he hesitates. But only for a moment. Then, slowly, cautiously, his hand reaches out, and for the first time in a long time, we're standing together again. And maybe, just maybe, that's all it takes to start the healing.

The seconds ticked by slowly as if the universe itself were holding its breath, waiting for him to make a choice. But even as I stood there, fingers still outstretched toward him, I could feel the air between us thickening, like an invisible wall was being built, one brick at a time, with each passing moment of indecision. I almost wanted to laugh, but it would have been a bitter thing. I hadn't come here to fight. I'd come to salvage whatever was left of us, to remind him that even in the darkest corners, there was still a spark of light. But I had no idea whether he could see it.

He wasn't moving—still, solid, like he was afraid that any movement would shatter the fragile quiet that had settled between us. And for a fleeting, maddening second, I wondered if I'd been wrong to hope, if perhaps the man I loved was too far gone. His eyes were searching mine, or maybe he was trying to see past me, looking for something, anything, to hold on to. I held my ground, not willing to let this moment slip through our fingers.

"You think it's that simple?" His voice cut through the silence, low and harsh. "You think I can just decide to walk away from this after everything?"

I bit back the urge to tell him how long it had been since I'd been walking this tightrope with him—waiting, wondering, praying that he'd find his way back before we both collapsed under the weight of it all. "I'm not asking you to forget it all," I said, my voice surprisingly steady. "I'm asking you to choose something else. I'm asking you to choose us. Choose me."

His gaze flickered briefly, like a candle flame fighting a gust of wind. "I don't know how," he admitted, his voice soft now, uncertain. "I've spent so many years wrapped up in this that I don't know what else I'd be without it."

A laugh, bitter and hollow, left my lips. "You'd be free, Evan. You'd be free."

The words hung between us, heavy, waiting for him to catch them. And, just when I thought he might finally take them—when I thought, maybe, just maybe, he'd step into the light with me—he stepped back instead, his hands pushing into his pockets as he looked down at the ground.

"I can't just let it go," he muttered, almost to himself. "If I let go of the revenge, then what am I? What's left of me?"

I closed my eyes for a moment, holding onto my patience with all the strength I had. "You're the man who used to make me laugh," I said, my voice a little softer now. "The one who held me close when the world seemed too big. The one who told me we could face anything together."

His jaw clenched at my words, but when he met my eyes, I could see it—a flicker of recognition. A moment where he realized just how much of himself he'd lost, how far he'd gone from the man he used to be. And maybe, just maybe, a part of him wanted to come back. But that part was buried deep beneath layers of bitterness and regret. He didn't know how to let it go, didn't know how to put down the mantle of revenge that had been his only companion for so long.

"I'm tired," he whispered, his voice raw, as though the weight of the words had taken everything from him. "I'm so tired of fighting."

I wanted to reach for him then, to pull him close and tell him that the fight didn't have to be this way, that we could find another way. But the distance between us felt insurmountable, a gulf of years and memories that had both made us and broken us. I could almost feel the words I wanted to say clawing at the back of my throat, desperate to break free, but I held them in check. There was no sense in trying to make him see reason if he wasn't ready to hear it.

Instead, I let the silence fall over us like a blanket, each of us lost in our thoughts, tangled up in a history we couldn't escape. I wondered, for a moment, if we were even the same people anymore—if the spark that had once burned so brightly between us had long since been snuffed out, leaving only ashes.

The air between us grew colder as the minutes stretched on, and I could feel the time slipping away, like sand through my fingers. I thought of everything we had once been—of the easy laughter, the quiet moments spent in each other's company, the plans we'd made, the dreams we'd shared. And it all seemed so far away now, so distant, as if it had never really been ours to begin with.

When I finally spoke, my voice felt strange, as though I were talking to someone else entirely. "I don't know what you need from me anymore, Evan. But I can't keep living like this. I can't keep waiting for you to find your way back. I've given you every part of myself, and I don't know how much more I can give."

He didn't say anything at first, but I could feel his gaze on me, heavy and unreadable. Then, in a voice thick with unshed tears, he spoke again.

"I don't want to lose you," he said, the words so soft that I almost didn't hear them.

I looked at him, at the man who had once been everything to me, and I saw him then—not as the shadow of vengeance he'd become, but as the person I had once loved. The person I still loved, despite everything. The realization hit me hard, like a slap to the chest. But even as I wanted to reach for him, to pull him back, I knew that I couldn't do it for him. He had to choose this. He had to choose us.

"I don't want to lose you either," I whispered back, my voice barely a breath. "But I can't fight this fight alone anymore."

And just like that, the silence took over again. But this time, it was different. This time, I could feel the walls beginning to crack.

The moment lingered between us, a delicate stretch of time, as fragile as the breath that held it together. The silence was heavy, wrapping us both in its uneasy embrace, as if waiting for one of us to take the next step. The walls around us seemed to close in, the echoes of our past reverberating like the distant hum of an old song—one we both used to know but had forgotten the words to.

I had hoped that the ache in his eyes would be enough to sway him, that the brokenness I saw reflected in his gaze would make him understand just how far gone we both were. But instead, he looked at me, his expression unreadable, as though my words had barely reached him.

I'd never felt this disconnected from him. Not in the beginning, not when we first collided like a hurricane and a summer storm. It was always us against the world, always some shared space where we could exist in harmony, like two halves of the same coin. But now? Now, it was as though he had slipped away, and I was left holding onto the echo of the man I once knew. And he? He was still lost in the haze of what was long past, still tethered to the ghost of a version of himself that didn't belong here anymore.

His gaze finally flickered to mine, something dark and almost apologetic flitting behind his eyes, though I wasn't sure whether it was regret for what he had done or for what he had become. "I don't know how to come back from this, Leah," he muttered, the words thick with uncertainty. "Every step I've taken, every move I've made, it's been in the name of something that's been eating at me. I don't know who I am without it. I don't know who I am without this war inside of me."

I swallowed, fighting the bitterness that clawed at my throat. "I don't know who you are anymore, either. But I know that you're not the person I fell in love with. You're not the man who held me at night and whispered that everything would be okay. The man I loved didn't run toward destruction—he ran toward me."

The words were harsh, but they were the truth. The truth I had been swallowing for so long, hoping that one day he would hear it and come back to me. But maybe the truth wasn't enough anymore. Maybe it had to be something else.

He shifted, and I could see him fighting against something within himself, a silent battle raging beneath his skin. "I'm not sure I deserve to come back," he said, his voice quiet, hoarse, as though it physically hurt him to say it.

The words landed in the space between us, so heavy and raw that it took everything I had to not crumble beneath them. But this was the moment. This was the turning point I had prayed for—where we either took a step forward together, or we each continued down the separate paths we'd already started walking.

"You're wrong," I said, my voice thick with emotion. "You don't have to deserve it. You just have to be willing to try. You just have to choose to take my hand and step away from the darkness. I'm not asking for perfection. I'm asking for a chance. For us."

He hesitated, and in that pause, I saw something flicker in his eyes—a glimmer of something that resembled the man I had known, the man I had loved. And yet, it was gone before I could reach it. He turned away from me then, pacing in tight circles, running his hands through his hair, clearly wrestling with something deeper than I could comprehend.

"I don't know if I can," he muttered under his breath. "What if I can't walk away from this? What if I've done too much? What if it's too late for me to change?"

His words hung in the air, and I could feel the weight of them, pressing down on us both, making everything seem impossible. He didn't believe in redemption. He didn't believe in the idea of starting over, of shedding the skin of his past to make room for something new.

But I had to believe. I had to believe that we weren't just doomed to repeat the same mistakes over and over again. I had to believe that love was bigger than the mistakes we'd made, that it was strong enough to bear the weight of his regret and mine.

"Evan," I said softly, stepping closer to him, my hand reaching out, though I wasn't sure if he would take it. "I know you don't think you can come back. I know you think you've gone too far. But I don't believe that. I believe that you can still choose. I believe that you can still come home."

He stopped in his tracks, his back to me, and I could see the tension in his shoulders, the way he was holding himself together by a thread. "And what if it's too late? What if I've already ruined everything?" His voice cracked, the vulnerability in it almost too much to bear.

"I don't know," I said honestly. "But I do know this. It's not too late for us to try. You may not be able to undo everything that's been done, but you can make a choice now. A choice to fight for something that's real. Something worth saving."

He was silent for a long moment, and when he finally turned around, I saw the rawness in his eyes, the unspoken words that hung between us like a live wire, pulsing with uncertainty and fear.

"I don't want to hurt you anymore," he whispered, his voice trembling.

I took a breath, the weight of his words sinking deep into my chest. "Then stop," I said, taking another step forward, my hand trembling as it reached out to touch his arm. "Stop hurting us both. Come back to me. Come back to us."

He looked at my hand for a moment, his eyes flickering with something unreadable, and then—just as I thought he might finally reach for me, finally take that step toward the future I had been holding out for—there was a sharp knock at the door.

We both froze.

I glanced toward the sound, my heart pounding. It was too soon. Too soon for anything else to intervene. And yet, the knock came again—louder, more insistent this time.

Evan's expression shifted, his jaw tightening, and I felt the air between us grow colder, as if the world itself had just decided to rip the fragile thread of connection we'd been building right out from under us.

"Don't answer it," I said, though I wasn't sure if I was speaking to him, or to the universe itself.

But the door rattled once more, and Evan's face went pale. And in that moment, I knew—whatever was on the other side of that door, it wasn't going to be good.

Chapter 34: The Last Ember

The first flicker of light caught my eye before I even heard the scream. It was subtle at first, like the pulse of a distant star on the edge of a blackened sky, faint and teasing. Then came the sound—crackling, fierce, alive—followed by the unmistakable scent of burning wood, of memories set alight, of something ancient and wrong. A fire. And not just any fire. This one, it seemed, had purpose.

I turned to find Max beside me, the man who had once seemed like the very embodiment of calm, the rock around which I had rebuilt everything. But tonight, the flames did something different to him. They stripped away the calm exterior, revealing the storm beneath. His jaw tightened, and his hand clenched into a fist at his side, the tendons in his neck straining like taut wire. His eyes narrowed, locked on the rising inferno, as if he could will it to stop. But of course, it wouldn't. Fires like this didn't stop unless someone told them to.

"We have to go." My voice was nothing more than a whisper, but it seemed to shatter the moment between us, a crack in the silence we had been carefully maintaining for weeks now. His eyes snapped to mine, and I saw it then—the flicker of recognition. The fear.

"It's happening again." His words were low, guttural, like a man who had already lost too much and feared he might lose more.

I wanted to tell him that it wasn't possible, that this fire was just a freak accident, some poorly discarded cigarette or a lantern left unattended. But we both knew better. This wasn't just an accident. This was a message. And as much as I hated to admit it, I knew who it was meant for.

The town was eerily quiet, save for the distant sound of the fire growing, licking at the sky, its flames dancing like mocking fingers. The wind had picked up, carrying the smoke toward us, and I could feel it on my skin—sharp, acrid, bitter. It reminded me of the nights we used to spend in the small cottage on the hill, when the air smelled of damp earth and pine, when things were simpler, before the world had caught fire in ways neither of us had been prepared for.

Max didn't move. His gaze was locked on the flames, his features unreadable. I wanted to reach for him, to shake him, to do anything to pull him from the darkness that had always followed him. But something in the air—something in his posture—told me that this time, he wasn't going to run.

"You don't have to do this," I said, my voice suddenly sounding small, lost against the enormity of what lay ahead. "We can leave. We can go far away, start over. We don't have to go back to this."

Max finally turned toward me, his face illuminated by the orange glow of the fire, and for a brief, terrifying moment, I didn't recognize the man I had known so well. There was something different in him now—something older, more resigned. It was as if the fire had already claimed him, and all that was left was the smoldering remains.

"I can't," he muttered, his voice rough, raw. "This isn't just a fire, Nora. This is him. This is the past coming back for me. For us."

I swallowed hard, the pit in my stomach growing heavier. I wanted to argue, to find a reason why we should walk away from all of this and never look back. But the truth—God, the truth—was too damn clear. Max was right. The man who had haunted him for years had finally caught up with us.

As we stood there, rooted to the spot, the fire continued to rage, its heat now pressing against my skin, relentless and unforgiving. The townspeople were starting to gather, but they kept their distance, as if they too could feel the weight of the moment, the gravity of what was unfolding.

"I have to go," Max said suddenly, his voice carrying an unspoken urgency. He turned away from me, his long legs carrying him toward the heart of the fire. "I have to stop it. I have to face him."

"Max, no!" I called out, my feet unwilling to follow at first. The word felt like it was choking me, but I pushed through it, scrambling after him, my breath catching in my throat as I moved.

He didn't stop. He couldn't stop.

The closer we got to the blaze, the more I realized just how much this was a part of him. The man who had walked away from this life—tried to bury it, hide it beneath layers of calm and routine—was now being dragged back into it, like a moth to the flame.

And there, in the center of it all, stood a figure in the distance, silhouetted by the flames. I could barely make out the features, but I didn't need to. Max's body stiffened beside me, and I felt the sudden pulse of anger, of pain, radiating off of him.

There was no denying it now. The man who had caused all of this was here, in this moment, ready to remind Max of everything he had lost.

Max took a step forward, but I reached out, grabbing his arm. "Max, please," I pleaded, my fingers digging into his skin. "Don't let him do this to you. We can walk away from this. You've done it before."

His eyes turned to mine, and in them, I saw something that terrified me more than the fire itself. A decision had been made, and I couldn't stop it.

"I'm not running anymore," he said quietly, and with that, he pulled away from me, his silhouette swallowed by the fire.

The fire seemed to swallow everything in its path, spreading its jagged mouth across the landscape as though it were a living thing, hungry and relentless. The wind picked up again, and the heat pressed against my face, searing through my skin. I could feel the flames even from a distance, each gust of air driving them closer to the heart of the town, but Max—Max was already gone.

It took all of my willpower to keep my feet rooted to the spot. Every instinct screamed at me to follow him, to grab him by the shoulders and pull him back from the precipice. But I knew it was too late. He had already made his choice.

I looked up, hoping to see some sign of reason in the sea of flickering light, something that would make sense of this madness. But there was nothing. Only the fire, and the figure moving within it.

For a moment, I thought I had imagined it. But no. There he was, moving with that same purposeful stride, a man on a mission he hadn't been able to escape, not in years. The man who had been waiting in the wings all this time, watching from the shadows, feeding on Max's fear.

I could hear Max's footsteps now, crunching against the gravel, the sound oddly steady amid the chaos. He wasn't looking back. He didn't need to. The fire was his past, and it was pulling him forward with an undeniable force.

I followed him then, not out of some misguided sense of loyalty, but because I knew I couldn't let him face this alone. If this was the reckoning, then I was damned if I would stand by and watch him burn in it.

"Max!" I shouted, my voice cracking against the roar of the fire. "Don't do this!"

But it was like he couldn't hear me, or maybe he just didn't care. His pace quickened, and he moved toward the dark silhouette now emerging from the flames—the man, the ghost who had been chasing him all this time.

I almost didn't recognize him at first, the figure so cloaked in shadows and smoke that he seemed part of the fire itself. But then he stepped into the light, and the face was all too familiar.

Jonah.

The name hit me like a punch to the gut, but I didn't have time to process it. Max was there, face-to-face with him now, their eyes locking in a silent exchange that spoke volumes. I could see the weight of the years between them in the way they stood, like two opposing forces, each unwilling to give ground.

Jonah smiled, and it was a smile that held nothing but malice. The kind of smile you'd expect from someone who'd spent years waiting, biding his time, savoring the moment when he could finally watch someone break.

"You thought you could outrun this, didn't you?" Jonah's voice was low, smooth—almost teasing. "But you can't, Max. You never could."

Max didn't respond at first. His jaw was set, and the muscles in his arms twitched with the urge to do something—anything—but he stayed still, staring at Jonah as if trying to weigh him, trying to find some trace of humanity in the man standing before him.

"You know why I'm here," Jonah continued, taking a step forward. The fire crackled behind him, lighting his face in a grotesque, almost theatrical glow. "You thought you could forget. But the past doesn't forget. It always finds a way to remind you of who you really are."

Max's fists clenched at his sides, the knuckles white with the force of it. His lips pressed together tightly, his expression unreadable, and for a moment, I thought he might actually let Jonah talk him into whatever sick game he was playing.

But then, Max moved.

In an instant, he was on Jonah, faster than I had ever seen him, and the air between them crackled with an energy I couldn't quite place. It wasn't just anger. It was something deeper—something raw, primal, like the very foundation of their rivalry had just erupted into the open.

Jonah staggered back slightly, but he didn't fall. Instead, he grinned, a dark, predatory grin, as if he'd been waiting for this.

"You've got some fight left in you, I see," Jonah taunted, wiping a small trickle of blood from his lip.

Max's eyes blazed. "You don't get to do this anymore," he growled, his voice thick with emotion.

I wanted to scream at them to stop, to remind them that there was so much more at stake here than their old grudge. But the words caught in my throat. It was as if the fire had consumed everything—everything that once held us together—and left nothing behind but the need for reckoning.

Jonah's smirk faltered for a moment, just a brief flicker, but it was enough. It was the crack I needed, the moment I'd been waiting for. I rushed forward, not thinking, not caring about the flames or the danger or the blood, but about getting through to Max before it was too late.

"Max, don't let him win," I pleaded, my voice raw with desperation. "This isn't the way. You don't have to fight him, not like this. Let's go—please."

Max froze, just for a second, his chest heaving as if the very air had been sucked from his lungs. His gaze flickered to mine, and for the briefest of moments, the intensity in his eyes softened. It was the first time I'd seen him doubt himself since this whole thing began.

But it wasn't enough. Not yet.

Jonah's voice sliced through the moment. "You think she'll save you, Max?" he sneered. "She's just a distraction. You can't run from what's coming."

Max's eyes hardened again, and with a final, guttural sound, he launched himself at Jonah. But this time, something had shifted. The fight wasn't the same. This wasn't just about winning. It was about surviving, about pushing through the fire. And no matter what, Max wouldn't let it consume him—not again.

Max was a storm in the center of it all, a force of nature battling against the winds that screamed through the night. His every movement was a challenge, each step an assertion that the fire, the man, the past—none of it would swallow him whole. The heat didn't faze him; if anything, it seemed to fuel him, burnishing the edges of his rage, sharp and clean like a blade's kiss.

Jonah, standing in the middle of it, was a snake that knew its prey. He wasn't bothered by the fire. No, the flames seemed to be his element, the very breath of life. His grin was wide, far too wide for my comfort, stretching across his face like a shadow that belonged to someone else. But there was something else in his eyes now—something faint, something he couldn't hide: doubt.

Max was relentless, driving him back with each strike. Jonah's movements were slower now, a bit more staggered, like he was trying to remember something he'd once known, trying to rekindle a flame that had long since burned out. Max, though, was a beast in human form. There was no hesitation in him. The moment Jonah had crossed the line, he'd ignited a fury Max hadn't allowed himself to feel in years.

And then, in a move that took me by surprise, Jonah stumbled, his shoulder colliding with the side of a half-burned building. The structure groaned, as if it were alive, as if it felt the weight of the years that had been thrust upon it. But Jonah didn't fall. He pushed off the crumbling wall and stood tall again, blood dripping from his lip. His eyes locked onto Max's, and for a fleeting moment, I could have sworn I saw something like respect in those eyes.

"I should've killed you back then," Jonah said, his voice low, but unmistakably cold. "You should have stayed dead, Max. And now I'll finish what I started."

Max froze, his fist raised in the air, poised for the next blow. But Jonah was faster, and before Max could react, Jonah reached for something hidden beneath his jacket—a glint of steel that caught the firelight just long enough for me to recognize it. A knife.

Everything seemed to stop. My heart slammed against my chest, every instinct screaming at me to move, to get in between them, but my feet wouldn't obey. I could only watch as the knife gleamed, the blade reflecting the flames like a cruel reminder of everything that had come before.

I couldn't breathe, couldn't think. Max saw it, too. I saw the shift in him, the tension in his shoulders as he adjusted to face the new threat. His eyes narrowed, calculating. But Jonah wasn't waiting. With a movement so fast I almost missed it, Jonah lunged, the knife aimed directly for Max's abdomen.

I don't know what happened in that moment—whether it was instinct or sheer willpower—but Max reacted before I could even scream. He twisted to the side, and the knife grazed his shirt, the fabric ripping under the force of the blow, but Max was already on him, fists swinging with everything he had.

The sound of metal against bone was deafening in the night air, and for a long moment, it was all I could hear. Max's body seemed to move with a rhythm I couldn't understand, his punches steady and deliberate, until he landed one final blow, sending Jonah stumbling backward. The knife clattered to the ground, lost in the chaos, its purpose fulfilled, at least for now.

Jonah's eyes were wild, his breath ragged. He wasn't finished. Of course, he wasn't. He'd never finish until Max was broken, or worse. He staggered, his back to the fire now, the heat licking at his skin, but he was still standing.

"Don't think this is over," Jonah spat, his voice barely a whisper. "You may have won tonight, but I'll be back. You can't escape me forever."

Max's chest heaved as he watched Jonah retreat into the smoke and the flames. His stance was wide, like a mountain unshaken by the wind. But I could see it in his eyes—the toll it had taken. He was exhausted, every muscle screaming in protest, and yet he stood there, waiting for the next battle, because he knew it was coming.

"You won't have to face him alone." I took a step forward, the words tumbling out before I could think better of it.

Max didn't turn to me right away. He stood there for a moment, letting the wind whip through his hair, his face etched with something far more complicated than anger. He was tired, and the fire wasn't the only thing burning inside him.

"You don't have to be part of this, Nora," he said finally, his voice soft but firm. "I can protect you."

"Max," I said, my voice trembling but resolute. "I'm already part of it. Whether you want me to be or not."

He turned then, his eyes meeting mine, dark and stormy. For a moment, I thought he might say something, might protest or push me away. But he didn't. Instead, he let out a breath, heavy and drawn-out, like he was carrying something too heavy to bear.

"I never wanted this for you," he muttered, almost to himself, the words like an apology wrapped in a confession.

"I know," I replied, taking another step closer. The fire was still burning, its light dancing across Max's face, making him look both invincible and broken at the same time. But it didn't matter. I wasn't leaving him.

Before he could respond, the ground beneath our feet trembled. It was subtle at first, like the faintest shiver in the earth, but then it grew, shaking harder, louder, until the buildings around us creaked and groaned as if they were straining under the pressure.

"Do you feel that?" I asked, my voice barely a whisper.

Max's eyes widened. "It's him."

Before I could ask who, the ground split open with a deafening crack, and the air was filled with dust and smoke as something—something huge—began to rise from the earth itself. I barely had time to react, but Max's hand shot out to grab mine, pulling me toward him as the ground began to give way beneath us.

And then, from the swirling dust and fire, a figure emerged. Taller than a man, its silhouette monstrous in the haze.

Jonah was just the beginning.

Chapter 35: Into the Fire

The air hung heavy with the weight of something unsaid, thick with the hum of unfinished business. I could feel it in my chest, like the warning tremors before an earthquake, a ripple of tension that surged up from the soles of my shoes to settle in my throat. Beside me, his hand was a vice—warm and trembling, but firm enough to make me certain he wouldn't break. He wasn't the man who'd walked into that room a decade ago, meek and lost, driven by shadows he couldn't name. No, that man was gone. He was standing here with me, at the precipice, his future in his grip, ready to burn everything that had once bound him.

The man across from us was a monster in a well-tailored suit, every inch of him a predator disguised in civility. His gaze was cold, calculating—a snake coiling slowly, waiting for the perfect moment to strike. I couldn't help the instinct to stand taller, to shield him from that glare. But he didn't need me. Not anymore. His eyes, now hard and defiant, locked onto the man who'd broken him over and over in the past.

"You've always been good at controlling people, haven't you?" His voice was a whisper at first, barely a murmur, but there was a weight to it now, a power that made the room feel smaller.

The other man sneered, his lips curling like a predator who'd cornered its prey. "You've grown brave, haven't you? How quaint. But that doesn't change anything."

I could feel the heat rising from him, the fire in his chest, stoked by years of silence, shame, and regret. He was a furnace now, burning brighter with every word. And the man who had once held all the power—the one who had made him cower and bend—was losing ground.

"I'm done with you," he said, his voice clear, steady. "You don't own me anymore."

The words settled between them like a stone, heavy and permanent. I squeezed his hand, not out of fear but out of sheer awe at the strength I was witnessing. It was like watching a storm being born—violent, unstoppable, and utterly righteous.

The other man's smile faltered, just slightly, before it returned, thin and humorless. "You think you're free? You think this changes anything?" He stepped closer, leaning in as if the physical proximity could break him. "You're still the same weak fool I shaped. You'll never escape me."

For a second, I thought I saw something flicker in him, a hesitation that betrayed the confidence he'd worn so thin. But before I could grasp at it, my focus shifted back to the man beside me. His grip tightened in mine, his knuckles white, but he didn't flinch.

"No," he said, his voice louder now, filling the space between us. "I'm not the same."

The words were a sword, sharp and cutting through the tension in the room. The air felt like it cracked, the stillness snapping, shattering, as though something had finally been broken in a way that nothing else could undo.

The silence that followed was so thick it could have suffocated me. But then, like the inevitable clash of thunder after a flash of lightning, he spoke again. This time, his words were low and deliberate, the kind that reverberated with history and fire.

"You had me once. You won't have me again."

The finality in his voice rang louder than any accusation, louder than any judgment. I could hear the release, the years of torment sliding off his shoulders like a mantle he no longer needed to wear. For the first time in a long while, I didn't need to protect him. He had already won.

And then, the unthinkable happened. The man in front of us, the one who had spent years twisting and contorting the truth to suit his whims, faltered. For the first time in years, he looked... unsure. It was a fleeting moment—just a flicker in his eyes—but it was enough. Enough to let us know we had done what we came for. We had broken the chains, severed the strings that had held him bound for so long.

But even as I felt that victory surge inside of me, as the air cleared, I couldn't ignore the gnawing sensation creeping along the edges of my mind. There was something not quite right. Something unfinished.

The man in front of us stepped back, straightening his suit as if he could restore his dignity with the flick of a cufflink. He gave us one last look, the kind you give someone you believe you've already defeated, before turning on his heel and walking away, his footsteps echoing off the polished floors.

It should have been over. And for all intents and purposes, it was. But as we turned to leave, the weight of the room pressing against our backs, I couldn't shake the feeling that the battle wasn't truly over. Not yet.

There was something else lingering, some unfinished thread that refused to break free. It wasn't over until it was, and I knew that. The man beside me felt it too, his fingers tightening just slightly in mine as if he understood that this victory, however monumental, was still only one step in a much larger war.

But for now, it was enough. He was free. And for the first time in years, so was I.

We stepped out of the building, the sharp slap of the doors closing behind us muffling the finality of the moment. The city stretched out before us, oblivious to the little war we had just fought. Cars honked, people bustled along the sidewalks, the hum of a Tuesday afternoon in full swing. But I felt none of it. My pulse was still pounding in my ears, my feet moving on autopilot, my mind tangled in the mess of what had just happened.

He was quiet beside me, his hand still firmly clasped in mine, the warmth of his skin grounding me. But I could tell the silence wasn't just from exhaustion; there was a storm swirling just beneath the surface of his calm.

"Are you alright?" I asked, the words coming out softer than I intended, but I couldn't help myself. He'd won, yes. He'd taken back his power, shattered the illusions that had held him captive for so long, but there was still that shadow behind his eyes. That flicker of something unspoken, something that refused to settle into peace.

"I should be asking you that," he replied, his voice rough, but not unkind. He wasn't looking at me, though. His gaze was fixed on the street ahead, distant, as though searching for something just beyond his reach.

"I'm fine." I squeezed his hand, offering him a smile that I hoped was more convincing than I felt. "I'm just worried about you."

He gave a half-laugh, not a real one, but a small breath of humor that didn't quite reach his eyes. "I'm the one who's supposed to be worried about you, remember?"

I rolled my eyes, the absurdity of the statement pulling me out of the heavy quiet that had settled between us. "Oh, please. You're not the one who's been hanging by a thread this entire time, trying to keep it together while the world falls apart."

He stopped walking then, his body stiffening, hand still locked with mine. There was something different in his stance, something not quite right in the way he stood—like a man who had spent so long walking a tightrope, trying to find his balance, only to realize that he had no idea what solid ground actually felt like anymore.

"You think I'm broken," he said, the words flat but heavy with meaning.

"No," I said quickly, my voice too high to be convincing. "No, I don't think you're broken." I stepped closer to him, instinctively reaching up to touch his arm. "I think you've been through hell, but you've survived it. You're not broken. Not even close."

He looked down at me then, those gray eyes of his softening just a touch. "Then why does it feel like I'm the only one who can see all the cracks?"

I had no answer for that. There were no words for the vastness of his pain, no simple phrase that could encapsulate the years of darkness he'd lived through, the weight of the things he'd kept buried. Not even the victory, so sweet and hard-won, could erase what had been done to him. What he had done to himself in the name of survival.

"I don't know," I said softly, truthfully. "But you're not alone in it anymore."

He nodded, though I could see the doubt still clinging to the corners of his expression. "You should be. You don't have to carry this with me. You shouldn't have to. I never wanted you to."

"You didn't have a choice," I pointed out. "Neither of us did."

He didn't respond, just exhaled a long, steady breath as if trying to rid himself of something too heavy to carry.

"Do you think it'll ever really end?" he asked after a long pause.

I hesitated, chewing on the question for a moment before I answered, the honesty creeping in despite my attempts to shield him from the weight of the truth. "I think you can move on. I think you've already started, whether you realize it or not." I leaned against him then, just for a second, a small gesture of comfort, of being there, together in this strange, unspoken space between us. "But the past... It's like the scar you can't see, but it's always there. It doesn't go away. It just becomes part of you."

His eyes flicked to me, a mixture of surprise and something else. Maybe relief. Or maybe just a recognition that I understood, really understood, in a way no one else could.

"Does that scare you?" he asked, his voice low, as if the question itself was too fragile to raise too loudly.

I smiled, trying to keep things light, but the truth crept in anyway. "Does it scare you?"

"I don't know what scares me anymore."

We stood like that for a while, the world continuing to spin around us as the city thrummed with its ordinary chaos. I could feel the weight of the unsaid things pressing in, filling the space between us, but I couldn't bring myself to speak them. Not yet.

"I don't want to run anymore," he said after a long pause, his voice barely a whisper against the noise of the city.

The words hit me like a punch to the gut, leaving me breathless. For the first time in I didn't know how long, he wasn't trying to outrun his past. He wasn't trying to bury it under layers of bravado or anger or isolation. He was choosing to face it head-on, even if the path forward wasn't clear. Even if it still scared the hell out of him.

"Well, lucky for you," I said, my voice light, "I'm not going anywhere either."

He met my eyes then, and for the first time in a long time, I saw something different in him. Something real. Something that wasn't guarded, wasn't hidden behind walls he'd spent years building. There was a crack in the armor. And in that crack, there was light.

"Thank God for that," he murmured, a quiet laugh escaping him, as though the weight of everything had finally shifted, even if just a little.

The air around us felt different now, charged with something new. Maybe it was hope. Or maybe it was just the quiet understanding that, no matter how the past tried to haunt us, we had each other now. And that was enough to face whatever was coming next.

We didn't speak much as we walked back toward the car, our footsteps muffled against the pavement. The world felt oddly silent, as if it, too, was holding its breath, waiting for the aftermath to settle. I kept glancing over at him, wondering if I could read the thoughts that flickered behind those unreadable eyes of his. But it wasn't that simple. He wasn't the same person he had been when we walked in, but he wasn't yet the man he was meant to be either. There were too many jagged edges, too many loose threads in the tapestry of who he was now.

"I still don't know how to feel about it," he said suddenly, his voice cutting through the quiet like a knife through the air.

"About what?" I asked, trying to sound casual, though I could feel my pulse quicken. I wasn't sure I was ready to dive back into all of this.

"The fact that I'm free," he murmured, his eyes on the street ahead of us. "It's all I've wanted, right? To be rid of him. To be done with it. But it feels... strange. Like something's missing. Like it didn't work the way I thought it would."

I stopped walking, unsure if I was the one who needed to break through the fog between us or if he was asking me to unravel something far more complicated than I was ready for. "I don't think it's about the 'freedom' part," I said softly. "It's about what happens next. What you do with it."

He turned to face me then, his expression unreadable, but there was a flicker of something in his gaze—something wild, something untamed, like he wasn't sure how to deal with what had just happened. Like he was waiting for the other shoe to drop. "And what am I supposed to do with it?"

I let out a sigh, brushing my hair out of my face, trying to find the right words. "Whatever you want. That's the thing, isn't it?

You've spent so long being told what to do, controlled by someone else's vision of you, that it feels... wrong to be in charge of your own life now."

His jaw tightened at that, and I knew I'd struck a nerve. "You think I don't know that?" he asked, his voice laced with frustration. "I'm trying, okay? I just—damn it, I don't even know what 'trying' looks like anymore."

"You're doing it," I said firmly, stepping a little closer. "You're facing it. The things you've been running from. And you're doing it on your terms now."

He looked down at our hands, the way they were still locked together, as if the simple touch grounded him in ways that words never could. "I don't know if I can keep doing it. I don't know if I'm strong enough."

I could hear the doubt in his voice, that tiny crack that had slipped past his usual defenses. I wasn't sure how to fix it, but I knew something. I knew that it wasn't about me trying to heal him or make him feel better. It was about letting him find his own path to peace, even if that path was full of sharp turns and unexpected detours.

"Why don't we take it one step at a time?" I suggested, forcing a playful smile. "I mean, I could really use a coffee. How about we head somewhere that doesn't have any ghosts hanging around? Somewhere you can just... breathe for a minute."

He raised an eyebrow, the tiniest hint of a smile tugging at the corner of his mouth. "Are you bribing me with caffeine?"

"Bribery?" I scoffed, faking a wounded look. "You wound me, sir. I'm offering you the simple pleasures of life. What more could a man want?"

"You know, I'm not exactly the 'simple pleasures' kind of guy," he said with a grin, though his eyes didn't quite meet mine.

"I know," I said quietly, "but sometimes, we have to start with the simple stuff before we're ready for the big things."

He nodded, but before he could respond, something caught his attention. A sound. A faint, almost imperceptible click from behind us.

I froze, my stomach flipping, every instinct on high alert. "What was that?"

He tensed, his eyes scanning the street as if he could will the world to stop moving. But there was nothing there. Just the steady flow of traffic and pedestrians, oblivious to whatever had unsettled us.

"I don't know," he said, his voice taut with unease. "But I don't like it."

We continued walking, but now it felt like we were moving in slow motion. Every step felt too loud, too deliberate. My heart raced, my mind spinning with a dozen possible explanations, none of them good.

"Maybe it's nothing," I said, trying to convince myself more than him. "Maybe just the wind, or—"

And then, from the corner of my eye, I saw it. A shadow, moving too quickly, too precisely to be a coincidence.

"Get down!" he shouted, pulling me roughly toward him, just as something sharp whistled through the air, slicing through the space where we had been standing moments before.

I barely had time to register the danger before he was already moving, pulling me toward an alley, away from the open street, his grip tight around my wrist. His pulse was hammering beneath my skin, the sharp thrum of fear and urgency coursing through him.

"Who the hell would—" I started, but his sharp tug cut me off.

"Stay quiet. Stay close."

We ducked behind a dumpster, the sound of footsteps approaching from the direction we had just come. My breath caught in my throat, panic rising like a tide I couldn't control.

"Are you sure—" I began, but he silenced me with a look.

The footsteps grew louder, closer, and then there was a voice. Low, familiar, and far too calm.

"Well, well, what do we have here?"

I froze. It couldn't be. But as the voice came into focus, I knew that the nightmare had only just begun.

Chapter 36: Rising Flames

I had just finished my morning coffee—dark, bitter, and just strong enough to keep me upright—when the first hint of something wrong brushed the air. It was a subtle shift, like the change before a thunderstorm. I was half-absorbed in the comforting hum of the kitchen, flicking through my phone, when the scent hit me. It wasn't smoke at first. More like something burning, a kind of acrid sweetness that stung the nose. I frowned and set my mug down.

The clock on the wall ticked too loudly as I rose, moving toward the window. Outside, the sky was still blue, the kind of morning that promises nothing more than the usual humdrum of life. Nothing out of place—until I saw the flicker. A small curl of grey-black smoke rising from the direction of the barn. It was almost hidden by the trees, an intentional camouflage, I was sure of it. My stomach dropped.

"Dan?" I called, my voice trembling even though I didn't want it to. I hated sounding scared. But I couldn't help it.

Dan came rushing in, his face tight with a sort of restrained panic. He didn't even need to ask. He knew.

"Stay here," he said, though it wasn't a request. His hand was already on the door. His shoulders were squared, the same way they had been when he'd first fought for me—when he'd made the choice to protect everything we had, even at the cost of his own peace. I knew that look. I'd seen it a hundred times. The same look he gave me when he told me, in the softest voice, that we were done running. That we'd put the past behind us. But it was clear now that I had been foolish to believe it.

I wasn't staying behind, though. I'd spent too much time standing in the background of my own life, watching him fight for both of us. Now it was my turn to be more than just a bystander. I grabbed my jacket and pulled it on over the thin cotton shirt I'd been wearing. The morning chill bit through, but the heat from the fire would soon make up for it.

The barn was already fully alight when we reached it. Flames clawed at the sky, hungry and relentless, licking at the trees as if they were long-lost friends. The heat slammed into us, even at this distance. And the smell—there was nothing like it. You think you've smelled burning wood before, but until you've watched something you love get consumed by flames, you can't truly know it.

I felt Dan's hand tighten around mine. His grip was iron. He wouldn't let go.

"It's him," I said softly, almost to myself. The words tasted bitter in my mouth. Of course it was him. Who else would it be? I didn't know what kind of monster we were up against, but I had learned enough about him to know that he wouldn't stop until everything—absolutely everything—was gone.

Dan nodded, his jaw set so hard it looked like it might crack. His eyes burned with something darker, a rage I'd only seen a handful of times, always on the verge of breaking through, but never like this. He was shaking, not from fear, but from the cold rage inside him that threatened to burn everything around us. He hadn't been the same since that night, and I had always believed it was my fault. My love. My fight that had dragged him into something even darker. But now I wasn't sure. We weren't just fighting for survival anymore. We were fighting for something more important: our chance at life. Together.

"We need to get out of here," he said, his voice clipped. There was no time for hesitation. He pulled me toward the house, but my feet were rooted to the spot. I couldn't tear my eyes away from the flames, from the devastation. The barn was our safe haven, our place to rebuild everything we had lost. Now, it was a pile of charred timber and ash.

"Dan, what if we—"

"We can't save it, Em," he interrupted, his voice low and dangerous. "This is bigger than that. He wants us to be consumed by this. To lose everything."

The realization hit me hard, the weight of it pushing me down. He wasn't just trying to burn our home. He was trying to break us apart, bit by bit.

As we ran toward the house, a thought struck me, sharp and sudden. "What if he's already inside?"

Dan didn't answer right away. But when he did, his voice was thick with something I couldn't place. "He won't stop. But neither will I."

The front door slammed open as we rushed inside. There was no sound, no evidence of anyone being there, but the air felt wrong, thick with tension, as if we were being watched. I scanned the space quickly, looking for anything out of place, but there was nothing. Nothing but the suffocating silence that surrounded us.

Then, out of nowhere, the phone rang. I froze. It was too soon. The fire was still raging, and yet someone had the audacity to call.

Dan's hand hovered over the receiver. He looked at me, searching my face for some sign, some hint that we were safe, that everything was okay. But we both knew it wasn't. I nodded, my heart pounding in my chest, and he answered it.

The voice on the other end was cold, distant, and yet all too familiar.

"I told you," the voice crooned. "This isn't over. Not by a long shot."

And just like that, the world tilted again, spinning us back into the very fire we had tried so hard to escape.

I didn't know how long we stood there, the phone still pressed to Dan's ear, the voice on the other end echoing in the silence. It wasn't just words—it was a declaration, a grim reminder that we were still trapped in a game we hadn't chosen. My stomach churned as I watched him grip the phone tighter, his knuckles white. I wanted to say something, anything, but the words were buried beneath the weight of what I already knew.

We weren't just running from him anymore. He was hunting us down, one step at a time, forcing us into a corner where there was no escape. This wasn't some petty revenge or misdirected rage. This was deliberate, methodical, and damn near surgical in its precision. And we had become the collateral damage in his twisted play.

"Is that all you've got?" Dan's voice was low, controlled, but the strain was evident.

The voice on the other end let out a slow chuckle, a sound so devoid of humor it made my skin crawl. "You're not as clever as you think, Daniel. You and your little princess, you can run, hide, whatever. But eventually, you'll burn too."

He hung up before Dan had the chance to say another word.

"Did you recognize the voice?" I asked, even though I already knew the answer.

Dan didn't reply right away. He didn't need to. His silence spoke volumes. We both knew. He didn't have to say the name; it was embedded in our lives like a permanent scar.

"I thought we were done with this," I muttered, my voice tight with frustration. I was angry, so angry I could feel the fire rising in me, threatening to burn away whatever resolve I had left. "I thought we'd left all this behind us."

Dan turned to me then, his gaze heavy with unspoken words. The kind of look that said everything and nothing all at once. His jaw clenched, the muscles in his neck tightening with the effort of holding everything back. But there was nothing left to hold back. We were past that point.

"Get your things," he said abruptly, his voice softer, but no less determined. "We're leaving."

It wasn't a suggestion. It wasn't even a plea. It was a command, wrapped in the same raw urgency that had driven him to protect us at any cost. And for the first time in weeks, I saw him as he was before—driven by a purpose that was singular and all-consuming.

I nodded, feeling the weight of his words settle deep into my bones. We weren't safe anymore. We hadn't been for a long time. But now, with everything that had been happening, with the fire, the threat, and the terror of it all, I could feel the pull of danger once again.

I moved quickly, grabbing the essentials—just enough to make it through whatever came next. I didn't stop to question anything. I couldn't afford to. Dan was already a step ahead, his mind clearly elsewhere, already formulating a plan that would take us out of this. I could see the tension in his body, the tight lines around his eyes, the furrowed brow.

And I hated that I wasn't enough to make him stop. Hated that even after everything we had gone through, there was still something outside of us that could tear us apart.

But I wasn't the kind of person to stand idly by, waiting for disaster to strike. No. I wasn't going to let that happen. Not again.

"We need to go to the cabin," I said, as I shoved a few more clothes into my bag. The cabin wasn't far, hidden deep in the woods where no one would think to look. It was the one place where we had always felt like we could breathe, the one place that had never been tainted by his presence.

Dan didn't argue, but I could see the hesitation in his eyes. He didn't want to go there. I knew it. It wasn't just the isolation or the danger—it was the memories. The way the walls seemed to hold everything we had once been. The place where we had first found a spark of something more, something real, before everything got complicated.

Still, he grabbed his keys from the counter and turned toward the door. We weren't going to let him win. Not this time.

The drive to the cabin felt like it took hours, though it was only a short distance. It was as if the world outside was stretching, bending, forcing us to linger in that strange space between terror and anticipation. Every rustle of the trees, every car that passed, every shadow lurking in the periphery seemed like a threat. But we didn't speak. What was there to say? The weight of what we were running from was enough to fill the silence.

When we finally reached the cabin, it was exactly as we'd left it—a little weathered, a little worn, but still standing tall against the odds. The small structure nestled into the trees, surrounded by the dense forest like a fortress, offering its protection, its isolation. It should have been a place of solace, a place to lick our wounds and regroup, but as we stepped inside, the air felt thick with something else.

It wasn't the same as before. The shadows seemed deeper here, and the silence pressed harder against the walls. It felt like something was waiting, hidden just beyond the edge of the trees, watching us through the windows.

"What now?" I asked, trying to keep my voice steady as I sat on the couch, wrapping my arms around myself for warmth. It wasn't cold yet, but I could feel the chill creeping into my bones, the cold from the outside finally seeping into my skin.

Dan leaned against the doorframe, his gaze distant as he stared out into the darkening woods. His fingers were drumming restlessly on the frame, a nervous habit I had come to recognize. He didn't answer, not right away.

"I don't know," he finally said, his voice quiet. "But we won't be alone much longer."

I knew what he meant. Whatever we had left, it wasn't going to be enough to protect us from what was coming. And we couldn't outrun it.

The cabin seemed to close in around us as the last traces of sunlight dipped below the horizon. The gentle murmur of the wind through the trees was the only sound that dared disturb the suffocating silence between us. Dan had settled into the armchair by the fireplace, though the hearth had long since gone cold. He was staring into the dark, his posture rigid, his thoughts far away. I could practically hear the gears in his head turning, the plans he was formulating—plans that I wasn't sure we had the luxury of time to execute.

I let my gaze wander around the room, the familiar rustic furniture, the worn wood floors that still creaked when you walked on them, and the little knick-knacks that had once brought a sense of comfort now seemed like relics from a different life. The life before everything fell apart.

"Do you think he'll come after us here?" I asked, though the question was more to break the tension than out of any real hope for an answer.

Dan's eyes flicked to me, and for a moment, I thought I saw a glimmer of something softer—maybe even guilt—but it was gone before I could be sure. He ran a hand over his face, rubbing the stubble there in a way that made me want to reach out and stop him, to ease whatever burden was weighing him down. But I knew better. There were some things I couldn't fix.

"He won't stop until we're dead or broken," he said, his voice low and harsh, but with an undercurrent of something else. Something I couldn't quite name.

It made me shiver, the coldness in his words. He didn't sound like the man I had fought beside, the man who had always protected me with everything he had. This was the man who had been hollowed out by loss, by fear. It was the man who was still haunted by things he wouldn't talk about. Things I couldn't fix.

I shifted, uncomfortable in the quiet that had stretched between us like a canyon. We had danced around the edges of these conversations for months, but now, with everything spiraling out of control, there was no ignoring it any longer.

"Are you sure this is about us?" I asked, my voice trembling just a little. I hated how fragile I sounded, but I couldn't help it. I was tired of being strong, tired of holding it together for both of us. I wanted to scream, to punch something, but I'd long learned that nothing would change if I did.

Dan's gaze snapped to me, and for the first time, I saw the weariness in his eyes that mirrored my own. He let out a sharp breath, standing up and pacing in a tight circle.

"I thought I was done with this," he muttered, his words barely above a whisper. "I thought if I just... kept fighting, if I kept you safe, it would all go away." He paused, looking out the window, his jaw tightening. "But I can't outrun this. No matter how fast I go, no matter how far I push you, he's always there. Watching. Waiting."

I stood then, unable to stay seated any longer. My heart was pounding, an unease blooming deep in my chest, but I forced my voice to stay steady. "Then why keep fighting? Why not just... let it go? We can disappear. We could—"

"We can't disappear, Em," he cut me off, his voice sharp now. "You think I haven't thought of that? You think I haven't considered just walking away and never looking back?"

He was pacing now, like he couldn't stand still for even a second. His hands were raking through his hair in frustration, and for the first time in what felt like forever, I saw the cracks—the places where the perfect mask he had built was starting to fracture.

"Then why don't you?" I demanded, my voice breaking just a little. "Why are we still doing this? Why can't we be normal? Why can't we just—"

Dan's head whipped around, and for the briefest moment, I saw a flash of something raw in his eyes. Something dangerous. Something that scared me more than I wanted to admit.

"Because if I stop fighting, if I let it all go, I'll lose everything," he said, his voice low and dangerous, vibrating with an intensity I couldn't comprehend.

It hit me then—what he was really saying. This wasn't just about protecting me. This wasn't just about fighting for survival. This was about something deeper. It was about his guilt. His shame. The things he couldn't let go of.

He wasn't fighting for us anymore. He was fighting for himself.

The realization sank into my bones, and I felt the ground shift beneath me. How had I missed it all this time? How had I allowed myself to believe that his fight was for us both when it had always been for him?

I swallowed, forcing the words past the lump in my throat. "And what if you lose anyway?"

The room went silent. Even the wind outside seemed to hold its breath. Dan froze, his back to me, his shoulders rigid with the weight of what I'd just said. His words came out hoarse, raw with something I couldn't place.

"Then we're both dead anyway."

I felt a chill settle in my chest, the weight of his words pressing down on me. I couldn't breathe. The man I had loved—the man I thought I knew—was crumbling in front of me. He was so far gone in his own battles that he couldn't even see what was right in front of him.

I opened my mouth to say something, but the sound of something—someone—outside froze me in place.

A soft crunch of gravel underfoot. A shadow against the window.

My pulse quickened. My instincts screamed at me to run, but I couldn't move. The silence was too thick, too heavy.

Then the door creaked, just the slightest bit.

Dan didn't move. Neither of us did.

Another crunch. Closer now.

A knock.

A sharp, deliberate knock on the door.

I felt my heart stutter in my chest.

"Em," Dan whispered, his voice shaking just enough for me to hear. "It's him."

And in that moment, I knew—whatever I thought was coming had just been replaced by something worse.

Chapter 37: Smoke Signals

The air smelled of wet earth, the kind that soaks into your boots and sticks to the soles like secrets you're not ready to share. It was one of those mornings when the sky couldn't decide whether it wanted to be overcast or promise the hint of a sunbreak, teasing us with the possibility of warmth before retreating back into a cloud-covered gray. I sat against the moss-covered rock, the cold stone seeping through the thin fabric of my jacket, but the discomfort was a small price to pay. It wasn't about comfort anymore—it was about survival.

Beside me, the crackle of a dying fire echoed in the dense silence of the forest. We didn't have much, just the remnants of a flame that we dared not let die completely. Smoke curled lazily into the heavy morning air, a thin, dangerous trail of evidence that could just as easily be seen by an enemy as a sign of life, something worth extinguishing. I could feel it in my bones—the ever-present weight of danger, lingering just beyond the treeline, the quiet hum of tension hanging between each of us like a thread too thin to cut.

"You really think we'll make it out of this?" Milo's voice broke through the stillness, a mixture of disbelief and dark humor coloring his words. He was trying, as always, to mask the weight of his own fear, but I saw through it. Milo wasn't one for vulnerability, but after everything we'd been through, there wasn't much left to hide.

I glanced over at him. His face, usually sharp and unreadable, was drawn in a way that made him look younger than his years. His dark hair was matted to his forehead, dirt smudged along his jaw where he hadn't bothered to shave in days. There was something about the way he held himself, half-leaning against the tree as if he might fall over at any moment, that made my heart ache. He wasn't the kind to share, but somehow, with the world falling apart around us, we had both started talking more. More than either of us were prepared for.

I took a deep breath, feeling the coolness of the air fill my lungs, grounding me. "We have to," I said, my voice steady, even though my own doubts gnawed at the edges. "We've made it this far, haven't we? And I'm not about to stop now."

Milo snorted, his lips curling into a smirk, though it didn't reach his eyes. "Well, you've always been stubborn. I can't say I'm surprised."

I shrugged, a small smile tugging at the corners of my mouth. "What can I say? I'm a woman of conviction." It was my way of deflecting the truth—of pretending that the gnawing fear in my gut wasn't real, that the weight of every choice didn't feel like it was slowly crushing me. But Milo didn't push. He never did. Instead, he shifted his weight, eyes scanning the horizon before turning back to me.

"You know, I never thought I'd end up here," he said quietly. His words, unspoken up until now, felt like a confession—heavy, raw, unfiltered. "I always thought I'd die in some boring office job, pining for the thrill of... well, whatever it was we had before all of this." His words trailed off, like he couldn't quite finish the thought. Like he didn't know how to say the things that were buried under the surface.

I nodded, understanding the unspoken truth. Before all of this, we were different people—carefree, unburdened by the weight of constant danger. It was hard to imagine that version of us now, when every step felt like a trap waiting to be sprung. I'd forgotten what it was like to breathe easy, to smile without wondering if someone was watching, waiting.

"But you didn't end up there, did you?" I asked, my tone soft but firm. "You ended up here with me. And whether we like it or not, we're making a difference." I paused, feeling the heat of my words, knowing they weren't just for him. They were for me too. We had chosen this. We had chosen each other, even in the midst of the chaos. "I didn't plan on being here either, but now that I am, I'm not backing down."

He met my gaze, the intensity in his dark eyes more than enough to show that, despite his words, he was in this. There was no escape, no running anymore. We were too deep into it all. The world had shifted beneath our feet, and there was no going back. But even in the midst of the tension, I couldn't help but feel a strange sense of relief. Maybe it was the comfort of knowing that, for all the fear that surrounded us, I wasn't alone.

"I'll follow you," Milo said, his voice low, but steady. "To the ends of the earth, if that's what it takes."

A weight lifted off my chest at the sincerity in his voice. It was all I needed to hear. There was no uncertainty now. No second guessing. Just a simple, undeniable truth: we had each other.

The fire flickered weakly, casting a soft, flickering light that was both comforting and dangerous. The embers still glowed, but I knew it wouldn't last much longer. We had no choice but to move again. The cycle was relentless, and it didn't care if we were ready or not. But as I stood up, my legs stiff from hours of sitting on the cold earth, I didn't feel the familiar dread that usually followed such decisions. For the first time in weeks, I felt a strange sort of clarity, the kind that comes only when you know exactly what's at stake. And in that moment, I was certain: we were ready.

The dampness of the forest pressed in on us, thick like a cloak we couldn't shrug off. The trees, tall and stoic, seemed to be watching us, their branches bowing under the weight of time and their own secrets. Each footstep was muffled, swallowed up by the wet earth beneath our boots, and the silence between us stretched out longer than was comfortable. I could almost hear the blood pulsing in my ears, a rhythm that matched the drumming of my own thoughts. Every second felt fragile, as if the world itself might fracture if I breathed too loudly.

We moved through the woods, not speaking, not even looking at each other, as though somehow, if we didn't acknowledge the gravity of the situation, it wouldn't land so heavily on our shoulders. But it did. There was no escaping the truth, not anymore. The threat was real, and it had followed us too far, too close to where we thought we could escape. My fingers brushed the cool metal of the knife at my side, a constant reminder of how little I could trust the world around me.

Milo kept pace beside me, his eyes darting between the trees, scanning the horizon as though at any moment, a threat would materialize from the undergrowth. He wasn't saying much anymore, just the occasional glance that told me everything I needed to know. There was a plan, but the details were murky, like smoke lingering in the distance, impossible to catch and hold. For all the time we had spent together, I could feel the space growing between us, a tension that wasn't just born of the danger that haunted our every move. It was the silence of things left unsaid, of dreams not shared, of the weight of all we'd been through threatening to suffocate us in its suffocating embrace.

The clearing ahead caught my eye, a brief glimpse of light filtering through the dense canopy, and for a fleeting moment, I dared to believe we might be able to stop, to breathe without fear of what came next. But the sound of footsteps—too light, too quick to be ours—snapped me back into reality.

I reached out instinctively, grabbing Milo's arm before he could turn toward the noise. His body tensed beneath my grip, but he didn't pull away. Instead, he stayed still, eyes narrowing as he tried to pinpoint the source. His lips barely moved when he spoke, the words low and sharp. "Don't let them see us. We don't need this right now."

I nodded, swallowing the bitter taste of fear that rose in my throat. We had no choice but to wait, to become shadows, blending into the earth as though we were just another part of the landscape. My breath hitched as I crouched low to the ground, my knees protesting the sudden movement, but I ignored them. We couldn't afford to make a sound.

The minutes stretched long and thin, the tension coiling tighter with every passing second. Then, just as the sounds of footsteps seemed to be retreating, I heard something else. A voice. Soft at first, too muffled to make out, but then clearer, closer. I could hear the shift in the air, the heavy exhalation of a breath held too long. It wasn't just a scout anymore. It was someone searching for us, and they were too close. Too damn close.

Milo's hand slipped to the small of my back, steady and grounding, before he leaned in. "We move now," he whispered, his lips grazing my ear. "We don't stop."

I didn't need to hear more. I didn't need to debate the strategy or weigh the risks. We were moving, and we were moving fast. My heart hammered against my chest, but I ignored the panic clawing at my ribs. We didn't have time to feel anything. We just had to keep going.

The trees blurred around us as we cut through the underbrush, my feet finding their rhythm in the uneven terrain. The air was thick, the dampness of the earth and the weight of the forest pressing against us like an invisible force. Each step was louder than the last, each rustle of leaves a reminder that we were not alone, that someone was watching, hunting us.

But there was something else in the air, too. A feeling I couldn't quite place, a sense of inevitability that settled deep in my gut. It wasn't just the usual danger—the close calls, the near-misses. No, this was different. This time, I could feel the endgame coming, closing in with the precision of a hunter.

Milo's pace quickened, his steps almost silent despite the roughness of the terrain, and I forced my legs to keep up, my breath coming in shallow bursts. He didn't speak again, but I could feel the urgency in his movements. We were no longer just running from a threat; we were heading into something. Something bigger. Something that had the power to change everything.

The trees began to thin, the shadows of the forest giving way to the open sky. We were nearing the edge of the woods, but it wasn't a safe distance, not yet. We could still be seen. We could still be trapped.

Milo glanced back at me, his jaw clenched, eyes intense. I saw the unspoken question in his gaze, the silent plea for confirmation. It was now or never.

I nodded once, curtly. There was no more time for hesitation, no more time to wonder if we were ready. We had come this far, and we weren't going to stop now.

With a final glance back, I pushed forward, my legs carrying me faster, my pulse racing in time with the pounding of my heart. Ahead, the sky was a pale blue, stretching wide and open, but I couldn't focus on that. I couldn't focus on the promise of freedom that it might hold. Not yet.

The moment we crossed the threshold of the woods, I felt it—the weight of everything that had led us here, crashing down in a single instant. It was a mix of adrenaline and fear, of anticipation and dread. The danger wasn't over. It was only just beginning.

The silence between us grew thick and heavy, clinging to the space like an unwelcome fog. My breath came in shallow bursts, my senses honed to an almost painful sharpness as the world around me seemed to hold its breath. Milo's hand brushed against mine, the brief contact a reminder that, despite everything, we weren't alone. We were still in this together, even if the weight of what we were facing seemed too much for either of us to carry.

We had crossed into the open, the woods now a distant memory, but the ground beneath our feet felt unsteady, treacherous in ways that weren't immediately obvious. Every rustle in the grass, every snap of a twig, made my heart race as I searched the horizon for any sign of movement, any hint of danger. It was impossible to tell where the threat might come from next, and that uncertainty gnawed at me, a constant companion.

Milo turned toward me, his face drawn, his expression unreadable. "What now?" The words hung in the air between us, a simple question, but one that carried the weight of every decision we'd made up until now.

I scanned the landscape, my eyes darting between the tall grass and the open fields ahead, trying to make sense of it all. The terrain was unfamiliar, and the realization hit me—there was nowhere left to hide. We had no choice but to confront whatever was waiting for us, no more running, no more ducking out of sight. We had been running for so long, and I was exhausted—exhausted in every possible way.

"We wait," I said, the words coming out more firmly than I felt. "We don't move until we know who's out there."

Milo snorted, a sharp sound that cracked through the tension. "And if they know we're here?"

I shot him a look, the sharpness of his tone cutting through the fog of fear. "Then we make sure they wish they hadn't found us."

For a moment, there was a strange kind of stillness between us, the kind that made me wonder if I was becoming numb to the danger, or if I was just pretending I wasn't terrified. It was impossible to tell, but the truth was, we didn't have the luxury of fear anymore. Not when everything we had fought for was at stake.

We crouched low, both of us moving silently, instinctively, knowing that any noise could be the difference between survival and death. The world felt too quiet, too empty, and my mind began to race with every worst-case scenario I'd ever imagined. My heart pounded in my chest, but I kept my focus sharp. It was all we could do now—focus.

The days of running were behind us. Now, we had to be clever. We had to outsmart whoever was hunting us. I glanced at Milo, who seemed to be thinking the same thing. His face, usually so inscrutable, was taut with concentration. There was something in his eyes that hadn't been there before—a glimmer of something hard and dangerous. He was ready for this. And somehow, that made me feel more sure of myself, even though the uncertainty still clung to my ribs like a second skin.

"Tell me this wasn't part of the plan," I muttered, my voice barely audible.

He glanced at me, a wry smile tugging at the corner of his mouth. "You think I planned to get us into a corner again? That wasn't on the agenda."

The humor in his voice did nothing to ease the knot tightening in my stomach, but I appreciated the effort. Milo was always good at making light of things that were anything but.

"I don't think we have an agenda anymore," I said. "I think it's just us and whatever comes next."

He looked at me, and for the first time in what felt like forever, I saw something softer in his gaze, a flicker of understanding. "We'll make it. We always do."

And maybe we would. I wanted to believe that. I needed to. But with every passing second, the silence of the field seemed to press in harder, as though the very air was thickening with the weight of what was coming.

And then, without warning, the sound of footsteps—heavy and deliberate—cut through the stillness. My pulse spiked, every muscle in my body tensing in response. They were close, too close, and the realization hit me like a blow to the chest: we had been found.

Milo was the first to move, his hand on my arm, pulling me down lower to the ground, signaling me to stay out of sight. His eyes were scanning the area, sharp, calculating. He didn't say a word, didn't need to. We both knew that if we made a sound now, it could all be over.

I held my breath, my heart a deafening rhythm in my ears, every instinct screaming at me to run, to fight, to do something. But I did nothing. I stayed perfectly still, my eyes locked on the movement ahead, praying that whoever was out there wouldn't see us, wouldn't notice the faint outline of our hiding spot.

The footsteps grew louder, closer, until they stopped just beyond our hiding place. A rustle of clothing, a shift in the wind, and then silence. They were so close I could almost feel their presence, their breath mingling with the cool air.

A voice—low and unfamiliar—broke the stillness. "They're here. We've got them."

I couldn't see them, couldn't hear anything beyond the pounding of my own blood in my ears.

Then, a soft snap—something small, something breaking—and in that instant, I knew we were out of time.

Chapter 38: The Final Blaze

The house was still, too still, as if it had sensed what was coming. The kind of quiet that settles deep into your bones, pulling at your nerves with the weight of unsaid things. I stood in the entryway, my fingers pressing into the cool wood of the doorframe, grounding myself to something solid. I could almost hear the house breathing with me, the faint creak of the floorboards beneath the weight of our steps. I glanced over at him, standing just a little too close, the tension between us taut and electric, thick with the kind of silence that makes every move feel like an explosion waiting to happen.

His jaw was set, eyes narrowed in that way that had always made him look like a man too far gone, too tangled in his own fury to see beyond it. But tonight, something was different. There was no rage in his gaze—only a kind of cold resolve. He was ready, and I knew it as surely as I knew the back of my hand. This wasn't about the past anymore. It wasn't about the things he'd done, or the things that had been done to him. This was about the moment right now, this second, when everything could change. And we would face it together.

I took a deep breath, the weight of what we were about to do pressing down on me. "You're sure?" I asked, though I already knew the answer. My voice felt small, tentative in the grand scheme of things, as if the question wasn't just about him, but about me too. Could I do this? Could I stand by him, in the middle of this mess, and face the one thing we'd both been running from for so long?

His lips twitched, just the faintest curve, like a promise. He didn't speak, but I could feel the quiet strength in his presence. It was enough. It had always been enough. I pushed open the door, and the night air hit me like a slap—cold and sharp, carrying the scent of rain and something else. Something metallic. There was no turning back now. The trap had been set, and we were the ones walking straight into it.

We moved through the yard in silence, our footsteps muffled by the wet grass, the world around us swallowed by the dark. The trees loomed like dark sentinels, their branches reaching out in strange, twisted shapes, as if trying to warn us. Or maybe to protect us. But there was no protection here. No escape. Just the wait for the inevitable.

"Do you ever wonder..." I started, the words slipping out before I could stop them. "Do you ever wonder how we got here?" I glanced at him, expecting to see something in his expression, some hint of the man I used to know, the man before all this. But there was nothing. He was gone, or maybe he'd never really been there to begin with.

He didn't answer right away, his gaze forward, scanning the horizon. I could see the tension in his shoulders, the way his fingers flexed at his sides. But there was no hesitation. He knew exactly why we were here, just like I did. "I wonder," he said, his voice low, but it had an edge to it. "I wonder if we're doing the right thing."

I wanted to tell him that we were. That we had no choice, that we couldn't keep running from this—whatever this was, whatever we'd become. But the words got stuck in my throat. I didn't know if it was the cold, or the weight of his question, or the fact that I didn't have the answer myself. Maybe that's what scared me most. We were walking into the fire, and we were both so damn tired of being burned.

The closer we got to the old barn, the tighter my chest felt. The place was like a wound, raw and bleeding, the air thick with memories that clung to the rafters and whispered through the cracks in the wood. This was it. This was where it had all started, and now, here we were, ending it. Or at least, trying to.

The door creaked open, a long, drawn-out sound that felt like it could shatter the night. Inside, it was darker than I remembered, the shadows pooling like ink, swallowing everything whole. But I could feel him there, his presence as sharp and familiar as the ache in my chest. He was waiting. Watching. The man who had haunted us for so long, the one who had made us both into something we never asked to be.

"Ready?" His voice echoed in the silence, a challenge, a taunt. It didn't matter if we were ready. We didn't have the luxury of choice.

I stepped inside, my eyes adjusting to the darkness. And there he was, standing in the middle of it all, his hands folded in front of him like he was some kind of twisted saint, waiting for us to do what we'd come to do.

"I should have killed you years ago," the man said, his smile cold, calculating. "But then again, I never thought I'd get this far."

"You don't get to make the rules anymore," I said, stepping forward, my voice steady despite the way my pulse was racing. "This ends tonight."

His eyes flickered to me, and for a split second, I thought I saw something like recognition—or maybe it was fear. But then he laughed, the sound low and guttural. "You really think you can walk away from this? You've been dancing around it for years. What makes you think this time will be different?"

I glanced at him, the man beside me, the one who had been with me through all of this. And for the first time, I saw it—the quiet understanding that we didn't need to play his game anymore. This was our game now.

"This time," I said, my voice a whisper, but the conviction in it was all I needed. "This time, we win."

The air in the barn was thick with dust and something else, something sharp, like the taste of regret mixed with the sting of betrayal. I stood there, just a step behind him, watching as the man across from us shifted on his feet, that smug, almost amused look still glued to his face. I was sick of it. Sick of the games, sick of the endless dance we'd been forced to perform for so long, like puppets on a string. And now, here we were, tangled in the final knot, with nowhere left to run.

"Do you remember the first time you betrayed me?" the man said, voice smooth like silk, though there was an edge to it now. His fingers twitched at his sides, like he was testing the air, waiting for us to make a move. "You were so sure of yourself back then. So full of fire. I almost respected that."

I could feel the man beside me stiffen, the muscle in his jaw flexing as his hands tightened into fists. It was like watching a kettle on the verge of boiling over, the tension in him so thick I was certain I could taste it in the air. But he didn't snap. Not yet. He was holding himself back, waiting, calculating, like he always did. I wanted to ask if he was okay, if he was ready, but I didn't. We both knew that asking wasn't necessary. Words were cheap at a time like this. What we needed now was action.

"I didn't betray you," he said, his voice low but steady. It was the calm before the storm. I could tell he was reining it in, keeping himself in check. He wasn't going to give the man the satisfaction of seeing him break. "I was just trying to survive."

The man's smile faltered for the briefest moment, and it was all I needed to see. We were getting to him. That was the crack in the armor. The one that would eventually break it open.

"Survive?" The man scoffed, his laugh a little too loud, too manic. "You think this is about survival? You think it's ever been about that? This is about power. Control. You never understood that. You still don't."

I couldn't help it; I stepped forward, the words slipping out before I could stop them. "And you think you've got control? Look around, pal. You're about to lose everything."

His eyes flicked toward me, narrowing like a predator catching scent of something more dangerous than it expected. I held my ground, matching his stare, but my heart was pounding. I couldn't afford to show fear now—not with him so close, not with everything at stake. But I could feel him, the past, clinging to me like a weight I couldn't shake.

"You're not as clever as you think you are," he said, but there was a tremor in his voice now, just barely noticeable, like he was trying to hold on to something that was slipping away from him.

"Neither are you," I shot back, my voice sharper than I intended, but I didn't care. The sharpness felt good. It felt like the first real step toward putting this nightmare to rest. "You've spent all this time holding onto power, but you've never had control. Not really."

Something flickered in his eyes, something I couldn't quite place, but I wasn't about to give him the chance to recover. This wasn't about talking anymore. This was about ending it.

The man beside me was moving now, his body tight, every muscle coiled, ready for the strike. But I saw it before he did—saw the flicker of motion from the corner of my eye, saw the flash of something metal in the dark. The trap. It had been waiting for us, just like we'd planned.

A loud crack filled the air, followed by the shriek of metal scraping against wood. It was so sudden, so sharp, I didn't have time to brace for it. But I didn't need to. The man beside me was already stepping forward, his body a blur as he moved with the kind of speed that only comes from years of practice. He wasn't just reacting anymore. He was leading.

In one fluid motion, he had the man pinned against the wall, the metal knife pressing hard against his throat. There was no hesitation, no second thoughts—just pure, unrelenting precision. The world seemed to slow down around me, the air thick with the promise of something final, something irrevocable. I could feel the pulse of my own heartbeat in my throat, the rhythm of it steady and calm, as if everything I'd ever done had led to this one moment.

"You're done," the man beside me said, his voice quiet but full of finality. "I'm not the one who's been holding onto the past. You are."

The words hung in the air, heavy and suffocating, and for a moment, it felt like the world had stopped moving. The man pressed against the wall didn't speak, but I could see it in his eyes—the flicker of something more than anger. It was fear. And it was something I'd never seen before. Not in him. Not in the man who'd spent so long pulling the strings.

"Go ahead," he spat, the words thick with contempt. "Kill me, if you think that's what it'll take to win. You think this will fix it? You think this will change anything?"

I couldn't look away from him. I had to hear it. I had to hear him say it, because I knew, deep down, that this wasn't just about the man in front of us. This was about us. About how we'd let ourselves be shaped by him for so long.

And then, the man beside me took a step back, dropping the knife. The sound of it hitting the floor echoed in the silence like a death knell. The past—the grip he'd held on both of us—was over. It was done.

"You don't get to control me anymore," he said, voice low, like a vow, but there was something softer in it now. Something lighter. And for the first time in years, I felt like I could breathe.

The man's eyes were wide now, a mixture of disbelief and something darker, but there was nothing left to be said. There was no more fight. Not from him. Not from us. The flames had burned through everything, and all that was left was the ash.

The moment the knife clattered to the floor, everything shifted. There was no dramatic flourish or sudden rush of emotion, just a quiet, aching realization that this was the end. Not the end of the fight, perhaps, but the end of the chains that had bound him for so long. I could feel the weight lifting from his shoulders, see the way his body relaxed just the tiniest bit as if the years of carrying the past were suddenly too much to hold. I didn't know what would happen next. None of us did.

But the silence stretched, like an invitation to something neither of us was ready for, even as it beckoned. I moved toward him without thinking, my feet almost betraying me as I crossed the floor, closer to where he stood, still staring at the man who had made our lives hell. My breath was shallow, my skin pricking with awareness. I had come here to fight, to help him, but standing next to him now, in the aftermath, the air between us felt unfamiliar, as though we were both standing on a threshold we hadn't noticed before.

He didn't look at me, though I knew he could feel me there. I wanted to say something—anything—but the words wouldn't come. There was nothing left to say. We had burned the bridges, torn down the walls, and now all that was left was this strange, heavy space between us, full of things unspoken. We had done what we needed to do, but now, now what?

A sound cut through the tension—the scraping of boots against the wooden floor behind me. I turned just as a figure emerged from the shadows. It was him. The man who had been pulling the strings for so long, his smirk still firmly planted on his face, even in the face of defeat.

"You think it's over?" he asked, his voice mocking, though there was a tremor there now. A crack in his own confidence.

The man beside me stiffened, his eyes snapping to the figure. It wasn't fear, not anymore. There was something else. Something colder.

"You had your chance," the man beside me said, his voice low, but with a calm finality that made the hairs on the back of my neck stand up. "Now you'll have to deal with the consequences."

The other man laughed, but it was brittle, like broken glass. "Consequences?" he echoed, his eyes flickering between us with a sort of panicked curiosity. "You don't even know what consequences are."

I didn't know whether to be insulted or amused. He wasn't wrong. We'd been dancing around consequences for years—him, because he thought he could control us, and us, because we hadn't had the strength to break free until now. But this wasn't about consequences anymore. This was about something deeper. Something he couldn't understand. And if he had any idea what was coming next, he would have been terrified.

"You can't keep running from yourself," I said, my voice cutting through the thick air. My words sounded braver than I felt, but that was the point. We weren't running anymore.

The man's face hardened at my words, but his eyes told a different story—fear. Fear that had been simmering just beneath the surface all this time. Fear of losing control. Fear of losing everything.

He took a step back, like he was about to bolt, but I saw it coming. The flash of movement. The knife. He wasn't done yet. In the blink of an eye, he lunged, the glint of the steel blade flashing in the dim light. Time slowed, as it always does when you're not sure if you're about to live or die.

But it wasn't the man beside me who moved first. It was me. I didn't even think about it. My hand shot out, instinct kicking in, and I grabbed the first thing I could—a heavy metal pipe lying discarded on the floor. I swung it with everything I had. The sound of metal connecting with bone was sickening, and for a split second, the world went absolutely still.

He staggered, the knife slipping from his grasp, a grunt of pain escaping him. And I knew, with perfect clarity, that we weren't going to win by playing nice. We had to end this, once and for all. But the twist was in how we were going to do it.

Before he could regain his balance, the man beside me moved. In an instant, he was at the other man's side, grabbing him by the wrist and twisting it with precision. The sound of bones cracking was like a gunshot in the quiet barn, and the man cried out in pain. It was almost poetic, the way everything fell into place—the last few years of rage and desperation spilling out in that one single, calculated motion.

But I knew this wasn't the end. It couldn't be. There was something still gnawing at me, a nagging feeling that we hadn't accounted for everything. He was too calm. Too willing to be overpowered.

And then I saw it. In his eyes. The glint of something more sinister than just a man on the edge.

The floor beneath us began to shift. The barn creaked as if in warning, and for a split second, I thought the building was going to collapse on us. I turned sharply to look behind me. My stomach dropped. The fire—the one that had been flickering outside—had spread. The barn was starting to burn. And this time, it wasn't going to stop.

"Move!" I shouted, but it was too late. Flames were already licking at the beams above us, the heat sweltering as the fire began to consume everything in its path.

I looked back at the man beside me. His face was grim, but I could see something there—something raw, something that said we were going to get out of this. Together. But as the smoke thickened, and the flames rushed toward us, I couldn't shake the feeling that something worse was coming.

And then, just as I was about to turn, I heard a noise from behind us. A rustle, a shuffle.

I whipped around just in time to see him— the man—grinning like a wolf. "It's not over," he hissed, his voice low, lethal. The last words I'd hear before the world around us exploded into chaos.

Chapter 39: After the Ashes

The scent of scorched wood lingered in the air, thick and heavy, as if the earth itself was still catching its breath. It clung to the skin like an old memory, and every step I took on the cracked earth felt like I was treading on the remnants of something we had both fought so hard to escape. The world around me was as muted as a faded photograph, the colors of life washed out by the fire that had once consumed everything in its path. And yet, there was a strange serenity in the stillness. The trees, now skeletons of their former selves, stood like sentinels, witnesses to the chaos, waiting for the world to begin anew.

He walked beside me, his hand wrapped around mine with a warmth that contradicted the chill of the morning air. We didn't speak at first—words felt unnecessary here, where the weight of everything that had happened seemed to hang between us like the smoke still curling in the distance. I didn't need to look at him to know that his eyes were locked on the same ruins that stretched out before us. He was a man reshaped by fire, his past burned away like the old timber, leaving behind a version of him that I couldn't yet quite recognize. I could feel the tension in his shoulders, the quiet war he fought within himself, but I knew better than to press him for answers. In time, he'd share what needed to be shared. For now, we had nothing but this moment, and it was enough.

The sound of my boots crunching against the charred earth was the only noise that filled the air, the silence between us speaking louder than anything else. When we reached the edge of what had once been a meadow—a patch of green where the wildflowers had grown thick and free—he stopped. I did too, unwilling to break the fragile calm that had settled around us. He turned to me then, his face still soft with the remnants of a smile, though it didn't quite reach his eyes. I could see the battle in him, a storm that no one else could touch, but I also saw something else, something that flickered in the depths of those dark eyes. It was hope, fragile and tentative, like the first crack of light at dawn.

"We survived," he said, the words low, as though he couldn't quite believe them himself.

I nodded, swallowing the lump in my throat. "We did."

A soft breeze stirred, pushing through the ruins and carrying with it the scent of the earth beginning to heal. For a moment, everything seemed to pause, as if the universe itself was holding its breath, waiting to see what we would do next. I squeezed his hand, willing him to feel what I felt—how, in spite of everything, there was still a future ahead of us. The ashes might have claimed everything in their path, but they hadn't claimed us. Not yet.

"I never thought I'd be here," he murmured, his voice cracking with a vulnerability that he rarely allowed to show. "I thought... I thought the past would always haunt me."

"I know," I replied softly, reaching up to touch his cheek, tracing the lines there with my fingers. "I know. But you're not that man anymore. You're not defined by what's come before. This"—I gestured to the ruins around us—"this is just... the beginning. You've laid the ghosts to rest, and now it's time to build something new."

His eyes softened, the tightness in his jaw relaxing just a fraction. He looked down at our joined hands, as if he needed the reminder that we were together in this. "I don't know what the future holds," he confessed, a faint smile tugging at the corners of his lips, "but I know that I want it to be with you."

The words were simple, but they landed between us like a promise, fragile yet unbreakable. We didn't need to say more. The air was thick with the weight of everything unspoken—the years of turmoil, the ghosts that had followed us both—but now, for the first time, we were looking ahead instead of behind. We had a future, a shared one, and no matter what it might hold, we would face it together.

"We'll make it," I said, my voice steady, certain. "Whatever happens, we'll make it."

He nodded slowly, then pulled me closer, his arms enveloping me in a way that felt like both protection and surrender. There was no more fighting, no more running. What had been broken could be mended, piece by fragile piece, and the cracks that ran through us both would become the places where light could get in.

When we pulled away, I looked at him and saw not just the man I had loved before, but the man who had been rebuilt by fire and loss, someone who had learned to stand tall in the ashes and not crumble beneath them. His hand brushed my cheek, his thumb grazing over the scar that marked me, the one I had come to accept as part of who I was.

"You're beautiful," he said, the words so soft they almost seemed to disappear in the wind.

I smiled, my heart full. "We're both still here. That's all that matters."

And just like that, the world seemed to open up before us, wide and full of possibility. The past no longer had its hold on us. The future was ours to shape, and we would build it with the hands that had been scarred but had also learned to hold steady. The ghosts of what we had once been were gone, and in their place, we stood together, ready to begin again.

We didn't speak much as we moved further into the remnants of what used to be home. The landscape was unrecognizable—charred earth, broken walls, and twisted metal that had once been sturdy support beams now lay crumpled like discarded toys. Yet, there was something oddly soothing about the chaos, as though the universe was in the process of figuring itself out again, piece by broken piece. In a strange way, it felt like we were, too.

I couldn't stop the laugh that bubbled up from my chest, unexpected and tinged with both bitterness and relief. "I guess we won't be hosting dinner parties here anytime soon."

He turned to look at me, one eyebrow cocked in that way I knew too well. It was that same mischievous glint that had always made me feel like maybe we were playing on the same side of the universe's joke. "Not unless you've got some marshmallows in your bag," he replied, his voice warm with a hint of playfulness.

I smiled back, though it was small, just a twitch of my lips. "I think the only thing we'll be roasting is the idea of ever getting the smell of smoke out of our hair."

His expression softened as he took my hand again, squeezing it just enough to remind me we were still tethered to something solid. It wasn't much, but it was enough. We walked for a while, the silence between us no longer uncomfortable but companionable, as though we were letting the land speak for itself. It had been broken, burned to nothing, and yet it still held an odd kind of power. Maybe because the earth was patient.

We found what was left of the garden—a scattering of scorched vines and singed flowers that had once bloomed in bright defiance. I crouched down, brushing my fingers across the brittle remains of a lavender plant. The scent was faint, but it was there, a whisper of something that hadn't quite given up. I inhaled deeply, letting the memory of it fill my lungs. There was no returning to what had been, but there was a quiet promise in what still lingered—proof that even the most stubborn of life forms could survive, somehow.

"Do you ever wonder if we'll just keep walking in circles?" I asked, my voice a little hoarse, though not from the smoke. It was more the weight of the question, the kind that always seemed to linger in the back of my mind.

He squatted down beside me, his hand grazing mine as he reached for the wilted lavender. "I think we're already walking in circles," he said, his tone a mixture of thoughtfulness and that sharp wit of his that never quite let me off the hook. "The trick is knowing when to stop and make a new path."

I glanced at him, searching his face for the familiar shadows of doubt, the ones that had never quite gone away even when he smiled. But all I saw was a man who was more himself now than I'd ever known him to be—gritty, broken in ways that couldn't be undone, but unafraid to embrace it. "So, what, you think we can just... start over? Like nothing happened?"

He shrugged, but there was a slight smile at the corner of his mouth. "I think we already have."

I wanted to ask him more—about his thoughts, his plans, his heart—but something held me back. The answers weren't something he could give in one breath, not after all that had happened. I knew that. Instead, I let the moment sit, letting the soft rasp of the wind through the dead grass speak louder than words could.

Our pace slowed as we wandered deeper into what had once been our sanctuary. The house, or what was left of it, stood in the distance—its silhouette an odd, twisted mockery of the home it had been. I found myself walking toward it, almost without thinking. There was a kind of unfinished business here, a need to witness it in its entirety, to look it in the eye and claim it wasn't stronger than us.

I climbed over a pile of rubble and found myself standing in the wreckage of what had been the living room. A pile of blackened furniture lay in the corner, a once-loved armchair reduced to a heap of cloth and soot. I could still see the outline of the fireplace, though it was filled now with debris rather than warmth. The windows were gone, the frame shattered, and the floor beneath my boots was uneven, the boards warped and cracked.

It was here that I felt the pull. I stood in the center of the room, my arms hanging loosely at my sides, as if waiting for the walls to speak to me. "It's...gone," I whispered, more to myself than anyone else.

"Gone, but not forgotten." His voice was quiet, close, his presence suddenly behind me, just enough to make the hairs on the back of my neck stand up. "This place doesn't define us, not anymore."

I nodded, swallowing hard against the lump in my throat. "I know. But it's hard to shake off, you know? The memories are embedded in these walls, like they're part of the very structure."

He stepped closer, placing a hand on my shoulder. "We're not those people anymore, and this place—" He glanced around the wreckage. "—this place doesn't hold us. Not anymore. We decide what's next."

I turned to face him, looking up into his eyes, those eyes that had seen so much and yet still held something—something that refused to give up. There was no grand epiphany in his words, no sudden burst of brilliance. It was the quiet certainty of someone who had walked through hell and had the courage to keep moving forward. And maybe, just maybe, that was enough.

"I think I'm ready," I said, my voice steady, though it trembled just slightly at the edges.

"Good," he replied, offering me a crooked smile. "Because I've got a feeling that whatever's coming next is going to be far better than anything we left behind."

The words hung between us, and for a moment, it felt like we were standing on the precipice of something new, something that had been waiting for us all along.

The world around us was still as we stood there, the remnants of what had been our life scattered like confetti in the wake of a storm. The quiet stretched long, thick with memories we hadn't quite learned how to shed. His hand was warm in mine, and as we lingered in that strange, suspended moment, I couldn't shake the sense that something was shifting. Not just in the land around us, but in him, in me, in everything that had once felt like it was slipping through our fingers.

"Do you ever feel like we're being watched?" I asked, half-expecting him to laugh it off.

He didn't. Instead, his gaze flickered toward the overgrown brush at the edge of the ruins, eyes narrowing just slightly. "I thought I heard something earlier," he said, his voice steady, but there was an edge to it, like a rope pulled tight and ready to snap.

My heart skipped a beat, that old instinct kicking in, the one that told me to be alert, to not let the comfort of this new peace lull me into a false sense of security. It had been too easy, too smooth a transition from chaos to calm. "You think it's someone? Or... something?"

His hand tightened around mine, and though his face remained impassive, I could feel the tension running through him. "Not sure," he replied, his voice low. "But I don't like it."

We stood there for a moment, the stillness pressing in on us like the weight of an unspoken truth, a warning neither of us wanted to acknowledge. "Maybe it's nothing," I said finally, trying to shake off the sudden unease that had settled in my chest.

He didn't reply, and when I glanced at him, his eyes were scanning the horizon, his jaw clenched in that way that always made me think of battles fought long ago. "I hope you're right," he said, and there was something in the way he said it that made my stomach tighten. "But I've learned not to trust that kind of silence."

We began walking again, more slowly this time, the sense of being watched hanging in the air like a thick fog. His gaze never wavered from the distant trees, the piles of ash, and the jagged remnants of what had once been a home. He was scanning every shadow, every shift in the wind, the way a soldier does when the war isn't over, even if the enemy seems to be gone.

I wanted to ask him what he was thinking, but I could see the question was already there on his face. The ghosts of his past hadn't been as easily laid to rest as I'd hoped. They lingered in the periphery, waiting to come back.

And then we heard it. A rustle, low and deliberate, just on the edge of the woods. It was a sound so faint, so insidious, that it took a moment for it to register. But once it did, the hairs on my neck stood straight up.

He turned to me, his eyes sharp, alert. "Stay close," he muttered, his voice tight with the same edge I had heard in his words earlier. Without waiting for a response, he moved toward the trees, his movements swift and purposeful.

I hesitated for a heartbeat, but then I followed him, my boots crunching softly in the dirt. The world had grown impossibly still around us, save for that faint rustling, and I found myself holding my breath, waiting for whatever it was to reveal itself.

We reached the edge of the forest, the trees looming like silent sentinels, their bare branches creaking in the breeze. He stopped, and I almost walked right into him. His hand shot out, gripping my arm to steady me, and his voice was barely a whisper. "I don't know what's out there, but it's not good."

I nodded, heart racing, as I scanned the darkening shadows. There was something here, something that didn't belong, something that had been lying in wait, patient as the fire had consumed everything. And now, as we stood here, in the aftermath of it all, I had the sinking feeling that whatever it was, it wasn't about to let us rebuild in peace.

The rustling grew louder now, more distinct. And then, just as I thought it might be an animal, something—or someone—stepped into view.

It wasn't an animal. It was a figure, tall and shrouded in dark clothing, moving through the trees with the kind of grace that made the hairs on the back of my neck stand on end. I couldn't make out any details—just the outline of someone who seemed to have emerged from the very shadows themselves. I opened my mouth to say something, but the words caught in my throat, lodged there by the terror that was beginning to knot my insides.

"Stay behind me," he said, his voice a low growl, as he took a step forward, his body a solid barrier between me and the stranger.

I didn't argue. I could feel the tension in his muscles, the barely-contained readiness to spring into action. It was the kind of danger we hadn't seen since before the fire. And now, it was here again, bringing with it a familiar unease, the kind that had followed us through every dark alley, every alleyway of our shared past.

The figure took another step forward, closer now, and I could see the faint glint of something metallic in their hand—shiny and sharp. My pulse quickened, my mind racing to make sense of what was happening. Who was this person? And why did it feel like the past had come alive again, its tendrils reaching out to pull us back into the very nightmare we had worked so hard to escape?

And then, without warning, the figure spoke, their voice cold, detached. "I was wondering when you'd come back."

I froze. The words landed like a slap in the face. "Come back? You..." I trailed off, struggling to process the weight of those words, the recognition of something I hadn't even known I'd been running from.

The figure stepped forward again, and this time, I could see the outline of their face—a mask, a pale white thing that made their expression unreadable, even as their eyes glinted with a hint of something... familiar. And then it hit me. The shadow of a memory I had thought buried long ago, a name I hadn't allowed myself to speak.

My breath caught in my throat. "No..."

But the figure only smiled, and the world went dark.

Chapter 40: Hearts on Fire

The first thing I noticed when I woke up that morning was the smell of coffee wafting through the air. Strong and warm, the kind that makes you feel like everything's going to be alright. It was my favorite part of the morning, this quiet moment when the world hadn't fully woken up yet, and I could still pretend that nothing had the power to ruin the peace I'd found in the space we'd built together.

I rolled over in bed, a stretch pulling at the edges of my body, muscles still sore from yesterday's hike, but satisfied. The weight of our shared history—the complicated, messy past that had once threatened to tear us apart—had settled into something solid, something I could finally breathe in without choking on the tension of what might have been. The house felt different now, too, warmer, somehow. Even the walls, which had once felt cold and distant, seemed to hum with the life we were building.

He was sitting at the kitchen counter when I wandered downstairs, sipping from his mug like he had all the time in the world. I caught a glimpse of his eyes as he looked up—like there was a secret there, something he was only willing to share with me, something that made everything else fade into the background.

I leaned against the doorframe, watching him for a moment. There was a kind of contentment in the way he moved, a quiet assurance in the way he held himself now. The fire that had once burned between us, fierce and scorching, had settled into something deeper, something that simmered with a quiet intensity. There was a gentleness there too, the kind of gentleness that only comes after you've fought your way through the storm together and come out on the other side.

"Good morning," I said, my voice a little hoarse from sleep, but there was a smile on my lips as I crossed the room to join him.

He didn't say anything at first, just reached out and pulled me into his arms. I melted against him, the way I always did. There was something about the warmth of his body, the way it felt like home, that made it impossible to resist.

"You're up early," I murmured, fingers tracing the edge of his mug as I sat down beside him.

He grinned, a teasing look in his eyes. "Can't help it. I've got a wife who can't seem to sleep in. You've got a busy mind, don't you?"

I rolled my eyes, playfully nudging him with my shoulder. "Well, I'm not the only one. You've been up for hours, haven't you?"

"Maybe," he said, taking another sip of his coffee, eyes glinting with mischief. "But I wasn't the one who got up at the crack of dawn to chase that perfect sunrise."

I laughed, the sound light and carefree, something I hadn't heard from myself in a long time. It felt good, good to be here, good to be with him, in this little house that had quickly become our sanctuary.

The day stretched out in front of us like a canvas waiting to be painted. The air was crisp, the sky a clear blue, and even the trees outside seemed to be settling into the rhythm of our lives, their leaves fluttering in the breeze like they, too, were content. I felt it then—the shift, the unspoken promise between us. We were no longer just surviving. We were living. And not just living, but thriving. The past, with all its pain and uncertainty, had finally been replaced by something steadier, something real.

As we moved through the day, side by side, I could feel the heat of his hand against mine, a subtle reminder of everything we had overcome, everything we had built. The way he looked at me sometimes, as though I was the only person in the world who mattered, made my chest tighten with something that wasn't quite sadness, but something deeper. A kind of gratitude, perhaps. Or maybe it was just the knowledge that the fire between us—though it had tempered—would never fully go out. It was there, simmering just beneath the surface, always ready to flare back to life at the smallest spark.

We spent the afternoon on the porch, the air growing cooler as the sun began to dip lower in the sky. I curled up against him, resting my head on his shoulder, and we watched the day fade into night. There was something perfect about it—something simple, yet profound. The world was changing, the seasons turning, but here, in this quiet corner of the world, nothing seemed as important as the feeling of his arm around me.

"You know," he said after a long stretch of silence, his voice low, the words weighing heavily in the stillness between us, "I think we've made it, don't you?"

I smiled, turning my head to look up at him. "We've made it through the hardest part," I said, my voice steady, but my heart a little softer than it had been when I first arrived. There was an understanding there now, a connection that didn't need to be spoken aloud to be felt.

He chuckled softly, brushing a strand of hair from my face. "I mean more than that. I think we've finally figured it out. Whatever this is, it's ours. And nothing—nothing—is going to take it away."

There was a fire in his eyes, something fierce and unwavering, but it wasn't the same fire that had once threatened to burn us alive. This was different. This was a steady flame, one that would keep us warm no matter what storms lay ahead.

I nodded, the weight of his words settling over me like a comforting blanket. "I think you're right," I said quietly. "This is just the beginning."

It was in the quiet moments, when the world outside seemed to hold its breath, that I found myself falling in love with him all over again. Not in the grand gestures or passionate speeches, but in the way he would stand in the kitchen, humming under his breath while making dinner, as though he had all the time in the world to wait for the perfect pot roast to slow-cook. Or the way he'd press a cup of coffee into my hands, his eyes crinkling at the corners as though he knew a secret joke I wasn't in on.

There was no grand revelation, no moment of fireworks when I realized how deeply I felt. It was more like the quiet certainty of the stars, distant and silent, yet ever-present. The kind of love that settles into your bones and makes you feel like everything—no matter how messy or uncertain—could somehow be okay because he was here, next to me.

We didn't need to talk about it much anymore, that love. It lived between us, pulsing like the hum of an old song you don't quite remember the words to, but you recognize the rhythm, the way it moves you.

Of course, it wasn't all perfect, not by a long shot. No one ever tells you that life, even the good parts, is layered with friction, that even the gentlest of flames can catch a gust of wind and suddenly flare into something unpredictable. A misstep here, an off-handed comment there, and things could spin out of control faster than you could blink. But we had learned to navigate that, hadn't we? We'd learned how to fight with fire and still come out unburned.

"I swear, if you touch that spoon one more time," he said, his voice low but teasing, as I hovered over the stove, stirring the sauce for the third time in as many minutes. I glanced over at him, finding his smirk and narrowing my eyes in mock warning.

"It's not my fault," I said, half-smiling despite myself, "that your cooking is so... unpredictable. I'm just trying to make sure it doesn't end up looking like charred cardboard again."

"Ah, so it's my cooking skills you're worried about?" he teased, one eyebrow raised in playful challenge. He leaned against the kitchen counter, arms folded, looking every bit the cocky chef he fancied himself to be.

"Your cooking skills," I agreed. "And the fact that you're setting the fire alarm off every time you try to make dinner."

"Fire alarm is a necessary life skill," he said, almost seriously. "How else would you know you're living on the edge?"

I snorted, shaking my head, amused. "Living on the edge?" I said, tossing the spoon in the sink, "You're setting off alarms every time you go near a frying pan."

"Hey," he defended himself, "it's a talent."

I watched him for a moment, leaning back against the sink, arms crossed, and a look of mock indignation on his face. There was a streak of something almost childlike in the way he acted, something that made me want to reach out and pull him close, just to see the softer side of him that he kept tucked away beneath layers of bravado. He could be hard sometimes, prickly like the bark of a tree, but when he let his guard down, it was like discovering a new world.

"Fine," I said, after a moment of consideration. "You're a culinary genius, and I'm the one with the unrefined palate."

"Damn right you are," he said, winking as he swept past me, his arm brushing against mine in an accidental but intimate gesture. "Now, let's see if we can salvage this dinner. I'd rather not spend the night on takeout."

The air between us shifted, as it so often did, when we found ourselves on the brink of something unspoken. The banter had lightened, but the tension hadn't completely dissipated. There were days when I could feel the smoldering heat of his gaze, the flicker of something deeper and older that we both still hadn't fully explored. The passion between us hadn't gone anywhere, not really. It was just… quieter now, like a storm gathering on the horizon, waiting for the right moment to break.

"You know," he said as he stood next to me, reaching for a pair of tongs and turning the roast, "it's funny how things turn out."

I glanced up at him, trying to make sense of the way he said it. It wasn't regret, not exactly. But it wasn't the casual remark I expected either.

"Funny how?" I asked, eyes narrowing a little.

He paused, his expression thoughtful, like he was choosing his words carefully. "Just... a year ago, we were barely speaking. Now, look at us."

A shiver ran through me at the reminder. A year ago, we hadn't known if we could ever really make it. The wounds we had inflicted on each other, the betrayals, the lies—it felt like a weight we would never escape from. But here we were, our own little corner of the world, putting together meals and talking about silly things like fire alarms and ruined dinners.

"We made it through, didn't we?" I said, my voice softer, the weight of what we'd been through settling heavily between us. "We're still here."

He turned to face me, and for a moment, the mask slipped. I saw something raw in his eyes, something that spoke of everything we had been through. And in that moment, I realized we weren't just here. We weren't just surviving.

We were rebuilding.

"Yeah, we are," he said quietly, his hand brushing against mine, his fingers lightly grazing my skin, sending a jolt of electricity up my arm.

And in that moment, it wasn't just the tension between us that simmered. It was the quiet certainty of how far we had come—and the undeniable pull of what was still to come.

I was standing at the kitchen sink when he came up behind me, his presence quiet at first, like a shadow inching into the light. He didn't say anything right away, just stood there, close enough that

I could feel the heat of his body against mine, his breath warm on my neck as he reached for the dish towel hanging by the counter. For a moment, I forgot the plates I was washing, the water running over my hands, because it was hard to focus on anything other than the way his fingers brushed against my skin, that subtle touch that made my heart beat just a little faster.

"You know," he said softly, "I'm getting really tired of being in second place." His voice was teasing, but the hint of something deeper lingered in the air between us. Something not quite playful, not quite serious, but entirely real.

I turned, giving him a half-smile, trying to hide the flutter that went through me. "Second place? And what exactly am I supposed to be winning?" I raised an eyebrow, the playful deflection a way to cover the tightening in my chest.

"Well, if you insist," he said, stepping closer, the movement slow, deliberate. "I'm second place to your work, second place to your friends, second place to whatever you're thinking about when you get that look on your face." He was standing so close now, his hand brushing against the small of my back, sending a wave of heat through me.

I felt a spark of defensiveness, but I hid it behind a smirk. "I didn't know you were keeping score."

His lips twitched at the corner, but his eyes remained serious. "Maybe I am. And maybe I'm ready to take the top spot."

My breath caught in my throat, his words not quite what I expected. There was something in the way he said it, something in the quiet intensity behind those simple words, that made the air between us crackle. It was the first time in a while that I could feel the fire building again, slowly but surely, like the kindling of a flame that had been smoldering beneath the surface.

"Is that so?" I asked, leaning into the counter, giving him the kind of smile that I knew could go either way. "And what makes you think you've earned it?"

He didn't flinch, didn't look away, his gaze steady and unfaltering. "I think I've earned it every damn day since we decided to rebuild this thing between us." His voice dropped lower, the words carrying a weight that I hadn't anticipated. "I've been patient. I've been more patient than I thought I could be. But there's only so much space left in my life for second place."

I felt a pulse of heat—not from the oven, not from the warmth of the kitchen, but from something deeper, something undeniable that stirred inside me. His words were both a challenge and a confession, raw in a way that left me exposed, left me wondering if I'd been blind to the depth of his feelings.

I couldn't find my words for a moment, my mind racing to catch up with my heart, which seemed to be beating louder in my chest than usual. And then, the walls I had carefully built around myself, the ones I thought were solid and unbreakable, suddenly felt thinner, like they were nothing more than paper and air.

Before I could respond, he reached out, his fingers finding mine, the touch light but certain, like he was pulling me out of something deep inside myself. "I'm done standing in the background, watching. I'm done being patient. I want to be your priority, not a second thought."

I pulled my hand back, suddenly aware of how vulnerable I felt, how raw the space between us was. "It's not that simple," I said, my voice shaky, betraying the calm exterior I tried to maintain.

He didn't seem fazed by my resistance. Instead, he stepped closer, the tension between us building with every inch. "Maybe it isn't," he said, his voice low, almost too soft. "But I'm not afraid of complicated anymore. Are you?"

I swallowed hard, feeling the weight of his question press against me. The air was thick with unsaid things, things we'd both kept hidden from each other, things we hadn't dared to voice for fear they'd be the spark that set us off again. But there was no avoiding it now. Not with the way we were standing there, inches apart, feeling the heat of something too strong to ignore.

He tilted his head slightly, as if he were waiting for me to make the next move, and in that moment, I realized just how much of this—of us—had been about waiting. Waiting for the right moment, waiting for things to settle, waiting for the past to stay buried. But the truth was, no amount of waiting could change the fact that we were both standing on the edge of something.

"Are you ready?" he asked, his voice barely above a whisper, his eyes never leaving mine. His question wasn't just about now. It was about everything that had come before, everything that was still to come.

I opened my mouth to answer, but the words never came.

Just then, a loud knock echoed through the house, sharp and unexpected, making both of us freeze in place.

We exchanged a glance, the moment between us fracturing, the tension breaking like glass. He moved first, stepping back, but the look in his eyes didn't waver. "I guess we're about to find out."

The knock came again, louder this time, insistent. My heart skipped a beat, a wave of unease sweeping through me.

"Who could that be?" I asked, my voice too soft, too unsure.

He didn't answer at first, just walked toward the door, his steps heavy on the wooden floor. And as he reached for the handle, I felt it—a ripple of something deep in my chest. The kind of unease that only came when something big, something life-changing, was about to unfold.

He paused, hand on the doorknob, and turned back to me, his expression unreadable.

"Stay here," he said, his voice low, dangerous.
I nodded, the knot in my stomach tightening.
And then he opened the door.

Chapter 41: A Love Rekindled

The sun dipped low behind the horizon, casting a golden sheen over the waves that lazily lapped against the shore. The air was thick with salt and the unmistakable scent of the sea—fresh, untamed, and alive. The sand beneath my bare feet was cool, soft, still warm from the heat of the day. My heart hammered in my chest as I watched him—Carter—standing at the water's edge, his back straight and his gaze fixed on me, as though he were waiting for something only I could give.

I shifted nervously from foot to foot, feeling the weight of this moment pressing against my ribs. There were no grand declarations, no fireworks or over-the-top gestures, just the quiet certainty of a promise made in the most intimate of settings—this small patch of earth, touched by no one but the tide and the sun. The breeze tousled my hair, making it cling to my face, but I barely noticed. My eyes were locked on him, on the way his jaw was set in that familiar, stubborn line. He was the same as I remembered, yet everything had changed.

We'd spent years avoiding this moment, dancing around it like two people who knew better than to believe in the kind of love that could survive the years of hurt we'd inflicted on each other. But here we were. All of it—the anger, the heartbreak, the years apart—had somehow led us to this point. There was no longer any room for doubt in my chest. The past was gone. The future, still unwritten, stretched before us like the vast expanse of ocean at our feet.

The small crowd around us had grown quiet, watching, waiting. Friends, family—people who had been part of our story, our fractured journey. They smiled, but their eyes held the same flickering uncertainty I felt inside. Would this work? Could we rebuild the wreckage we'd left behind?

My fingers brushed the delicate fabric of my dress, a simple thing, with no frills or lace, just a soft, understated elegance that felt like it belonged to this moment. It wasn't the kind of dress I imagined wearing for a day like this—too simple, too real—but it was the kind of dress I'd wear now, after everything we'd been through. No more grand illusions, no more empty promises. Just raw, unvarnished truth.

The officiant—someone I barely recognized, a friend of Carter's from years ago—cleared his throat and smiled, but his voice faltered slightly, unsure. I couldn't blame him. How do you speak the words that tie two lives together again after everything? The silence between us hung heavy, not uncomfortable, but charged with a thousand unsaid things.

I took a deep breath and walked toward him, each step an effort to calm the jittery energy that buzzed beneath my skin. His eyes never wavered, never strayed, and it was as though time itself had paused, just for us.

"How do we always end up here, on this same shore?" I whispered, the words slipping out before I could stop them. They were for him, but they were for me, too.

He smiled then, a small, crooked thing that made the space between us feel impossibly small. "I don't know," he said, his voice low, but steady. "Maybe we were always meant to be here. Or maybe we're just too stubborn to stay away."

The corners of my lips tugged upward at that, despite myself. "That sounds about right." I reached out, touching the cuff of his sleeve, as though anchoring myself to him once more.

The ceremony moved forward slowly, methodically, as though each word spoken could alter the fabric of the universe. The vows were simple, grounded in a quiet understanding that we'd already been through it all, that this was less about promises and more about the acknowledgment of what had always been. We'd come full circle, from the messy beginnings to the painful middle to this point, where the end was no longer something we feared.

His hand found mine as the officiant spoke the final words, sealing the deal.

"I do," Carter said, and I felt the weight of it settle into my chest, a comfort, a balm for the old scars.

"I do," I replied, the words slipping out more easily than I expected, as though they were the only truth I'd ever needed.

The moment lingered, stretching on forever, but in the best way. The wind picked up slightly, tousling my hair again, and I could hear the faintest cry of gulls overhead. But it was the sound of Carter's breath, steady and deep, that grounded me. The rush of the sea faded into the background, and in that instant, nothing else mattered but the two of us standing together, in the heart of this vast world, making a quiet promise to each other.

We turned, walking down the aisle—if you could even call it that—our hands still tangled together, our steps in sync. The crowd erupted into applause, but it felt distant, like a memory we could barely touch. I felt as though we were the only two people in the world.

A slight breeze swept in from the sea, cool and soothing against my skin. The tension that had gnawed at me for so long—the uncertainty, the fear that we were just one more failure in a long line of them—was gone. And with it, came something else: the unmistakable feeling of home.

We didn't need to say it out loud, not yet. But in the space between us, between the softness of his touch and the steady rhythm of our hearts, I knew. This time, we were different. This time, we would make it.

The reception was an unexpected affair—simple, yet perfect in its chaos. The beach house, only a few hundred feet away from the ceremony, was alive with laughter, music, and the mingling of voices. There were no extravagant decorations, no towering cake, just the warmth of the fire pit crackling in the corner and the low hum of a guitar in the distance. The air, still heavy with the salt from the ocean, felt fresh, almost like it was giving us a second chance, like it was holding its breath, waiting for us to finally take the plunge into something real.

Carter had been quiet ever since the vows. Not in a bad way, but in that contemplative, "I've just said the most important thing I've ever said in my life" way. I could tell it was still settling in for him, the gravity of it. He wasn't a man of many words, but his silence was the kind that spoke volumes, the kind that filled the spaces between us in the most profound way.

I walked up to the table where a small group had gathered, the clink of glasses and the soft chatter around me blending with the distant sound of waves crashing. I found Sarah first—my best friend, my partner-in-crime since forever. She was sipping from a wine glass that looked way too delicate for someone as formidable as her, her eyes bright, a mischievous grin playing on her lips.

"You look... well," she said, arching an eyebrow as I slid into the chair next to her. "You're doing this whole 'married' thing way too effortlessly. It's unsettling."

I laughed, the sound escaping a little too freely, a little too loud. It felt good to be back here with her, with someone who understood the mess I'd made of everything, who had seen me at my worst and still somehow stuck around.

"I'm just as surprised as you are," I said, glancing back over my shoulder where Carter stood, speaking with his cousin. He looked every bit the man I had fallen in love with years ago, but now he was also someone new, someone I was still learning to trust. We were figuring it out together, piece by piece.

Sarah didn't miss the glance. She was too sharp for that. "You're doing fine," she added with a wry smile. "But let's be real for a second. You're never going to let him live down that ridiculous dance you two did at the reception. I swear, it looked like a synchronized disaster."

I snorted, the first genuine laugh in what felt like days. "We both know that was a mistake from the moment we agreed to it. But I swear, that man has no rhythm. He's got the grace of a bull in a china shop."

Sarah leaned back in her chair, her arms crossing over her chest. "Oh, I know. I was watching, and all I could think was, 'Is this what a love story looks like in real life? Because I'm here for it.' It's messy, and it's awkward, but it's real. And that's exactly what you two need."

I nodded, turning my attention back to Carter. There were times, especially over the last few months, when I wondered if I was making the right decision, if I was simply chasing something that was already gone. But when I looked at him now, I didn't feel like I was clinging to a ghost. I felt like I was stepping into something new, something I couldn't fully understand yet, but that I was willing to figure out.

"Maybe we're just too stubborn for our own good," I muttered to Sarah, unable to tear my gaze away.

She chuckled, a deep, knowing laugh. "You two are nothing if not stubborn. It's probably why you're still standing here."

I hesitated. "You think I'm making the right call? I know you're my best friend, and you've always been the one to remind me to think things through, but this... this is different."

Sarah's eyes softened, and for the first time that day, there was a quiet wisdom in her gaze, something I hadn't seen in a while. "Do I think you're making the right call? No. But I think you're making the call you need to make. And I know you won't regret it. You've both fought hard for this. And, if anything, that says a lot more than all the doubt you're carrying around."

The words settled over me like a blanket—comforting, heavy, and familiar. The doubts I'd had seemed so much smaller now, now that they were spoken aloud. It was always easier to hold on to uncertainty when it was quietly gnawing at the edges of your thoughts, but now that someone else had given voice to the possibility of redemption, I could breathe a little easier.

I glanced back to where Carter stood, still engrossed in conversation. There was something about him that made my pulse quicken, something that had never faded, even in the years we'd spent apart. Despite all the distance and time, he was still the first person I thought of when I woke up and the last person I thought of when I closed my eyes.

A voice, familiar and smooth, interrupted my thoughts. "Is this the part where we get to toast to second chances?"

I turned, startled, and found Carter standing beside me, his hand outstretched toward my wine glass. His eyes were mischievous, but there was a depth to them now that hadn't been there before—a kind of quiet strength that made the air around him feel different.

"Absolutely," I said, raising my glass to meet his. "To second chances."

"To not messing it up this time," he added with a wink.

The words hung between us for a moment, charged with the kind of tension that comes when two people have spent years circling around each other, trying to figure out if they're brave enough to take the leap. But in that moment, I realized that we already had.

And we had done it together.

We clinked our glasses, the sound ringing out against the distant roar of the waves. And for the first time, I truly believed we might just make it.

The night felt like it had its own rhythm, its own heartbeat. The waves didn't crash anymore, just murmured against the sand in a soft, steady lullaby, while the flickering lights from the fire pit cast strange, golden shadows over the faces of our friends and family. The laughter and conversation blended in the cool evening air, the tang of saltwater and the scent of woodsmoke mixing with the faintest perfume of the flowers strung up in the nearby arbor.

Carter and I lingered just a little to the side, watching as our guests mingled, danced, and celebrated the fact that we had somehow, impossibly, managed to do what we had set out to do—make a promise that felt real. The world seemed so much quieter now, softer, as though everything was still adjusting to the weight of what we had done. The firelight danced across Carter's face, and I couldn't help but trace the curve of his jaw with my gaze. His eyes found mine, and there was a flicker there—something raw and full of understanding. His fingers brushed mine, light as a breath, and I realized then, truly, how much I had missed him.

"I should probably go mingle with the others," I said, my voice not quite as steady as I wanted it to be. It was odd, how easy it felt to slip back into this comfortable familiarity with him, and yet how terrifying it still was to be this close, this vulnerable.

He raised an eyebrow, but there was something in his expression—something that dared me to stay just a little longer, to let this quiet moment stretch on until we were the only two left in the world. "We could always just run away," he suggested, his voice low and teasing, but his eyes told a different story. "You, me, the beach, the stars. I think we could both use a little more time alone."

I laughed, half-genuine, half-nervous. "Is this your idea of a romantic elopement? Because if it is, it's not going to work. I'm not abandoning our guests to get lost in the night with you. Not this time."

He smirked, clearly enjoying my discomfort, and then slowly, without breaking eye contact, he took a step closer. "It wouldn't be abandonment. I'd say it's an...extended honeymoon. One with no interruptions." His hand slid to the small of my back, a comforting, possessive gesture that sent a jolt of heat through me.

It was then, in that brief, but intense moment, that I felt something shift in the air between us. It wasn't a grand gesture or a sweeping revelation, but something simple and undeniable. Something that had always been there but had been clouded by time and distance.

"You always were a hard sell," I said, half-laughing, half breathless, trying to steady myself.

He raised an eyebrow. "Only for the things that truly matter."

I stared up at him, his face so close to mine, his lips just barely brushing against my hair as he leaned in. For a moment, I thought he was going to kiss me, right there, with the world watching, or maybe without it. But he didn't. He let the moment stretch between us, as though he knew that we were standing on the edge of something that could tip either way.

And just as quickly as it had come, the tension shifted. Carter stepped back, his hand dropping from my back, his expression unreadable for a split second. But I saw the way his jaw clenched, the way his fingers twitched at his side, and I knew. He was thinking, just like I was, about how we had always been this close and yet so far apart.

"I think we need a drink," he said finally, his voice steady, but with an edge of something I couldn't quite place. "Before either of us says something we might regret."

Before I could respond, someone else interrupted us—thankfully, it was Sarah. She was approaching with a smile that had always been more knowing than friendly. She held two glasses in her hands, one of them tipped precariously with a cocktail that looked like it might have a little too much rum in it.

"I thought you two might need some company," she said, her eyes darting between us. "What's going on over here? Do I need to intervene?"

I shook my head, a little too quickly. "No intervention necessary. We're just... taking a breather." I took the drink she offered, more grateful than I cared to admit for the distraction.

She smiled, her eyes lighting up as she glanced at Carter. "Taking a breather, huh? You're lucky I don't have the energy to keep playing matchmaker, or I'd start asking about the kiss. But I think we've all had enough drama for one night."

Carter grinned, his earlier tension melting away in the face of Sarah's relentless teasing. "Don't worry," he said, tipping his glass toward her. "We're fine. Really."

She didn't look convinced, but she let it slide, choosing instead to grab a seat nearby and engage in an animated conversation with some of the other guests. I watched her, then glanced back at Carter. There was a brief, unspoken understanding between us, a shift that neither of us acknowledged out loud.

But just as I thought we might settle into this moment, just as I thought the evening would stretch on peacefully, a voice broke through the air—sharp, and suddenly filled with urgency.

"Lena," it called, a familiar, unwelcome sound.

I froze, my heart skipping a beat. There, standing at the edge of the group, was Adam. The one person I had spent years avoiding, the person I had never wanted to see again. His eyes locked on mine, and my stomach churned as a thousand questions collided in my mind. Why was he here? How had he found me?

And then, just as quickly, my gaze shifted back to Carter. His jaw tightened. His expression went cold, unreadable.

In the space between us, a silent war began to simmer.

Chapter 42: The Eternal Flame

The wind tugged at my coat as I stood by the window, watching the gray clouds roll across the sky in waves. The air was crisp, thick with the scent of wet leaves and the promise of a storm. It was a familiar scent, one I had grown used to over the years. The city had its way of reminding you that nothing lasts forever, that change was inevitable, that you had to keep moving, or you'd be swept away. I was learning to embrace that change, even if I didn't always understand it.

I turned from the window, my fingers brushing the cool glass before I let it drop to my side. The house behind me was quiet now, a peaceful silence that felt too heavy for my heart. Every corner held memories—some I welcomed, others I wanted to bury deep beneath the floorboards. But memories don't stay buried, not really. They find their way to the surface, whispering in the quiet moments, in the spaces between breaths.

His voice broke the stillness. Soft, but steady. "You're a long way from running, you know that, right?"

I smiled without looking at him, the sound of his footsteps moving closer as familiar as the rhythm of my own pulse. "I'm not running." The words were quiet but resolute, a promise I hadn't realized I was making to him, to myself.

"You sure about that?" His voice was thick with something I couldn't quite place. "I've seen you try."

I turned to face him then, my eyes tracing the familiar lines of his face, the way his hair fell in soft waves against his brow, the way the light danced across his features. He was my calm in the storm. No matter how much the world changed around us, no matter how much we both shifted in ways we never expected, there was something constant about him—something I could trust. Something I could hold on to.

"I'm sure," I said, taking a step toward him, my breath hitching slightly. The distance between us had always felt like a universe, even in a room as small as this. But now? Now the space was different. Less an ocean, more like a river—still flowing, but not so far away.

He reached out, taking my hand in his, his fingers warm against mine. "I'm not going anywhere," he said, his voice soft but filled with a certainty that made something inside me flutter.

I swallowed, trying to steady my heartbeat, but it was impossible. He always had that effect on me. "I know," I whispered. The air between us seemed to thicken, charged with a static that made everything feel too real, too present. I could see the future in his eyes—a future that stretched out in front of us, full of possibilities, of new beginnings and old ghosts.

But I wasn't afraid of those ghosts anymore. They didn't have the power to haunt me the way they used to. Not with him by my side.

"You've been carrying a lot, haven't you?" His words were soft, more of a statement than a question. But they hit me harder than I expected. I wanted to argue, to tell him I was fine, that I didn't need anyone's pity or concern. But I couldn't. Not when he was looking at me like that, with those eyes that saw straight through to the parts of me I kept locked away.

"Yeah," I admitted, my voice cracking slightly. "I guess I have."

There was a beat of silence before he pulled me into his arms, his embrace wrapping around me like a cocoon. I closed my eyes, letting myself sink into him, feeling the steady beat of his heart against my chest. For a moment, I allowed myself to believe it. That maybe, just maybe, I didn't have to carry the weight alone anymore.

"Let it go," he murmured, his breath warm against my ear. "Let all of it go. You don't have to hold it anymore."

I nodded against him, the words swirling in my mind like a tangled mess. Let it go. It was easier said than done, but in that moment, with him, it almost felt possible. Almost.

"I'm scared," I confessed, the words slipping out before I could stop them. I could feel him tense slightly, but he didn't pull away. He didn't flinch. He just held me tighter, his fingers pressing against the small of my back as if grounding me to him, to us.

"I know," he said quietly. "But you don't have to do it alone. Not anymore."

The knot in my chest loosened, just a little. I had lived so long with the fear that I would always be alone, that I would always be running from something—either from my past or from myself. But here, in this moment, with him, I realized that maybe I didn't have to be.

We had both been through our own storms, fought our own battles, and somehow, despite everything, we had come out the other side, together. It was strange, how life worked that way. You could spend years wandering in the dark, convinced that you would never find your way, and then suddenly, everything clicks. The path becomes clear. The storm passes.

"I don't know what the future holds," I whispered, my words lost in the soft murmur of his breath. "But I know I want to face it with you. Whatever it is."

He pulled back slightly, just enough to look into my eyes. There was a fire there, a quiet intensity that made my heart race. "We'll face it together," he said, his voice low, filled with a promise that made my skin tingle. "And whatever comes next? We'll handle it. We've made it this far."

And for the first time in a long time, I believed him.

The sound of the kettle whistling from the kitchen pulled me from my thoughts, and I gave a soft laugh as I wiped my eyes. Funny how a simple noise could remind you that life was still humming along, despite all the heavy moments. It was a reminder that we were still here, still moving forward. We might not know exactly what was ahead, but we had each other, and maybe that was enough for now.

I made my way into the kitchen, the warmth from the stove spreading over me, comforting in its familiarity. He was leaning against the counter, his sleeves rolled up, a mug of coffee in hand. His eyes followed me as I moved around the room, like he couldn't quite help himself from watching. I couldn't blame him. I'd caught myself doing the same thing more times than I could count, when he thought I wasn't paying attention.

"Have you ever noticed," I asked, pouring hot water into the teapot, "how you never really know someone until you make them coffee at four in the morning?"

His lips curved into a smile, though it was a quiet one. He was the kind of man who wore his smiles like a secret, not a badge of honor. "I think I learned everything I need to know about you when I saw how you make tea."

I turned to look at him, eyebrows arched. "And what's that supposed to mean?"

He raised his mug in mock salute. "I'm just saying, you're the only person I know who makes tea like it's a science experiment. It's... kind of impressive. You could be running a lab somewhere, brewing up something that could change the world."

I snorted. "Well, if the world is really in need of better tea, I suppose I'd be the one to save it." I tilted my head, watching him. "Maybe that's my true calling—global tea reform."

He let out a quiet laugh, the sound warm and easy, like a blanket on a cold day. I couldn't help but smile back, my own heart lightening at the sound. There was something about him, the way he could make everything feel effortless, even in the moments that weren't.

"You always did have a knack for making the impossible sound like it's no big deal," he said, setting his coffee down on the counter and crossing the room toward me. "But then again, you've been handling impossible things for a long time, haven't you?"

There was no bitterness in his voice, no judgment. Just truth. It wasn't the first time we had danced around that topic. We had both carried our fair share of baggage, and we had never been afraid to look at it, pick it apart, and lay it all bare. Maybe that was why we worked so well—because we had nothing to hide from each other.

I met his gaze, my fingers tracing the rim of the teacup absentmindedly. "I think the thing with impossible things," I said, my voice quiet but firm, "is that they don't stay impossible forever. Not if you're willing to try. Over and over, if you have to."

His hand brushed mine, warm and steady, before he pulled back just slightly, giving me room to breathe. "And that's why I think we'll make it," he said. "Because you've never given up. Not on anything. Not on yourself, not on the people you love, and definitely not on me."

I blinked, the weight of his words settling in like a heavy quilt. It was a strange thing to hear, even stranger to believe. For a long time, I wasn't sure anyone could see me that way—not truly. Not in the way he did. But with him, I started to think that maybe, just maybe, I didn't have to keep fighting alone.

I leaned into him then, my face pressed against his chest as I took a deep breath, inhaling the scent of him—the musk of cologne, the trace of fresh coffee, the faintest hint of something woodsy that clung to his clothes. "I don't know how I got so lucky," I murmured, my voice muffled.

He chuckled softly, fingers brushing my hair. "Lucky?" He paused, his voice turning lighter, teasing. "You were the one who nearly ran away from me a dozen times, remember?"

I pulled back to look at him, narrowing my eyes in mock offense. "You were insufferable back then. It was practically a survival instinct."

"Ah," he said, raising his hands in surrender. "I was just being a good, stubborn man. Doing my job, making sure you didn't miss the obvious."

I rolled my eyes. "Sure, sure. You've convinced yourself of that. But I didn't need saving."

"No, you didn't," he agreed, his tone turning serious. "You needed someone who understood when to push and when to let you be."

I swallowed, his words stirring something deep inside me. It was strange to think that, for all the times I had thought I was alone, there had always been someone right beside me—someone who never really gave up, even when I wanted to.

"You've been my rock," I whispered, my voice catching. "I don't know how to tell you how much that means to me."

He didn't say anything at first, just took my hand and squeezed it gently, as if the gesture was enough. And for a moment, I believed it was. He didn't need to speak every word. His actions, his presence, were louder than anything his voice could say.

The kettle on the stove whistled again, louder this time, cutting through the soft stillness of the room. I stepped back, taking my tea from the counter and pouring it into the cup. The warm steam curled around me, and as I inhaled, I couldn't help but feel that maybe, just maybe, this was the beginning of something new—something I could believe in. Something that had been worth all the struggles, all the battles, and all the heartache. Something I wouldn't run from. Not anymore.

The morning light crept through the curtains, casting soft shadows across the room, and for the first time in a long time, I felt like I was breathing in sync with the world. The chaos, the noise, the endless questions—they all seemed so far away now, like distant memories from another life. Here, with him, there was only this moment. Only the warm, steady pulse of a love that had quietly transformed from a flicker of hope into something undeniable.

I caught sight of the clock and winced. It was almost time. Time to face the day. Time to face the world outside. But for a few more minutes, I wanted to savor this quiet. The kind that only existed when you were alone with someone who had come to mean everything to you.

He stirred beside me, his breath slow and even, like the rhythm of a song you never wanted to end. I glanced at him, half expecting him to be awake, but he was still lost in the haze of sleep, his face soft, almost childlike. A far cry from the man who had walked into my life with such purpose, such conviction. That same man now lay beside me, tangled in the sheets, vulnerable in ways he hadn't allowed anyone to see before.

I could still remember the first time he'd let his guard down, just a crack, when he looked at me in a way that made my heart skip a beat. No one had ever looked at me like that—not with tenderness, not with understanding. He'd come into my life like a storm, shaking everything I thought I knew about myself. And somewhere along the way, I had stopped fighting it.

His hand shifted on the bed, and I froze, thinking he was waking up. But no, it was only a dream, his fingers twitching like he was chasing something in the deep recesses of his mind. I couldn't help but smile. He always seemed to be chasing something—whether it was answers, or me.

I gently brushed his hair back, watching him sleep for a few moments longer, until I couldn't resist the urge to wake him. Carefully, I leaned over and kissed his forehead, a quiet gesture that felt more intimate than any whispered confession. His eyes fluttered open, slow and lazy, and for a moment, I thought he was still somewhere between the realm of sleep and reality.

"Morning," he mumbled, his voice rough with sleep.

"Good morning," I replied, my fingers tracing the lines of his jaw. "How long are you planning on pretending you don't want coffee?"

He chuckled, the sound vibrating through his chest, and for a second, everything else faded away. "I wasn't pretending," he said, his voice thick with humor. "I just didn't want to move."

"Smart man," I teased. "But you can't hide from the inevitable forever."

He groaned, and I could practically feel his body protesting the idea of moving. "It's not that," he said, rubbing his eyes. "It's just... I've never really been a fan of mornings. But with you? It doesn't seem so bad."

That made me pause. His words, simple as they were, carried more weight than I expected. I looked at him, his eyes now fully awake, staring back at me like he was seeing me for the first time all over again. In his gaze, I saw the same raw honesty that had drawn me to him from the beginning—the kind of honesty that left no room for pretense or lies.

"Are we really doing this?" I asked, my voice almost a whisper, unsure whether I was talking about the moment or something much bigger.

His lips twitched, but there was no hint of hesitation in his gaze. "Doing what?"

"This. Us," I said, waving my hand between us as if that could somehow encompass everything. "Being... real."

He tilted his head, studying me in a way that felt like he could read every thought I had, like he knew exactly where my mind was going. "I thought we were already there," he said quietly.

I hesitated. "Are we?"

He didn't answer right away, instead reaching for me with that same deliberate calm he had whenever he was truly trying to understand me. "I think we are," he said, his voice low, "but if you're asking if we're ready for whatever comes next... then I think we're as ready as we're ever going to be."

I swallowed hard, the weight of his words pressing on me in a way I wasn't sure I was prepared for. We had already crossed so many lines, already been through so much. And yet, the future still loomed like a shadow, casting doubt where certainty once lived.

The silence between us grew heavy, like the pause before a storm, but then he shifted again, pulling me closer, his chest warm against mine. "I know this isn't easy for you," he said, his voice more serious now, the playfulness gone. "I know you've got your walls up, and I know they've been there a long time. But if there's one thing I'm certain of, it's that I'll keep knocking until you let me in."

My breath caught in my throat, his words stirring something I hadn't even realized was buried deep inside me—fear, hope, the possibility of something more. He was giving me something I had never asked for. Something that terrified me more than anything.

"I'm not sure I know how to let you in," I whispered, the words barely audible even to myself. "I'm not sure I can."

His hand cupped my face gently, his thumb brushing across my cheek in the kind of tender motion that made it hard to breathe. "You don't have to know how," he said, his voice quiet but firm. "You just have to trust me enough to try."

Before I could respond, before I could even process the weight of his words, the doorbell rang—sharp and insistent. My heart stuttered, my mind racing with a thousand possibilities. Who could be at the door at this hour?

His eyes met mine, his expression unreadable. "You weren't expecting anyone, were you?"

I shook my head, the unease settling like a stone in my stomach. "No one. Not that I can think of."

But the ringing continued, louder this time, and something deep inside me told me that whoever was on the other side of that door wasn't there for a friendly visit.